BACKSTAGE

John M. Argos

John M. Argos

BACKSTAGE

ACKNOWLEDGEMENTS

I would like to thank my husband Bob Ross for his encouragement and support. And a huge thank you to my mom, Jeanne Argos and my aunts: Margaret Argos and Marie Williams for their wit and wisdom. I would like to thank Naomi Rose and Vanessa Bruhm for their help in navigating the self publishing world. I would also like to thank my sisters Nikki Laliberte and Mary Argos. And thanks to the many friends who have read this book over the years especially my friends Ruth Yanka and Cheryl Carr. Finally, I would like to thank Michelle Hoover from Grub Street.

CHAPTER ONE

———∞———

I was drawn to the flashing lights. Police cars, news vans, crowds of people milling about, even the beginning of a traffic jam. In Mason City, Iowa? Things like this didn't happen here where the corn grew right up to the back door of Wal-Mart. It was so incongruous I blinked to make sure I was seeing what I was seeing. I looked again; nothing had changed. I stopped running and walked across the field in front of the local high school to a group of people all staring across the street.

"Somebody die?" I asked.

"You don't know?" a woman who looked vaguely familiar asked. She had a small camera dangling from her neck.

"Really? Somebody died?"

"Arthur Graves, God rest his soul." An elderly woman standing next to her, her permed, grey hair a helmet around her plump face made the sign of the cross.

Arthur Graves, why did I know that name?

Seeing the confusion on my face, the woman with the camera said, "You know Arthur Graves, Benjamin's father. You *must* know who Benjamin is." She said it with such certainty that I wanted to say no, I did not know who Benjamin Graves was but of course I did.

"Benjamin is home," she said as she took a step closer. "Which means he is right across the street. And do you know this is the first time since April of 2005 he has been in Iowa? Thirteen months to the day since he last saw his parents!" Her voice rang with indignation. She yanked the camera off her neck and began taking pictures. I looked in the same direction. I saw a hill with a stand of trees, which we all knew, hid a house; so, what was she taking pictures of?

I walked through the crowd. No one was looking at each other; all eyes were across the street. Moving away I leaned against a tree to stretch out my tightening legs.

Benjamin Graves, the movie star, in Mason City again, unbelievable. I closed my eyes and felt the tidal surge of my old infatuation with him flood through my chest.

I was back in high school watching him win a race at the state track meet. Then I was in the auditorium of the public high school watching him star in his senior class play. The next time I saw him he was on television. Now he was the biggest star in Hollywood.

I looked over and saw Jesse Clinton, the reporter from H! Television, walking toward me. You could ask how I knew who he was. Suffice it to say I just did.

"Yo, dude," he said, "are you from around here? Where are we again?" Jesse looked back towards the van and signaled to a stocky guy with a shaved head who hurried toward us carrying a camera. I wiped the sweat from my forehead and adjusted my shorts. Jesse smiled broadly at me, his teeth so white and perfect it almost hurt to look at them. He had on jeans, sneakers, and an untucked white dress shirt open two buttons at the throat, just as he always did on television.

"You're in Mason City, Iowa," I replied.

"A fly over state," the cameraman muttered. I shot him a look. I had heard that phrase so many times during my ten years in Boston that when someone said it now I felt instant annoyance.

"Are you from around here?" Jesse asked.

"Yeah, I grew up here." I turned away to continue my run.

Jesse grabbed my arm. "Hang on," he said, "I just want to ask a few questions. What did you say your name was again?"

"I didn't."

"So what is it?"

I stared at him for a few seconds before replying. He made a few notes in a small spiral notebook and then moved closer to me.

"Liam Ashby, how do you feel about the death of Arthur Graves?"

"Huh?"

He stepped even closer. I could smell his cologne. It had a bitter edge. His eyes had softened and looked slightly filmy, almost as if he was going to cry.

"Are you a Benjamin Graves fan?"

"Sort of." Behind us a car drove by with its windows down and rock music blasting. Jesse closed his eyes, signaled to his cameraman and took a step back. When he opened his eyes they were moist again.

"Are you a Benjamin Graves fan?" he asked again.

"Didn't you just ask that?"

Jesse signaled to his cameraman again and scowled at me. "Dude, can you work with me for a minute?"

A voice in my head was shouting to get the hell out but my feet were rooted to the ground. Jesse closed his eyes again and when he reopened them they were dry and blank. I wondered if he knew his eyes hadn't moistened as before.

"Are you a Benjamin Graves fan?" he asked.

"Yes," I replied trying not to smile, feeling like I was auditioning for a commercial.

"Then you must be upset."

"Why?"

"His father died. Surely you know that?"

"I just found out a few minutes ago."

"I'm sure you can imagine how hard this must be for the Graves family." Jesse's earnestness was pouring from his eyes.

"Yes I can imagine how difficult it is for them, it was for….."

"Was for…..?"

"Nothing," I said. I had no intention of telling him about my dad's death.

Jesse took a step forward. Now his eyes were alive with sorrow. He turned and faced the camera with one hand on my shoulder. It felt hot and wet against my skin. He positioned us so we were side by side.

"We have it from good sources that Benjamin Graves arrived here from Tokyo's Narita Airport early this morning. We believe he is staying with his mother and sisters across the street." He pointed to where the cops were standing.

"Why are you talking to me?" I asked.

Jesse's face went blank for a second, reverted to a concerned look and then he smiled. "Turn off the camera Kurt." He put his notebook in his pocket and started laughing. "I'm bored, that's why. They sent us to the middle of bum fuck Egypt to try to get a story that we are never gonna get."

"See ya," I said as I turned away.

"Hey, don't run away." Jesse's face had reverted to his earnest look. "You look like a serious runner." I ignored his question and retied my shoes.

"Were you and Benjamin friends?" he asked.

"That's a really dumb question," I replied.

"How old are you?" He looked at his notebook. "Liam Ashland."

"Ashby."

"Liam Ashby."

"Thirty-two."

"You're the same age and you both grew up here so why is my question so stupid?"

4

"Do you think if we were friends I would be standing here in my running clothes outside his mom's house right after his dad died talking to you?"

"Good point." Jesse smiled what seemed like a genuine smile, his first one. "Did you ever meet him in high school or when you were kids?"

"No," I said, "not technically. He went to the public high school; I went to Newman, the Catholic school. There was no reason for me to meet him."

"What do you mean, not technically?" Jesse's eyes narrowed.

"I saw him at a couple of things," I muttered.

"What things?"

I looked around in several directions wondering why I was still standing in the same place and not miles away on a dirt road. I could feel the muscles in my legs start to ache; I would have killed for a Gatorade.

"Our senior year I saw him in a play and then again at a track meet in Des Moines."

"Then why didn't you meet him?"

"This isn't *Little House on the Prairie*," I said. "Benjamin was just another kid from the public high school." I wondered if he could tell I was lying.

"Didn't someone tell us that Benjamin was quite the big star in high school?" Jesse asked his cameraman who nodded his assent. "What play was he in?"

"*The Taming of the Shrew*," I replied.

"Shakespeare, in this town?" Kurt said.

"What the hell do you know about this town?" I asked.

"Nothing."

"Then stop judging something you know nothing about."

"I thought Midwesterners were supposed to be friendly," Kurt said. I took a step toward him.

"Whoa, you two," Jesse laughed as he stepped between us. "We don't work for Jerry Springer… we're just trying to come up with some local information about Benji. So—what was he like?" Jesse put his moist hand on my shoulder again. "What role did he play? What was his event in track? Did he win?"

I knelt and pretended to tie my shoes again. My race that day had been one of the first and I had hours to kill before the bus ride home. The last race of the day was the 100 meters. I was watching my teammate, who was favored to win. Benjamin had unexpectedly won that day. When the race was over I had found myself a few feet away from him. His coach was congratulating him. I had stared at him: he was tall, trim, muscled and unbelievably good-looking. To my surprise, Benjamin looked back.

I stood up. I couldn't tell Jesse that story, after all, what had it meant? Would it kill me to tell him what I remembered of the play? My memory was crisp.

"As I said, I did see him in the play." I looked at Jesse who was nodding at Kurt. The camera was pointed at me but I wasn't looking at anything. I was no longer standing outside the high school; I was inside it, sitting in the third row, my eyes glued to Benjamin's every move.

"A group of us from Newman went to see it." I remembered how much trouble I had rounding up a group to see the show. They hadn't understood my motivation and neither had I. "Within minutes of the show starting it was clear we were watching someone really special. He was sensational, magnetic, moved like a dancer; and those green eyes, they were just amazing. I would have traded places with her in a heartbeat."

I blinked several times and noticed the camera staring at me. Jesse was smiling at me. My mind raced: did I say those last few words out loud or just think them? I had no idea.

"Thanks, that was quite informative." He turned and faced the camera. "Anything else you would like to tell the millions of viewers of H! about your fond memories of Benjamin Graves?" I mumbled no and bolted away. Had I just come out on national TV? I looked back for a moment to see that the camera was still trained on me.

Feeling tightness in my left hamstring I came to a stop and thought about what I had just said. I wondered if it was too late to fix it but convinced myself they would never show it to anyone. I slowly jogged home.

Lying on my living room floor trying to stretch out my hamstring, I kept reliving my conversation with Jesse Clinton. I was sure I remembered most of it and wished I hadn't said ninety percent. I hated this familiar feeling, instant regret for something I said. I knew it would haunt me for hours as I worried my way through the memory. My only solace was that no one would see an interview with a sweaty runner from Iowa. Would they?

CHAPTER TWO

———∞———

The day I left Boston three months earlier, it had been twenty-five degrees with a biting wind blowing in from the ocean. My life had been upended in a matter of months. The summer before while in Iowa for my mom's surgery, my boyfriend Justin called to say he had started seeing someone else. When my dad died six months later from a heart attack, I felt overwhelmed by life. On an impulse I put my condo on the market and it sold within a week. When I called Mom to tell her my condo had sold, she told me how happy she was I was moving home.

Afterwards I had no recollection of telling her I was coming back to Iowa.

Several weeks later, I was standing on the sidewalk in front of my former condominium, hands shoved deep in the pockets of my coat, my ears red, my nose running. My best friend Gregg stood several feet from me, his head turned away. When I told him I was moving back to Iowa, he accused me of running away.

I hugged him good-bye. My eyes started to fill until I looked at his stony face. Driving up Dartmouth Street, I looked at the familiar landmarks: Copley Place, Back Bay Station, the Copley Plaza Hotel, and the Boston Public Library, but felt no connection. I realized in that moment that Boston had never been my home, even after ten years.

I turned onto the Massachusetts Turnpike and headed west. Fourteen hundred miles and I would be in Iowa. Fourteen hundred miles to wonder if Gregg was right.

The first night in my hotel room near Erie, Pennsylvania, I ordered a pizza. I sat on the bed, the buzz of the adjacent room's television not getting under my skin for a change, nursing a Corona. My first bite brought back memories of summer nights with my sisters, watching late night television after our parents had gone to bed, the phone number for the local pizza restaurant embedded in our heads. I felt a glow of something that was either nostalgia or my second beer. Whatever the cause, for that night I believed I had made the correct choice.

The next morning I wasn't so sure.

The weather had warmed up but not in a good way. Now it was sleeting and my car was rear wheel drive. I wrestled with it for hours before giving up after only making half the distance I had hoped for. After checking into the first hotel I found, I slid across the street to an Outback restaurant and ordered a Glenlivet. It was five thirty and the place was quiet. There was an elderly couple in the next booth: the woman probably in her late seventies, the husband even older. He kept saying "What?" every time she said something.

When I brought the scotch up for a sip, I stopped, inhaled and I was in my grandparents' dining room for a family dinner. The clink of the ice against the glass, the smell of the alcohol mixed with cooking food, Grandpa at the head of the table, Dad at the other end: how many Sundays had we spent at their home?

I ordered a burger as a group of teen-agers sauntered in, the open door sending a blast of frigid air into the room. The boys were bumping into each other, the girls on their cell phones while the waitress shot a glance at the cook. The kids didn't see either the elderly couple or me. They left the front door ajar and the waitress rushed over and slammed it closed.

When I entered high school, my dad assumed I would try out for the football team. I was 5' 5" my freshman year and weighed 130 pounds. I had stared at my skinny body in the mirror, a mop of black curly hair, anxious blue eyes staring back at me, wondering if he saw something I didn't. When I told him I was trying out for track, he argued with me and then ignored me. I remember being surprised at how easy it was to be ignored by him.

Finishing my drink, I watched the elderly couple as they slowly got out of their booth. She had to help him to his feet and it took a few seconds for him to find his balance. She smiled at me.

My chest tightened as I remembered when Grandma died. It was 1990 and I was sixteen. The day after her funeral Dad asked me to stay at my friend Sue's house as he claimed my crying during the night was keeping everyone awake. I showed up at Sue's house with my stuff shoved in a backpack. Her mom welcomed me with no questions asked. I stayed there for a week.

When I returned home I asked Dad why he had wanted me out of the house. He looked at me with confusion. *Hadn't it been my decision to stay with Sue's family?* He asked me. When I reminded him that he had asked me to leave, he changed the subject and ignored me again.

The next morning the sun was out and the roads were dry. I left at seven and didn't stop until I was outside Chicago. After eating something forgettable at a McDonalds, a group of high school students had walked into the restaurant. Considering their general geekiness, I had to assume they were in a high school band. I would recognize them anywhere, as I had been one of them.

They seemed so young and dorky and zitty and metallic. Initially they annoyed the hell out of me but as they dispersed into smaller groups and sat down around me, I began listening to their conversations and I was right back with them. They were on their way to a contest of some kind in downtown Chicago. Their excitement level bordered on hysteria.

I had attended several of these contests. For most of these trips I shared a room with my best friend Jim. I played the clarinet and he played the trumpet. We had been friends since kindergarten. Sometime around the age of 12 or 13, our relationship became sexual.

During our junior year, we were at a hotel in Decorah, Iowa preparing for a contest at Luther College. It had been midwinter and the room was stifling. I remembered lying in my twin bed, waiting for him to join me and when he hadn't, I got into his bed. He had rolled away from me. I had asked him what was wrong and he claimed he was just tired. But when he didn't call me to hang out the following few weekends I knew it was over. The sex stopped that night in the hotel and then the friendship stopped. My parents didn't understand why Jim didn't come around any longer and I couldn't tell them.

As I walked out of the restaurant, I remembered the last time we had had sex. Over the years our sex had progressed from jerking off across the room to mutual masturbation and then some awkward oral sex. But that last time, we kissed for what seemed like hours until my lips were chapped and swollen. I had never kissed anyone before.

And then, a few weeks later, it was over.

My adult assessment of the experience was that I had been the initiator of the sex and he had been the terminator. He had the satisfaction, if that was the right word, of ending it, and I was left with the shame of having started it. Had I forced him into something? It was a question I couldn't answer.

When I arrived in Mason City four days after leaving Boston, I drove across town until I was a block from my childhood home. I pulled into a parking lot that was the site of my former grade school. I got out of my car and stood in the middle of the ice-covered parking lot that had once been our gym and auditorium. I remembered standing on the stage for our annual St. Patrick's Day concert, staring out at the parent filled room, nauseous with fear. I sang *Danny Boy* and when my voice cracked and creaked and I saw the rolling eyes of the crowd and the red faces of my parents, I knew I had only imagined I could sing. Afterwards my sisters teased me for weeks, imitating my singing voice until one day I exploded in anger. My fury silenced them.

I walked across the lot to where the entrance had been. The kindergarten classroom had been across the hall from the principal's office. I stood where I imagined my desk had been and remembered the first time I saw Jim. I had felt an instant attraction with no understanding of what it meant.

I jogged back to my car; my hands and feet numb and drove the short distance to the serpentine alley that split my childhood block in half. As I inched forward I began seeing ghosts—not exactly ghosts since I don't believe in them—but my memories almost became flesh, so defined that it was as if the alley was crowded with people from my past.

I saw my dad, his ever-present cigarette hanging from his lower lip. I saw my sisters racing each other on their baby blue Schwinn bicycles. My dog Snoopy was running in front of me, a tennis ball in his mouth, his back legs dragging slightly on the ground. None of us ever spoke about what his odd way of moving meant until it was too late to do anything about it.

An ancient oak tree dominated our back yard, a tire swing hanging from a muscular branch. My sisters and I spent countless hours swinging, sometimes twisting the rope so that we spun out in a rush of motion, our legs thrust forward as we looked up into the twisted branches of the tree. When we jumped off the swing we would be so dizzy we would stumble around, exaggerating the effect until Dad would shout at us to stop acting stupid.

In the early spring the blue sky pierced the canopy, but by midsummer we looked up into a blanket of green. Only two people could fit on the swing and to make it work their legs had to rest on top of each other. My sisters rarely included me and when I asked my friend Ronny to swing with me one summer day when I was ten, he called me a homo.

I stopped in the alley behind our house and saw Mom looking out the window, her face relaxing into a smile. I pulled in behind the garage, got out of the car and looked around the yard. Tired rose bushes shivered in the February cold. The poorly shoveled back steps alarmed me. I imagined her slipping as she walked into the house carrying a bag of groceries.

Inside I hugged her tightly. She cried in my arms, something she had only done once before: at Dad's wake. It only lasted a few seconds and then she backed up to remove herself from my embrace. I stuck my hands in my pockets to avoid reaching out to her and looked around. The kitchen was completely empty. She was moving out and I was moving in, as a tenant. I had tried to buy the house from her but she had resisted.

I opened the spotless white refrigerator looking for water and laughed to see it fully stocked. There was the crunchy peanut butter and apricot jelly I had loved as a kid, milk, eggs, and cheese. I pushed things around looking for a bottle of water, and spotted French's mustard, bologna, mayonnaise, and cottage cheese she must have thought I still ate. My tastes had changed so much in the ten years I had been away. That was the first time I asked myself the question: why had I moved back home?

CHAPTER THREE

———∞———

I shook my head clear of memories, got up from the living room floor and walked into the kitchen. I poured a glass of water and sat at my kitchen table flipping through the latest issue of *Vanity Fair*. Benjamin was on the cover in a leather skirt, sandals that laced up to his knees, and no shirt. The article purported to be about the concern in Hollywood that this latest version of *Alexander the Great* might bomb just like the one with Colin Farrell. As usual, the whole point of the cover story was to get the actor in as little clothing as possible. I pushed it away.

A wave of loneliness swept over me. I missed my friend Gregg so much that at times it hurt like a toothache. Even though we had just spoken the night before, I called him again.

"Two phone calls in less than twenty-four hours?" Gregg said. "I wonder what that means?"

"It means I miss you, asshole."

"You know how I feel about phone displays of affection," Gregg said. "Oh what the hell, I miss you too. So when are you moving back to your real home…Boston?"

I started to tell him to move on to the next topic but he interrupted me.

"I gotta tell you Liam, I miss you so much it almost feels like we were more than friends. Are you sure we didn't fuck?"

I remembered one time early in our friendship; we had gotten drunk and passed out on my bed together. I had awakened to find myself curled up next to him, his back against my chest. He had looked over his shoulder and we kissed, simultaneously started laughing and fallen back asleep.

"Has it broken sixty degrees yet?" I asked him.

"Of course not." He sighed into the phone. "You are so lucky not to be here. It is pouring rain, wind gusts of thirty miles an hour, fifty-five degrees and overrun with young scary lesbians. They should reschedule Memorial Day in Provincetown to late June when the sun finally comes out and the birdbaths thaw. My hair is a mess, my skin is chapped, and my libido unfulfilled. Speaking of libido, do you remember that guy, Paul, I told you about last weekend? The one I was planning to marry? Did I tell you he looks exactly like Clive Owen except for the fact that he is blond and short?" I heard someone in the background ask if anyone wanted their screwdrivers freshened. "Guess what I saw him wearing this morning?" Before I could say a word, Gregg said, "A full length black leather trench coat!"

"So?"

"Liam, Liam, Liam, you know as well as I do that you can never date someone who would wear a full-length black leather trench coat. I guarantee you on weekends he is training Rottweilers and studying genetics." I heard ice clinking as Gregg yelled, "And put some vodka in it this time." He paused to say good-bye to someone. "I may go home today. I had my back waxed for nothing. Where have all the gay boys gone?" he sang. I toyed with telling him about my moment with Jesse Clinton but decided I was too thin skinned to take the heaps of grief he would throw my way.

"I don't know where all the boys are but I do know where Mr. Number One Box Office is right now. Have you heard the news about Benji?"

"Of course I have. Are you listening to me? We've barely been able to go outside, and since I'm not getting laid, we've been watching TV. H! Television is treating this as if the father of the president died. Where is he from again? I know it's one of those I states, it's Indiana, right?"

"What if I told you that he is about two miles from where I'm standing? That I ran past his parent's home a few hours ago and….."

"And what?"

"Nothing important, just…just a few local TV stations were there."

"Whenever you start stuttering, I know there is a lie built into what you said but I am not in the mood today. I know how long it can take to get you to spill it so we'll move on. So what did you say about Benjamin, my future husband?"

"He is literally two miles away from me."

He gasped. "Now I know why you moved back to the Middle East! You are a stalker, plain and simple. Have you seen him yet? You have to see him; I insist that you see him. I need to know what he looks like in real life. Does he wear lifts; are his teeth really that white and his eyes that glowing shade of green, does your gaydar go off in his presence? Oh, what am I saying? You don't have any gaydar! Why the fuck didn't I take you up on your offer to spend this weekend in Iraq or Indianastan, wherever the fuck you are. This is so unfair," Gregg yelled to whoever was in earshot, "Liam Ashby is minutes away from Benjamin Graves and I'm stuck in a typhoon with 3000 drunken dykes pretending they are in a version of *The L World* meets *The Real World*."

"Even if you were here, Gregg, you can't get close to where he is… there are cops everywhere. You'll see more on television. Now get out of that moldy house and go spread your magic, or spread something. I have to get ready for work. You know Gregg, some of the young lesbians are kind of cute. Hell, they may even find your man breasts protrude enough to pretend you're a girl."

I threw my cell phone onto the couch and flipped on the television to H! To my shock I saw my own face in a close up saying, "Within minutes of the show starting it was clear that we were watching someone really special. He was sensational, magnetic, moved like a dancer; and those green eyes, they were just amazing. The joke with my friends was that he should have tamed that shrew before the end of the first act. We all wondered what she was fussing about. I would have traded places with her in a heartbeat."

Now I had my answer.

"Once again, that was Liam Ashland, a former classmate of Benjamin Graves," Jesse Clinton said, "providing us with a glimpse into the real life of Benjamin back in 1992 before he became the icon he is today. As you just saw, even in high school Benji cast quite a spell," Jesse paused for effect, "apparently on men as well as women." I watched in disbelief as a body that was wearing my Nike running shorts ran away from the camera.

"Fuck, fuck, fuck!"

Had I said it that way? Did I really finish my sentence?

"What an idiot!" I shouted to my empty house.

Did anyone in Iowa watch H! Television? My cell phone rang.

"Ashland?" Aunt Margaret snapped at me. "The Ashlands live in Clear Lake for God's sake. They're white trash and Baptists. How could you screw up your own name? If I were with you right now, I'd slap you upside the head. You may not go to church anymore but do you have to pretend to be a Protestant?"

"Slow down Aunt Margaret." I should have known she would be watching. "He completely screwed things up. Don't you know me better than that?"

"Liam, he just said your name was Ashland, where did he get that if you didn't tell him that?"

"He wasn't listening to me."

"I just can't imagine they would make such a big mistake."

"You don't suppose Mom was watching, do you?"

17

"Of course she wasn't. She thinks watching PBS is daring," she said. "But trust me, someone in that nursing home she calls a neighborhood will have seen it. It's probably being dissected in the bingo hall as we speak."

"You know she hates it when you talk about her subdivision like that."

"Would you ever choose to live in a development where the average age is pushing 75?" My landline rang. It had to be her. She refused to call my cell phone.

"Don't take any of her guff."

"Hello?"

"Hi honey. Shouldn't you be on your way to work?"

I looked at my watch. I still had an hour before my shift started. A dog barked sharply in the background. "Aggie, shut up!" she cried. "Wasn't it a beautiful day?" Before I could answer she added, "How was your run?"

"I was hoping to go fifteen miles but…."

"Marie called," she said. Marie was her older sister. There wasn't a topic invented that she didn't know how to instantly bludgeon. "She said she saw you on television…in your running shorts." I said nothing. "Who were you speaking with?"

"Some television guy," I said. "Arthur Graves died, you know, Benjamin's dad?"

"Yes, I heard, the poor man. Locked up in that house with that, with that woman." She paused. "What did he want to know?"

"You know, it was kind of a blur. I don't remember a lot of it. I know I told him I didn't know Benjamin at all but then I did remember seeing him a couple of times back in high school so we talked about that."

"Marie said you sounded like you were good friends with him, *exceptionally good friends* is how she put it."

I began cracking my knuckles. "Why would she say that?"

18

She sighed. "Marie said you might as well have been wearing a button saying you are a homosexual." I started to say something but she kept talking. "You know I don't care about any of that but you also know how private I am."

"Why can't Aunt Marie stay out of our family?"

"Liam, she is my sister, she is your aunt and she is our family."

"But...."

"I may not agree with her on many things, Liam, but she is still my sister." She sighed loudly enough for me to hear. "What will Father Schmidt say tomorrow?" she asked.

"About what?" I had an image of Father Schmidt talking to the boys in my eighth-grade class about sex with his right hand jiggling in his pants pocket.

"That you're gay. What else could we be talking about?"

"Father Schmidt...."

"We are not going down that road, Liam," she said. There was a long pause. "Okay, I've said my piece and that's that, but honey, can you do me a favor?" she asked. "If you see any more television cameras, please run in the opposite direction." She hung up.

When I returned to the living room, there was a live shot of a Town Car, its windows blackened, slowly making its way down the driveway of the Graves home followed by three police cars. I turned the volume back up.

"We have it from reliable sources that in that car are Benjamin Graves and his sisters, Elizabeth, and Veronica. We have been told they are on their way to a funeral home to make final arrangements. Our sources also tell us that Benjamin's girlfriend, Alyssa Wheelock, will be arriving by private jet later today," Jesse Clinton said. "There are unsubstantiated rumors that John Bankman, Jamie Diego and Rose Wizenwood will be attending the funeral. Are there any A-list actors left in Hollywood this weekend?"

The H! News truck got in line with the others, cameras rolling, as they followed the procession of police cars. When they returned from another endless commercial, I saw the Lincoln pull into the driveway in front of Major Erickson, a local funeral home. I sat down to watch as I realized that I was actually going to see Benjamin, the elusive star. There was no place for him to escape since both the front and back doors to the funeral home were completely in the open. Now I understood why H! was here: access to a Hollywood star in a setting he couldn't control.

The camera zoomed in. He was dressed in faded jeans, cowboy boots, and a body hugging, cream-colored shirt. Sleek black sunglasses covered his eyes and his hair was blond again, just as it had been in high school. Glancing over his shoulder at the convoy following him, Benjamin shook his head slightly and disappeared into the funeral home trailed by his sisters, neither had inherited his looks. Mason City's finest lined up to block the entrance, chests puffed out for the cameras. Jesse Clinton began speaking and I hit mute. I watched for a few seconds and something caught my eye. Behind Jesse was a garage door. As the camera pulled back I could see that the garage was connected to the funeral home by an enclosed walkway. I was wrong, Benjamin could have gone into the funeral home without any attention. I turned off the television.

With a quick look at my watch, I realized I was running late for work. I threw on my gear: black pants, a white shirt and a black vest. I backed out of the garage and lowered the top of my convertible. I could hear my Aunt Marie's voice. Every time she saw me in my car she would say how goddamn stupid it was to drive a BMW in Iowa. "Rear wheel drive in this climate?" she would say. "I thought you were smarter than that. Don't come skating over to my house when you can't get that toy out of your garage next winter." I asked her once if they still sold snow tires in Iowa but when I saw the *don't make waves* look on my mom's face, I changed the subject. Ten minutes later I was at work, wondering how long the kick of not having to deal with heavy Boston traffic would last.

CHAPTER FOUR

———∞———

Pulling into the parking lot, I was surprised to see Sue Flanagan's car. She was rarely at work this early; as head waitress she could show up right as the doors opened. I walked through the kitchen saying hello to the cooks and bus boys. I caught a few smirks and I felt my face start to burn. When I walked into the bar, my interview with H! was playing on the television. I found the remote and snapped it off.

At that moment, Sue strode out of the dining room humming "Greensleeves." She had short brown hair, and a slightly too large nose. She was trim from years of waiting on tables and raising two daughters alone. Back in high school my mom thought Sue was the perfect match: Irish, Catholic, smart, and cute. To me, Sue had been more like a sister. She was at our house so often my family used to tease her about where her bedroom was. However when I came out to my parents in college, my mom had briefly acted as if it was Sue's fault. Mom had believed for a few weeks that if only Sue had shifted her affection to me, everything would have turned out differently. Then when Sue got pregnant, married and divorced all in the same year my mom's attitude towards Sue turned to pity with a dash of relief.

"What are you doing here so early?" I asked.

"Liam, what are we going to do with that paranoia of yours? We're one waitress short tonight so I had to help set up. You really need to stop fussing." She continued on into the kitchen. I heard her say, "Julio, you look magnetic tonight!"

Obviously she had seen the interview, which meant everyone else had as well. I knew from experience Sue would not let go of something this juicy until she had beaten it to a pulp. I opened the cash register drawer and saw a white slip of paper taped in the slot for twenty-dollar bills. In large block letters, as if a ransom note, someone had written *sensational* in green ink. I looked over my shoulder to see if anyone noticed me crumpling it up and throwing it in the trash. I began searching for other evidence of her handiwork. In the dishwasher there were three glasses lined up with different slips of paper taped to each, all in green ink with the words, *sexy, graceful, and amazing* in large flowing cursive writing. In the small refrigerator where I kept the garnishes, there was a length of green crepe paper hanging across the opening like a banner at a prom dance with the line: "Everyone would have traded places with that shrew in a heartbeat. He made me wet all over!" Looking up I saw the manager, Georgia Dee, heading in my direction followed by several waitresses all of whom were laughing. I felt my cheeks burning.

"Okay everyone," Georgia said, "the joke's over. We have a full slate of reservations tonight and I need you to focus. Some of the news people are coming in and I want to show them we're not a bunch of hicks." Sue walked into the room with her trademark smile, one part warmth and one part condescension.

"Liam's not a hick," Sue said as she walked towards the bar. "He might be El Jefe of the 'Homos for Benji' fan club, but he's not a hick! Or should I say La Jefa?"

"That's enough out of you," Georgia Dee said, "our first reservation is going to be here any second."

"Jesus, Liam," Sue sat on the edge of a bar chair, "don't you know better than to talk to the press? They always misquote people."

22

"How do you know that, Jacqueline Anderson?" I said referencing her favorite actress.

"Don't you think she and I would be great friends?"

"Can you believe this shit?"

"I bet she's lonely."

"What?"

"Jacqueline, I bet she's lonely." Her eyes were closed. They snapped open. "Oh and don't worry," she said, "you know as well as I do that most people have IQs of slugs. By Monday morning no one will remember one iota of your riveting interview."

"Liam, can I talk to you for a minute?" Georgia Dee motioned me to a corner. I looked over at Sue. For a second her face was open as if saying, *can I come as well,* but when she wasn't asked to join us, it disappeared as quickly as it had appeared. "I got a phone call from someone who said he was representing the Graves family," Georgia Dee said in a whisper, her breath ripe with cigarettes. "They need to hire two people to work the reception following Arthur Graves' funeral on Monday. Do you want this?" Nothing was registering. I stopped listening to her. "Of course you want this, the money is incredible," she said. She snapped her fingers in front of my eyes several times. I tried to imagine being in the same room with Benjamin Graves and then suddenly I was in a sailboat with him, the sun beating down on our bare chests as we were whisked towards our private island. "Liam, do you want this or don't you?"

I came back to Iowa. "Can I bring Sue?"

She sighed. "I suppose, but you have to make her promise not to say anything inappropriate. I know that mouth of hers. I swore to this guy that whomever I recommended would be completely professional about this and not someone impertinent and unpredictable. His dad died, after all. This isn't a Hollywood party." She waved Sue over. "You have a good friend, Sue. I'll let Liam tell you what is going on." One of the cooks stuck his head around the corner and motioned at Georgia Dee. "Now what?" she muttered under her breath.

"What is she talking about?" Sue asked.

I was back on the sailboat again. Of course, I didn't know how to sail but hopefully Benjamin did. Sue poked me in the chest.

"The Graves family needs wait staff for the funeral reception on Monday," I said. "We're going to be inside the Graves house serving cocktails to fucking Benjamin Graves. Can you believe this?"

"Are you bullshitting me?"

"I couldn't make this up."

"How much are they paying us?"

"Who cares?" I said. "I am going to be standing right next to Benjamin Graves!"

"Liam, get a grip. We're not all star fuckers like you. How much are they paying?"

"I don't know, Georgia Dee said it was incredible."

"Okay, now you've got my interest. Incredible is a sum I can work with." She started to walk away from me and hesitated. "Jesus Liam, you're white as a sheet. Are you going to be able to handle this?"

"Of course I can," I said. "What's the worst thing that can happen?"

"Vomit, diarrhea, gas." She headed towards the dining room.

"You are not fooling me," I said as I followed her. "You're as big a celebrity junkie as I am."

"No one is as big a celebrity junkie as you are." She stopped behind the bar and found her purse tucked on a shelf. "However, my family is going to die when I tell them." She dumped the contents of her purse on top of the bar, rummaged through it, found her lip gloss and then returned it all in one two handed scoop. As if on cue, Georgia Dee reappeared.

"Did I mention the confidentiality agreement you have to sign?" she asked.

"Oh, who cares about those," Sue said.

24

"This is serious, Sue." Georgia Dee shot me a look. "Here's the deal, you will sign a document in which you will swear that you will tell no one, not even your mother, what you see on Monday. If you won't sign it, you can't go. If you tell anyone what you see and it makes it into the press, you will be sued. Understand?" Georgia Dee said.

"How much are they paying us?" Sue asked.

"Liam, take care of this." Georgia Dee walked into the dining room.

"Are you deliberately trying to screw this up?" I asked. Sue had a stubborn look on her face. She looked at her reflection in the mirror behind the bar and fixed her hair.

"Can you bring it down a notch?" I asked. "She'll ask Barb or Mary in about two minutes if you don't start groveling a little."

"Oh, all right," she said, "but only for you."

Before I had time to wonder what was going on with her, my first customers arrived. As I reached for beer glasses, my reflection in the mirror startled me. There was a slight tremor under my left eye, and my chin was twitching. I could feel nervous energy roiling in my gut.

Pacing behind the bar, I saw the local news start on TV and realized it was only five thirty. I felt like a ten year old on Christmas Eve. I wanted to be able to bend time to race through the next thirty-six hours. Why couldn't Mason City be the hometown of Tom Cruise? I wouldn't cross the street to see that one. I decided to call my sister Leah in Minneapolis, which required a trip to my car as Georgia Dee prohibited cell phones inside the restaurant.

"Leah, I have thirty seconds to say this and ten seconds of that is you swearing that we never had this conversation. Do you swear?"

"Of course," she replied sounding slightly disinterested.

"I am working the Graves family funeral reception on Monday. I have to sign a statement saying I will never tell you or anyone else a thing about it afterwards."

25

"Are you drunk?"

"Of course not! I'm at work." Georgia Dee came outside to smoke a cigarette and pointed at me. "Shit, my boss just found me. Gotta go."

"You looked really cute on TV," she said as she hung up.

Jesse Clinton and the cameraman were sitting at the bar when I returned. Jesse was tapping a cigarette on the back of his hand. "I thought you could smoke indoors in Iowa." Seeing them again, I felt a strange combination of embarrassment and anger.

"It's up to the individual owners." I knew that I sounded pissed off. "This place is nonsmoking."

"Hey, I know you, don't I?" Jesse asked. "You're that guy from this morning, the runner, aren't you? You wouldn't believe the reaction we've been getting to that piece. It was Leo something, right?"

"No, it's not Leo. It's Liam…and it's Ashby, not Ashland. You screwed up my last name."

"Hey…dude…chill." The cameraman returned my glare.

"Have you been on TV before?" Jesse asked. I shook my head no as I moved away to wait on the couple sitting next to them.

"You'd never know…you were a natural, wasn't he Kurt? It was almost as if you were lost in a dream. You spoke out loud what millions of women," Jesse paused, "and men feel about Benjamin Graves. You just had the balls to say it in front of a television camera. The camera loved you by the way." He put his unlit cigarette in his mouth. "I would kill for a Ketel One dirty martini," he said, "you do have Ketel One don't you?"

"Make that two," Kurt said.

I served them their drinks and then ignored them. Sue appeared at the waitress station, looking twitchy. I caught her eyes and then looked at Jesse Clinton. She raised an eyebrow and smiled.

"What do you need Sue?" I asked.

"A green apple martini and a glass of Chardonnay."

"Oh come on."

"Seriously Liam, that's what I need."

"Hi, I'm Jesse Clinton, H! Television." Jesse stood up and extended his hand while staring at Sue from the neck down.

"Sue Flanagan," she shook his hand and smiled. "H! Television… not sure I've heard of that." Jesse frowned as he took a sip of his cocktail.

"What's everyone saying about all this?" he asked.

"All what?" Sue asked.

"You know," he took a gulp of his drink, "the Graves funeral… all the reporters in town."

"Did someone die?" Sue looked concerned.

"Yes," Kurt said, "Arthur Graves died, you know, Benjamin's father?"

"Oh that," Sue said, "I was sorry to hear about that but the rest of this? This kind of thing happens all the time. Why, it was only forty some years ago when the premiere of *The Music Man* was held here. By now, everyone is a bit jaded by all this Hollywood stuff. Plus, when you live here you see Benjamin Graves everywhere: church, bowling alleys, the Super Wal-Mart, why I've even see him at my 4 H meetings." She picked up her tray of drinks and strolled into the dining room. I turned my back to them.

"What was all that about?" Jesse asked. I looked at his reflection in the mirror.

"We all get a little tired of people from the East and West coasts acting like people in Iowa are from a different planet. I lived in Boston for years and whenever I told people that I had grown up here, they would inevitably say, 'oh, that's where they grow potatoes, right?'"

"Boston's a great city," Jesse said, "I've been there many times. I interviewed John Bankman in his old Dorchester neighborhood. Nice guy, short, but basically a nice guy." I moved away to make a few drinks for one of the waitresses; Jesse continued on as if unconcerned whether anyone was listening. "Of course that was before he made it big. Now he's a jerk just like all the others."

Finishing off his martini, his manner softened by the alcohol, Jesse asked, "You remember the popular crowd in high school?" He pointed at his empty glass. "A bunch of assholes, right? Mean spirited, smug, and exclusive—tell me I'm wrong."

"The woman who just left was the most popular girl in my high school and was the complete opposite of what you are describing."

"So there's one. Anyway, what was I saying?" He moved his empty glass back and forth several times. "Oh yeah, the A-listers make that old high school crowd seem kind. When they're on the rise they need the press, and suck up to us like we are the A list crowd. But once the rare few get there, then all of a sudden they hate us, hate the red carpet, and hate the paparazzi."

"Such phonies," Kurt said.

"Hey come on Kurt, they're the reason we have a job, right? Anyway, who do you have to fuck to get another drink around here?" My head snapped around to tell him to relax but when I saw his eyes, I knew he was kidding. "Anyway, where was I...oh yeah, when most of them begin their inevitable slide to Lifetime movies or dinner theater, then all of a sudden they love the press again. It's all so transparent. And then of course there's Benjamin."

"What about him?" I asked.

Jesse looked around as if looking for someone.

"What are you doing?" I asked.

"Needing to make sure none of his people are here."

"What people?"

"His minions. They're sort of like crazed Scientologists."

Kurt choked a little on his martini.

"Is that redundant?" Jesse asked.

"Oh come on," I said.

"Am I exaggerating, Kurt?" His buddy shook his head no. "Benjamin has thought police everywhere. This guy controls everything, he has set the bar so high, no one else comes close. I'll give you an example, if one of his staff was at this bar, right now, hiding inside the costume of a Midwesterner and heard what I just said, my cell phone would ring in a few seconds and it would be my boss telling me that my job was on the line if anything I had just said went public."

His cell phone rang. The color drained from his face. He let it ring a few times before picking it up. He looked at the caller and then slugged Kurt on the shoulder. "You're a real fucker, aren't you?"

"So if they are all assholes or Nazis why don't you change careers?" I asked, handing him his drink. He gave me a studied, pensive look.

"Hell dude, I couldn't change careers, this is in my blood, man!"

I walked away. A few minutes later I looked back to see Jesse deep in conversation with a young couple next to him. They looked smitten.

At the end of the night Georgia Dee, Sue and I were sitting at the bar with three stingers lined up in a row. Sue was counting her tips.

"Jesse Clinton is a bit of an ass but his table left me a 50% tip." She began sorting her cash by denomination. "Once they were into their second bottle of wine, they ended up being a lot of fun."

"It drives me crazy that you sort your money as if you still work at United Bank."

She waved her hand in front of her face as if dismissing me.

"I think the cameraman was hitting on me but I wasn't sure." She leaned back on her bar stool and crossed her legs. She had the best legs of any woman I knew. "I hate it how the sexual lines are blurring, I can't tell anymore who is gay, straight, bisexual, asexual, transgender, in transition…God, it's all so confusing!" Her face lit up as if she were on stage.

"Do you need a soap box?" I asked. I took a long swig from my drink; the alcohol sizzled across my tongue.

"Hey, I'm just getting warmed up." She looked through me. "You know what I think? I think people should have to wear a button stating what gender they want to have sex with. They can change it the next day; hell, they can change it hourly. But when you are talking to someone you should be able to know if they want to fuck you or color your hair. Is that asking too much? I made $400 tonight," she added as she finished counting her money. Georgia Dee grimaced as Sue said fuck but she let it go. She was one stinger in already.

"How are you two holding up?" Georgia Dee lit a cigarette. She gave herself permission to smoke inside the restaurant but no one else. I realized that for the first time all night, I had stopped thinking about Monday for a few minutes but when she asked it all came rushing back. The knot in my stomach returned.

"By the look on your face, Liam, I would say not well." She took a long slug of her drink and a lengthy drag on her cigarette, the smoke streaming out of her nose. "I'm so jealous of you two. I'm as big a groupie of Benjamin Graves as you are. I just don't talk about it." I had to stop myself before promising that I would tell her everything. "I haven't obsessed about anyone like this since Elvis." Sue put her hand over her mouth to stifle a laugh. "The early version of Elvis, not the Vegas one."

Sue and I were standing next to her car, I had my arm around her shoulder and she was leaning into me.

"What was up with you when I told you about the job on Monday?" I asked. "You reacted like you'd been hired to rake my mom's yard."

"That's an ugly thought, all that Pomeranian dog poop everywhere."

"Aggie is a Sheltie, not a Pomeranian."

"Whatever, all I know is she barks too much."

"Answer my question."

"Not sure," she pulled away from me. "You want the easy answer?"

"I'll take any kind of answer."

30

"I guess I couldn't believe it, still can't. Things like this don't happen to me. Are we really going to make $3500 each?"

"That's what Georgia Dee said," I replied. "Don't you think we're worth it?"

"I know I am, not sure about you." She walked back to me and leaned against my shoulder again and her body relaxed. We stood together for several minutes in silence.

"You know Liam, this is just like after senior prom, a warm spring evening… the glow of alcohol…the smell of sex in the air," she said.

I was barely listening. The sailboat had just deposited Benjamin and me on the beach. We were setting up camp for the evening.

"Me wanting to have sex with you and you dreaming about giving Mark McSweeny a blow job. Isn't it interesting how some things never change?"

Whipped away from reverie, I remembered what Mark McSweeny looked like naked. His skin had a creamy texture that from a distance looked soft but when you were close to him you could sense the strength just under the surface. He had a small tuft of hair between his pectoral muscles. He was a runner as well. His calves and legs were muscular and lean. We had gone to the Drake Relays together and shared a room. The same Drake Relays where I saw Benjamin win his race. I was brushing my teeth and Mark was in the shower. The water stopped and he opened the curtain and stood there with the water streaming down his body. I had forgotten myself and stared at his penis without inhibition. I looked up and Mark was glowering at me. The rumors about me started then, rumors that kept me in the closet until my junior year in college.

"Why didn't you tell me?" I asked.

"Honey, after our tenth slow dance and getting no response despite my amazing pelvis grinding into your crotch, I figured you either had the smallest dick in the world or you were gay. Since I have been told that most Irish men have good cocks and observed a handful on my own, so to speak," she added in her best Mae West imitation, "I just assumed you were gay. And no, I am not hitting on you but I sure wish you liked girls. We would have made a great couple." She gave me a small kiss on my cheek. "What do you think Monday is going to be like?"

"Right now, I think it will be a hoot but I will probably be scared to death. Maybe we should have a few cocktails first."

"Perfect! We'll be nice and messy and dump drinks all over Benji's crotch and you can blow dry him off, so to speak." She laughed at her own joke. "Can you imagine dropping a Bloody Mary in his lap? His handlers would have a cow. I am assuming that his handlers will be there or do you think the death of your dad allows you to act like a normal human being for a day? Probably not."

"We can't have that attitude on Monday, can we?" I said. "We have to act like we are in the presence of American royalty, all deference and self-abasement. That shouldn't be hard for you to pull off, at least that's what your second or was it third husband told me."

"Bitch." She got into her car after giving me another kiss.

Before leaving the parking lot I checked my cell phone for messages and saw that Gregg had called several times. I only listened to the last one.

"Liam Neeson, call me the second you get out of work. Doll, you're famous! You're having your fifteen minutes of fame and you're stuck in that hellhole. Oh my God, you should have seen what happened when word got around the bar that I am your dearest friend. It was the best time I have ever had, well maybe the second best time, nothing will top St Bart's, 2002. Anyway, call me ASAP. A guy I swear looks exactly like Daniel Craig wants to talk to you…the way things are going tonight, maybe it is Daniel Craig. He wants to know how long it takes to drive to Iowa City."

For a second I toyed with ignoring the message but knew how pissed Gregg would be if I didn't call. To my surprise, his phone was turned off.

CHAPTER FIVE

I drove the speed limit to my mom's house. I had not heard from her in two days. My car inched forward until I was in front of her townhouse. Pulling into her driveway, I saw Mom sitting on her patio with her two sisters, the card table set up, snacks on a TV tray, drinks warming in the unusually hot spring sun. I looked at my watch; I was five minutes late. When I kissed them all hello, Aunt Marie looked at her watch as well.

"Aunt Marie, can I talk to you for a minute?" I asked.

"Your beer is in there." Mom pointed at a yellow cooler sitting next to the empty chair.

I opened a beer and stood next to her.

"We're ready to play cards Liam," Marie said, "can't this wait?"

"No," I said, "it can't. Can we go inside?"

"I have no secrets Liam. Whatever you have to say you might as well say it in front of all of us." Marie lit a cigarette.

"It's about the television thing."

"Is that all?" Marie barked out a laugh. "I thought you had something important to talk about."

"It is important to me."

"For Christ's sake Liam, let it go. No one remembers it anyway."

Mom put her hand on my arm and looked me in the eyes. I knew what she wanted. It was what she always wanted. I let it go.

Aunt Margaret said, "Did you hear that Bill Thompson's mother died?"

"That one," Aunt Marie said, "she couldn't put a meal on the table if her life depended on it."

"Didn't you graduate from high school with him?" Mom asked. Her mouth smiled at all three of us but not her eyes. It dawned on me that she wasn't drinking beer, which was the proof I needed to know that she was upset. When she was angry, she gave up beer and cheddar cheese. My sister Deirdre called them her Lenten mood swings: they could happen any time of year; usually we didn't know what caused them but this time I did.

"Yes, I did graduate with him," I said, "but we were better friends in grade school. It's funny though, I have no memory of his mom."

"Of course not," Aunt Margaret said, "she was a Campbell."

I burst out with a laugh. "What does that mean?" My family was used to my laugh by now. Sue thought I sounded like a trapped jackass.

Aunt Margaret adjusted her cards and the score pad into perfect right angles. "Grace Campbell always thought she was better than everyone else. Why she wouldn't even talk to her first cousin and they barely lived one block apart. So of course she wouldn't have spoken to you, a mere Ashby. Colleen, didn't you teach your son anything?" She glared at my mom as she announced her bid of 53.

"55," Aunt Marie said taking a drag on one of the excessively long cigarettes she favored. "It's a beautiful afternoon, let's not spoil it by recreating the Campbell family tree."

"56," my mom declared. "Although I don't know why I'm bidding." She took another look at her cards, "I've never seen so many strangers."

"I have no intention of recreating anything, Marie. I was just answering my nephew's question."

"He's my nephew too." Smoke drifted out Marie's nose.

"How old was she?" Mom asked.

"Well, let's see," Margaret looked skyward.

"Here we go," Marie muttered.

Margaret shot her sister a look. I stuffed a handful of potato chips in my mouth.

"When I started at Holy Family High School, Grace was a senior so that made her approximately four years older than I was."

"Approximately?" Aunt Marie said, "You don't know the exact number of days between your birthdays?"

"She was best friends with Rose O'Malley. You remember her, don't you Colleen? They were inseparable. They usually dressed alike for special occasions. I remember what they wore for the Mistletoe Dance as if it happened yesterday—green velvet dresses with fox collars and white gloves. They looked like movie stars. When they handed me their coats I couldn't stop smiling."

"You know what they would say about two high school girls dressing alike today," I said softly. Aunt Marie laughed out loud.

"I don't know how the hell you remember this stuff," Marie said. "I can barely remember what day of the week it is, let alone what somebody wore to a dance forty years ago. Sometimes I think you have the most vivid imagination of anyone I've ever met."

Aunt Margaret looked at my mom with determination. "To answer your question Colleen, Grace Campbell graduated in the class of '54 so that would have made her seventy on April 17."

"You know her birthday? Now I've heard everything," Marie's voice was deep, throaty and echoed of the thousands of cigarettes she had smoked.

We played several hands of pinochle with Aunt Margaret bidding on every hand. She was a much better card player than either my mom or Marie, which drove them both crazy. I watched my mom for any hints of what was going on inside her. She gave away nothing. She could have been a Cold War spy, if captured; she wouldn't have told them a thing.

"Liam, are you ever going to bid or are you going to sit there with a dazed look all afternoon?" Marie said this without looking at me.

"I'm a little rusty at this, in case you hadn't noticed."

Three pairs of eyes bore through me.

"For a smart boy, you can be awfully dumb." Margaret set her cards down again. "This is not a hard game. A pinochle is the queen of spades and a jack of diamonds. That counts four points. But most importantly, you need a marriage to bid which, if you remember, must be a king and a queen of the same suit." She finished her drink. "I just had a thought, Liam. When you play pinochle in Massachusetts do two kings count as a marriage?"

I had just taken the last swallow of my beer, some of which came out my nose.

"Are you all right honey?" Mom moved to take hold of my hand but then stopped.

"Margaret, you never know when to keep your mouth shut, do you?" Marie lit another cigarette.

"Aunt Margaret, that's one of the funniest things you've ever said to me." I couldn't stop coughing.

"Then why do you sound like you're dying?" Marie exhaled a long plume of smoke in Margaret's direction. At that moment Aunt Margaret rattled the ice in her empty low-ball glass. I knew my cue.

"Anybody need another drink?"

Mom picked up her wine glass and threw back the last drops.

"More coffee for you, Aunt Marie?"

"Why the hell not, it's only four."

"What do you think of the beer I bought for you, Liam?" Mom asked, her tone providing the correct answer.

It was Leinenkugel Creamy Dark, which I liked well enough. "It's great, although I better take it easy today, tomorrow is a big day." As soon as I said these words, I regretted them. I could sense my mom and Margaret's disapproval at the mere suggestion that I might be done drinking for the day. It made them uncomfortable if people stopped drinking, especially before dinner.

"It is beyond me why you can't tell us…" Margaret stopped her sentence at a stern look from Mom.

"Who really cares?" Marie handed me her coffee cup, which had a bright red lipstick smudge on the edge.

"I still don't understand why you aren't selling real estate. This town needs a young, good looking, energetic salesman," Mom said.

"Leave him alone Colleen," Aunt Margaret said.

"Are we going to plan Liam's life or play cards?" Marie said.

"You know as well as I do that it is possible to do both," Margaret said with a look at her empty glass.

"Margaret, I swear if you don't concentrate on this game, I am going to walk home," Marie said.

I started coughing again thinking of this sixty-seven year old walking three miles home in her bright pink high heels with ankle ties.

"Do I need to remind you who is winning?" Margaret asked.

CHAPTER SIX

———∞———

Monday morning was a more typical spring day in northern Iowa: overcast, spitting rain and around sixty degrees: a perfect day for a funeral. The night before had ended abruptly. After dinner Mom made it clear that she was done for the night by taking away Margaret's dessert plate even though she had several bites left of her apple pie.

I was relieved to go home.

I had gone to bed early and slept for seven hours straight. After a fast three mile run, I took a quick shower and pretended to shave. Sue teased me endlessly about my lack of facial hair, wondering how long I had been taking estrogen.

As I ran a comb through my hair I wondered what the Graves family was going to be like. My biggest worry was that they would be rude. I hated rude people, the result of many years working in the restaurant and real estate industries. There was something about eating or buying a home that brought out the worst in people.

Sue walked in my front door without knocking. I was sitting on the couch, anxiety inching up my body. I stood up and she kissed me lightly on the lips.

She looked at me. "What's wrong with you?"

"Why?"

"You hide your feelings about as well as I do."

"Other than I'm going to meet the man I have dreamed about marrying—nothing's the matter."

"My God, you are such a lesbian. Is that all?" She sat down next to me. "Hey, I've been meaning to ask, how does your family like having a famous member, hell you're almost as famous as Benjamin Graves. I would watch my back if I were you today. I've heard he's nasty when he's jealous."

"My mom is not happy."

"Why?"

"I'm not exactly sure, it's not like she pretends I'm straight or anything."

"She'll get over it."

"I'm not sure it's that simple."

"Of course it is, it always is."

"Maybe in your family, not mine."

We walked into the kitchen together and I poured her some coffee. "I was thinking Sue, if we lived in LA, we could market ourselves as the duo that handled the Arthur Graves funeral. We'd probably have to turn business away."

"You're right. When this is all over, let's talk about doing just that. I never wanted to spend my best years in Iowa; think of the money we could make!"

"Hold on," I said. "If you recall, I just moved back here. I'm not going anywhere."

"Along with your apparent lack of a sex drive, that is another thing about you that I don't understand. I love having you back in Iowa but Liam, I had to come back. You chose to come back." She put an index finger over my lips. "I know all about your Florence Nightingale fetish, but your mom is fine, she is better than fine. She just about ran me off the road the other day in front of Target. I swear she was going fifty in a 25-mile zone. I started to give her the finger but recognized her at the last second."

39

We drank our coffee in silence as I studied her. I could tell by the slight tension in her shoulders that she was as nervous as I was. Her bravado was an act, but very few people would be able to tell. I wished, not for the first time, that I could hide my anxieties as well as she could.

As I backed my car out of the garage, Sue reached over and put a hand on my shoulder. The tension had moved from her shoulders to her face. "Please help me remember what happens today. I want details, I want to know what Benjamin smells like, I want to know how tall he is, how big his hands are, how broad his shoulders are… oh my fucking God, I can't believe we are going to meet him in a few minutes!"

"I was just thinking about how jealous I am that you can hide your neuroses."

"Sorry, lost my mind." Her voice was back to normal, her guard back up. "You do realize of course that nothing like this will ever happen to us again. In a few years no one will care if we talk and this is a story that I want to remember."

"I'll do my best although I do tend to have short term memory loss when I'm nervous."

"Are you aware that you just ran a stop sign?"

"Fuck." I took a deep breath and tried to concentrate. "Before I forget, Benjamin's mom is still alive. If we don't screw up today, maybe he'll ask us back to handle her funeral."

"She better die soon while I still have my figure." Sue reapplied her lip-gloss in the vanity mirror.

I slowed down to a crawl as we neared the Graves home. There were two cops guarding the entrance to the driveway, arms extended outward, and palms up. I rolled down the window.

"Not so fast," an overweight fifty-something cop growled at me.

"We've been hired for the funeral reception." I flashed my yellow pass at him swallowing my irritation at his manner. Sue was fumbling in her purse. I noticed that the young cop on her side of the car couldn't stop staring at her cleavage. When she handed her pass to him, she looked up and burst out laughing.

"What's so funny Miss?" the older cop snarled.

"I was just ogled by my cousin Tommy!" She reached through the window and hit Tommy on his arm. He turned five shades of red before saying, "Please don't tell my mom."

"Don't you love small towns!" she replied between fits of laughter.

Creeping up the driveway I looked through the trees to the point across the road where I had talked to Jesse Clinton. H! TV would love to know that their gay poster boy was on his way into the Graves family home. As I approached the crest of the hill, the home came into view: two stories with a portico supported by eight white Doric columns, looking more like the White House than Tara. There were rose bushes lining both sides of the driveway and surrounding the house, every bush the same size and covered in the same type of red rose.

Another cop waved us on, pointing at a service road that continued past the house and then disappeared to the right. Behind the house there was a parking area for staff and a small stone walkway I assumed would lead us into the kitchen. To the left I saw a large swimming pool, the water a steely gray in the murky light.

"That pool is big enough for my entire extended family including all ex-husbands and the ten or so in prison," Sue said.

There was a slate patio area with two groupings of wrought iron furniture. Behind that was a tennis court and what seemed to be a guesthouse in New England shingle style. I could see an electric fence discreetly hidden among the evergreen trees, which created a rectangle around the house. I vaguely recalled an article I had read a few years ago about this house and how unhappy Benjamin's parents were living in it. I wondered if the fence was to keep people out or in.

"Are you ready?" Sue whispered.

"As ready as I'll ever be."

"Why am I whispering?" she said in a loud voice. She gave herself a small slap on the face. "I need to grow a set if I'm going to get through this day."

I laughed and then blushed. Even to my own ears, my laugh seemed several volumes too loud.

"My God, Liam. Don't do that again. You might raise the dead, which I supposed wouldn't necessarily be a bad thing today, would it?"

At the end of the path was a door painted beige with a wooden plaque that said *Welcome* in several languages. There were small Dutch girls, geisha girls, and harem girls dancing around the border. I knocked several times. Finally we heard a woman scream, "What!!!!!" The door opened and we walked into the kitchen. I saw a thin, short, fortyish woman with shoulder length brown hair, pursed lips, and translucent skin. Fury was streaking from her eyes. She looked at us quickly. "Who the fuck are you two?"

"We're the wait staff," Sue said, heat in her voice. I felt my breath shorten. Sue hated women like this.

"You can't be," she spat out. "Gretchen, get the fuck in here now," she yelled. 'And you two…out!" A young mousy woman flew into the room, headset on, Blackberry in hand.

"Yes, Theresa?" she was out of breath.

"What the fuck is going on? Where are Roberto and Oscar?" Gretchen started to say something. "Don't tell me that they're still in LA. I do not want to hear that!" She glared at us as she moved in close to Sue.

"Do you have any idea who is going to be here today? Do you?" Sue said nothing. "Donato, Rose, John, Jamie, Dustin, Helen, Edwina, Dawn!"

She moved over to me, I could smell her breath: frosty wintergreen mixed with coffee.

42

"Not today, I cannot handle the likes of you two today. Get the fuck out of here." She rubbed her index finger back and forth beneath her nose.

"Where the fuck is my purse?"

Gretchen pulled Theresa aside and said something that I could not hear.

Theresa erupted again." Get Manuel on the phone now!" She looked at us again and said, "Why are you two still here?"

Her voice was low and rumbled with volcanic anger. I couldn't look at Sue out of fear that she would say something that would get us fired on the spot. Somehow Gretchen was able to simultaneously make a phone call, hand Theresa her purse and talk into her head set while throwing an apologetic smile our way.

"Manuel," Gretchen said quietly into the phone, "Theresa needs to talk to you."

Theresa grabbed the phone out of Gretchen's hand, "If you don't tell me that Roberto and Oscar are on a jet right now, minutes away from this god forsaken hell hole..," she was walking in a tight circle,

"What? FUCK!!!!!"

With that she flung the phone at Gretchen who deftly caught it with her left hand. Theresa stalked off through a door into what I assumed was the main house but not before shooting a look at Sue. "Button that shirt up missy, this isn't a strip club." Sue and I stood there in stunned silence.

"Oh my God," Sue said, "Who was that?" She buttoned her blouse.

"That is Theresa Armstrong," Gretchen replied as she checked messages on her Blackberry. "She's handled every one of Benjamin's functions for the last five years but always in LA and you won't be surprised to hear this, with her own staff." I looked at Sue whose shoulders were no longer up around her ears. "Not sure how she forgot that the wait staff was local, guess she didn't want to believe it." She looked at us and smiled. "Don't worry, I'll keep her out of your way. Once she accepts the fact that you belong here she'll move on to the next crisis." In the distance they heard another loud, "I do not want to hear that! Where are the caterers? They're lost? FUCK!"

"See," Gretchen said, "next crisis already. Now let's get you two to work. Oh, and see me at the end, I have your pay." She put a hand on my shoulder and moved me towards the door. "But first a tour of the house, well at least the part of the house you'll see."

She led us into an oval dining room. The table had chairs for sixteen, and it was covered in a burgundy damask tablecloth, the walls covered in mauve patterned wallpaper. I peered into the next room. It appeared that all the furniture was in Wright's signature look. Gretchen must have noticed me looking at the furniture.

"Benjamin loves Frank Lloyd Wright's designs. We all think he is a frustrated architect. Aren't there some Wright buildings in this town?" She asked me over her shoulder. "I thought I overheard Benjamin telling Donato that this morning."

I smiled at the way she referenced Donato DiStefano as if we all knew him.

"One of the few Wright designed hotels is in the center of Mason City," I said. "Plus we have the largest concentration of Prairie School homes outside the Chicago area. Across the street from where I live is a house designed by Walter Burley Griffin, a colleague of Frank Lloyd Wright. I always fantasized about living there." I noticed Gretchen's eyes nervously darting around the room. "Sorry."

"It's no problem, I just have a lot to do." She pulled her Blackberry out of a pocket. "By the way, there is nothing to be nervous about. Trust me. They won't even know you're in the room. They only notice each other. Sort of like when a dog sees another dog on the street, except they don't smell each other's butts. They have people lined up to kiss them instead."

She looked at her watch and shepherded us into the next room. "The caterers, once they find their way here," she laughed, "will fill this table with various types of finger food, of course leaning toward the healthy side, always healthy for this crowd." She was circling the table, her eyes taking in everything. "We'll need you to mingle with trays of food as well. Alternating with food, we need you to come through with red and white wine. That is all the alcohol Mrs. Graves is allowing today. She doesn't drink and doesn't approve of it but has compromised on this for Benjamin's sake. She would like you to make sure that no one has too much to drink. If you see anything out of the ordinary, please let Theresa or me know and we will speak to them but please don't refuse them anything. We do not want any scenes today!" I looked at Sue and raised an eyebrow—how were we supposed to keep track?

As we continued walking through the house it felt like we were walking through a museum dedicated to Frank Lloyd Wright's greatest hits. While beautiful to look at it seemed self-conscious and appeared to have no one living in it. I wondered why this tribute to Wright hadn't extended to the outside of the home.

As we made our way out of what I supposed was the family room, I stopped to look at a photo sitting on a bookshelf, the one piece of evidence that a family lived in this house. It was of Benjamin with his parents at an awards show, Benjamin and his dad in tuxedos and his mom in a shimmery peach gown, Benjamin clasping his award by his side. Benjamin was sporting a huge smile, bigger that I had typically seen in photos of him. He was beaming, his dad looked nervous, his mom unhappy.

"That was at the Golden Globes last year when he won Best Actor for *Flag Day,*" Gretchen said. I had picked up the photo to get a closer look. Gretchen took it from me and looked at her watch.

"Thanks, but I know that. I know pretty much everything about his career," I said. Gretchen looked at me sharply. "Don't worry," I said, "I won't drool over him. I am going to disappear into the wood work."

"Don't disappear too much. They expect to get what they want, when they want it," Gretchen said.

Theresa yelled from somewhere, "It's about goddamn time you showed up. Gretchen…I need you…now!"

I know that Sue and I were busy helping the caterers, making sure that everything was ready to go the moment the Graves family appeared but when I try to piece together that day, most of the hour or so before they arrived is lost to me. My anxiety level was so high it was almost as if I had no ability to retain memories. I do remember finding a small bathroom off the kitchen where I hid for a few minutes, and I remember Sue nervously rapping on the door ordering me out. When I opened the door I saw Gretchen talking into her headset looking worried. She looked at me and said, "That was Theresa. The motorcade just left the cemetery. They'll be here in about ten minutes." Sue jumped out of the bathroom, her eyes darting around the room.

"Benjamin's personal assistant, Sydney Ross, just arrived,"

Gretchen's eyes were distressed.

"Just do what she says and you'll be fine. However if I were you I would stay out of her way. She makes Theresa look like she should add "Mother" to her name."

At that moment, the door from the dining room slowly opened and a middle-aged woman took two steps into the kitchen. She easily filled the doorway and as my mom would say was built like a linebacker. Her shiny auburn hair was swept back from her round, handsome face, which was accented by small square glasses, perched on her nose. Her gaze swept across the room.

"On the surface everything looks fine. Is that the case, Gretchen? I suppose I don't need to say that I hope so, but then again, I just said it, didn't I?"

Walking in a deliberate manner towards Gretchen, who had lost her coloring, Sydney asked, "Where is Theresa? I really need to talk to her now."

Gretchen ran out of the room.

46

"Oh, and you two," Sydney pointed at Sue and me. "Since you both look terrified, you must be the local help. I need to tell you a few things."

She spoke softly and deliberately, which had the effect of causing me to lean towards her, which was the last thing I wanted. She stood between us and put an arm around our shoulders in a maternal way. She moved us to the back door and outside. The drizzle had stopped but it was still cloudy and chilly.

"And you are?" she asked. I blurted my name, Sue muttered hers. She frowned at Sue. Sydney moved closer to me. She smelled of roses.

"I know these things can be a bit stressful, especially for novices, but everything will be fine if you listen only to me. Theresa is adequate in her -what's the word—arena, and normally I wouldn't bother with such minor details as this."

She looked me straight in the eye.

"But it is utterly vital that today goes well. The Graves family is in shock...as I am."

I looked in her eyes. I didn't see shock.

"Benjamin has banned all personal assistants today, no publicists, no managers. Several guests don't know Benjamin that well. They will be uncomfortable and that is where you come in. They will need extra attention, especially Edwina and Rose." My heart raced when she said those names. She was speaking to me as if Sue had walked back in the house. "I need you to make them your priority."

"Why are they here if they don't know Benjamin?" Sue asked. Sydney glowered at her.

"I don't have time to answer that," she said without looking at Sue.

"You understand, don't you handsome?" She slid her hand down my arm with a quick squeeze of my bicep and turned toward Sue and said loudly, "Is anything getting in to you dear? You're not high or drunk are you?" She leaned in as if to smell Sue's breath. "Because if you've taken anything or had anything alcoholic to drink, I want you out of here now."

Sue muttered something.

Her voice turned into a whisper. "When I ask you something, I want a response I can hear, okay dear?"

Sue's face flushed. "I understand completely." Her voice was firm and clear.

"That's better dear."

Sydney moved us back towards the house. "I want you two at the front door to take coats."

When I opened the door for her, Theresa was standing there with her hands deep in her pockets. "Theresa darling," Sydney gave her a slight kiss on each cheek, "so good to see you." She kept walking as she marshaled us towards the dining room.

"Where the fuck are you taking them?" Theresa asked. "I need them in the kitchen."

"Always so gratifying to see that your language skills have remained at such a high level, Theresa, but we really don't want to hear that word again today, now do we? You should know by now how Mrs. Graves feels about filthy language. Surely you realize how upset she must be but then again, you've never met her, have you?"

As we entered the dining room, she said without turning around, "Theresa, I would love a decaf cappuccino, one lump of sugar."

I looked at Theresa out of the corner of my eye and saw her face threaded with anger. We went directly to the front of the house. I only had a few seconds to look at the tables that were overflowing with food.

"Okay, where was I?"

Sydney slowly turned in a circle.

"I want you," she pointed at Sue, "to stand here and offer to take their coats." She positioned her to the immediate right of the front door. "And you, what was your name again? I want you to hang their coats in the closet over there."

She pointed to a door somewhat hidden under a staircase that curled away to the second floor. The staircase didn't seem attached to the wall. I heard a car door close and my heart rate accelerated. We stood at attention as the mahogany and stained-glass door opened. I held my breath and I could feel sweat dripping down my sides. One part of my brain felt like it had frozen shut while another part was yelling at me to remember everything. I closed my eyes for a second and when I opened them, there he was, Benjamin Graves, an arm's length away.

I squinted trying to recognize the person in front of me. While it was certainly Benjamin Graves, he didn't look anything like he did in photos or movies. What I saw was a grieving man. His arm was wrapped around his mother's shoulder, his green eyes were blood shot and he looked tired, very tired. Sydney stepped forward to squeeze Benjamin's hand. She said, "Mrs. Graves, I am so sorry for your loss."

Benjamin helped his mother out of her coat, which he handed to Sydney, who handed it to Sue who handed it to me. His mom was familiar to me as I had run into her over the years at the garden store near their home but I had never met her. She was pale, her mouth turned down, the flesh around her chin sagging but her eyes were clear.

I remembered when my own dad had died and my eyes filled with tears. I remembered how lost my mother had seemed those first few days. I looked down, took a deep breath and didn't exhale as I tried to control my emotions. When I raised my head I realized that Benjamin was looking in my direction. I glanced at him and he stared back for a second with a quizzical look on his face. It only lasted a second; I wasn't even sure it had happened. I looked at Sue who was helping Benjamin's sister out of her coat.

The rest of Benjamin's family came into the house. I recognized them all. For the first time in my life I realized how odd it was that I knew so much about a man and his family whom I had never met.

I felt a rush of energy as the celebrities arrived. Donato Distefano, Helen, Rose Wizenwood and Edwina Sharp handed us their coats, said hello to Sydney and disappeared into the living room. Then John Bankman zipped by, an athletic bounce to his step. It happened so fast, I wasn't sure it was real. Sue continued asking for coats until Theresa materialized in front of us.

"Okay you two, you're done here. I need you in the kitchen!" She glanced around as if she was being tailed. She pointed us to a door behind the staircase that led down a hall back into the kitchen. "Having you as coat check girls was...." Her voice was thin and shrill. I looked behind her and saw Sydney staring at us.

Sue and I loaded up trays with glasses of red and white wine and walked into the dining room, which was filled with family. We worked opposite sides of the room and to a person they declined a drink. The next room held the actors. Our trays were emptied in seconds.

Alternating between food and wine, we went about our jobs. I realized after a few minutes this was no different than any other private party: we had a job to do and we were being ignored. I also realized that it made little difference that it was Donato Distefano taking a glass of wine from my tray and not Donato Smith. After all the nervous energy of the past few days I felt deflated.

When I reentered the room with the actors a hush had fallen. I glanced behind me and saw Benjamin standing in the doorway holding his mother's hand. It was almost as if I had seen an impostor earlier at the front door and now the real Benjamin Graves had arrived. His eyes were no longer blood shot, his hair was perfectly imperfect, and the dark smudges under his eyes were gone. He helped his mother to a chair as I watched his every motion. The muscles of his back made small ripples in the black fabric. When he knelt down to ask his mother something, I could see his quadriceps push out against his pants.

When he stood up he nodded at me. We were on a beach and I was handing him a cold beer. The sweat was running down the side of his face as he guzzled the beer and then ran into the ocean. I felt a nudge in my back and I was pushed forward. I remembered what I was supposed to be doing and realized that Benjamin wanted a glass of wine. I walked across the room, my eyes on the floor to make sure I didn't trip. When I looked up, Benjamin's green eyes swept across my face. "Thanks," he took a glass from the tray, his gaze back on his mother. I stood still, forgetting where I was, again, until I felt pressure on my shoulder and realized that I was being pushed again by Theresa back towards the kitchen. Once inside, she angrily whispered in my ear, "Listen you dumb fuck, we were promised that you would not be star struck. If I catch you acting like that again, you are out of here. This is a fucking funeral, not some goddamn charity event for dumb fuck local yokels who want to meet their favorite movie star." She stalked back into the dining room. I was embarrassed by what I had done and as much as I hated to admit it, she was right.

When I entered the living room, Rose and Edwina were standing near the entrance.

"Had you ever met him?" I heard Edwina whisper to Rose who shook her head no. "I hadn't either until today. You know, we're working together next year for the first time."

Walking slowly to the next group, I thought about what kind of person Benjamin must be that he would want complete strangers at his dad's funeral. John Bankman was talking to Helen as I approached them. "Had you ever met Benjamin's dad? I heard he was a great guy." I was amused to hear traces of his Boston accent that he had so studiously tried to eliminate or so I had read in *People*.

"I was hoping to meet Arthur Graves," Helen replied. "We did a show on the fathers of superstars and Benjamin promised me that his dad would show up but I guess he got cold feet. Benjamin showed up in his place. The audience went crazy." She took a scallop from my tray. "You know, Benjamin never does talk shows." She was looking at me as if I were a peer. "I guess never is the wrong word since he did mine." She spoke quickly and without an obvious intake of breath. "Cold feet...I wonder who was the first person to ever say that in this context?" John looked befuddled.

After several more failed attempts to hand out food, I switched back to wine, which was also steadfastly refused. I began to feel superfluous and wondered if they would let us leave earlier than planned. I worked my way to the front of the house and then walked quietly through the empty entryway. Stopping for a second, I looked up at the second floor, wondering where Benjamin's bedroom was. Not wanting to get caught by Sydney, I headed toward the hallway that led back to the kitchen. I opened the door and almost collided with Benjamin. He was taking a gulp from a silver flask, John Bankman looking on approvingly.

"Shit," Benjamin said, "busted."

"It's just the waiter," John replied. His accent reminded me of the Filene's Basement salesman who tried to sell me a tuxedo once. I kept moving.

"Hang on," Benjamin said a little too loudly and to my ear, a bit drunkenly. His hand reached over and brushed against my bicep. I jerked back from the unexpected physical contact. "It is you...Liam Ashby, John, it's Liam Ashby." His eyes had narrowed to half their size. John stuck out his hand and pumped my arm.

"You're that guy that Jesse interviewed, aren't you? I thought you looked familiar but when he said your name was Liam Ashland, it just didn't register." Benjamin took a step closer to me, close enough that I could smell him, a combination of cologne, soap and Scotch. His mouth was only inches from mine. I stared at his lips. On screen his lips were like plump pillows you wanted to fall into. I wanted to kiss him.

"When I saw you at the front door, I started to put two and two together. He screwed up your name, didn't he? If it's not on a cue card, they fuck things up." He took another pull from the flask. "Did you know that I ran track in high school?" I nodded yes as my mouth would not form words. "I followed your times in the Globe Gazette. Boy have you changed, you were a twig in high school," he said. "Didn't you win the mile at the Drake Relays?"

I nodded. "I saw you win the 100 meters," I muttered.

"The only race I ever won. It was a fluke. You set a record that day, didn't you?"

"Yes, I did Mr. Graves." He took another step towards me and placed a hand on my shoulder and gave a small squeeze. It felt large and hot against my shirt. I could feel sweat pouring down my sides and a stirring in my groin.

"Dude, call me Benjamin." I winced at the word "dude"—it carried such an assumption we all played for the same team. "By the way, I'm glad you liked my performance in *The Taming of the Shrew*. I thought I sucked. I'll have some wine. Do you want any, John?" he asked.

"Nah, I'll stick to Scotch, that stuff gives me a headache."

Benjamin grabbed two glasses, one of which he threw back in a second and as he replaced the glass on my tray, he looked me in the eyes and smiled. "Nothing to say to me, Liam?" At that moment, I heard Theresa from the kitchen. "Has anyone seen that local waiter, Leyland, Lawton, Larry. I am going to fire him right after I kill him." The door swung open almost knocking the tray of wine glasses to the floor.

"There you are," she said, "where the fuck?" She stopped when she saw Benjamin standing against the wall. Two red circles appeared on her cheeks.

"Theresa, don't be mad at Liam, I was just talking to him. This is my fault, not his. Liam and I both ran track back in high school. We're old friends." Benjamin gave me a tap on my shoulder and said with a big smile, "Thanks for the drink and for talking to me for a few minutes. You did talk, didn't you?" He put his empty glass on my tray. "God it was good to have something else to think about," he said softly.

I returned to the kitchen in a daze. Where the hell was Sue? I could still feel the pressure on my arm and shoulder where Benjamin's hand had been. I felt sweaty and had the beginning of a headache. What I wanted was either a stiff drink or to go for a fast, hard ten mile run. I looked across the room and Sue waved at me.

"I really need to talk to you," I whispered into her ear as I pulled her into the foyer.

"You don't look well," she replied. "You're pale and moist. What happened?"

"Benjamin Graves was just talking to me, he knows my name and he remembers me from high school."

"Liam, I need you to smile. And then I need you to raise both arms," Sue said, "now tell me your name."

"What the fuck are you doing?"

"Making sure you're not having a stroke."

"I can't believe this. I cannot fucking believe this."

"What's the big deal?" she asked, "after today, you'll never see him again, unless you buy a ticket."

I looked at her. She was right, as usual.

"Come here," Sue ordered. "You need to calm down." She wrapped me in her arms. I burrowed my nose into her neck and breathed in her perfume. My hands ran up her strong back, developed from years of carrying trays of food.

"Jesus." She shoved me away.

"What…what did I do?"

"I just felt that thing between your legs. Is that real?"

I looked down and blushed bright red.

"Do I know you?" Sue asked, "I thought you didn't have a sex drive."

54

"Of course I do," I said, "you didn't seriously believe that, did you?"

"To be honest, I did," she said, "I've never seen you even look at a man since you've been back in Iowa." She took me by the hand and we walked into the kitchen. "We need to keep moving before The Wicked Bitch of the West finds us again and before you pop out of your pants."

On the island in the middle of the room, there were dozens of glasses filled with wine. Sue and I looked at each other. "We could start dumping them on the plants," she whispered. She stayed next to me, "I can't tell you how relieved I am that your sex drive is erupting. Your eunuch act never made sense to me."

My hard on pushed against my briefs as if asking for a treat.

I heard a clock chime the hour and realized we had at least two more hours of work. I began picking up empty plates and glasses; it was all I could do not to start taking things from people in the hope they would leave sooner.

I began to resent everything about this day, especially the money. Our silence had been bought and for what? I hadn't seen one thing out of the ordinary. These people were no different from anyone else and it was ludicrous that we all made them into something they weren't and I was one of the worst offenders.

Entering the living room I saw Benjamin standing next to his sisters, Alyssa Wheelock right behind him with her hand around his waist. They were all crying. This day had been so strange that I had almost forgotten someone had died. I heard one of Benjamin's sisters say, "I can't believe Daddy is gone, what am I going to do?" in a choked voice that could have easily turned into a wail. My eyes filled up when I saw Benjamin fall into Alyssa's arms, his body shaking with sorrow.

"Why don't you and your friend take a fifteen minute break," Sydney Ross whispered in my ear, appearing out of nowhere.

"What about Theresa?"

"Don't worry about that." She smiled at me and pushed me lightly towards the kitchen. Sue was washing her hands at the kitchen sink when I entered. I took her by the arm and we walked to the back door and out to my car.

"We're on a break." I looked at Sue's tired eyes. "By order of Commandant Ross."

"God it feels good to sit down. I am pooped." She yawned and closed her eyes.

"What do you think so far?" I asked her as I yawned too. I could smell my breath and found a tube of Lifesavers in the door pocket.

"Boring." Sue grabbed them out of my hand. "If it wasn't for the money, it would be no different from any other event I've worked. Plus about the third time you say to yourself, *that is Rose Wizenwood sitting in that chair*, you realize, so what?"

I looked up at the house and saw Sydney waving at us to come inside.

When we were back in the kitchen Sydney said, "Coffee, tea and desserts need to be set up." She looked at Sue and then turned her back on her. "Benjamin and some of his guests will be going to the guest house in a few minutes and they might need help with drinks, that sort of thing. Liam, I need you to make sure everything is in order."

The second I opened the back door, it began raining and I raced across the patio and burst into the guesthouse. I looked around at the sparsely furnished room: wicker furniture shoved in a corner, a dusty television on the wall, and several plants that were thirsty. Walking towards a small bar I spun around as I heard footsteps descending a staircase and then stop.

"How could you, Benjamin?" a woman said, "I asked one thing of you today, one simple thing and could you do that for me? Of course not." The disgust in her voice was thick. "What's even worse is that I had expectations. I am such a fool."

"I'm not drunk, Mom," Benjamin replied.

"Of course you are, just listen to your voice."

"I've only had a couple of drinks."

"I don't believe you, which is one of many things about you I don't believe. Take Alyssa for example." Her voice began to quaver.

"What about her?"

"Just remembering that day when—" she said.

"Stop," Benjamin said angrily.

"On top of everything else today you have made me remember the worst day of my life."

"Worse than Dad dying? Are you fucking kidding me?" Benjamin shouted.

The footsteps resumed. "Benjamin, I want you to leave," she said. She came around a corner and saw me. "Who are you and what are you doing here?"

"Liam Ashby, Mrs. Graves. My mom is Colleen Ashby." I stuck out my hand that she touched with her fingertips. She gave no sign of knowing my mom or me as she walked out the door.

I heard footsteps retreat back upstairs. I stood in the middle of the room unsure what to do. What the fuck was all that about? Footsteps began descending again and Benjamin came into the room looking distraught.

"Hey Liam, sorry you had to hear all of that, we're a little strung out today."

"Hear what?" I said.

Benjamin's shoulders relaxed. "I wanted to let you know how sorry I am for your loss," I said. "My dad died recently so I know what you are going through. It's really hard."

"Thanks, I appreciate that," he replied, his eyes glistening. "You're right, this is so much harder than I ever expected." He rubbed his eyes with the back of his hand. "What the fuck am I talking about? I didn't expect this. Did I?" He sighed. "I have no idea what I am saying."

"What can I get you?"

"Huh?"

"Sydney said that some people are coming out here and she wanted me to cover the bar."

"Fuck no, that is the last thing I want. Why would she think that?" He looked around the room, glanced at his watch and left. I watched him walk across the patio oblivious to the rain. Looking at the water streaking down the window, I wondered if I had expected my dad to die. Does anyone? The back door of the house opened and Sydney hurried across; rainwater had left large marks on her silk suit.

"Change of plans," she said, "people are leaving which means you can leave soon. I think your girlfriend could use some help."

"No problem." I began walking toward the door. Sydney stopped me, "Before you go, tell me what you thought about all of this."

"Why?"

"I have my reasons."

"Why would you care what I think?"

"Because you don't want anything from me."

"How do you know?'

"Oh God, not you too!"

I laughed, "You're right, I don't want anything from you." Sydney's face relaxed.

"Now I can trust what you say," she said.

"Does that mean you don't trust anyone in LA?"

"Yes, that is exactly what I mean."

"Guess I'm not surprised...much." I thought about the day. "I guess the most surprising thing is that Benjamin seemed like a regular guy. I expected that someone that famous would be kind of obnoxious." Sydney smiled and nodded in agreement. "Many are," she said.

"But it was weird that some of the actors didn't seem to know Benjamin very well."

"They don't."

"Then why are they here?"

"They had to be, it's expected."

"By whom?"

"By you, no doubt."

"You don't know that about me."

"Come on Liam, you wouldn't have found it strange if no other celebrities were here today?"

"That's not my point, of course I would assume that Benjamin has friends that are actors. However you're telling me that total strangers attended the funeral of his father."

"John is a good friend of Benjamin's."

"So one actor here today is his friend. Bizarre." I thought for a few seconds. "Benjamin could have chosen a very private funeral. No one needed to know the guest list."

"He did. We're in Iowa, aren't we?" She walked to the bar and poured herself a Scotch. She took a swallow and sighed. "Finally, I can have a drink." She polished it off and poured another. "If this had been in Southern California it would have been a zoo. There would have been hundreds, maybe thousands of fans outside the funeral home, outside the church. You must know what people are like." I remembered when Benjamin had filmed a movie in Boston and the hours I had spent hoping to catch a glimpse of him, which I never did.

"I suppose you're right," I said.

"Of course I am," she said. "What else do you have to say about today?" I looked at her relaxed eyes.

"The thing that really blew me away was that Benjamin remembered me from high school."

"Enjoy it because he won't remember you tomorrow."

"That's harsh."

"Why?" she asked, "I'm just being honest." She patted me on the hand. "It's better to believe what I say, trust me on that." I shook my head. I didn't want to. "There really wasn't anything you could do today to cause him to remember you short of shooting him." She laughed at her own comment. "Anything else?"

I looked at her and decided that giving my opinion of the day didn't seem to matter much anymore. "No," I said.

"Sorry," she said, "I didn't mean to throw cold water on you." She put her arm around my shoulder. "Come on, tell me one more thing." A blast of Scotch infused breath washed over my face.

I hesitated. "Well...I can say one thing that has nothing to do with Benjamin or LA. Sue and I were told to watch out for you, that you were impossible but I just want to say I thought you were great. Not sure what the warning was about. Theresa on the other hand...."

Sydney laughed loudly. "Thanks Liam, that's one of the nicest things anyone has said to me in a long time and you know what the best part is? I believe it. You made my day." She crushed me in a hug.

"You smell great," I said as I took a sniff. "What is it?"

"Clive Christian #1. Benjamin gives me a bottle every Christmas." She looked pleased. "Let's go inside, I'm sure Sue is looking for you."

When we entered the kitchen, Sydney went down the hallway to the front of the house. The caterers were cleaning and packing. Sue walked in carrying a tray full of dirty plates and glasses.

"So nice to see you taking a break but really Liam, aren't you supposed to be working?" She scowled at me and pretended to be looking through glasses. "Anything juicy happen out there?"

"I'll tell you later," I said, "let's finish up and get the hell out of here." Thirty minutes later we were done, had found Gretchen and gotten our checks. Sue kissed hers before she folded it and shoved it in her purse. When we stepped outside the rain had stopped and the sky was brightening to the west. We both plopped down into the seats of my car and exhaled simultaneously.

"You seem back to normal. Did you and John Bankman have a quickie in the guest house?" Sue asked.

"No, but I did overhear a conversation between Benjamin and his mom. I'll tell you on the way home." As I pulled to the side of the Graves house, I looked up at the second story and for a second it seemed like someone was looking down at me. Driving across the front of the hill, I was tempted to stop and cut a dozen roses from the blossoming bushes that lined either side of the driveway but figured one of the over amped Mason City cops would probably shoot me. When we pulled out onto the road, I was surprised to see all the news vans parked across the street. "I suppose they're hoping for one last shot of Benji for the next *People*."

"Preferably crying," Sue added. "Hey, are we being followed?" I looked in the rearview mirror and saw the H! van behind us.

"Oh my God," she said, "we're being stalked."

"Calm down Britney, they are probably on their way to the airport." However, as we made our way to Sue's house, they stayed right behind us. "If they don't leave my porch in a few minutes, call the police," she said.

"Why do you think they are going to follow you?" I asked.

"You really are blind to my hotness, aren't you?" But as she ran up the stairs into her home, no one got out of the van. I looked in the rearview mirror and they looked back. I sat for a few minutes thinking about my options and then decided the only sensible option was to go home. I pulled into my alley and quickly into my garage. They continued up the alley and I breathed a sign of relief. However when I turned on the light in my kitchen, my doorbell rang. Suspecting that they would not go away if I tried to ignore them, I went to the front door and yanked it open. Standing there was Jesse Clinton and Kurt with his camera pointed at me.

"Now what?"

"Liam Ashby," Jesse said, "is it true that you were hired to work at the Arthur Graves funeral reception today?"

"I can't talk about it," I said, wishing I had said nothing.

"So it is true," Jesse said, "we'd like to come in and talk to you for a few minutes. There are millions of Benjamin Graves' fans that need to know how Benjamin is holding up. Surely you can talk about that."

"I can't," I said, putting a hand over my mouth to cover my yawn. Jesse turned to Kurt and said, "Stop taping for a second." Turning back to me he said, "You know Liam, we pay people for information and we pay well. The response to our interview with you from Friday has been unbelievable. This would be the perfect ending. Can't you help us out?"

"Sorry, no can do," I said, "and you know what?" The camera was pointing back at me. "Have you forgotten that a man's father died? Don't you think he is upset enough already without you guys parked across the street? These things are private or at least they should be. How would you feel if it was your father that died and you had some jerk trying to film your every move?" I closed the door and turned off the light. I went to the refrigerator and popped a beer. I sat down in my empty living room staring at nothing with images of Benjamin Graves invading my mind. I quickly jerked off into my t-shirt. Without feeling hunger, I ate a bowl of leftover pasta salad. I walked into the bathroom and jerked off into the sink. The face looking back at me was unfamiliar. This reflected face looked rattled and exhausted.

I turned on my television, turned it off, thumbed through a *New Yorker* and tossed it on the coffee table. Nothing interested me except the thought of Benjamin Graves: standing next to me, touching my arm, remembering me. The argument with his mom ran on a tape in my head. I could see the headline: *Benjamin Graves's secret drinking problem! Drunk at his own father's funeral!!*" I went to my computer and scrolled through my folder of photos of him. I stopped at a picture I didn't normally look at: a stock studio photo of Benjamin when he was in his early twenties. I was struck by how open he seemed, his smile was wider, his eyes less guarded. He still had a whiff of Iowa about him. I scrolled through more photos. To me, Benjamin had an unusual combination of the wholesomeness of Matt Damon, the slightly off kilter looks of the young Harrison Ford and the sexual swagger of Daniel Craig.

I drank another beer, jerked off again and went to bed not caring it was only nine. I couldn't stand to be alone with myself. I hoped sleep would happen. It didn't.

CHAPTER SEVEN

———∞———

Thursday night, a few days after the Graves reception: the restaurant was swamped. As I raced around making drinks I thought about the photo and article on the front page of the local paper of the entire Graves family, including Benjamin, boarding a private jet for the family ranch in Montana. It said Benjamin planned to spend the summer there with his mom to work through his grief. I laughed when I read it. Working through their anger might be a better plan.

Customers were lined up four deep around the bar, some jostling to cut off other people, but I knew who was next. Usually the aggressive ones were the heavy drinkers and I could hear the hint of impatient anxiety in their voices when they ordered their drinks. Sue had the night off. Work always seemed like work when she wasn't around.

As the evening wound down a few seats opened at the bar. I was talking to Barb, one of the waitresses, when I noticed a man heading in our direction. He was wearing a Boston Red Sox cap, a dress shirt, and blue jeans. I could tell by the way he walked that he had been drinking for a while. He sat down in front of us and began reading his Blackberry. Barb turned her back on him and smiled. I mouthed at her; *do you know him?* She shook her head and headed into the dining room.

He ordered a draft beer and a Scotch chaser. While his walk had been unsteady, his voice was clear. As I handed him his drinks

I did a quick assessment. He had broad shoulders, his eyes hidden under heavy black glasses with tinted frames, a muscular neck, long brown hair and a dark brown beard. His voice had a slight southern twang. But there was something familiar about him. I thought back to high school wondering if he had been in my class. After about twenty minutes he ordered another round. I decided to give him one more and then cut him off. The rest of the bar had emptied by now and the waitresses were gone. Georgia Dee had called it a night. I just needed to get rid of him, close out the cash register and I could leave. When I saw him raise his hand to signal a third round, I walked over to him to give him the bad news.

"I'm sorry sir, but I cannot serve you anymore. I believe you have had too much to drink to safely operate a car," I said in a practiced manner.

"I didn't drive so you have nothing to worry about," he mumbled under his breath.

"How will I verify that?" I asked. I always hated moments like this. It was sometimes difficult to determine if someone was really drunk and I didn't want to get into an argument with a guy this big.

"I won't leave until the bar closes and then you can watch me get into a cab, deal?"

"The bar closes in thirty minutes." I gestured towards the empty room. "You're the last customer."

"You sure about that?" I nodded yes. "Forget the Scotch, how about just one more beer?" There was a threat in his voice that I didn't like. I served him his beer and walked to the other end of the bar where I stood and stared at him for a few minutes. He was sitting still, looking at the back of the bar. He formed a fist and smacked his leg a couple of times. I was relieved there was a house phone under the bar. I knew the police could be here in a few minutes if he refused to leave. I finished putting away the fruit and olives, cleaned out the sink, turned the dishwasher on and waited. I looked over as the man took his last swallow of beer.

"Do you want me to call you a cab?" I looked at my watch. "The bar is closed."

He stood up, walked towards me, his hand grabbing the backs of chairs for support. I reached under the bar for the phone. His eyes were glossy and unfocused. He took off his hat but when he went to set it on the bar, it fell on the floor. He put his hand up to his face and started doing something with his beard but seemed to get distracted. He looked away and then looked back, raised his hand and with a yank pulled his beard off one side of his face. He removed the dark glasses and looking back at me were instantly recognizable green eyes.

"Liam, how are you?" he asked.

"Fuck."

He tried to shake my hand but lost his balance and grabbed the bar.

"I...I saw the photo in the paper this morning, you left with your family," I said.

"That wasn't me. Can I have one more drink? I swear I'm not driving."

"Why aren't you with your family?"

He hesitated. "Guess I just wasn't ready to leave Iowa yet. I feel like I haven't said a proper goodbye to my dad." He looked away and rubbed his eyes. "When you told me on Monday that your dad had died, I knew I had met someone I could talk to, someone from around here." His voice slurred and then broke. "I wanted to talk to you about how it's been for you. I couldn't think of a way to approach you other than this." He looked at me, his eyes full. "Can I have that scotch now?"

"Sure," I said.

"Are you going to have a drink?"

"Hang on, I'll be right back."

"Where're you going?"

Ignoring him I walked into the kitchen made sure the cooks and busboys were gone, turned off the lights and locked the back door. I stopped for a moment in the darkened room, my heart thumping. I crossed to the front of the restaurant, locked the door, and turned off the external lights.

I stood near the hostess stand and closed my eyes. Benjamin and I were swimming naked in the warm ocean. We stumbled out of the water and dried each other off with enormous beach towels.

My eyes refocused and I walked back behind the bar.

"I've changed my mind, I'll have whatever you're having," Benjamin said, using his normal voice with no hint of the South. He yanked his wig off and threw it on the bar. He ran his hands through his hair and pushed it off his forehead.

"I'm having a stinger, do you want one?"

"Sure." He scratched his scalp a few times. I paused to stare at the movie star sitting just a few feet away. I shook my head in disbelief.

"I know exactly what you're thinking," Benjamin said, "and I don't want to hear it. No BS, okay?"

"How do you know what I'm thinking?" I pushed his drink across the bar.

"I can see it in your eyes. I've seen it before. I don't want to hear what a big fan you are or how much you liked me in whatever fucking film I was in. I am here to talk to you man to man about what it's like to be thirty-two years old and not have a dad, that's it. No other agenda, deal?"

I took a gulp of my drink. He did know what I was thinking and it pissed me off. I walked around the bar and sat two chairs away from him. I gave him a quick once over. He had on loose blue jeans and a denim shirt with a white T-shirt showing at the collar. With the wig and hat he could have passed for just about anybody in Iowa. I took another long slug from my drink.

"So Liam, how long has it been since your dad died?" His head was propped up on one arm. I looked at his glazed eyes and realized that he was on the verge of being very drunk. I wasn't sure I wanted to talk to a virtual stranger, let alone a drunk one, about my dad. Then again, this wasn't your typical stranger; I knew more about Benjamin Graves' life than I did either of my brothers-in-law.

"Six months ago," I said.

"What happened?"

I pushed my drink away. My face was suddenly hot.

"Heart attack," I said. Benjamin raised an eyebrow. "What?" I asked.

"You're in such good shape, just figured everyone in your family would be as well."

"My dad was a heavy smoker when I was a kid," I said. "He quit smoking about ten years ago, but it was too late." I finished my drink and went behind the bar to make another one, carrying in my head a full color image of dad in his bed at the hospice. I had missed saying goodbye to him by an hour or so.

"Were you close?" Benjamin asked.

Were we? I thought. I supposed the answer was no. "Yes, we were, in our own way," I said. "Although he wanted a football player and a ladies man. What he got was a gay runner."

"A gay runner," Benjamin echoed. "That's funny. There's gotta be a joke there somewhere. What's the difference between a gay runner and a straight runner?" He was starting to slur his words even more. I said nothing hoping he wasn't going to say something ridiculous or even worse—insulting—but he was too drunk to find a punch line. He looked at me as if the last sentence out of his mouth hadn't happened.

"Things got a bit weird when I came out to him when I was twenty-two," I said. "I thought being honest with him would take things to a different level...suppose it did, just took awhile."

"What do you mean?" Benjamin asked.

"Not tonight, I don't want to talk about that tonight. I don't know you at all."

"Were you there when he died?" Benjamin asked.

"No." The grief rose up inside me. My sister Deirdre had begged me to come home to say good-bye one last time but I had resisted, telling everyone that he would pull through as he always had. But I was wrong.

"I wasn't home either," Benjamin took a long swallow from his drink, grimacing as he did. "This drink sucks. I should have stuck to Scotch."

"Nobody's pouring it down your throat," I said.

Anger passed through his eyes. Throwing back his drink in two swallows, Benjamin said, 'you know what? I'm really drunk. Where's the bathroom?" he asked, slurring his s.

"Back of the room, second door down."

I wondered if he needed help. Gregg would have helped whether he wanted it or not. I realized I was pretty high myself with straight alcohol on an empty stomach. And I had to drive. I dumped my drink out and filled the glass with ice and water.

With a stumble, Benjamin made his way back to the bar, fumbling with his fly.

"One more for the road?" he asked too loudly.

"I'm calling you a cab."

"No fucking way, one more and I want you to have one too."

"That's not going to happen, I have to drive, plus the owner of this place sometimes shows up in the middle of the night with one or two of his many girlfriends. And then his wife invariably shows up as well, gets pretty ugly. Last weekend we heard there were knives and melons flying."

Benjamin looked at me, his eyelids half open. "I don't want to wait for a cab." There was a tone to his voice that implied that he wasn't used to waiting for anything. "I want you to take me home. Is that a problem?" He put his wig back on with a skill that surprised me. He bent down and retrieved his beard and hat from the floor. As he stood up he lost his balance and grabbed the bar.

"Uh…uh…sure," I answered, nervous energy pulsating through my frame. Benjamin fucking Graves in my car! Gregg was going to shit when I told him. "It's out back through the kitchen."

Benjamin moved slowly in the direction I had pointed, bumping off the wall a couple of times. I turned off the lights around the bar and followed him. My eyes were fixated on his strong buttocks as they moved against the fabric of his blue jeans. He stopped in the middle of the kitchen, lost his balance again and looked at me like a puppy just separated from its mom.

"Follow me," I said. I led him to the back door with a slight push on his back. We walked to my car with a few shoulder taps and turns to keep Benjamin moving in the right direction. "Nice car," Benjamin said as he made his way around the back of my BMW. "CBS gave me one of these when I was on *Buddies*. Right after they killed me off. A plunging elevator? So unoriginal. God I was pissed about that."

"Didn't exactly hurt your career," I said.

"That was kind of a prickish thing to say." His eyes were half closed. "How would you like it if I started ridiculing your career?"

I remembered that after his brief television career, Benjamin had gone on to make a movie that grossed over $100,000,000. A mediocre movie based on an even more mediocre Anne Rice novel.

"Bartending is not my career, I don't have a career and I wasn't ridiculing you."

Benjamin sat down in the passenger seat. When I slipped in behind the wheel I got a sense of how large he was. His shoulders were almost touching mine. He was staring out the window as I pulled on to the highway.

"How did your dad die?" I asked him.

"Same as yours, heart attack, actually it was his third in ten years," Benjamin said. "He hung in for three days. I was in Japan. I hadn't seen him since Christmas. Now I'll never see him again. How do you forgive yourself for that?"

"You can't," I replied, "or at least I can't."

"Liam, I don't want to go home. Is there someplace we can get a drink around here?" He opened the window and stuck his head out and breathed in deeply.

"No, it's too late. Unless you want to come to my house? "

"Fine with me as long as you have alcohol."

"I'm Irish, there's plenty of alcohol."

We rode the rest of the way in silence. My heart was thumping so loudly I wondered if Benjamin could hear it.

We walked up the steps of my back porch, Benjamin holding on to the railing. Inside he stood in the middle of my kitchen staring at my cabinets, several of which had their doors ajar.

"Why are the doors open?" he asked.

I looked at my cabinets and then looked at him. "It always seems stupid to close them when I know I'm going to open them again," I replied.

"Lived alone long?" Benjamin laughed.

I felt my face redden. "Why don't you go to the living room?" I pointed to the front of the house. "Scotch ok?" I pulled the shades down.

"I thought you said everyone would be asleep," he scratched his head roughly.

"They are but you just never know."

"Paranoia, I know it well."

"You have a reason. I didn't have ten news vans parked on the street when my dad died."

"I don't want to talk about shit like that. We had a deal, right?" He walked into the living room.

"You're a bit of a prick yourself," I said to his back. He made no acknowledgement.

When I entered the living room, Benjamin was looking at a family photo from five years ago. "You look just like your dad," he said without looking up. "He was a good looking guy."

"I guess so. I don't think of my parents that way."

"Well he was. Are these two your sisters?" I nodded yes. "Cute." I didn't think I would share this tepid review of their looks.

Benjamin sat on the couch; I was in a chair across the room with the coffee table between us. There was an awkward silence. I took a drink from my Scotch. He leaned forward and picked up the *Vanity Fair* with his photo on the cover. He glanced at himself and then put it on the floor. Underneath the magazine was a DVD of his movie, *Alone in a Field of War,* costarring John Bankman. He picked this up as well. Underneath that was his movie, *Flag Day.* He turned it over.

"Did you fly to Montana and back in the last three days?" I asked.

Benjamin frowned. "No, that's someone I hired years ago, he doesn't really look like me up close but from a distance he's a dead ringer."

"Did he go on vacation with your family?"

"No, of course not," Benjamin said. "He flew out with my family, he'll stay in a guest house we have and when I join them this weekend, he'll go back to LA…." He looked at me with annoyance. "How'd you get me talking about this?"

I shrugged. Benjamin leaned back into the couch and looked up at the ceiling. He closed his eyes. For a second I wondered if he had fallen asleep. He sat up again, rubbed his eyes and took a long swallow of scotch. His head was bobbing back and forth as if not connected to his neck. "None of my friends have lost a parent. Do you miss him?"

Not really, I thought. "Yes I do, I think about him every day," I said. "I moved back to Iowa a few months ago and while I didn't think my dad's death was the primary reason, now I'm not so sure." *You know why you moved back here and it had nothing to do with him,* a voice countered.

"Your mom's okay?"

"She is now, she had a rough go a couple of years ago, breast cancer." My eyes filled up.

"How much of that conversation in the guest house did you hear?" Benjamin asked, looking me right in the eye.

"Nothing that made any sense and to be honest I'm pretty lit right now…I can't remember much of anything."

"She had a rough day. You know when you're really unhappy or sad you tend to take it out on someone else?" Benjamin asked.

"Yeah, I know that well." I remembered arguing with both of my sisters during the funeral reception. It had seemed so vital at the time. I had a vague memory it was about seating arrangements. "My mom lives close to your parents, sorry, your mom's house." There was a long silence.

"Guess I'm going to have to start getting used to saying that as well," Benjamin said, choking back a sob. His shoulders shook as he started to cry. I stood up and placed the Scotch bottle on the coffee table. He poured himself a full glass and proceeded to drink half in one swallow. I finished what was in my glass. I was now officially drunk.

Benjamin fell back against the couch. "I can't fucking stand this…" he murmured as his eyes shut and his head fell back against the corner of the sofa. Soon he was snoring with his mouth slightly agape.

"Shit," I said. I moved over to the end of the couch and sat down, staring at this prostrate figure. "Shit," I repeated. I stared at him for a long time. I shook his leg slightly and nudged him. No reaction except his snoring became louder. I reached for the Scotch and poured myself another shot. Unsure what to do I decided to do nothing but go to bed. I finished my drink, stood up, swayed and collapsed back down. I sat for a moment trying to focus my eyes to see this beautiful man passed out on my couch and realized through my fog that I was just about ready to pass out as well. I forced myself to my feet and left Benjamin where he was. I made it half way across the room and sat down in a different chair. At least I was getting closer to my bed. Staring off into space, I listened to Benjamin's snoring. I realized I was in an unbelievably unique situation. There were millions of people around the world who would have traded their souls to be in this spot right now, people who would have figured out a way to turn this moment to their advantage either sexually or monetarily. But I wasn't like most people, was I? And anyway, if I tried to have sex with him, wasn't that "sort of rape"? I laughed at the concept of "sort of rape". I rubbed my eyes..fuck I was drunk. I stumbled to my bedroom, tossed my keys, change and wallet onto my dresser. Pulling off my shirt, I had to reach for the wall to steady myself. As I pulled off my pants and underwear I fell forward and landed on my bed. I fell asleep instantly.

I was having the most wonderful dream. Benjamin Graves was lying next to me in my bed. His erect penis was pressed against the mounds of my butt. His hands were around my torso, his fingers insistently brushing my nipples. His head was next to mine, soft sweet breath gently blowing across my face. I turned to lie flat on my back and with a start woke up. I was not alone in my bed. I turned to my right and from the dim moonlight that provided a grayish blue tint to the room, I saw a shirtless Benjamin Graves asleep next to me. I let out a long sigh that bordered on a whistle. Benjamin was sound asleep, his head flat on the bed, his hands crossed on his chest, the sheet hovering around his belly button.

I took in the hairless upper body, the deeply defined pectoral muscles, the biceps that bulged even in slumber and I moaned with delight. I stared for what seemed like hours until I realized I needed to pee. What if I woke him? Would he think I had made a pass at him? As I listened to Benjamin's breathing I realized he was deeply asleep. Sliding to the left, I slipped out of bed, my engorged cock bouncing in front of me as I walked to the bathroom. I turned on the vanity light to see a bloated face staring back. I also realized that I had the worst breath imaginable and though one part of my brain said *why are you doing this* the other part of my brain knew exactly why, so I flossed and brushed my teeth.

Returning to my bedroom I stared at this hulk of a man asleep in my bed. I was as sexually excited as I had ever been. Since Benjamin had shown up in Mason City I had been a walking hard on. I had moved back from Boston partly to avoid sexual feelings and now they were at a level I had never experienced before. I thought for a second that I should go sleep in the guest room but then thought, *fuck it,* this is my house and my bedroom and he made his way into my bed. He's the one who should leave.

As I got into bed, Benjamin turned to his left side and the sheet that had been covering him slipped down his thigh. I saw his cock and balls hanging loosely across his leg. Benjamin continued turning until he was lying flat on his stomach, the sheet just below his ass. My breath came in shallow exhalations. I was on the verge of an orgasm just by looking at him. I ached to touch him. I put my hand a few inches over Benjamin's ass resisting the urge to grab it. I turned onto my back and with just the slightest brush against the tip of my dick, I came. I calmed my breathing, turned onto my stomach and tried to fall asleep but couldn't. I kept turning over to look at this naked man, this naked movie star in my bed. Eventually I dozed off, and the next thing I knew, the sun was shining through the window and I was alone in bed. I walked through the house, the bottle of Scotch was on the coffee table but there was only one glass. The magazine was back on the coffee table. No evidence of any kind that Benjamin had been in my bed.

CHAPTER EIGHT

———∞———

I sat at the kitchen table. I had drunk so much alcohol that my memories were fuzzy even though I was only a few hours removed from them. I could remember the evening until we got home and then I vaguely remembered Benjamin passed out on my couch. What had happened between then and waking up with him in my bed? I had no idea. A blackout, I had a blackout. Great. Now I wasn't even sure he had been in my bed.

I stood in front of the window looking out at my backyard, seeing nothing and guzzling water in an attempt to purge my body of alcohol. I forced myself to eat something and still felt like shit. I was exhausted but knew I couldn't sleep. I also knew that I couldn't run in this state. Nothing interested me; I turned on the television, surfed through a few channels and turned it off. After sitting at the kitchen table, my mind a blank, I forced myself to stand up feeling nausea roiling in my gut. I stumbled to the bathroom and drank half a bottle of Pepto-Bismol.

Knowing I needed to do something physical, I grabbed my garden tools and walked the two blocks to Aunt Marie's house. Every time I had been there I had looked with dismay at her garden. I was twitchy to clean it up but Aunt Margaret had told me to mind my own business. I started to knock on her front door and then decided, *screw it*; I am just going to start weeding. Who wouldn't want that done? I felt a wave of nausea and leaned against her house for a few seconds.

I frowned at what I saw. Roses defoliated by Japanese beetles, withered strawberries, and swarms of aphids. Just as I began to work, Aunt Marie's disembodied voice floated out of a window.

"Liam, what in the hell do you think you're doing?"

"Hi, Aunt Marie, how's your day going?" I had already begun to pull a few weeds.

"Considering how much I lowered my expectations years ago, it's just about perfection." A cloud of cigarette smoke billowed out the window. "To repeat, what the hell do you think you're doing?"

"I am weeding." I pulled a handful of dandelions and threw them on the sidewalk.

"Why in the name of God would you do that? Did your mother put you up to this?"

"No."

"Then, what are you doing? How would you like it if I just showed up at your house and started washing windows?"

"My windows don't need washing."

"My garden doesn't need weeding."

I stepped towards the window. Her face looked younger through the mesh of the screen. She had been beautiful as a young woman but decades of smoking had aged her far beyond her years. The screen hid the lines and it was as if I could see the face hidden underneath her seventy-year-old skin. "Your garden looks like shit," I said, "and I'm going to weed it whether you like it or not."

She blinked several times, brought a cigarette to her lips, lit it, took an extra long drag and started laughing. Her laugh embodied every cigarette she had ever inhaled. "It's about goddamn time you showed some spunk. I was beginning to think it had been surgically removed by some East Coast hack. Go to it, have a ball." Her head disappeared leaving behind a cloud of smoke that got caught in the tiny squares of her battered screen.

I pulled and organized, and watered and pulled some more. Every time I thought about Benjamin I worked faster and harder. Two hours later I was covered in sweat, my hands were caked with dirt and my back hurt, but her garden looked better, or so I hoped. I felt almost back to normal, almost.

Based on the way I smelled, it seemed most of the remaining alcohol in my body had come out my pores.

As I picked up my tools, Aunt Marie called to me from her front porch. She was standing on the front steps holding two glasses of lemonade. A cigarette was dangling from her lip, the ash just about to fall into one of the glasses.

"Here," she handed one to me.

"Thanks." I drained the glass in one gulp. We stood there in silence for several minutes. Aunt Marie was looking down the empty street as if expecting someone.

"What are you doing?" she asked.

"Having a glass of lemonade."

"Don't get cute with me, what are you doing back in Iowa? If you think your mom or Margaret need you here, you're mistaken."

"In case you've forgotten, my mom was sick barely two years ago, and she's still not 100%."

"She's fine. You seem to be the only one who hasn't noticed that."

"What's that supposed to mean?"

"Oh hell, I don't know, how about you treat her like she's ninety instead of sixty -seven and with half a leg in the grave. Sometimes I think you just want to push her in and get it over with."

I could feel my back straighten and the blood rush to my forehead. "What the fuck does that mean?"

"Guess I struck a nerve. I haven't heard that kind of language since oh hell about four hours ago when I yelled at that jerk who lives behind me with the two pit bulls. I swear to you, I am going to shoot those two sons of bitches one of these days, maybe the owner as well. Anyway, where was I?"

"You have a gun?"

She looked at me without answering.

"Okay, here's the deal Liam, and don't say a word until I'm done." She lit another cigarette with the butt of the first one. " You pander to your mother and you never challenge her on anything. This phony attempt at being the perfect son makes her feel like you think she is going to keel over tomorrow."

"Did she tell you this?

"She didn't have to. I know her as well as I know just about anyone and I know you are driving her crazy. Of course your little stunt on TV didn't help." She smiled at me, showing all her teeth. The only time she smiled like this was when she knew she had scored.

"Why do you care, of all people?"

"Don't you get sassy with me young man," she said, "we may not have much of a relationship but I care about your mom and she's worried about you." She paused as she lit a third cigarette. "Why in God's name would someone your age and…and…your kind move back to Mason City, Iowa, for Christ's sake."

I stood there wondering what I could say, what I should say and I froze. I knew Aunt Marie well enough to know that I could not change her opinion about me or about anything for that matter. Trying to engage her in a discussion seemed like a waste of time. "I like it here."

"Bullshit."

"You don't know me at all."

"That's true, I don't but I know that a normal, single thirty-two year old man, especially a gay one, would not willingly come back to Iowa."

"Are you calling me abnormal?"

"Yes."

I picked up my glass. A sole ice cube lay at the bottom. I threw it back and began splintering it between my teeth. "You came back."

79

"You know very well why I came back, three husbands, three burials and one bankruptcy. I had no choice, you did and still do for that matter."

"What gives you the right to question my motivation?" I asked. "I didn't ask for your opinion of me, my relationship with my mom or my attempts to be a good son to her—something someone I know—could do a much better job at. My mom has never said one thing to me about my moving back here that indicated she is worried about me. In fact, I think she's thrilled to have me here."

She stared at me for several minutes. She reached in the pocket of her navy stretch pants, pulled out her lighter and rolled it back and forth in her hand. "Believe whatever you need to believe." She turned to go back into her house. "Paul does the best he knows how." She said it softly and with so much sadness, I felt instant regret.

I walked home, took a shower and went to bed.

CHAPTER NINE

———∞———

Several days later, I was again playing cards with my mom and aunts, this time in Aunt Margaret's backyard. I had learned there was an unspoken rotation between Mom, Margaret and Marie. At mom's house we played pinochle. At Aunt Marie's we played cribbage and at Aunt Margaret's we played 500. At mom's we always ate something basic: roast pork or chicken. At Aunt Marie's we always ordered take out because she had never learned to cook which according to my mother was the reason she had buried three husbands. Then there was Aunt Margaret. She would always whip up some unusual meal that invariably irked my mom. Mom could never understand why Margaret would take a beautiful pork roast or filet of beef and add some God-awful spices that nobody liked or had even heard of. The last time we had eaten at Aunt Margaret's she'd prepared a pork loin stuffed with prunes and coated in curry. The look on my mom's face when she bit into the one piece of pork she had eaten that night was a perfect combination of disgust and judgment.

"So, what's for dinner tonight?" Marie asked as Margaret shuffled the cards. Mom sat up straight in her chair as she prepared for the bad news. It was as if her doctor was giving her a death sentence. Aunt Margaret beamed as she began organizing her cards.

"Tonight we're having grilled swordfish. It will be served with mango salsa, jasmine rice and fresh asparagus. For dessert we're having coconut cream pie, homemade of course." As my mom let out a gasp, Margaret continued, "If I remember correctly Liam, swordfish is one of your favorite meals."

They all looked at me. "Well, I am fond of swordfish, I wouldn't necessarily say it's my favorite meal of all time but it's in the top ten." I hoped this was a good enough compromise to appease my mom.

"Bingo." Marie said looking directly at me.

"What does that mean?" Margaret asked.

"Liam knows."

My face reddened. Marie looked at me, her lips wide apart, all of her teeth showing.

"Swordfish! Margaret, I swear." Mom spat out. "Where the hell did you find swordfish in Iowa? And more importantly, how long has it been dead?"

"I got it at Fareway. You know Colleen, they actually have a fish section in that grocery store. Al Simons assured me that this fish was caught yesterday off the coast of Massachusetts, flown to Minneapolis last night and driven down to Mason City this morning." She sniffed. "Sometimes Colleen, you act like we are in Siberia. Seven clubs."

"Eight diamonds," Marie took a long drag on a cigarette, "Margaret, if you believe that fish was alive yesterday morning, I've got a bridge to sell you."

"Nine clubs," I bid, not sure if I was supposed to bid or not. I was hoping my card playing skills improved soon.

"See Margaret," Mom said with a note of triumph in her voice. "Why I bet that fish died before Liam even started his drive back home in February. Liam, tell her how long it takes before a fish makes it to market in Boston, let alone Iowa. I pass."

Marie sat up, her eyes bright, her grin splitting her face in two. I looked at the three of them: Marie triumphant, Margaret confused, my mom expectant.

"I need to pee." I stood up.

Marie let out a honk. "Some things never change. Liam sit down, we're going to finish this hand." I sat back down.

"It will be delicious," Margaret said.

"Where did you find a mango?" Marie asked between exhalations of smoke.

"What's wrong with a simple pork roast and potatoes?" Mom threw in. "It's a good thing I had a big lunch. You aren't serving one thing that I will eat!" She folded her arms across her chest.

Aunt Margaret looked like she was going to scream or cry.

"Anybody need a drink?" I asked.

"Liam, once again, sit still," Marie ordered. "No one's going to die from alcohol withdrawal if we finish this hand. By the way, I intend to set you."

After losing at cards again, I found myself in the kitchen with Aunt Margaret. She was flouncing around her narrow galley kitchen, yanking things out of cupboards and the refrigerator.

"Sometimes she is the most irritating person in the world." She said this almost in a whisper as if afraid of getting caught. "Just because I use spices other than salt and pepper she thinks I'm odd. Could you grab the fish out of the fridge?"

When I handed the swordfish to her, I caught the distinctive smell of old fish. Mom and Marie had been right; this particular swordfish had been dead a long time. But I knew I would choke it down.

"Do you want me to handle the grill?"

"Of course." She put a hand on my arm. "Why I let that woman get under my skin is beyond me. She has been doing this to me her whole life. When we were kids it was about the way I dressed, now it's about food. Sometimes I could just...."

I started to feel the need to defend my mom. Aunt Margaret looked at my eyes and said, "I love you so much Liam. Life has improved 100% for me since you moved back home. Now if one of my ungrateful wretches would come back...even just a visit." She smiled as she said this but I knew how much it pained her that none of her four children had been to visit her in months, years in one instance.

I poured myself a glass of wine. "Do you think I suck up to my mom too much?"

Margaret spun around and quickly made herself a vodka and tonic. "Why would you ask that?"

"You know why and you know who said it." I could see the unease in her eyes. "I want the truth."

"Did I ever tell you the time that Uncle Leo and your grandmother got into an argument over the lumps in her gravy? They didn't speak for six weeks!"

"Will you please answer my question?"

"No, Liam, not this time." Her eyes were moist. "This is between your mom and you, it's none of my business. I could wring Marie's neck sometimes."

"Guess I got my answer."

"No, you didn't, you do not know how I feel about this but for once in my life I am not going to walk into the middle of something that is none of my business. I made a promise after your mom got sick," she swiped at her eyes, "never mind any of that." The pan with the rice bubbled over. "Now will you please start the grill?" She turned her back to me. "When are you going to tell me what happened at the Graves house? Don't you trust me?"

Startled by her question, I almost knocked my wine glass over.

"Of course I trust you, you know better than that." I walked toward the back door. "Let's have lunch on Thursday at my house? I'll tell you everything." *Most everything,* I thought.

"Absolutely, Liam Conor." I could feel her love rush across the room and wrap around me.

As I lit the grill, I looked over at mom who was looking sheepish.

"Was I too hard on Margaret?" she asked. "Marie just told me that I was an ass."

84

"I didn't say ass, Colleen, I said jackass. I don't like being misquoted." Marie turned her head to blow out a stream of smoke.

"Well, maybe you were a bit harsh," I replied, "but then again you don't like fish, right?" I could see Marie watching me.

"No, I don't and she knows that."

"Is it going to kill you to miss one meal, Colleen?" Marie asked. "You know that most of the food Margaret prepares isn't to your liking. What's the point of telling her over and over that you don't like her cooking?" Marie looked up at the twilit sky. "Sometimes it seems that you two never left the farm and are still fighting over what Katherine was going to make for dinner." Marie and her mom had never gotten along; she always referred to her by her first name.

"I suppose you're right, I will never say another word." Mom took a long swig of her beer. "But I will certainly always have a big lunch before I show up for one of her so-called dinners."

"Do you want me to ask her if she has a chicken breast I can throw on the grill?" I asked.

"No, no I'm fine. I'm really not that hungry."

"Colleen, don't start this victim crap," Marie stated, "If you're hungry, eat something. You've already hurt her feelings. There's nothing to be gained playing the martyr."

I could feel my anger growing. I looked at my mom who mouthed: *let it go.* I turned my back on them and focused on the grill. Marie and my mom began to talk about my sister Leah's recently announced pregnancy and Marie's strong belief that Leah's husband wasn't ready to be a dad and how much she disliked my brother-in-law.

"I really cannot stand him, Colleen…why—" Just as I was about to say something, Margaret waved at me from the kitchen window and pointed at the grill. I cleaned it, made sure it was the right temperature and slapped the fish onto it getting one more whiff as I closed the lid.

I took a deep breath and remembered Benjamin in my bed, the sheet slipping off his hips, and the glimpse of his thigh.

"What are you looking so happy about?" Marie asked, "And don't you think you should flip that fish? Margaret will kill you if you burn it."

"I was thinking about how much I love all of you," I said, startled at the ease of my lie.

"You should be selling fish at Fareway," Marie said as Mom burst out laughing.

"She got you there, even though I prefer to believe your answer." She got up from her chair and walked over to me. "I'm sorry about the food comments," she said into my ear. "Life's too short to get upset about something so unimportant."

"Life's too short to get upset about a lot of things," I said.

She looked at me with surprise. Her eyes began to drift away but then they returned, confused but strong.

The next night at work I tensed up when Sue walked through the door. We hadn't worked together much since the funeral reception and I had resisted several offers to hang out with her out of fear that I would start talking. However, I now realized that the events of that one night had turned into a dream that was locked away inside me. I knew I wanted it private from the moment it ended but didn't trust myself to stay quiet but now I did. I felt the tension leave my shoulders.

"What are you looking so pensive about?" Sue punched me on the shoulder. "Benjamin haunting your bedroom again?"

I spun around and looked at her but relaxed when I saw her eyes.

"He showed up again at 5 am today and insisted on massaging my man parts until—"

Sue put her hands over her ears and said, "TMI, TMI." Then she stopped and looked at me, "On second thought, spill it, I haven't had a good sexual fantasy in ages, might as well be yours."

"Hells bells, I'm glad to see you two together again, why don't I schedule you the same night more often?" Georgia Dee said as she shoved her purse behind the bar.

"Because the hotness quotient goes through the roof when we're both in the same building," Sue said.

"Of course, how could I forget?" Georgia Dee said. "Well, I need you two hot things to be on your game tonight. We're booked solid and fortunately it is our kind of people. Thank God those other kind only come around here about once a century." She picked up the reservation book and headed to the front of the restaurant. "I'm sorry," she said.

"What for?" I asked, but Georgia Dee did not reply.

"Oh Liam, don't be so dense," Sue walked towards the dining room.

"What's she sorry for?"

"For sending us to the Graves house in the first place," Sue said with exasperation. "You really are thick as a brick sometimes, aren't you?"

"What the hell are you talking about?"

"You've been ignoring me, you've hardly said two words to anyone since the funeral reception and you look pissed enough to put your fist through a wall but nothing other than that." She stepped back into the bar and glared at me. "And I don't understand why. We had virtually the same experience and you don't see me acting like a huge weirdo. You're holding something back, aren't you?"

CHAPTER TEN

———∞———

I had never seen the bar so crowded. Every seat was taken and there were two or three people standing behind each bar stool waiting for their drinks. With no time to think about anything except making sure I was waiting on people in the right order, I was in high gear: pina coladas in the blender, sweating metal shakers filled with ice cold gin, the customer grinning in anticipation; people shoving empty beer bottles at me demanding instant replacements. Sometimes if I waited on someone out of turn, I could feel the hostility of the overlooked.

The bar began to empty around eleven. I followed one of my regulars to the front of the restaurant to make sure she was okay to drive. When I returned I saw one couple I had not noticed before sitting near the dance floor. The man had his arm around his date's shoulder, she laughed loudly and nervously. I walked up to their table.

"Can I get you anything else?" I hoped the answer was no. They were the only two people left. I was planning my second fifteen-mile run in the morning and I was ready to go home and sleep. The woman was blond, thin and attractive enough in the subdued lighting. She looked at her glass and glanced at the man next to her. His arm slipped away from her shoulder. Jumping out of her chair, she said, "No thanks, I really need to get home." She gave the man a quick kiss on his cheek. I could sense her disappointment that the evening was ending.

The dark haired man paid the bill and headed towards the bathroom. I breathed a sigh of relief. I just needed to close out the cash register and I could go home. Sue had left thirty minutes earlier after inviting me over for dinner the next night. She was a lousy cook but I couldn't say no. I just hoped her mom would do the cooking. With a grin, I realized I was worrying about one meal just as my mom always did.

After counting the money, locking it in the safe and saying good night to the few remaining cooks, I returned to the bar to turn off the lights. To my annoyance, the dark haired man was standing at the far end of the bar staring at me. I headed in his direction saying loudly, "Sorry sir but we're now closed for the night." As I approached I took a look at this man who had not moved. He had black hair, a closely cropped black beard and blue eyes. There was something oddly familiar about him. "I really need you to leave sir."

"Liam," the man said in a familiar voice.

"Fuck," I replied.

"Good to see you too," Benjamin said.

"What the fuck are you doing here?" I turned out the lights and headed to the kitchen not waiting for an answer. I was not going to put up with this shit again. Everything was almost back to normal. As I strode out of the restaurant, the heat and humidity hit me with a punch. The moths were circling the parking lot lights, seemingly with no control. As I reached my car, I felt a hand on my shoulder.

"What do you want from me?" I asked.

"The conversation we never had the other night," Benjamin said. "This time I'm sober and I really do want to talk to you."

"Do you even remember what happened that night?" I asked.

"Of course I do." Benjamin took a step back. "I threw up in your bathroom and passed out on the floor next to your tub. I woke up in the middle of the night, cold and sick." He turned away from me. "I tried to clean things up as best I could. I hope I didn't leave too

89

much of a mess. I'm really sorry about what happened." He looked back at me, "I knew you'd be upset with me."

"Upset is not exactly the word I would use, pissed is more accurate." I said. "You don't remember taking off your clothes and climbing into my bed in the middle of the night?"

"Bullshit," Benjamin said.

"Bullshit? You were ten times drunker than me. I woke up and there you were," I said, "I had no idea what was going on. I was scared to move."

"You're making this up."

"You don't know me. I would not make something like this up." I wiped my brow free of sweat.

"You didn't take a picture of me, did you?" Benjamin's voice was wary.

"That's it, I'm out of here." I yanked the door open to my car.

"What? What did I say?" Benjamin tried to close the door before I got in.

"Do you know what you just accused me of?" The sweat was pouring down my face. "Don't you think if I had taken a picture of you, you would know by now?"

"How?" Benjamin asked, "Maybe you just haven't found the right buyer?"

"Fuck you." I tried to open my car door but Benjamin was blocking it. I moved forward towards him and Benjamin took a step away. "This is unbelievable. Even if I had taken a photo of you, which I didn't, I wouldn't have any idea how to sell it."

"It's not that hard."

"Of course not...to you...and ...your kind," I said. "You live in that world. I wouldn't have a clue."

"You've never heard of *People* magazine? How about your friend Jesse Clinton? He could have told you what to do."

"He is not my friend, I did not take a picture of you, and you are an asshole if you think I'm the kind of person who would do that."

"Liam, calm down." Benjamin put an arm around my shoulder. "A few years ago my best friend, my fucking best friend sold some photos of me when we were on holiday in Phuket. I was naked on the balcony with my girlfriend. My best friend did this to me for a few thousand dollars. Can you believe that shit?"

A flash of empathetic paranoia ran over me. Taking a deep breath I said, "Yes, I remember seeing those." Benjamin had just started dating Alyssa. I had stared at those photos for hours. I let out a long exhalation. "Okay, I get it now. However, for the last time, I did not take any pictures of you. In fact, no one knows anything about that night, not even my best friends." I leaned on my car and thought for a few seconds. "You know what? I have no idea what to say to you. Let's pretend we never met."

"Why?" Benjamin had a hurt look on his face, the same hurt look he had used in *Alone in a Field of War*.

"I just had a flash of insight into what you might be feeling," I said. "Let's see if you can return the favor. You're a bartender in a small town in the Midwest. For some odd twist of circumstance, you wake up in the middle of the night and Jamie Diego is lying naked next to you in your bed." Benjamin looked unfazed by the concept. "Needless to say, you're surprised to find her sleeping next to you. While in your heart you know this is just some bizarre fluke, there's a part of you that fantasizes that maybe she got into bed with you for reasons other than sleep."

"But I'm not gay," Benjamin said.

"Not the point." I didn't try to hide my impatience. "You're trying to imagine what I might be feeling. You're an actor, pretend you're me." Benjamin looked befuddled. "Okay, I'm going to spell it out." I decided I had gone this far, I might as well say it all. An alarmed voice in my head began shouting, *you will never see him again Liam, shut up, shut up, shut the fuck up!!*

"I have fantasized about you since I saw you in that play in high school." I paused and looked up at the sky, which was filmy with humidity.

"I have dreamt about you." I looked at him to see if his expression changed, but it hadn't. "I have imagined being your boyfriend, living with you in LA, the whole thing." I shoved my hands in my pockets. "I've seen every movie and television show you've been in, including the bombs. I have hundreds of pictures of you on my computer."

I closed my eyes assuming when I opened them he would be gone. I was wrong.

"Then one night, I find you sleeping naked in my bed. Can't you imagine that might be confusing for me? I know you're not gay, you don't have to say it again," I said as Benjamin started to open his mouth. I felt frustrated that apparently I wasn't making my point. "My fantasy came alive that night. You came alive that night and it fucked me up." I tried to get into my car but Benjamin had blocked it again. "I have a good life here and I don't want anyone, including you, especially you, to screw things up for me."

"But all I want to do is talk to you about losing your dad," Benjamin said. "I'm sorry I apparently got into your bed but you have to believe it wasn't intentional. I was drunk."

"I know that," I said. I wondered for a moment if Benjamin had been so drunk that he had no memory of getting in or out of my bed.

"Then, what's the problem?" Benjamin asked. "You're kind of making a big deal out of nothing."

"Nothing? How can you say that? Why are you being so dense about this?"

"About what?" Benjamin asked, "What are we talking about again?"

"You genuinely do not get this, do you? I suppose you can have anything and any woman in the world you want." I paused. "What's it like to not have any fantasies?"

"You're a funny guy," Benjamin said as he let go of the car door. "But I think I'm beginning to see your point. Can we go somewhere and talk?" I shook my head no.

"Why not?"

"For one thing," I said, "I'm doing a fifteen mile run tomorrow." Benjamin stared blankly at me. "I'm running the Twin Cities Marathon this fall and I'm on a training schedule."

"Hey, I have a great idea," Benjamin put both hands on my shoulders and turned me to face him, "let's go to your home, you can grab your gear for your run and then we'll go to my parent's house. We don't have to worry about neighbors, we can have that conversation I've wanted, and then we can go for a run together in the morning."

"No," I said.

"Oh come on," Benjamin squeezed my shoulders. "It's perfect. There are eight empty bedrooms. You can have your pick of the lot. Hey, you can even lock the door and not worry about naked movie stars showing up in your bed in the middle of the night." He grinned. "Shit, you never know, maybe John Bankman this time." I scowled at him.

"I'm just teasing you Liam, jeez, lighten up." He swung open my car door. "I know a great run near my parent's house, all on gravel roads, easy on the knees, like I have to tell you that. I measured it out when I was in high school. It's a five-mile loop. I'll do it once and then you can run yourself ragged." I stood frozen next to my car with sweat running down my back. "I won't take no for an answer," Benjamin said. He pointed to an older, tired looking blue car. "I have my dad's old car, it's that Le Sabre over there. I bought him a Bentley but he sold it. He would only drive that junk. Can you believe that? Let's go, I'll follow you."

I sat immobile in my car, annoyed and distrustful. Switching on the ignition I continued staring off into space trying to figure out what I was going to do until the headlights on the car behind me were switched on and off several times. Driving like an eighty year old, I drove the exact speed limit to give myself time to think. I opened all the windows to feel the damp wind on my even damper skin. My shirt and pants were stuck to my body. I felt my sex drive knocking on a door begging to be let in.

I willed myself to think of cold things. I thought about walking down Tremont Street in Boston, a March Nor'easter howling in off the ocean, my clothing soaked and my teeth chattering. Then I thought about the glimpse of Benjamin's cock I saw as the sheet fell off his body. Biting my lower lip, I thought about blizzards when I was a kid, the temperature fifteen degrees below zero, two feet of freshly fallen snow whipping about in the aftermath of the storm, my dad hounding me to go out and shovel. Then I thought about Benjamin's loose, downy balls draped over his thigh. Sitting up as straight as I could, I thought about the first time I dove into the ocean off the coast of Maine, the water so frigid I thought I was going to have a heart attack. Then I remembered what Benjamin's ass looked like and I sighed. I felt my hard on push insistently against the zipper of my pants. I knew I was going to spend the night at the Graves home.

In my bedroom, I found a small duffel bag. I tossed in my running shorts, tank top, shoes, socks, sunscreen and a baseball cap. Rummaging through my closet, I found the belt I wore to carry the several bottles of water I was going to need to do a long run in this heat. I ripped off my clothing, my dick standing straight up, damp at the tip. I laughed out loud to think what a joke it was to pretend that I could control my sex drive. I stuffed myself into briefs, put on a pair of shorts and light blue Polo shirt. I looked in the mirror and wondered if I should wear a different shirt. A voice popped into my head asking why I was worrying about how I looked. I batted it away. Sliding my feet into a pair of sandals, I found my shaving kit, made sure I had my toothbrush and toothpaste and walked out the back door, trying to look nonchalant.

"You certainly look more comfortable," Benjamin said as I got into his car. It smelled of ancient cigarettes. "I can't wait to get out of these clothes. I don't remember it being this humid so early in the summer when I was a kid."

"Global warming," we said in unison. We looked at each other. He turned away first. Benjamin had taken off the black wig and beard and removed the contact lenses. I was startled again at the transformation.

"I can see you're in great shape," Benjamin said as we pulled up my dark, empty alley. "Maybe we can get in a workout tomorrow too. There's a gym in the basement. I haven't been as religious about exercise the last couple of weeks, and boy can I feel it."

"Uh, maybe." I remembered the number of times I had read articles about Benjamin's exercise regime and how you too could look just like him.

"Maybe?" Benjamin said. He started to say something and then stopped.

As we drove up the Graves driveway, I remembered how it had felt to pull into this same driveway ten days earlier. I could see Sue's cousin staring at her breasts, I could remember Theresa Armstrong screaming to come in when we knocked on the back door and I remembered the first time I saw Benjamin, his eyes bloodshot and tired. When we stepped out of the car, floodlights filled the back yard, illuminating the pool and patio.

"Let's go to the guest house first, that's where the beer is," Benjamin said. "My God it's hot." He pulled his shirt over his head and threw it on the table next to the pool. He raised his arms and stretched his back. His loose fitting khakis had slipped down in back, showing the waistband of his boxer shorts. I crossed the patio and stood next to him. There was a tiny area of blonde hair at the center of his lower back.

"Do you like Belgian ale?"

"Sure, that would be great," I said. A voice warned me to not have more than two, as it would mess up my run in the morning. *Screw it,* a different voice countered, *you can run any day.* A third voice said, *shut the fuck up* and for once they did. Benjamin came out of the guesthouse and handed me a bottle of Affligem Ale. "Come on, let's find you a bedroom." He put a hand on my shoulder and pointed me towards the back door. I felt his hand even after it was gone.

Striding through the back hallway where I saw Benjamin drinking with John Bankman, he bounded up the staircase taking two steps at a time with me right on his heels. Pointing to his left, he said, "My parent's bedrooms are down there."

"They slept in separate bedrooms?" I asked. I could see the *Enquirer* headline: *Benjamin Grave's Parents in a Loveless Marriage* or, *Separate Bedrooms for Benji's Parents, Father Gay?*

"Yeah, my dad was a champion snorer, they slept in separate rooms for years." The headlines disappeared, the real story too mundane. Benjamin led me to the right side of the house. "I always sleep in the first bedroom here. You can choose from any of the others. I'm going to rinse off and then meet you at the pool in a few. Okay dude?"

I winced at that word again and shook my head yes as Benjamin closed the door to his bedroom. Not particularly caring which bedroom I slept in, I took the one directly across the hall from his. Turning on the light, I saw a sparsely decorated room: mahogany platform bed, white duvet, and hardwood floors. Feeling greasy and wondering if I smelled like olives and gin, I decided to take a shower as well.

A mirror filled bathroom was next to a large walk in closet. I stepped into the rectangular shower, wondering if I should jerk off.

The stall had four showerheads. Not being able to figure out how to turn on all four I settled for one. When I washed my cock it sprang to life. I turned the water to cold to make it go away.

I dried off with a towel that seemed about five times thicker than the ones in my own bathroom. I scrubbed my teeth; made sure my hair looked as good as I knew how and then stopped and stared at my reflection. *What do you think is going to happen?* I sat down on the bed and remembered the exact words Benjamin had said to me several times: *but I am not gay.* I felt anger at the part of my brain that could so blithely ignore those words. I took a long swig of my beer, the sharp taste of the ale mixing oddly with the toothpaste.

Benjamin was standing in the hallway when I walked out of my room. His hair was wet from the shower. He was shirtless and wearing baggy shorts that hung off his hips. Considering the amount of flesh that was showing, it appeared he wasn't wearing any underwear. He smiled at me. I was dazzled.

"Come on, let's go for a swim." Benjamin headed for the staircase.

"But...but...I didn't bring a bathing suit."

"So what?" Benjamin replied, "There's nobody here but the two of us."

Jumping down the stairs as quickly as he had gone up them, Benjamin disappeared down the hall. When I came out the back door, he was walking out of the guesthouse carrying two more beers. He handed one to me. Turning his back, Benjamin pulled off his shorts. The lights from the pool cast flickering shadows across his body as he dove into the pool. Surfacing at the other end of the pool he called to me, "If it were up to me, I'd be naked all the time." He splashed some water at me. "Why the hell are you still dry?"

"Benjamin," I said, "I'd rather just sit here by the pool."

"Stop being so modest. There's nobody else around."

I looked at him and then looked at my crotch. This erection was going nowhere.

"I have an erection."

"What?"

"You heard me, I have an erection."

"Why?"

"What do you think?"

He disappeared under the water for a few seconds and then popped up like a bobber on a fishing line. "You know for a second, I forgot that you're gay."

"I am and I do."

"You do…what?"

"I'm not going to say it again."

"So what?" Benjamin was right below me by the edge of the pool. "You know, I've seen plenty of erections and in case you hadn't thought about it, straight guys get them too."

"What do you mean, you've seen plenty," I asked.

"Haven't you?" Benjamin asked.

"No, I haven't."

"Isn't that unusual?"

"Guess you're assuming I've slept around."

"No, no, that's not what I meant," Benjamin forced a laugh.

"Of course it's what you meant and why have you seen plenty?"

"Because every time I go to a public gym, I get hit on a fair number of times. It really doesn't bother me. I think it's kind of flattering," Benjamin said. "Although it can be a little awkward when I go in to take a shower and some guy with a hard on follows me."

"That's not how I operate."

"Okay, I get it, you're the vestal virgin of the gay world. Good for you. Now get your ass in this water, you have no idea what you're missing."

I looked at him smirking at me, his hair plastered on his forehead, dim lights creating a murky atmosphere and I ripped off my clothing. I stood at the edge of the pool, my erection bobbing and pulsating with blood. I saw Benjamin staring at my cock. I dove in over his head and broke the surface as he emerged next to me.

"That's better." He wiped the water from his face, his lips only inches away. I had seen those lips kissed so many times I felt I knew them better than my own. I pulled back.

"Hey, are you hungry?" Benjamin asked. "I'm starving. Let's see what I can rustle up in the kitchen." He swam to the far side of the pool; put both hands on the edge and pulled his muscular frame up with little effort. He stood facing me, the water rushing down his body. I looked at his strong legs and flat stomach. He had a long cock that curved to the right. It was a beautiful dick, an exact match to the body. He toweled off and walked naked into the house.

"I'll be right in," I said as I looked down to see that I was still hard. I dried off and pulled on my underwear and shorts. When I walked into the kitchen, Benjamin said, "You're a real piece of work. There's nobody around but the two of us and I've already seen you naked, so what's with the clothes? You're not some sort of religious fanatic are you? God I hate people like that." He had pulled cold cuts, pickles, mustard, and cheese out of the fridge. "But don't quote me."

"No, I'm not," I grabbed a handful of potato chips, "Obviously you know I was raised Catholic but I'm not religious anymore. I just don't feel like standing in your kitchen with no clothes on and an erection. Would you?" It was irritating to me that he was naked, almost as if taunting me that he was beyond issues about nudity and self-consciousness.

"Of course I would," he replied, "do you want me to get one?"

"W…w…what?"

"Kidding." He looked into my eyes, "Do you have a sense of humor?"

"Of course I do but I don't see anything funny about what is going on."

"I'm just jacking with you Liam. What kind of sandwich do you want?"

"Are you flirting with me?"

"Of course not." He finished making a ham and cheese sandwich and looked at me expectantly.

"Then why are you naked?"

"Because it's hot and because I like being naked. Can we move on?" He took a large bite out of his sandwich. The fog in my head disappeared along with my erection. I took off my shorts and underwear, reached over and took half his sandwich. "Hey, that's mine," he said.

"Not any more," I replied with my mouth full. "How about you rustle up another one?" Benjamin looked at me with a slight frown, paused and then made two more sandwiches. He put them on plates and then grabbed several handfuls of potato chips, one of which he shoved in his mouth.

"I bet you don't eat like this often," I said.

"I eat whatever I want, don't you?"

"Maybe in the next couple of months when I'm running sixty miles a week but usually I try to eat healthy. I thought your kind were all health nuts."

"Nuts maybe, but health nuts?" Benjamin said. "Not really."

"That's what I read all the time."

"Do I need to say the obvious to that comment?" Benjamin added another fistful of chips to his plate. "Let's go eat by the pool."

Benjamin found the nearest chaise lounge and settled in with his plate of food covering his crotch. He took a slug of his beer and said, "Here we are and you know what? I don't want to talk about my dad, isn't that weird?" He drained the bottle. "All week I've wanted to have that conversation with you but now I don't want to go there. I'm in too good a mood." He let out a sigh. "Maybe my mom is right about me."

"What does that mean?"

Benjamin filled his mouth with food and looked away. "Nothing...at least nothing important." I started to ask him again what he was talking about but then remembered how oddly my mom had acted those first few weeks after my dad died and I let it go.

"I can tell you that when my dad died, after a week or so, I was more than ready for even a few minutes of normalcy."

"Thanks," Benjamin said with a smile that was so genuine for a second I didn't recognize him.

He set his empty plate on the table next to him and put his arms under his head staring into the starless sky. His eyes closed and mine opened. I looked up and down his body. His legs were slightly apart, his balls on the chair, his cock resting on his thigh.

"How about another swim?" Benjamin asked without opening his eyes. He stood up and dove into the pool. I finished my sandwich knowing now that I would never forget what he looked like naked. I walked to the edge of the pool, my erection waving side to side.

"It appears that Boner Boy is back," Benjamin said with a laugh. I jumped into the pool in a cannonball, trying to splash as much water as I could into his face. Staying along the bottom, I jumped up right behind him. I put my hands on his shoulders and tried to dunk him. However he had at least thirty pounds of muscle on me and I could not move him. Benjamin grabbed me by the arms, whipped me around in front of him and dunked me instead. I popped to the surface gasping for breath between fits of laughter.

"Boner Boy," I said. "Wait til I tell my friends my new nickname. I'll be called BB for short…shorthand for something long!"

"Hey," Benjamin said. "Maybe you do have a sense of humor, BB." He turned me around and with both hands on my waist, picked me up and threw me several feet in the air. Sinking to the bottom of the pool, I paused for a few seconds and then swam across and rose directly in front of him. I put my hands on his shoulders again but this time I kissed him full on the lips. Benjamin pushed me away as he wiped the back of his hand across his mouth. I glared at him. Had he really just wiped his lips?

"Where did that come from?" Benjamin asked. He stepped away from me, pulled up and sat on the edge of the pool.

"Did you really need to wipe your mouth?" I asked, "I don't have rabies."

"Did I?" I shook my head yes. "Sorry about that, I didn't mean anything by it," he said. "You do remember the fact that I'm not gay."

"Of course I do but...*but what?*" I asked myself. *Should I apologize?* I started to but he cut me off.

"No need to apologize Liam, I know I'm a flirt. I can't help it. I flirt with anyone, men, women, young, old, stray cats, the homeless...even people I hate. It's just my personality." He stood up. "I'll go put some clothes on, meet me in the guest house."

I climbed out of the pool, toweled myself off and put my shorts back on. All the different aspects of me were having a war in my brain. I listened for a while to see who was winning. I gave a slight edge to my anger over my embarrassment. When I walked into the guesthouse, Benjamin was opening a beer, which he offered to me. He had put on a pair of shorts.

"No, I'm fine, I would like a glass of water, however." He handed me a bottle of Pelligrino, which I inhaled.

"What are you doing here?" Benjamin asked.

A wave of anger swept across my chest. "You invited me."

"That's not what I meant," Benjamin said. "Why are you back in Iowa?"

"I'd rather talk about what just happened."

"What do you mean?"

"I kissed you."

"Hell, I forgot it already." He opened another beer.

"I can't decide if it was your fault that it happened or mine. I'm leaning toward you."

"Why?"

"I think you're a cock tease."

"You're right, I am." He walked towards me. "I thought we had already established that. Anyway, where were we? Oh yeah, how could you move back to Mason City after living on the East Coast for so long? There's not exactly a lot to do around here."

"You sound like my friend Gregg. Minneapolis is only two hours away," I said, annoyed that the conversation wasn't going where I wanted.

"What about friends, what about sex? Clearly that could use some attention."

I blushed, cursing that I had no power to stop it.

"I would like to see how you would handle this situation if you were in my shoes and Jacqueline Anderson was sitting across from you naked."

"Bad example," he said, "she's like a sister to me. But I do get your point, now if it was Jamie…." "Do you have a boyfriend back in Boston?"

"No."

"That makes no sense, a good looking guy like you, in great shape and with that wonder boner. Why the fuck are you single?"

"I had a boyfriend until about last fall." *Wonder boner?*

"What happened?"

"I don't want to talk about it."

"Why?"

"Because it ended badly."

"Don't they all?"

"I wouldn't know. I've only been in one serious relationship."

"I've been in many. And every break up sucks. Either you want it to end or they don't or vice versa." Benjamin stood up and said, "Let's go back outside." As we walked across the patio, Benjamin stepped out of his shorts, never breaking his stride as he strolled into the pool. Coming to the surface, he said, "As my Dad used to say, come on back in, the water's fine…among a variety of clichés."

"I know, I know, I'm just not ready yet." I wondered if I would ever be ready again.

"Maybe someday you'll tell me about it." Benjamin said.

I lay down on a lounge chair with my arms behind my head. Someday implied a future relationship, didn't it? I could hear the rustle of the trees and the rhythmic splash of the water as Benjamin swam several laps.

Could I stay in the moment with him? My mind fought over the concept. I had always believed that if you didn't work a conversation to death it meant you were shallow. Was I? Was he?

Taking a deep breath and letting it out slowly, I let myself imagine that I was living with Benjamin in this house. I closed my eyes. Benjamin would step out of the pool, lift me up and kiss me deeply as he ran his hands across my chest. We would kiss for what seemed like hours. I let out a sigh as I felt drops of water hit my forehead. I opened my eyes to see Benjamin staring down at me, a curious look on his face.

"You look awfully happy," he said, "what were you thinking about?"

"Nothing in particular."

"I don't believe you." Benjamin wrapped a towel around his waist. "I'm pooped. See you in the morning." He put a hand on my shoulder and walked into the house. "And don't forget to lock your door. I may not be able to trust myself with you under the same roof!"

"Fuck you," I said. He turned around and smiled.

CHAPTER ELEVEN

———∞———

I was stepping out of a limousine right behind Benjamin. We had arrived at the Academy Awards. Benjamin was nominated for best actor and was favored to win. I had adjusted his bow tie just before we got out of the car and been rewarded with a long kiss. His breath smelled of coffee and mint. Holding hands we walked the red carpet, fans screaming Benjamin's name as the flashing cameras lit our way. Just ahead of us were Julia Roberts and her husband and right behind us were Brad and Angelina. I smiled at Angelina; we had plans to meet later at the Vanity Fair party. Ryan Seacrest began asking me which designer had made my tuxedo but someone was tapping me on the shoulder. I turned to see which pesky reporter it was. I opened my eyes to see Benjamin lying on his side next to me in bed. He was dressed in running shorts, shoes and socks. His head was propped up on his hand.

"See Liam, I couldn't stay out of your bed after all."

I sat up, looking for a clock, feeling like I had done something wrong.

"What time is it?" I asked.

"Time to get your ass moving." He yanked the sheet off my body. "I've been waiting for you to wake up for two hours. I'll be downstairs." He jumped off the bed and disappeared out the door. I found my watch; it was just after 9 AM. I swung my legs over the side of the bed and fell forward to stretch out my lower back. My erect cock pushed against my chest. Benjamin was acting like it was noon for God's sake. I put on a pair of running shorts, ran a damp hand through my hair, put my contacts in and brushed my teeth. I drank two large glasses of tap water.

Walking into the kitchen, I smelled freshly brewed coffee, toast and bacon. I looked around to see if there was anyone else in the room.

"Did you do this by yourself?"

"Don't condescend to me," Benjamin said, "I am perfectly capable of feeding myself as evidenced by the sandwiches I made not that long ago."

"I could use a cup of coffee." I raised my arms over my head and stretched out my back several times.

"You put caffeine in that ideal specimen of a male form?" Benjamin poured me a cup. "I thought you were healthy."

"It's too early for this." I opened the refrigerator looking for milk. "I can't drink this black. Do you have milk or half and half?"

"Oh my God, you really are a philistine." Benjamin ate a slice of bacon. "There should be half and half on the door."

I took several sips of coffee feeling Benjamin's eyes on me.

"Can we go now?"

"You're kidding, right?" I asked. "I won't be ready for at least an hour. I have things I have to do."

Benjamin sighed. "I don't want to know what you do in that time frame." He poured himself a cup of coffee. "I'll be outside reading, just let me know when you're ready to roll."

I finished my coffee and found a bottle of water in the refrigerator. We were no longer on the beach, now we were looking at co-ops on the upper west side of Manhattan.

An hour later, hydrated, stretched, water bottles filled, sunscreen on, I was ready to go. I had so much adrenaline running through my body it felt like I was heading to the starting line of the Boston Marathon. When I walked outside, Benjamin was asleep in a chair.

"Are you finally ready?" he asked without opening his eyes. He sat up. "I feel like I've been waiting for my co-star to come out of wardrobe."

"If you were going for a fifteen mile run instead of a two mile walk, you might have a little more understanding of what you need to do to prepare."

"Are you teasing me?" Benjamin asked. "Good, I like that in a friend." It took me a few seconds before it registered that Benjamin had just called me a friend.

He walked towards a garage that had room for five cars. I saw one empty space, two Mercedes Benzes, the old Le Sabre and an Audi. Benjamin chose the Buick. I threw my stuff in the back seat and got in.

"My family owns about 400 acres or so behind the house." Benjamin scratched his unshaven face. "We need to drive to the far end." He pulled behind the guesthouse onto a gravel road. We were soon in the middle of acres of grasslands.

"I've been trying to restore this land to what it was before farming took over." Benjamin said. "Have you ever run out the bike path to NIACC?" he asked. I nodded yes. This path led from my mom's subdivision through farmland out to the local community college. I tried to imagine running this path and seeing Benjamin running towards me.

"I got this idea from them. There is a small section where they've been restoring the land to what it looked like hundreds of years ago." I looked over. He was biting his lower lip.

"You do seem to forget that I am from here as well." I rolled down my window. "I've seen that a million times."

"Did you know that in less than 150 years almost all of Iowa had been plowed? There were 30 million acres of grassland that had existed forever and in a century and a half it was all gone. By the time I'm done, I'm hoping to have one of the largest grassland preserves in Iowa. I'm thinking maybe someday I'll donate it to the state." He paused. I looked over again. His eyes were full. I reached over and touched his shoulder.

"My dad loved this," he said.

"It's a great idea," I said, "I remember in high school we studied the travels of Cortes and his army when they explored this part of the Midwest. I think I read that the grasslands were taller than their heads. Of course they were about four feet tall back in those days."

Benjamin laughed and said nothing more and neither did I. As we drove down a slight decline, I could see a metal gate in the distance. Benjamin reached over and pressed a button on a device that looked like a garage door opener and the gate swung inward. Driving through the gate I could see security cameras on poles at several junctures near this entrance. We turned right and a short bumpy ride later; he pulled the car over to the side of the road. Now we were back in farm country. To our right was a large wooded area set back about a quarter mile. There was a narrow dirt path leading away from the road. On our left as far as I could see was farmland. The corn was only a few inches high at this point in the season. In some sections the land was flat but in others it rolled away in a series of hills. Stepping out of the car the only sound I heard was the wind stirring the trees. Benjamin was already stretching as I came around the front of the car.

"Are we still on your property?" I asked. I was amused that my mom hadn't told me that the Graves family purchased all this land. Then again, maybe she didn't know? I thought about telling her but then again how could I tell her how I'd found this out?

"No," Benjamin said. "Although I have been trying to buy this land for years."

He reached inside the car and pulled out a small bag. Within a few minutes, he had attached a beard and popped in blue contacts; a New York Yankees cap covered his hair.

"So where does that path lead to?" I asked.

"I'll show you when you're done with your run."

I started jogging, unsure what pace to set. Benjamin came up behind me, took hold of my shorts and pulled them down. He raced past me. "Come on, get the lead out!" he called over his shoulder. I yanked up my shorts and took off. I blew past Benjamin as if he were standing still.

"Does this pace work for you?" I asked.

Benjamin made it to my side but I could see he was struggling. I slowed down gradually, allowing him to find his breathing. Soon we were comfortably running side by side.

"When did you measure this run out?" I asked.

"My sophomore year," Benjamin said, "that's when I really got into running. Do you remember Scott Jensen?"

"Of course," I said, "he was plastered all over the sports section our senior year."

"He was my best friend...then," he said, "his family owns this land. This was his run. We did this route several times a week all summer."

"He was a hunk," I said. "I always thought he could have been an actor."

"Yeah, he was a good looking guy, but then again aren't we all?" He twisted his face into something Picasso would have loved. "He was unbelievably self conscious except when he was on the football field. We won the state tournament that year."

"Excuse me," I reached over and gave him a knock on his forehead. "Is there anybody home? Once again, in English...I...grew...up...in...Mason City. The only people in this town who didn't know that your football team won the state championship were either infants or in a coma."

Benjamin reached over and made as if to pull my shorts down again but I sidestepped his reach and pulled his down instead. He stumbled forward without attempting to pull them up. I stopped running and watched as he fumbled a bit longer with his shorts around his knees. His backside glistened with sweat. I began jogging again and caught up with him. As I did, Benjamin yanked up his shorts high above his waist, the fabric jammed into the crack of his ass. He pointed his feet together and ran a few steps pigeon toed with his eyes crossed until he burst out laughing.

"You're a real squirrel, aren't you?"

"That's one word for it." Benjamin turned around and I followed suit. There was nothing to see except a long, straight gravel road. In the distance there was a small grove of trees surrounding the next farmhouse.

"There's nobody here except us, I can do anything I want!" Benjamin yelled as he pulled off his shorts and took off racing down the road. I hesitated and then pulled my shorts off as well. I had never run outside in the buff. My dick was bouncing up and down and sideways. The belt I was wearing filled with small water bottles was bouncing off my hips.

"Well if it isn't BB himself," Benjamin said, "hey what's wrong? Where's your wonder boner today? You're not sick, are you? You don't find me attractive anymore, do you?" He put the back of his hand to his forehead and said, "I knew I shouldn't have had those potato chips last night. I look bloated, don't I?"

"You're right. I'm leaving you for Tom Cruise. He would never eat junk food!"

"Bastard! You'd leave me for that freaky dwarf?"

Coming to a sudden stop, Benjamin put his shorts back on. I looked around wondering what I had missed.

"We'll be on a paved road soon," he said, "usually there's no one around but you never know." I put my own shorts back on as well surprised at how quickly his mood had shifted.

As we resumed our normal pace, I asked, "What happened to Scott Jensen after high school?"

"He went to the University of Iowa, full football scholarship and then screwed up his knees his first year on the team and never played again. Last I heard he was a lawyer living in Des Moines with a wife and kids. I haven't talked to him since high school."

"Why? What happened?"

"Nothing really, we just drifted apart."

"I thought you said you were best friends. How do best friends stop speaking to each other?"

"Are you still friends with your old high school buddies?" Benjamin asked.

I thought of Jim. I didn't want to tell him that I didn't have high school buddies, only Sue.

"Good point," I said.

We ran the rest of the loop in silence. Benjamin had a look on his face somewhere between indifference and sadness. When we returned to the car he waved me on. "I'll be waiting for you right here," he said, "have a ball."

I took off. I didn't care what my pace was. I wanted to do this run but I wanted it over as well. When I came around the loop again, Benjamin was gone. I started running even faster and was back at the car in thirty minutes. I walked a bit making sure my body had responded well to this hard exercise. I needed to find a place to lie down and stretch.

"Liam," I turned around and Benjamin walked out of the woods. He had removed his beard. He waved me over. I jogged down the path and into the stand of trees. Sunshine filtered through the branches, the cooler temperature a welcome break from the heat of the road. Benjamin was striding away from me. As the trees grew thicker, the trail began a slight ascent. I could see a beam of sunlight at the end. We were standing on a shelf of rock ten feet or so above a quarry. The sunlight was ricocheting off the water creating a light so bright, I had to put my hand over my eyes in order to see.

"Wow," I said, "this is incredible."

"I know. Scott showed this to me. He claimed this was one of the first quarries dug by the Brick and Tile Company back in the 20's.

He also said that very few people knew about it. I didn't believe him at first but we came here a lot and I never saw another person. Of course that was a long time ago."

Benjamin stripped off his shorts, shoes, and socks.

"I always have to brace myself for this," he said. "The water's pretty cold this time of year." He thrust himself up and forward and did an effortless swan dive into the water, emerging seconds later. He whooped several times with his voice echoing off the walls.

"I think my balls are up around my liver right about now. Wow this is cold." I leaned over the edge as he disappeared into the wall of rock. Seconds later he was standing next to me, his body covered in goose bumps. I looked down at his dick. It had shrunk down so much that only the head was showing.

"I think you scared it away," I said. Benjamin self-consciously pulled at his cock.

I stepped out of my clothes, sucked in a gulp of air and dove in. I hit the water and my breath was knocked out of me. I had never felt water this cold in my life, not even at the beaches in Maine. I broke the surface and yelled, "Fuck, fuck, fuck!" I looked for a way out and it took a few seconds before I saw the footprints Benjamin had left behind on the rocks. I yanked myself out slapping my hands against my chest to bring some warmth back in, clambered up the path with my teeth chattering. The sun had momentarily gone behind a cloud and the wind was cold on my skin.

"I...I...I could really use a towel," I said. I rubbed my head several times to shake the water out of my hair.

Benjamin stepped forward and enveloped me in a bear hug.

"I'll warm you up," he said.

I was so startled I felt my body tense into a knot. I resisted the hug and tried to pull away but Benjamin did not let go. He rubbed his hands on my upper back while pressing firmly into my body. I felt myself become aroused as I relaxed into his embrace with my arms at my side.

Benjamin slowly let go of me. Looking down he said, "I guess you find me attractive after all, BB."

He lay down on the sun warmed rock platform. He put his hands behind his head, crossed his feet, and closed his eyes. I stood frozen in place, my erection bobbing up and down, angry with myself for not being able to control my body. I was tempted to jump back in the water to make it go away but didn't want to feel that cold again. I knelt and then lay face down on the smooth granite shelf. I looked again to see if Benjamin was aroused. He wasn't. I could not make sense of any of this. In my mind people were gay or they weren't. While I knew there were men who called themselves bisexual, I hadn't met any and I had never bought the concept. And right now I couldn't buy that Benjamin was motivated solely by flirtation.

I wished there was someone watching us who would tell me the truth.

Breathing in and out, trying to calm down, trying not to look at his cock, my mind began darting from memory to memory. I had played a game with my sisters and cousins years before. Our parents would tell us they would give a dollar to the kid who could lie still the longest without making a noise. We didn't realize then the motivation was simply to give our parents a break from a group of noisy children.

I felt about ten years old again as I lay on the ground wondering if I was being manipulated and if so, why?

My stomach rumbled with hunger and I was in our backyard, playing croquet next to the large oak tree, hamburgers and hot dogs sizzling on the grill. My dad was holding court over the BBQ, mom setting out bowls filled with broccoli and cheese casserole, baked beans, and potato salad. My dad was looking at me with a question in his eyes.

Then I was in our neighborhood church, the pallbearers pushing my dad's casket down the aisle, mom steadfastly not crying but her body shaking with the effort of withholding so much emotion. I looked up at the altar and I was no longer at my dad's funeral but instead preparing for a Christmas mass. I was thirteen years old and I had been chosen to do several readings with Jim.

On that cold Wednesday night with all the doors locked, Jim and I were alone in the church. A few candles glowing in the front of a statue of Mary and Joseph created waving shadows that washed across the crucifix that dominated the back wall. Jim and I had run back and forth across the altar, not bothering to genuflect. We had hugged each other right there in the middle of the altar, our hands reaching down to squeeze each other's erections through our wool pants. We ran into the sacristy, pulled out bags of communion wafers that we shoveled into our mouths as if eating Fritos. Jim held up a bottle of wine but we were too afraid to drink it. I remembered hugging him over and over, desperate to kiss him but instead settling for a hug and a pull at his rigid cock.

The following day I woke with a start, surprised I was alive. I had assumed that Jesus was going to smite me dead for the sacrilege I had committed in His house. Several weeks later when I was doing just fine, the seeds of doubt about my Catholic religion began to sprout.

Feeling a twinge in my hamstrings, I turned on my back and began doing a series of stretches while Benjamin dozed next to me. My muscles were tight and I realized that I was incredibly hungry and thirsty. I felt a pair of eyes on me.

"You're pretty good at that. Maybe you can show me? Madonna tried to a few years ago but I...." he stopped himself and turned bright red. "I'm starving, let's go home."

"I'm assuming you meant the Michigan Madonna and not a visitation from heaven?"

"Forget I said that." He jumped to his feet and put his running shorts back on.

When we walked into his kitchen, he pulled a bowl of pasta salad out of the fridge. He handed me a fork and we inhaled it, not bothering to spoon it out on separate plates. We chased this with ham sandwiches, potato chips and water. I sat slumped at the kitchen table feeling a big let down beginning. Benjamin raised his arm and smelled his armpit.

"My God, I stink. Why didn't you say something? I need to be hosed down." He disappeared down the hallway.

When I walked into my bedroom, the let down I had made a feeble attempt at keeping away took over. I felt like an addict who had been told that there were no more drugs. Benjamin surely wasn't going to keep showing up and since he hadn't said a word about his dad, I assumed he had changed his mind about having that conversation with me.

I took my time with the shower, ultimately figuring out how to turn on all four showerheads. I let the hot water beat down on me. I felt nothing but warmth as I imagined myself lying again on the rock shelf, Benjamin at my side. I lost track of time.

"Young man, don't you think you've been in there long enough?" The voice was deep and authoritarian. "You know young man, I may not be able to see what you are doing there but Jesus can. HE knows what despicable things you're capable of. Get out here now."

I started laughing as I dried myself off and walked into the bedroom with the towel around my waist. Benjamin stood in the middle of the room. His eyes swept up and down my body.

"Fuck if I know why you're single," he said. "You're a knock out." I started to protest but he waved his hand as if to say don't bother.

""Okay, I have some things I need to do this afternoon so I'll run you home." He began to walk out of the room. "What's a good time for you to come back tomorrow morning to work out?"

"How about ten?" I asked feeling a surge of adrenaline flood my chest.

"It's late but I can work with it."

As we pulled down my street, Benjamin stopped the car in front of the house. He looked at me and put a hand on my shoulder.

"This is the best time I have had in years. I think we're going to be great friends." He squeezed my shoulder. "See ya in the morning, call me on my mobile so I know when to expect you." He handed me a card. "And one more thing and please don't get your back up again." He was unable to hold my gaze. "I don't want to say this but I have to. You...you won't tell anyone that you and I are friends, right?"

"You already know...."

"You know I'm supposed to be in Montana," he interrupted. I wondered if I had thought my words and not said them out loud. "But it's not really about that," he continued. "I haven't had a friend of my own...with no strings attached...since high school. If anybody gets wind of this, well everything will get really fucked up. Promise?"

"I already told you that I haven't said anything but yes, I promise I will continue to keep this between us."

"Thanks." He briefly held my arm. "See you tomorrow."

I watched the blue LeSabre pull away and wondered how I was going to keep all of this to myself.

CHAPTER TWELVE

———∞———

I walked inside my home and headed straight for the bathroom where I jerked off in about ten seconds. Warning bells were clanging inside my head. Benjamin thought he had a new friend. I thought…I thought what? None of this felt like a new friendship to me; it felt like what had happened with Justin.

I was pacing through my house, unsure what to do. My phone rang and rescued me.

"Hey little man," Gregg said, "why haven't you called me? You move to Indonesia and you never call. I miss you."

"I miss you too."

"What have you been up to?" Gregg asked.

"I've been kind of busy."

"Doing what?" he asked. "Other than mixing a few cosmos and jerking off, what else is there to do in that god forsaken place?"

"You'd be surprised." I instantly regretted the tease.

"What's that supposed to mean?"

"Nothing." I muttered.

"Anyway, enough about you." Gregg said. "You know we've never talked about what happened to moi in Ptown. Aren't you in the least bit curious about who I fucked?"

"I didn't want to pry."

"Oh spare me Jane Austen, you know you want the dirt. Well here it is. His name was Zack, don't you love that name? I am starting to get a woody just saying it out loud. Anyway, he was a myriad of muscles but, drum roll please…he was a PH LTD!"

"Oh my God, no!" I said. This was an acronym we created that stood for 'Pubic Hair Longer Than Dick.' I knew that to Gregg this was the ultimate one-nightstand nightmare.

"Oh my God, yes," he said. "Tiny dick plus he was into some sort of unnatural natural thing. He didn't shave his balls or clip his pubic hair. His dick was lost inside his grotesquely large bush. It needed a GPS system to find its way out. Quelle horreur!" Gregg sighed into the phone, "It was such a shame, he had the body of death. But you know me, when I have a nostril hair longer than a guy's dick, no amount of muscle is going to turn Mr. Miracle on."

"Oh well, there's other fish to fry," I said.

"Okay spill it."

"Spill what?"

"I know you as well as I know the head of my cock that when you start blathering clichés you're hiding something from me."

"I am not hiding anything." I remembered hugging Benjamin at the quarry.

"I can tell you're smiling," Gregg said. I looked over my shoulder for a hidden camera. "What are you so happy about? Have you met someone? Is he a farmer? Does he wear bib overalls without underwear? Is he blond?"

"I haven't met anyone."

"Don't you lie to me missy, I can smell your lies from half way across the country. There can't possibly be any other gay people in that *Harvest Home* hellhole. So who could you have met? Who does that leave for little Liam?" There was a long silence as I held my breath. "I tell you Liam, if you fall for another SOB story, I will never speak to you again."

I felt myself bristle. "You know I hate that one. 'Sort of bi.' What does it mean?"

"You know very well what it means, you dated one, remember?"

I ignored that. "I haven't met anyone."

"I don't believe you," Gregg said, "wasn't one enough?"

"I don't know what you're talking about."

"Was Justin gay?" Gregg asked. "Was he straight? Was he bisexual?"

"I don't want to talk about this."

"If I don't talk to you about this, who will? Nobody else has the balls." Gregg said, his voice full of heat. "You know you have this thing for falling for guys who are vague about their sexuality."

"I've only been in one relationship."

"Oh come on Liam, there was only one Justin but how many other men did you have crushes on, 5,6,10? And they all fit the same description. You'd never know they were anything but straight except occasionally they'd let a guy suck their dick."

"Did you call me to say hi or just to harangue me?"

"So I'm right!" Gregg said. "I knew it. Why is it so hard for you to find a man who is willing to say out loud, yes I'm gay? I thought you had learned your lesson when Justin left you to marry Penny."

"I'm hanging up now but before I do, the next time I want your psychoanalysis of my personality, I'll ask first. Got it?"

"Oh come on Liam," Gregg said. "You know I only want the best for you. You deserve to be with someone who appreciates who you are and just as importantly understands who they are. Please don't get involved with another head case, that's all I'm saying."

"Justin wasn't a head case, he was just a little confused."

"I am not going down that road," Gregg said. "On another, far more pleasant topic, you're still planning on visiting me next month, aren't you? I've inked you in my book for the weekend of July 14th."

"Of course I'll be there," I said. "But you have to promise not to bring this up again. Will you promise me that?"

"I will do no such thing and what good would it do anyway?" he asked, "you know I never keep my promises. Must run, love you, kisses." The line went dead. I stared at the phone, all the old arguments about Justin flooding my brain. I didn't need Gregg to remind me what a mess the relationship had been.

I remembered every detail of the morning we met. My boss had insisted on me hosting an open house that Sunday morning. I knew no one would show up, the neighbors had already walked through the empty townhouse on Union Park. It was the holiday season and the weekend forecast was for temperatures around ten degrees. I arrived at 9 A.M. to light fires in the parlor and kitchen fireplaces. It was so cold in the house I had left my hat, coat and gloves on. I had my coffee and the *Boston Globe* figuring I had several hours to read the paper—alone.

Justin Thornton walked in by himself, my first and only prospective client of the day. He had on a stocking hat, black pea coat, jeans and LL Bean boots. His face was bright red from the cold, his lips a bit chapped and his chocolate brown eyes watering. He had pulled off his hat, his hair matted from the static electricity. He smiled at me. He had beautiful white teeth, and a strong handshake. He had opened his coat to let in the warm air from the fire. He smelled of Tide and Safeguard. I could see his chest outlined through the black cashmere sweater he was wearing. He was funny, sarcastic, flirtatious and smart. He was five years older than me, single, worked in banking and had grown up in Concord, Massachusetts. He was an only child and had been educated at Deerfield and Harvard. His family had been in banking for generations.

I sold him the house. When our relationship was over, I found out that Justin had never liked it.

I stopped myself. What was the point of reliving this again?

I went outside and began picking up sticks and pulling weeds, I felt stubborn about the idea that Benjamin might be another Justin. While Benjamin was an overwhelming flirt, he seemed completely at ease with his sexuality, something Justin never was. I cursed as I

stepped in a pile of dog shit courtesy of our neighborhood hippies'
dog Jerry.

As I hosed down my sneakers, I thought, even if Benjamin is a
SOB story, he didn't live here so how far could anything go?

CHAPTER THIRTEEN

———∞———

I arrived at Sue's house at 7 P.M. on the dot. She was standing at the doorway looking at her watch.

"You're three seconds late." She pulled the bottle of red wine from my hand and kissed me on the cheek. I walked into her foyer just as her two daughters, Heather and Haley, came running downstairs. Their cat, Xerxes, followed and wound his way around my leg. When the two girls saw me they stopped and hid behind their mom.

"Enjoy this," Sue pushed them in front of her to shake my hand. "They are about five minutes away from considering you a relative, and once that happens, you better deadbolt your front and back doors."

I knelt down and shook their small hands. Heather, who was eight, looked like her mom. Five-year-old Haley looked like her dad although I was beginning to have trouble remembering which of Sue's husbands had been her father. I loved to tease Sue that she couldn't remember either.

"Let me get a couple of beers and I'll meet you outside. It's too damn hot to sit in the kitchen." I could smell lasagna baking in the oven as we walked into the kitchen.

"Doesn't your mom know how to make a cold pasta salad or chilled cucumber soup?" My shirt was sticking to my back.

"No, I don't," Sue's mom Clara said as she walked into the kitchen and gave me a hug. The fact she would hug me was viewed by the Flanagan family as a shocking public display of affection. What Sue and her siblings got instead of hugs were wisecracks and a built in cook and babysitter. "My boneheaded daughter asked for lasagna and lasagna is what she got. She'll probably ask for potato salad in February." Sue rolled her eyes at me.

"They'll be ready to be picked up any time tomorrow morning after eleven unless Father Schmidt carries on again in his sermon. Last Sunday I thought Mrs. Herzog was going to have a stroke." She took a quick look at her lasagna, a cannon blast of hot air filling the kitchen. "I heard her say that her sausage, cheese, green bean and French onion casserole, an old family recipe no doubt, was going to be ruined all because of that man. She had tears in her eyes when she said that, can you believe that Liam? Tears over a casserole? I told her to buck up for God's sake, it's just one ruined casserole out of the hundreds she has served every Sunday at the exact same time for the exact same people having the exact same conversation."

"You did not say that to her, Mom," Sue said.

"Well I thought it, that's just as good." Clara turned the oven down. "There are so many more important things to worry about such as finding boyfriends for the two of you. I swear I'm going to rustle up a man for Sue. I just have to find one that won't be frightened off by her impertinence. And I'm going to look under every bush and behind every tree until I find another gay man in this town. There has to be at least one here, doesn't there?" She rummaged through her purse for her car keys. She only lived three blocks from Sue but never walked. No one in Mason City walked.

"Enjoy the lasagna. I had to fight off eight of Sue's cousins when it came out of the fridge." With that she was gone, one granddaughter on either side of her, the children carrying pillowcases stuffed with pajamas, dolls and books. Sue handed me an Affligem Ale and we went outside.

"Just what I need." Sue plopped down onto a chaise lounge. A few feet away was a small garden, a swing set and Barbie's dream house, its contents strewn all over the patio. "My mom as my Yenta. She's already tried to hook me up with Eric Schwartz. Do you remember him in high school?" I nodded yes. "Do you recall what he looked like?" Before I could reply she said, "Red hair, chubby, covered in zits, breath that smelled like over worn running shoes and a personality that hinted at animal torture." She took a sip of her beer. "Well, the current version has no zits, no hair, more chub, breath that could peel wall paper and a Jesus agenda. I suspect years of electric shock therapy. My mom couldn't understand why I wouldn't go on a second date with him and what's worse, she met him!"

She looked up at the sky and then looked at me. "What the hell is eating you?"

"What are you talking about?"

She stretched out on the chair. She had on white cotton shorts, a peach tank top and sandals. She looked good in just about anything. "Let's see how many anxiety tics I can count. A forehead so furrowed you could lose change in it, greasy skin and shifty eyes. Do you need any more?"

"Fuck you."

"I can't help it that you are as transparent as Saran Wrap."

"I'm not sure I want to talk about it. I was just that close to forgetting. But now that you brought it up, my friend Gregg is lecturing me about men and his concern that I am going to fall for the wrong kind of guy and what is much worse, Aunt Marie was harassing me on why I moved back here in the first place. She had the nerve to call me abnormal. Can you believe that?"

"You are a little weird but then again, does she own a mirror?" She kicked a tennis ball into the garden. "What's Gregg worried about? But before you answer that, have you met someone? There's an element of sexual energy oozing out of you. Usually you come across as a castrated monk, tonight you look like a man whore. I haven't seen this since the Graves funeral reception."

"No, I haven't," I said. "Maybe you're projecting."

"Maybe, I have been feeling kind of-god, I hate the word -horny, there must be another word," Sue said.

I raised an eyebrow.

"Yes Liam, women do have sex drives. Not that you've ever given that a thought. We all know that with men, El Grande Penis gets all the focus. Anyway, it's much more than about getting laid. I'm really lonely." She stood up and walked over to her garden where she retrieved the tennis ball. "Having you back in Iowa is great and I love our friendship. But the disadvantage is that it has pointed out to me that I want the same kind of relationship with a straight man, with some sex thrown in as well."

"There must be at least one man in this town who would be your fuck buddy."

"Fuck buddy? How inelegant."

"Sorry, sometimes I forget that you're not a gay man."

"With this body? Are you blind?" She finished her beer. "I need a strategic planning session. You worked at a big corporation, you must know what I'm talking about."

"Yeah I do," I replied, "We had endless planning sessions which produced endless lists of urgent recommendations, all of which were promptly ignored. Did I tell you about the time...."

"Hello! We're talking about me!"

I jumped up and went into the house to find paper and pen. "Okay, we're going to make a list of what you want in your ideal boyfriend. Ready? I want spontaneous answers, whatever pops into your head."

"Height?"

"6'2"

"So specific?"

"Are you going to ask or analyze?"

"Sorry, color of eyes?"

"Blue"

"Weight?"

"182 pounds"

"Muscles or on the flabby side?"

"Like you have to ask?"

"I have met lots of women who prefer their men squishy."

"Not this woman."

"Hair color?"

"Anything but red."

"Why?"

"Red pubic hair? Please!"

"Waist size?"

"Thirty-two"

"Speaking of inches, dick size?"

"I knew we'd get there eventually, I'm shocked it wasn't your first question."

"So?"

"Eight inches."

"That's it?"

"What's wrong with eight?"

"Nothing I suppose but if you're going to fantasize, why not go for it?"

"Does it really make that much difference?"

"Not to me but to every other gay man I know it does."

"Men. You're all alike. If you're gay you want a big cock and if you're straight you want big tits. Do you want another beer?" I hesitated but she shot me a look that said *don't be difficult*. As she walked out her back door she said, "This is really stupid. A man like I'm describing doesn't exist in this town except for you or Benjamin Graves. You're a major homosexual and he's back in California and living with that twit. Have you ever seen her show? Oh my God, it is so stupid. She plays her part like a cross between Pamela Sue

Anderson and Courtney Cox. A bitchy bimbo! You know, if I could have five minutes with Mr. Graves, he would dump Alyssa Wheelock in sixty seconds flat."

I smiled as I remembered Benjamin Graves hugging me on the edge of the quarry.

"What are you looking so happy about?" She placed the beer on the metal table that sat between us, two orange tinted Popsicle sticks stuck to the surface. "And I want the truth."

"I was just wondering what the difference is between a major homo and a minor homo?"

"Major, minor, regular, irregular. It's all words," Sue said. "I just don't get why straight men aren't more like gay men. And by the way, was that really what you were smiling about?"

"In what way?" I asked. "You were just lumping all men into one category a second ago, men obsessed with the size of body parts."

"Well you do have that in common. That's a given. I guess I'm talking about how comfortable I am around you and how I feel that I can tell you anything and you won't worry about being emasculated. I get so tired of worrying about that. I tell you if all men's dicks were as big as their egos, the latest obsession would be tiny cocks."

"My friend Gregg calls them PH LTD."

"What does that stand for?"

"Pubic hair longer than dick."

Sue had just taken a swallow of beer, which she proceeded to spray all over Barbie's pink convertible, which was next to the empty dream house. "I love that. Can I use it?"

"Of course, be my guest. Just be careful who you use it around," I said, "you never know where a PH LTD might be lurking, trust me, they're everywhere."

"How would you know? I thought you had only slept with about two men your entire life?"

"Because I've been in plenty of locker rooms. You wouldn't believe some of the things I've seen. There was this one guy, probably late fifties, very overweight, who would try to wrap his towel around his waist. But he was too chubby for the towel to meet in front. So he would walk through the locker room with this inverted V in front which of course caused you to look at his crotch. And what did you see? Pubic hair! Lots and lots of pubic hair and a miniature, scared penis lost amidst the forest. Why would you draw attention to the fact that you had a cock the size of your pinkie?"

"Maybe he didn't care?" Sue said.

I thought for a minute. "Then I guess I do qualify as a major homo. That never entered my mind."

"See what I mean? You're all phallic centric. Even a eunuch like you. And it doesn't seem to matter what country you're from. Have you ever seen those giant golden phalluses they carry around at Hindu festivals? You can't get any more cock obsessed that that."

"You should be having this conversation with my friend Gregg. He's really boned up on this subject."

"Have I ever told you how much I hate puns?" She yawned. "Are you ready for dinner?" I wasn't the least bit hungry for hot food but I nodded yes.

"Sit still. If you come in the house you'll start sweating and I know how much you hate that. I can still remember looking at you the day we graduated from high school and saw the sweat stains on your mortarboard. Not a pretty sight."

"My mom bought me wool pants if I remember right. Do you know that people used to swim in wool bathing suits?"

"No, I didn't know that. I can't imagine." She stood up and picked up my empty beer bottle. "You know," she said as she stretched her back, "if I could, I'd swim naked all the time.

I looked at her, my mouth slightly open.

"What, what did I say?"

"Nothing, just a bit of deja vu."

"That was weird," she looked at me with doubt in her eyes, "The last time a man looked at me like that, I got pregnant."

She disappeared into the house and I disappeared into my memories of the last twenty-four hours. The next thing I knew the table was set and my food was placed in front of me.

"You're a lot of company," Sue said, "This is turning into a typical bad date. I expect more from you."

"God, I'm sorry, I think the beer went right to my head." I wondered how much I could tell her without telling her anything. "I think it's the combination of the alcohol, the heat, the smell of summer. And at the risk of being called a copy cat, I'm a bit horny too." I grimaced as I said that word; to me it was something fourteen year olds would say. "How about randy? Is that better?"

"Hell no, when I hear that word, I think about Randy O'Leary. Didn't he go to jail for public exposure?"

"I was just remembering standing next to Benjamin, his lips only inches away. Can you imagine what he looks like naked?" I wanted to tell her exactly what he looked like without clothes.

"Well, you better have a vivid imagination because that is one sight you are never gonna see." She took a bite of her lasagna. "Just as good as always."

I took a bite as well and sighed with contentment as my appetite kicked in. "There are plenty of fake photos of him on the Internet. Guess they'll have to do." *Was it really necessary for me to say all of this?* I thought. Then again if I didn't say what I believed would be the expected response, Sue would know I was hiding something. I wondered how people had affairs, how did they keep their stories straight?

"Maybe your problem is your lack of cooking prowess," I said with my mouth full of pasta.

"Honey, if it were only so simple. I never even get to that point with a man." She speared a mushroom on her fork. She was a slow eater, which I liked. My family raced through their meals as if someone was going to snatch their plate away. "We have a date, usually over coffee. Then the second date is usually happy hour somewhere. If we get past that, then there will be dinner out. Then they expect sex, usually at my place. Then I tell them I have two daughters and two ex-husbands. The next thing I know I'm being dropped off here without dessert and with a promise of a phone call that never comes."

"Has it really been that bad?"

"Actually it's worse," she pushed her food around her plate. "Let's just say that a couple of times I didn't tell them about the kids or the exes for a while. Didn't matter, the ending was the same."

"Maybe we would all be better off it all men were gay and all women were lesbians. We could procreate via test tubes and the relationship part would be with our own kind. Men basically aren't monogamous anyway so they could fuck around all they want and since women are basically all lesbians, they could nest to their heart's content."

"I'll take overblown stereotypes for $800, Alex," she took my plate to bring me seconds, "although you may have a point."

"You'll find someone Sue," I held her hand for a second and she didn't pull away, "I'm going to keep my eye out for someone who has at least two of your requirements and who doesn't have a wedding ring on."

"Make sure they don't have a tan line on that finger." She withdrew her hand from mine. "I absolutely hate it when I sound so needy for a man. I have my children, my family and you. What else do I need?"

"Was it eight or nine inches? Where are my notes?"

She punched me on the shoulder and then leaned over and gently kissed me on the lips.

CHAPTER TWELVE

———∞———

The next morning I awakened feeling as good as I had since moving home. I had coffee on my patio, the sun peeking over the garage, a lawn mower humming distantly, hints of freshly mown grass stirring childhood memories. I heard the whistle of a train crossing through town, the wheels a faint rumble.

I showered and shaved while chastising myself for getting cleaned up before exercise. I wondered if I should bring a bathing suit, a change of clothes? I decided against either, as it would imply expectations. After all, I had been invited solely to lift weights. I brushed my teeth until my gums hurt, flossed twice and gelled my hair until I looked like a model for a cut-rate cosmetology school, took another shower and simply towel dried my hair. I avoided my reflection, annoyed at my vanity.

At 9:30 I was pacing in my living room, checking my watch every thirty-seconds or so. At 9:45 I decided to head over to his house. Benjamin was a morning person so clearly he must be up. When I turned on the ignition, I felt a jab of anxiety. What if Benjamin had forgotten the invitation? What if he didn't answer his phone? I pulled the card out of my wallet that Benjamin had given me: it was business card size with the initials B.G. embossed in the middle. His mobile number was on the back. I wondered what this would fetch on E Bay.

With nervous fingers I dialed the number. After the fourth ring I could feel the coffee swirling in my gut. Just as I was about to hang up, Benjamin answered.

"Hey Liam, where are you? What time is it?" His voice sounded groggy.

"Just leaving my house, is this a bad time?"

"Why?"

"You don't sound like yourself."

"No, no I'm fine, just tired, slept like shit. I'll open the gate in front, just pull in and come around to the back of the house. See ya in a few."

I felt somewhat mollified by his comment that he hadn't slept but I still drove very slowly to his house wondering the entire way if I should call back and cancel. My radar was up, detecting any hint that I might be overstaying my welcome. Any hint that he perceived me as a hanger on, and I was gone from his life in a second. As I pulled around the back of the house, I saw Benjamin standing in the doorway. I stepped out of the car with trepidation and as I closed the door he came down the stone path. He was wearing glasses, a wrinkled T-shirt and baggy black nylon shorts. No hint of the movie star today. I must have looked surprised because Benjamin said, "I know I look like crap. I didn't sleep all night, kept dreaming about my dad."

"You should have cancelled."

"Thought about it but I figured the exercise would help and I could use the company."

I stood next to my car unsure what to do.

"I'm not ready to start yet, do you want some coffee? I haven't had mine."

He came out of the house carrying two large mugs. He handed one to me and to my surprise it had the right amount of half and half. I thought to myself, *see Sydney Ross, they do remember.* Benjamin moved over to the metal table by the pool and sat across from me, holding his mug between two hands almost as if warming them. He looked so incredibly sad, I wanted to reach over and put my arm around his shoulder but I did not. I remembered what it was like those first few weeks after my dad died. I would be going along feeling as if things were returning to normal when suddenly there was a punch of grief so sharp, I would have to stop and catch my breath.

Several minutes went by, the only sound the hissing and swaying of the cottonwood trees that surrounded the house. Benjamin looked at me, his face etched with lack of sleep and sorrow.

"I keep having a variation of the same dream. They are all about my inability to get home. My mom would call and tell me that dad was in the hospital and that I needed to come home right now! My first dream I was in Aspen and there was this incredible blizzard, then I was at St. Bart's and there was a hurricane, then a terrorist attack, and an earthquake, on and on. Every version of the dream prevented me from getting here." Benjamin paused, his eyes full. "Isn't it ridiculous how your mind works? My dreams were all about an external event preventing me from coming home to see my dad one last time when in reality it was just my own stubbornness that kept me away."

"I know, I know," I said, "I was the same way."

"I remember you telling me that," Benjamin said, "That's why I didn't call and cancel this morning."

"Guess we're cut out of the same cloth, as my mom would say," I said.

"Two peas in a pod?" Benjamin offered, a small smile struggling to break through.

"Yup, exactly." I looked at Benjamin; he didn't look away.

Benjamin stood up, drained his coffee mug and said, "Enough of this crying in our beer, let's go work out." He headed towards the back door with me on his heels. We walked through the kitchen, down the hall to the other side of the house. He opened a door that looked like an entrance to a closet but instead was a staircase leading down to the basement. Benjamin flipped on several switches at once, the room suddenly over bright. I blinked a few times getting used to the overhead lights. Benjamin saw his reflection in the mirror and said, "Whoa, way too much unflattering light. I knew I looked bad this morning but I didn't realize I was a dead ringer for Jeremy Irons." He toned down the lights to middle range.

"Okay muscle man," Benjamin dropped to the floor and started stretching, "show me how you keep those guns so defined."

I did a few stretches and began working my biceps, feeling self-conscious. While my muscles were okay, they were small in comparison to Benjamin's. But after a few sets, my body warmed up and I lost myself in the exercise. We spoke little other than an occasional word of encouragement or counting out reps. We were both covered in sweat when we finished. While Benjamin's face still looked tired, his body was bulging from his efforts. He lifted his shirt to look at his stomach. His oblique muscles were beautifully defined and you could have washed clothing on his stomach muscles. He flexed his arms, turned sideways to look at his back and then shook his head.

"Please don't tell me you are unhappy with what you see."

"I kind of am," Benjamin said. "This is not normal for me, your body type is my old body type and I want it back. I feel like I'm turning into one of those muscles freaks in a magazine."

"Actually you do sort of look like one, I think her name was Debbie Atlas."

"Prick." Benjamin turned off the lights. "Come on, let's have some lunch and a swim, I'm starving."

As we made our way to the pool, Benjamin began stripping off clothing. It wasn't as warm as the day before but the June sunshine was still hot on our skin. Benjamin peeled off his shorts and walked over to an outdoor shower that I hadn't noticed before.

I stood next to the pool watching Benjamin soap down his body. He had his back to me, the scent of Dial soap and rosemary shampoo lingering in the air. The soapy water formed rivulets that streamed off the muscles of his ass.

I stepped out of my shorts, my erection bounding out of my jock strap. Before I could be subjected to any boner boy jokes, I dove into the pool and swam several laps waiting for Benjamin to join me. I floated to the shallow end and sat on the first step. My upper torso was exposed to the air as I laid back, lifted my face to the sun and basked in the warmth of the moment. I listened to the rhythmic sound of Benjamin swimming back and forth across the pool. I kept my eyes closed. After a while I felt the presence of Benjamin next to me. He was sitting in the same position; head tilted back, sun streaming over his face, his eyes closed. I studied his profile. It was not classically handsome in the way of a model. It was almost as if three different looks came together in one face. I wondered if his looks would have been as notorious a hundred years ago or if he was a product of his time. I thought about the stories that revolved around unparalleled beauty and wondered how Benjamin would have measured up. I began to have a thought that Benjamin had grown even more attractive as I came to know the person beneath the mask and then Gregg's voice was in my head slapping that thought back into the recesses of my mind. *You barely know him,* he would say, *get a grip and be a man* or something to that effect. Gregg took pride in being just as inscrutable about relationships as straight men.

Benjamin opened his eyes and smiled at me, his teeth a dazzling white against the golden color of his skin. "What's going on in that little brain of yours?"

"I was thinking about Apollo and wondering if he would have been jealous of you."

"What?" Benjamin sat straight up, a blush spreading across his cheeks.

"You heard me, I was just wondering how you would have measured up. What do you think?"

"Measured up against a mythical character?"

"You know what I mean. How you compare—looks wise—to other famous good looking men."

"Don't you think I am vain enough without thinking about things like that?"

"I don't think you seem that vain," I said. "You certainly weren't worrying about vanity about two hours ago when I arrived."

"That's because I'm comfortable around you, more so than I have been around anyone in a long time. Trust me, no one in LA sees me looking like I did when you got here."

"Let's get back to my question. But before you answer, let's keep this in the last few decades. And I'm not just talking about looks. How do you compare to Brad Pitt, Ryan Reynolds, or classic actors like Paul Newman or Montgomery Clift."

"Hold on, hold on." Benjamin grabbed my arm. "Let me think for a second. Well, at the risk of sounding like an asshole, I think I'm a better actor than Brad. Ryan Reynolds, come on, really? Now Paul Newman, forget it, I'm not even in the same league and Montgomery Clift? Well all I can say about him is that I'm not nearly as gay."

"Not nearly as gay!" I laughed my braying laugh.

Benjamin looked at me and said, "Where did that sound come from?"

"Sorry," I said, "I don't normally let that out of the barn until I've known someone for a while. It slipped out."

"No wonder you're single."

I reached over to try to push Benjamin into the pool. As I did, he stood up and dove in and to my astonishment, he had a semi hard on.

"What the fuck was that?" I said just as Benjamin surfaced in front of me, took hold of my feet and pulled me into the pool in one quick motion. As I felt myself being yanked forward, my upper body snapped back and I hit my head hard on the edge of the pool. The next thing I knew I was lying on the patio.

"Fuck," Benjamin yelled as I gagged trying to spit out the water I had swallowed. Benjamin was kneeling next to me, my head was tilted up and two fingers were placed over my nose. I drifted away for a second and then felt air being forced into my lungs. I pulled away from him, turned my head and vomited more pool water. Benjamin was moaning softly as he gave me more air. My breath was slowly returning to normal but my heart was beating furiously.

"Shit, Liam, I am so sorry. Why did I drag you into the pool like that? I am such a fucking idiot!"

I tried to speak but instead threw up again.

"We need to get you to the hospital. Now."

"No, no I'm fine," I croaked out.

"Tell me what hurts."

I looked up at him as he said those words, the same words he had said to Matthew McConaughey in *The King's Battalion*, and I started laughing and then threw up on his bare feet.

"My head hurts." I felt the back of my head; there was a large lump. Benjamin pushed my hand aside, "Shit you must have hit your head on the edge of the pool. That does it; we're going to the hospital. You probably have a concussion."

"No, that is not what I want to do." I sat up. "My name is Liam Ashby, I'm thirty-two years old and live in Mason City, Iowa. See? Everything is fine."

He felt the back of my head. "You need to ice that, I'll be right back." He ran into the house and seconds later was back carrying a plastic bag full of ice cubes. He moved behind me and pressed the ice into my head while rubbing my neck and shoulders with his free hand. I heard him say under his breath, "Shit that was scary, sorry." I started to protest that it wasn't his fault until I heard Benjamin say, "shhhhh" as he continued kneading my shoulders. I relaxed under his touch and leaned back. What seemed like hours later, I heard my name. I opened my eyes to see Benjamin looking down at me.

"Liam, wake up. I'm worried about you. Are you sure you're okay?"

I reached up to rub my eyes and pulled away from Benjamin's embrace. "Must have nodded off."

"Let's try standing up to see how your balance is." He put his hands under my arms and lifted me to my feet. I felt dizzy and stumbled a bit backward. Benjamin's arms were again wrapped around my chest as he led me to a chair. "You sit here. I'm going to get you something to drink. Are you hungry? How about a sandwich?"

"Sure, that would be great," I said, not feeling hungry but relieved he would leave me alone for a while. Benjamin went into the house and I slumped in my chair. I had never experienced anything like this, not even as a kid just learning to swim. Of course I had swallowed water over the years when a wave would hit me unexpectedly but nothing like this. It was the weirdest sensation. I couldn't tell if water had entered my lungs or not. It felt like it had but now that I was sitting up I suspected it had not. My breathing was fine. I was a little shaken and tired from the adrenaline rush and I had a bad headache.

I closed my eyes. I was floating in a warm ocean, the waves rocking me side to side. Benjamin was standing next to me, one hand supporting my lower back. I opened my eyes just as Benjamin leaned over to kiss me. I felt a hand on my shoulder.

"Come on Liam, wake up!" I sat up in my chair with a start. "Here, eat something."

I thought I wasn't hungry until I got a whiff of the ham and cheese sandwich he handed me. I ate it in four quick bites.

"Do you want another one?"

"No, I think I better see how this settles." I drank some water. For a few seconds I felt fine and then a wave of nausea hit me as I felt the sandwich coming back up.

"Oh my God, you're white as a sheet." Benjamin jumped up and led me towards the bushes that lined the side of the guesthouse. He held my head as I vomited up the food. It was as if everything I had ever eaten was trying to come up out of my stomach. I was vomiting so hard I was crying. I fell to my knees as wave after wave of retching wracked my body. Benjamin was kneeling next to me, his hand on my forehead and his arm around my back. He was murmuring something I couldn't understand. The vomiting finally subsided as I leaned against his leg. I wiped my mouth with the back of my hand.

"I better go home."

"You're not going anywhere." Benjamin wiped the tears from my face. "Come on, I'll help you up."

"But I have to work tonight." I stood up, my legs shaky, my knees dirty and my chin covered in saliva. I shivered in the shade of the pine tree we were next to. Benjamin put his arm around my shoulder and led me into the house and upstairs to the guest bedroom. I sat down on the bed while he went into the bathroom. A few seconds later I heard the water running in the shower.

"How is your nausea?" he asked, his eyes narrow and worried.

"It's over, I think."

"Good, we need to clean you up."

He led me into the shower and to my surprise he followed. The hot water was pounding off our shoulders as we stood facing each other. I could not stop shaking. The heat seemed unable to penetrate my skin.

Benjamin pulled me towards him and held me against his body. He pushed a spigot on the wall next to us and rubbed his hands together. He began washing my hair, his hands making gentle circles across the top and back of my head. No one had washed my hair since…I had no idea. I reveled in the feeling, strong hands rubbing my head, massaging my scalp, gently touching the lump on the back of my head. I closed my eyes and swayed slightly. Benjamin pushed me back so the wall steadied me. The water pounded down on me and this time the heat began to soak into my bones.

I felt two hands on my shoulders as I was turned around and Benjamin began washing my back. I smelled the clean scent of soap as my upper back was lathered. I felt a hand go under one arm and then the other. I leaned my forehead against the wall as I felt Benjamin wash the lower part of my back, moving his hands in a circular motion. My legs were pushed slightly apart. I felt two hands on my buttocks, and then felt one soapy hand reach between my legs.

I felt Benjamin's face near mine as he whispered, "Turn around."

I turned around making sure I was grounded as I was beginning to feel light headed. I felt two hands on either side of my face, washing first my cheeks, then my forehead, massaging the area under my eyes, moving down my nose and then my neck. A finger formed circles over my lips. The hands moved down my chest as they outlined the edges of my chest. Slowly the hands continued down to my stomach. I opened my eyes to see Benjamin staring at me, no expression on his face.

I closed my eyes again as I felt my balls cupped gently. A hand clasped my penis to wash it, first up and then down, two simple motions, no more. And then the hands were gone, moving down my legs. I looked to see Benjamin washing my feet. I was rinsed off and he was gone. I was alone in the shower. I was weak from dehydration and from the heat of the water. I turned off the shower, stepping out to find Benjamin standing there with a large white towel. He rubbed me down vigorously and then led me to bed. He pulled down the comforter and sheets and I crawled under them. Benjamin pulled the bedding up to my neck and sat down next to me with his back against the headboard. He put his arm around me and pulled me close.

"What is going on?" I asked.

"Not now, you need to rest."

"But I have to work in a few hours."

"It's only twelve thirty, what time do you have to be at work? Five?" I nodded yes. "Then you have plenty of time. I brought up some ginger ale." I sat up and had a drink. It tasted sweet, bubbly and cold. Perfect. The last person who had brought me ginger ale when I was sick had been my dad. I leaned against Benjamin's shoulder as I heard him humming quietly. It was a tune that was familiar but I could not place it. I had just about figured it out when I fell into a dreamless sleep.

CHAPTER FIFTEEN

---∞---

I woke up unsure where I was. I looked around the room trying to place the furniture and setting. It all came back to me, as the dull ache from the back of my head became forefront. I sat up and looked at my watch. It was 3 P.M. and while I had time, I knew I needed to get moving. I was alone in the room. I found a robe hanging in the closet and pulled it tight against my body. I felt thin and chilled and deeply thirsty. I walked downstairs and into the empty kitchen and drank a large glass of water. Outside Benjamin was asleep in a chaise lounge. I knelt down beside him. He was sound asleep but he didn't appear restful. His legs were twitching and there was a worried look on his face.

I went upstairs, dressed and went back to the kitchen to find paper and a pen. I left a note telling him I was fine, that I needed to work and asking him to call me in the morning. Stopping at the local grocery store on my way home, I bought chicken soup and soda crackers. As I ate the soup in the dim, cool light of my living room, I thought about everything that had happened. I was completely confused. I felt the back of my head and winced from the pain. In my freezer were various ice packs and I pressed one against my head and sat down.

I was unable to sew the threads of the past few hours together into a cohesive narrative. Had Benjamin been aroused? It had happened so quickly; I wasn't sure any longer. But what I was sure of was being washed by him. He had to be gay. There was no other explanation for his behavior, was there? Should I tell Sue what happened? Gregg? My head started pounding and I went to the bathroom for aspirin and a shower.

I drove to work feeling better but still weak. I was lightheaded and tired but grateful it was Sunday, usually the slowest night of the week. With any luck I would be home in bed by ten. The weather had turned during the time I was asleep at Benjamin's. Now it was cool, cloudy, and drizzling. People tended to stay home when the weather was poor. Walking into the bar, I saw Georgia Dee going over the reservations. She took one look at me, jumped out of her chair, and made a beeline in my direction.

"What the hell is wrong with you?" She put a hand on my forehead. "You look like death eating a soda cracker."

"Thanks, good to see you too."

"I'm serious Liam, you look awful. You're white as a ghost. Why are you here?"

"I think I had a touch of food poisoning this morning." The lie rolled off my tongue. "I slept all afternoon. I think I feel better."

"Think is not good enough, if you don't start looking better soon, I'm sending you home. I'll cover for you."

"Thanks." I felt my eyes water slightly at her generosity and then knew I was a mess.

Sue walked in. "Too bad George Romero isn't filming a movie around here."

"Didn't you feed him last night Sue?" Georgia Dee asked.

"Yes, why?"

"The poor guy got food poisoning and I'm putting two and two together. One lousy cook equals one sick bartender. You didn't leave the mayonnaise on the counter all afternoon again, did you?"

Sue was indignant. "Not that it's any of your business but my mom did the cooking and no I did not leave any mayonnaise out.

That was an isolated incident and it was years ago and I wish you would stop bringing it up."

"You almost killed Gertrude Anderson. I will not stop bringing it up and I don't appreciate your haughty tone." She walked to the front door. "I am still your boss and don't you forget it."

Sue walked over to me, put a hand on my shoulder and said, "You really don't look well, what the hell happened?" I looked away; I couldn't lie to her and look her in the eye. *Could I tell her what really happened?* Then I remembered the last time I told her something in confidence and her entire family knew within twenty-four hours. Her mom had mentioned a truncated version of it to my mom at the grocery store. I relaxed into my lie.

"I had a craving for an omelet this morning. I guess the eggs were old? I don't know for sure but whatever it was, I threw up for about an hour."

She put one hand on my chin and turned my face towards her. "Something weird is going on with you. You're holding something back from me. Aren't you?" I did not respond. "I don't like it. Good friends tell each other everything. At least I do with my friends." I walked away from her.

"There's nothing going on other than what I just said. I guess I'm not allowed to get sick?"

"That's not the point and you know it. I can tell you're lying to me and I don't appreciate it." She walked into the dining room.

"Shit," I said softly. I set up the bar for the evening but found myself forgetting where I normally placed things. I started to berate myself, remembered what happened and went and sat down at the far end of the bar, something that wasn't normally allowed. But I knew that Georgia Dee would give me a break for this one night.

The evening progressed as slowly as I expected, with only a handful of customers. The hands of the clock seemed to be stuck at 6 P.M. I did not banter with the few customers I had or with Sue.

In fact, she was acting as if she didn't know me. I thought about taking Georgia Dee up on her offer but I wasn't exactly breaking a sweat and decided to finish my shift. I thought again about what happened in the shower. Benjamin had to be bi-sexual although I wasn't convinced that was a real state of human sexuality. A straight man would not have washed my body, would he? But then again, we hadn't kissed or had sex. Was it simply what it was: one man washing another man's body? *Bullshit*, I heard Aunt Marie say. But then I thought about men giving other men massages, body waxing, body part piercing. I felt my headache coming back just as I looked up to see Benjamin walking in the bar, black beard and black wig, baseball cap firmly in place. He had a stern expression on his face as he walked directly up to me.

"What the fuck are you doing here?" he asked me so softly I could barely hear him. "You should be home in bed. And why did you leave my house without saying anything to me? I woke up around five and you were gone, no note, nothing. I called your house but obviously you weren't there. And one more thing, why don't I have your cell phone number?"

"I left you a note," I said feeling the headache working its way down the back of my neck. "On the metal table next to where you were sleeping."

"Never saw it."

"Not my problem." I got up to find some aspirin behind the bar. "You are no one to talk about leaving without saying anything."

Benjamin sat down at the bar, "Sorry. I don't mean to be such a hard ass. I'm worried about you. You had a traumatic experience today. Look at you. You look horrible."

"I wish people would stop telling me how bad I look. You may not want to own up to your vanity, but I'll own up to mine."

"How much longer do you have to work?"

"Actually I could leave right now. My manager offered to cover for me."

"Then, let's go," Benjamin said, "I'm taking you home. I looked across the bar to see Sue watching us. She had that look on her face that said, now I understand everything. She also looked very pissed off. I jumped off the bar stool and poured Benjamin a beer trying to pretend he was just another customer. I looked over at Sue again who was tapping her pen on the bar. I walked towards her.

"What can I get for you?"

"How about honesty? Do you serve that?"

"What do you mean?"

"Knock it off," she said, "it's clear that you and the hunk at the other end of the bar are into each other. Why couldn't you tell me that? What's the big secret?"

"We are not "into" each other."

"Do you know him?"

"Yes."

"Are you dating?"

"No"

"Is he gay?"

"No"

"Bi-sexual?"

"I don't know, I don't think so but I'm not sure."

"How did you meet him?"

"Here, at the bar, one night last week when you weren't working."

"You claim you've only met him once before, that you're not dating him, that you haven't slept with him and yet the two of you were just speaking to each other as if you are lovers." Sue's eyes flashed. "If you lie to me one more time Liam, well…I don't know what I'll do. All I know is that I've had enough lies in my life for three people."

I took a deep breath. I remembered that both of her husbands had cheated on her.

"Let's have lunch tomorrow. I'll tell you everything, okay?"

146

She continued glaring at me. I waited for a sign that her anger was dissipating. When nothing happened, I said, "Sue, your friendship is more important to me than anything." I reached over and held her hand. "I really do feel awful. I'm going home to bed."

"Okay Liam," she said, her eyes softening, "I'll pick you up at noon tomorrow. Now go home and get some sleep. I'll tell Georgia Dee that you've left." She came around the bar and hugged me tightly. "But I want the fucking truth," she whispered in my ear.

I walked back to Benjamin. "You're right, I need to be in bed."

"Now you're finally talking some sense. Come to my house, okay?"

"Where I go is not really forefront right now." I glanced back at Sue. "I need you to sit here and finish your beer. Make sure that my friend Sue sees that you're still here after I've left. She's convinced that you and I are lovers. If you leave with me, I will never convince her otherwise."

"Lovers?"

"Lovers."

"She thinks I'm gay? Huh, that's funny."

"What's so funny about it? Many people over the years have assumed that I was straight. I didn't find it amusing."

"We're not going to have that conversation now. Now get your ass out of here. I'll leave five minutes after you. I left the gate unlocked, just drive around back and I'll meet you there."

I looked back to make sure Sue was no longer in the bar. I walked up to the front desk to thank Georgia Dee for covering for me and stepped outside. It was pouring rain and chilly. I didn't have an umbrella so I cut back through the restaurant. As I passed the entrance to the bar I saw Sue talking to Benjamin. I felt my heart race as I ran to my car.

The streets were deserted. Even though it was June, there was something about bad weather that kept Iowans in their homes almost as if they expected a natural disaster at any moment. I shivered in the cold and turned on the heater. I was so numb, achy and tired that my brain shut down and I simply reacted. I stopped at home for dry clothing and more aspirin. When I pulled around the back of Benjamin's house, the kitchen lights looked welcoming through the downpour. I pulled up the hood of my sweatshirt and made a dash for the back door. I could see Benjamin standing near the stove. *Lovers*, I thought. *So that's what we looked like?*

I rang the doorbell, startling Benjamin, who spun around. "Come on in," he called out. The kitchen was warm and smelled of chicken soup. "This is my mom's cooking, the best chicken soup you will ever have." He looked over at me. "You still look frozen, here, wear my sweater." He handed me a white cotton sweater that was a couple of sizes too big. It hung down mid thigh and the sleeves were over my hands. Benjamin laughed as he took this in. "You don't seem that much smaller than me but I guess you are. You look about twelve years old in that."

"Maybe I'm shrinking."

"You probably lost five pounds today. You're looking thin, at least in the face. We need to fatten you up."

"You know I already have three moms in this town. I don't really need another one."

"Three?"

"The 3M's. My mom, and my two Aunts, Margaret and Marie. You should meet them sometime."

"Can I get you something to drink?"

"Ginger ale would work."

He poured us both a glass while we waited for the soup to warm.

"I feel awful about what happened today. That was hands down the dumbest thing I have ever done."

"Shit happens," I said knowing that I agreed how dumb it was.

"I wish I could be so nonchalant about almost killing you." He went back to the soup, stirred it and turned it up a notch. "By the way, I met your friend Sue. She's quite protective of you."

148

"How?"

"She walked over, introduced herself, never asked me my name and proceeded to tell me that outside of her family, you are the most important person in her life. I think she also said that if I fucked with you she would haunt me." He smiled. "Or something to that effect."

"She did not say that."

"Maybe I'm embellishing a bit but she did say that you are her best friend."

"Did she really not ask you your name?"

"We barely spoke for thirty seconds. As soon as she threatened me, I fled."

"You are so full of shit," I said. "What did she really say to you?"

"All she said was hi. I was reading between the lines. But I got the message loud and clear, don't fuck with my friend Liam."

"She didn't ask you any questions?"

"I think she would have if I hadn't run out of the place. Plus I realized too late that if I'm going to show up at your place of employment again I need an alias and a back-story. I decided to risk the embarrassment of acting the fool and getting the hell out of there. She strikes me as someone you don't want to screw with."

"You're right. She can sense a lie before you even say it. I've lied to her about four times in the last twenty-four hours and I don't like it."

"Why are you lying to her?"

"Benjamin, come on," I said, feeling cranky and exasperated. "How could I tell her anything about this morning without letting her know about you, or a version of you, that it never entered my head to create? She knows everything about my current life. She also knows that other than my family, she is my only local friend. So when she asked me who you were, I lied."

"What did you tell her?"

"That you were someone I met at the restaurant last week and barely knew."

"That works. Now what will my name be?"

I took a swallow of ginger ale, stood up and started pacing. I thought of Justin and all the subterfuge. I wasn't going to do that again no matter who the other person was.

"What is going on between us?"

"What do you mean?" Benjamin asked. "Other than we share a common background and are becoming friends. What else do you think is going on?"

"What about this morning?"

"Didn't I apologize already for that? I was a fool for yanking you into the pool. Sometimes when I'm around you I feel about fifteen years old."

"I'm talking about your semi hard on when you dove into the pool and I'm talking about the shower."

Disbelief clouded his eyes. "The former never happened and the latter…well…what about it?"

"You can pretend all you want, I know what I saw."

Benjamin turned his back to Liam. "Maybe I was thinking about Alyssa. I haven't gotten laid in a while." I could see a blush spreading across the back of his neck.

"And the shower?"

"What about it?"

"Are you deliberately being dense?" I asked. "You bathed me. You washed my entire body. Don't you remember that?"

"Of course I do. It was really nice."

"That's all you have to say about it?"

"What else is there to say?"

"Are you in the habit of washing the bodies of men?"

"You think I came on to you and I just won't admit it, right?"

"That would be a yes."

"Are you upset with me?"

"Confused is a better word."

"There's nothing to be confused about. It just seemed like the right thing to do at the time. It felt almost ritualistic to me. Maybe something the ancient Greeks would have done. I thought it was a lovely moment."

"It was lovely, that's not my point." I paused. "Are you bisexual?"

Benjamin stood up and walked to the other side of the kitchen. He filled two soup bowls full of steaming chicken soup. He placed them on the table along with crackers and more ginger ale. He ate his soup in silence. I was annoyed that he hadn't answered my question but I was prepared to wait him out. He wasn't going to dodge this one.

Benjamin finished his soup and pushed his chair back. "I'm just me, why do you have to label me?"

"So that is a no?"

"I didn't say that. In the hope that I don't sound like a bumper sticker, I reject all labels around sexuality. I have a girlfriend, we have an active sex life and that's about it."

"It's that simple for you?"

"Yes, I take it that it's not that simple for you?"

"No, it isn't, not at all." I had an image of Justin reaching over to touch me. "I had a bad experience with someone who was vague about his sexuality."

"I'm not vague. I just don't want to be labeled."

"Then why were you so insistent about making sure I knew that you're not gay? I think you've said, *but I'm not gay*, about twenty times since I met you."

"Maybe twice but I take your point. And to be fair to you, my attitude about labels is relatively recent. I've met some people the last couple of years that live their lives this way. I think it's a really interesting concept but it's still pretty new to me."

"Have you ever slept with a man?" I asked.

"Have you ever slept with a woman?" Benjamin responded as he picked up our dishes and put them in the sink.

"Yes, a couple of times in college," I said.

"So does that make you bisexual?"

"No, no it doesn't. I don't define myself that way. I'm attracted to men, in case you hadn't noticed."

"Thanks for clarifying that," Benjamin laughed. "You know, you're proving my point. Your primary drive is to have sex with men and be in relationships with men and yet you can physically have sex with a woman. Most people would say that if you can get it up for both men and women you are bisexual but you don't see it that way. So why get hung up on labels? They don't apply to you, do they? Why is it so important to shove everyone into such narrow categories?"

"I believe that the societal assumption about bisexual people is that their sexual attraction is equally split between men and women."

"Did you look that up in Webster's?"

"I'm just talking about assumptions, not some dictionary entry."

"I think you're talking about your own assumptions. You have no idea what other people think about this. For example, there are many people who don't believe that bisexuality is a true condition of human sexuality at all. That they're with a member of the opposite sex because they're afraid to come out of the closet."

"And those people also believe that everything can be explained away."

"Now we're getting somewhere." Benjamin sat up straight in his chair. "If someone doesn't believe in your definition of sexuality, then they are too rigid. But isn't your definition of bisexuality just as rigid? That's why we should throw out all labels," Benjamin said. "I think we're all basically bisexual anyway." He picked up both of our glasses. "Let's go in the family room. It's more comfortable."

I made my way through the dining room and two living rooms, wondering how I had gone from asking Benjamin if he wanted another glass of Champagne to whether he was bisexual. From the family room, a flickering light beckoned me. Benjamin was seated on the floor and motioned for me to join him next to the gas fireplace, which put out a surprising amount of heat. I felt warm for the first time all evening.

"I have a question for you," Benjamin said. "If a man marries a woman when he's in his early twenties, has several children, stays married but has sex with men on the side what does that mean? Is he a closet case? Is he gay pretending to be straight? Or how about two women who live together for twenty years and then one falls in love with a man?" He looked deeply into the fireplace; the flickering light made him seem older and younger at the same time. "I know men in the industry who have been married, have five or six kids, get divorced in middle age and spend their remaining years with a man. So what are they? Would you call them gay? I wouldn't."

"Alright already, you've made your point," I said. "But you are treading on dangerous ground. You are playing right into the belief of the right wing that we 'choose' to have sex with someone of the same sex. That we weren't born this way but somehow decided that life would be more interesting if I decided that I liked to suck cock and have people insult me on a routine basis." I finished the ginger ale in my glass and poured more. "Maybe someday we will all grow beyond labels but I don't see that happening anytime soon. And meanwhile, if your belief catches on, I see our rights going out the window again. Do you really think that gay marriage in Massachusetts would be legal now if your ideas were more widespread?"

"I'm not following," Benjamin said. "If all relationships were on an equal level then why wouldn't same sex marriage be treated the same way as opposite sex marriage?"

"Look at this way," I said, "When I worked in the business world, my employer opted to extend health insurance benefits to same sex couples but they did not extend benefits to opposite sex couples who chose not to get married. Why? Because they had the choice to marry or not to marry. Same sex couples did not have this choice. You know how people are, when they think that you have chosen to live a certain way or opt out of a societal tradition as marriage, there are penalties. If you choose one year to be with a woman and the next year with a man, then you are selecting a partner almost as if they were a color scheme. Gay marriage would be dead in the water. Why create an institution if people can choose to live with a man or a woman and enter into a heterosexual marriage? I think you have an interesting idea but I think you are naive."

"Perhaps," Benjamin said, "but I prefer this way of living my life. It works for me."

I moved closer to the fireplace as I heard the rain intensifying outside. The wind was blowing hard causing the windows to rattle in their frames.

"Do you envision yourself getting involved with a man someday?" I asked.

"I have no idea. What's wonderful about this is that I'm open to the concept. I'm shedding so many of my old prejudices it is unbelievable."

"Well, you have successfully avoided answering my question now for several minutes," I said, "So I'm going to ask it again, have you ever slept with a man?'

"You mean, other than the night last week when apparently I stumbled in to your bed."

"I'll stop using the euphemism. Have you ever had sex with a man?"

"No, I haven't," Benjamin said.

"Really?"

"Don't look so surprised, Liam." He slid across the floor, came behind me and started massaging my shoulders. "Maybe I just haven't met the right guy?"

"Stop flirting with me," I pushed him away and stood up.

"Sorry, I told you it is second nature for me."

"Your flirting is annoying and confusing and feels a bit phony so...please stop."

"Phony? That's a new one, hadn't thought about it that way." He closed his eyes and pulled his knees up to his chest. "I think I see your point but I didn't mean anything by it," he said. He opened his eyes and smiled and I remembered the scene from *The Swiss Family Robinson* remake early in his career where Meryl Streep had played his mother. His eyes had melted her and I feared they were beginning to have the same effect on me.

"You are currently in a relationship with a woman. Are you monogamous?" I asked.

"Alyssa and I are monogamous, 100%." He said this with so much conviction, I laughed out loud.

"What's so funny?" he asked.

"Never mind. It won't seem funny to you."

"I don't like being made fun of."

"I am not making fun of you, just at your flip flop. One minute you are Mister cutting edge sexuality and the next you sound like Oral Roberts. Guess I'm wondering who the real person is. Do you know?"

He looked at me with a befuddled expression. We were quiet for several minutes.

"I'm way too tired to continue this conversation," I said and walked over to a window. The rain was coming down in sheets, the cottonwood trees bending in the wind. It seemed to me that even if he did have sex with men, he wasn't going to tell me.

"I'm going to bed."

"Do you need anything?"

"Nope, I'm good. See you in the morning." As I walked past him, I laid a hand on his shoulder. It was almost imperceptible but I felt him pull away slightly.

I trudged up the stairs. My quadriceps were aching, my back hurt and I had a headache. I stripped down, brushed my teeth and was asleep before my head hit the pillow.

I woke up unsure where I was. I always thought this experience was a brief glimpse into what amnesia must be like. As I placed myself in my surroundings, I looked at my watch and saw that I had been asleep for three hours and I still had a headache. I went into the bathroom to ransack the medicine cabinet but couldn't find one. I smiled at my middle-class assumption that assumed every bathroom would have such a thing. This one was all flat, smooth surfaces.

I thought there must be some in the kitchen. When I opened the door to my room, I saw that Benjamin's door was ajar. There was a television on with the sound on low, the light from the screen spilling out into the hallway. I poked my head around the corner and saw Benjamin sitting up in bed, his eyes glued to the television. He had his glasses on and was shirtless, the sheet and blankets covered his lap. I looked over at the TV and saw that he was watching *Casablanca*.

He looked up and frowned, "Sorry, was the television on too loud?"

"No, not at all. I still have a bad headache. Do you have any aspirin?"

"Of course, come on in." He got out of bed. He was wearing white boxer briefs. I became uncomfortably aware that I was naked.

"There's a robe hanging on the back of the door," Benjamin said. I put on the blue terry cloth robe. He walked out of the bathroom with a glass of water and two pills. "This ought to do the trick."

"Thanks." I swallowed them dry.

"At the risk of being accused of coming on to you again, I think I can help you with your headache."

"How?"

"A massage."

"How will that help?"

"You'll only find out if you succumb to my magic hands." He began rubbing them together as if to warm them up.

"Now that we're just two dudes hanging out together, why not?" I winced as I said dudes. "Is that the way your kind talk to each other?"

"I wouldn't know, I don't have a "my kind" group."

"Please don't start your sociology lecture again, my head will implode from the weight of so many illogical thoughts."

Benjamin sat down on his bed, his back against the headboard. He spread his legs and patted the space between them.

"You lie here and put your head in my lap." I raised an eyebrow. Benjamin looked away.

I sat upright with my back to him waiting for some kind of cue.

"Why don't you take off your robe? I need to massage your shoulders too."

I stood up and removed my robe. Nothing else was standing up. Sitting down on the bed, Benjamin put his hands on my shoulders and pulled me toward him. He then pulled me down but the second my head hit his chest, I winced at the pain. I sat up again and pulled away.

"Sorry, talk about denial, I forgot all about your injury," Benjamin said. "How are we going to do this? Will a pillow help?" He had me sit up and placed a large pillow over his lap and chest. I slowly lowered myself again until my head was comfortably resting on it.

"I promise I won't go near that, I'll focus on your temples and forehead." He was whispering in my ear and I was already falling asleep again. He began rubbing my temples, slightly pushing in and then massaging my forehead and the crown of my head. His hands were caught up in my hair, and sometimes he would curl a lock around a finger. Within a few minutes I was asleep.

When I woke up the room was dark, my head was still resting on Benjamin's chest, rising and falling with the rhythm of his breathing. My headache was gone.

CHAPTER SIXTEEN

The next morning the sound of a shower woke me. The sun was streaming in the windows. I sat up in bed and thought: I just slept with Benjamin Graves. Not wanting to leave yet feeling like I should, I rubbed my eyes, stretched and looked around the room. Benjamin was a slob; his jeans, T-shirt and underwear were all on the floor. There was a pile of gym clothes in the corner and a few dirty dishes sitting on the desk in front of a window.

I was putting the robe back on when he walked out of the bathroom drying his hair.

"Good morning BB," he said as he toweled down his chest. "Glad to see you're back to normal. Trust you're ok?"

"I feel great, really great. That's the best I've slept in ages."

"Me too. I'm starving, how about you?"

"What are you cooking for me today?" I asked.

"Cook? I don't think so. We're going out to breakfast. I want pancakes, sausage, hash browns, toast, the whole works. Doesn't that sound incredible?"

"Beyond incredible. Can't you hear my stomach grumbling? I'll be ready in five minutes."

I walked across the hall pleased at how good I felt about everything. I had cleared the air with Benjamin. While I didn't agree with him, I also didn't necessarily disagree with him either. I just knew I couldn't live my life like that. My earliest memories of sexual feelings were always about boys. If that didn't make me gay, then what was I? And while I had had no trouble having sex with a woman, I had been 21 at the time. I could have fucked just about anything. When I walked out of room, Benjamin was walking out of his.

"Hang on, I forgot something," Benjamin said backing into his bedroom. "I'll be down in a couple of minutes."

The sunlight on the patio was beckoning as I walked through the kitchen. I stepped outside, the cool air causing me to shiver. The air was crisp, the sky a brilliant deep blue almost as if it was early fall instead of early summer. I pulled a chair into the sunshine and closed my eyes.

"Ready to go?" Benjamin asked as I looked over at the back door. Standing there was a man I didn't recognize. He had salt and pepper hair, a grey beard and a Minnesota Twins baseball cap. Baggy blue jeans, black sweatshirt and sneakers finished the look.

"Wow," I said, "You look at least fifty."

"It helps that my dad's clothes sort of fit me and that I'm really good at this shit." He turned around to give me a full look. "I have a question, what are the odds of you running into someone you know?"

"Why?"

"I woke up this morning with the realization that if I'm going to spend the summer here and be seen in public with you, I need to decide on a consistent look and persona. It's not exactly Hong Kong here, so eventually you will run into someone you know." He slapped his forehead. "This is all wrong, your friend Sue has already seen me and knows that we know each other. What happens if we run into her this morning? Then you'll have two people to explain to her."

"Trust me, she is sound asleep—she is not a morning person. Getting up early for her involves being up before eleven."

"But she has already met me and I didn't have grey hair or a beard. I'll be right back." He ran into the house and a few minutes later he was back outside with the black beard and black wig on.

"Okay, that issue is resolved, and since Sue and I didn't speak other than to say hi, I have carte blanche to create my alter ego. Here's what I've been thinking." He guzzled the remains of a diet Coke. "Somebody is going to see me either entering or exiting the driveway so I need a plausible excuse as to why I'm staying in this house. How does this sound? I met Benjamin in LA, moved there from, uh, Texas back in the mid-90's hoping to break into movies. I couldn't act at all so I ended up doing some stunt work. Eventually somebody noticed that I have the same build as Benjamin and I became his exclusive stunt double. So far so good, right?" I nodded yes, bemused at how much Benjamin was into creating this fiction.

"Over the years, I became a family friend and moved beyond stunt work. I've been a chauffeur, bodyguard, errand boy, pretty much any job they wanted. Mrs. Graves wasn't sure how long she'd be away this summer so she asked me to move in and keep an eye on things."

"Works for me," I said, "What's your name? And why Texas?"

"Because I love doing a Texas accent." He cleared his throat, stood up and turned around. He tucked his hands into the back of his jeans with his weight shifted to one leg. One shoulder was a bit lower than the other and when he turned around he was wearing a lop-sided grin.

"Hey, how y'all doing?" His voice had a resonant twang. "I'm fixing to go out for breakfast. I could use me a mess of bacon and grits. Can you rustle that up in these parts?"

I frowned at him. I thought he sounded like a reject from *Urban Cowboy*.

"What you frowning at boy?"

"You need to either bring it down a notch or pick a different state. How about Montana? I think a soft cowboy twang might work."

"The fuck you say. I was born in Waco but grew up in Katy. This is how my kin sound. You calling me a phony, boy? Cuz we don't deal well with that kind of talk back home."

"Cut!" I clapped my hands together. "Let's start this scene over, okay?" He took a step towards me and glowered.

Benjamin paced a bit and then turned to me.

"Name's Clay Davis. We go way back to Jefferson Davis and we are proud of our kin and proud of the way we talk. Got it?" He put a hand on my shoulder and squeezed. I looked for a semblance of Benjamin under the distorted face and began to think he had transformed himself completely.

"Got it, I definitely got it."

He rubbed his hand on my upper back and said, "What's your name, purty boy?"

I started to laugh but seeing Benjamin's eyes, I shut it down.

"My name is Liam Ashby." Apparently he was acting with a capital A. I wondered how long it would last.

"You sure got a purty mouth boy." He grinned lasciviously. He ran a finger over my lower lip. I pulled away.

"Jesus Benjamin, are you trying out for *Deliverance, Part II*?" His eyes opened wide and he smiled.

"Sorry about that, I was having so much fun I got a little lost. *Deliverance* is one of my favorite movies. I would kill to do a remake of that. Let's get the hell out of here; I got a hundred chores to do today. I'm gonna be busier than a one-legged man in a butt kicking contest." At that I let loose with my trademark laugh.

"Whoa, Nellie," he said drawing out each syllable. "That sounded just like my old horse Blackie the day she died. God rest her soul."

He walked over to me, cuffed me on the ear and said, "Hope y'all don't mind my old pickup. I think there's room between the deer I shot this morning and my gun rack for a purty little thing like you."

"Oh shit, what have you created?"

Benjamin started laughing and said in his normal voice, "Come on, let's go eat. Where are we going?"

"The Country Kitchen. Other than my mom's house, it's the best breakfast in town."

"Then why don't we just go to your mom's house?"

"You're kidding, right?" I asked. "I'm going to show up at 7:30 on a Monday morning with a total stranger, someone I've never mentioned to her. The deer won't be the only dead thing in your old pickup if we do that."

"You need to start talking about me. I want to meet the three M's." Benjamin got into the LeSabre.

"Yeah, yeah I'll do that." I felt a surge of energy and disbelief. Would he still be around tomorrow or the next day? "I told Sue last night that I met you at the restaurant. You came in, sat at the bar and we started talking. I think my mom will buy that. Not sure Sue did. I'm beginning to feel like a professional liar."

Benjamin looked at me. "I feel crappy about this. But it's the only way this is going to work. I'm sorry you have to lie to your family and friends."

"Guess it's not that big a lie, is it?" I wondered how I would feel if either of my sisters were in my shoes. Would I accept that it was a lie of necessity or would it feel like an unnecessary lie, a lie whose sole purpose was to keep people out of the secret?

Benjamin drove down the hill and out on to the road. "Maybe someday I can go public that you're my friend. But I don't want to do that yet. You have no idea what it would be like."

"I think I have a sense," I said. "And I have the good sense to know it would be awful. I mean just having Jesse Clinton follow me home after your dad's funeral reception was enough for me."

"He did what?"

"He and his cameraman followed Sue and me as we left your house. They came right up to my front door with the camera on. He wanted to know how you were holding up. I told him you were a fucked up mess and that you had sobbed in my arms." Benjamin's head turned sharply to look at me. "Not really. I reminded him that your dad had just died."

He put a hand on my shoulder. "Now I remember why Sue looked so familiar. She was with you the day of the funeral, right"

I nodded. "My friend Gregg said they played that clip several times. It was the bookend to my fifteen seconds of fame."

"Who's Gregg?"

"My best friend back in Boston."

"How did you meet him?"

"He was the friend of someone I met at my first job. He's a realtor. God I hope his ears are burning."

"Was he your boyfriend?"

"Hell no, not my type at all." We drove past my childhood church. "He's good looking but a bit overweight. Did that sound as shallow as I think it sounded?" I looked at him. "Forget it, don't answer that. He's just not my type. But he's smart and hysterically funny. At times he drives me crazy but he did stick with me through a pretty shitty time."

"So how many boyfriends have you had?" Benjamin asked.

"Just one."

"One?"

"Yep, only one."

"How many men have you dated?"

"Didn't I just answer that?"

"You've only dated one man your entire life?"

"Yes."

"How many men have you slept with?"

"Not counting you, two."

Benjamin looked over, his mouth agape. I cried, "watch out!" just in time for Benjamin to slam on his brakes and avoid hitting the car that had abruptly stopped in front of us.

"You've only had sex with two men?"

"Well, how many women have you slept with?" I asked.

"Hell, I have no idea. Plenty." Benjamin pulled into the parking lot of the restaurant. "But not nearly as many as I could have. Liam, what's wrong with you?"

"There is nothing wrong with me." I got out of the car and slammed the door.

"You bet your ass there is." Benjamin said as he ambled to the restaurant. "You're gonna be middle aged sooner than you think and you're going to regret not fucking around when you had a chance. And, you're not always going to be in the shape you're in now. Good morning y'all!" Benjamin said to the hostess, switching instantly to his Texas accent. "You sure as shootin smell good, Ma'am." He leaned in close to the thin, bleached blond forty-something woman who stared at Benjamin without censors. "My friend and I are about starving. We need food, lots of food. Do y'all think you can handle us?"

"Of course I can." She stood up straight, grabbed two menus and headed to a corner booth. "I just love your accent, where are you from?"

"I'm from Katy, Texas, Ma'am, just west of Houston. Ever hear of Katy?"

"Can't say that I have but I bet it's nice." I could hear the slightest breath of a southern accent creeping into her words. "And if the men all look like you do, I may have to pay Katy, Texas a visit, real darn soon!" She touched the back of Benjamin's hand as he flashed his million-dollar smile at her.

I started reading my menu. "By the way, does it bother you that you're falsely flirting with that woman?"

"What do you mean, falsely flirting?"

"Do you plan on coming back here and asking her out on a date?"

"No, of course not."

"She thinks you are, look." I glanced towards the hostess stand where she was staring at Benjamin.

"Maybe I will ask her out on a date." He sat up in the booth.

"Yeah right."

"What point are you trying to make here?"

"Nothing other than to show you that your flirtations have consequences, that's all." Benjamin started to say something but instead opened his menu. We ordered our breakfasts. Our food arrived minutes after ordering: pancakes, eggs, toast, sausage, and hash browns. I had forgotten how much I enjoyed this kind of food. Just as we were finishing, Benjamin's phone rang. He looked at the number, stood up and said, "Shit, it's my agent, again. I gotta take this." Ten minutes later he returned looking upset.

"I have to go to LA today," he said.

"Why?"

"Some of the money people behind my next film are getting nervous. Did you see *Alexander* with Colin?" I shook my head. "Not many did. It tanked. They're worried about our version. There are even some rumblings about canceling the whole thing, which would really piss me off. The script is great." He looked around to make sure no one was listening. "Also, they think I've been gone from LA too long. My agent has been trying to explain that my dad just died and I need a break. That worked for a while but it's running thin. They want me to do the LA scene for a couple of nights."

"But I thought you had a photographer taking pictures of your double in Montana?"

"How do you know that?"

"You told me, at my house, that first night."

"I did? Shit, I have no memory of that. God, I was toasted." He finished his coffee. "A plane is on the way, it'll be here in a couple of hours." He pulled out his wallet and left two twenties on the table. I looked at him and said, "Unless you want people to talk about you, I wouldn't recommend over tipping that much." He thought for a minute and pulled one twenty back.

As we left the restaurant, I could see the hostess try and plant herself in Benjamin's line of vision but he was lost in thought and walked by her without a word. I smiled and thanked her, but she barely noticed me. The drive home was quiet. This time the silence felt strained and awkward. I picked a hangnail until it bled.

When we arrived at Benjamin's, I got out of his car and walked towards mine.

"This really sucks," Benjamin said, "I was just settling in. Plus I feel like we have a bond since I just about killed you yesterday." I felt the back of my head; the lump wasn't as painful to touch today. "I promise I will be back here by the end of the week." He walked towards me. "This is the happiest I've been in years. I hate to leave." He stopped directly in front of me. "Come on, give me a hug." I moved forward and he put his arms around me. We embraced fully. I was overwhelmed with the smell and feel of his body. I felt myself becoming aroused and I didn't care. We stood that way for several minutes, neither saying a word. Then I felt him pulling his face back from mine. Our faces were so close we were almost touching. He leaned forward; I raised my chin up as Benjamin kissed me on the forehead.

"I'll give you a call as soon as I get back, ok?"

"Sure," I said. I had been so positive that Benjamin was going to kiss me on the lips that I almost believed it had happened.

Benjamin stood with his hands in his front pockets, a glum look on his face as I drove around the house, down the tree-lined hill and onto the highway.

He just kissed me. Benjamin Graves kissed me and though it was my forehead and not my lips, it was still a kiss.

CHAPTER SEVENTEEN

———∞———

Twitchy with impatience, I called my mom.

"Good morning, honey," she said. "Sure looking forward to seeing you tomorrow night. We're doing Chinese take out. Margaret can order whatever god-awful food she wants, as long as she doesn't expect me to share it. She could order duck lips for all I care."

"Do you need anything done around the house?"

"That's sweet of you but I'm fine. I've already been to the store, started a pot of beef stew, walked the dog and cleaned the bathrooms." She usually woke at 5 AM as if shot out of a cannon. I heard water running and then the garbage disposal. She raised her voice to compete. "You might check with Marie. Maybe before dinner tomorrow night, you could help her replant all the weeds you pulled on Saturday."

"She's not upset with me, is she?"

"Define upset."

"Mom, her garden looked like crap."

"Liam, honey, you're right. It did and it does but, and I'm only saying this for your own good, nobody tells Marie what to do, what to say or what she needs done around her house." I heard a squeaking sound in the background; most likely she was cleaning the front of her oven with Windex and a paper towel. "You could point out that her roof leaks but if she didn't notice it herself, she wouldn't have it fixed. Have you forgotten how she is?"

168

"Apparently. Don't you think she is the most stubborn and outspoken woman you have ever met? Do you know what she said to me on Saturday?"

"Yes, of course."

"There are no secrets with the three of you, are there?"

"No."

"Are you worried about me, Mom?"

"Worried is not the word I would use."

"Aunt Marie told me you're worried. According to her, you all think I was daft to move home. Is that true?"

"Liam, don't listen to her. Sometimes she says things that are true, and they may be hurtful. Then other times she says things for shock value."

"What was the point of shocking me?"

"In her own weird way, maybe she thought it would help you find someone?" She turned on the dishwasher. "I do have to say one thing—I hate it that you're single. You're a good, smart, handsome boy and you should not be single. And where are you going to find a boyfriend around this place?"

"It's funny you said that. I met a guy at the restaurant last week. He came in for a drink. His name is Clay Davis and you won't believe this, but he's a friend of the Graves family. He's caretaking their house until Mrs. Graves returns from Montana this fall."

"Is he gay?"

"No, I don't think so. I barely know him. But he's really nice and he likes to run. We went for a run together on Saturday."

"So he's just a friend."

"Right."

"Oh."

"I thought you'd be pleased."

"It's always good to meet new people but you need more than another friend. Then again, it's probably better that he's not gay since he's only around a few weeks. At least you don't have to worry about him breaking your heart when he leaves."

"You have a point." I smiled at her anxiety. "By the way, I told him that you make the best breakfasts in Mason City, so don't be surprised if we show up some morning after a run."

"Well shoot, I need to go back to the store." I heard her open the refrigerator and then slam it shut. "I'm low on eggs."

"Mom, Mom," I said laughing, "it won't be any time soon. He had to leave town for a few days. I'll give you plenty of warning before we show up."

"Doesn't matter, I better go in any event. You know I hate being low on things. Love you Liam. See you tomorrow night."

I paced through my living room, went outside, and worked on my garden for a while. After almost cutting off my index finger remembering Benjamin's lips on my forehead, I decided to put my gardening tools away. I didn't have time to run so I forced myself to do a few yoga poses. I stripped down to my underwear, stretched and moved into downward dog. It didn't work. My mind was filled with one image after another of Benjamin: naked with the plate of food over his crotch, in the shower, his lips inches from mine, his ass in the moonlight, stumbling down the gravel road with his shorts around his ankles.

I savored each memory; they were so real it was as if Benjamin was in the same room. I reached forward with my eyes closed, wishing with all my might that he was standing in front of me. I imagined holding his cock and balls in my own hands. I moved my hands back and forth languidly as I leaned up to kiss him. I fell to my knees and jerked off, my orgasm racking my entire body. I lay on the floor staring at the ceiling thinking of nothing until I heard a car pull in front of my house. I looked at my watch. Sue was right on time which wasn't like her; she was almost always thirty minutes late.

I ran to the bathroom, washed my face and hands and began rehearsing what I was going to tell her. I thought that if I repeated it over and over that eventually even I would begin to believe there was a Clay Davis.

I wanted to tell her. If she never told another soul then everything would be fine. But if she slipped, even once, word would get around, and if Benjamin found out then he would be gone from my life, and I did not want that.

Sue honked her horn four times. I took a deep breath, bracing myself for the lies I was about to tell.

"Hold your horses," I called out as I ran down to her car. "No one has honked a horn in this neighborhood in at least a decade. Someone might call the cops and trust me; I don't want another glimpse of Flanagan family incest." I slid into the passenger seat. "I will never forget the look on Tommy's face when he realized the breasts he was lusting over belonged to his first cousin."

"That was classic, wasn't it? I've told at least ten people that story, which means by now the entire county knows. I'm not sure he'll ever live it down. But then it does continue the legend of my nearly perfect breasts."

"Nearly?'

"One is slightly smaller than the other but it is quite imperceptible except to my critical eye." She gunned the car up the road. "Here's what I am thinking: why don't we stop at the grocery store and pick up some bread, cheeses, fruit and have a picnic? It's a perfect day to go to Clear Lake, warm enough to sit on the beach but not so warm that you would even think about going into that water and risk cholera."

"I haven't been to Clear Lake since I was about ten. For some reason we went in the water that summer. I remember getting this weird rash on my legs." I rubbed my thigh as if it still itched.

"According to my mom, there's enough run off fertilizer and chemicals in that lake to qualify it as a weapon of mass destruction. One errant match and all of North Iowa would go up." She raced through a yellow light. I grabbed the dashboard.

"O.K., enough about that bullshit, let's talk about your bullshit. What gives with the bearded hunk? I introduced myself and he just about ran out of the restaurant. He didn't say one word to me although he flashed a smile at me. His teeth are so white they just about gave me a migraine." She whipped into the parking lot and turned off her car. I started to get out but she hadn't moved.

"Time to spill it, Liam. What's his name? How did you meet him? Is he Catholic? You said he isn't gay, so what's his story? Is he from around here? Since he isn't on your team, I want you to have me over for dinner. He's the best looking thing I've seen around here…ever."

"Do you really think so? Guess I'm not into all that facial hair."

"Who cares about the beard? He can shave. Didn't you notice his eyes? His hands? And my God, those shoulders!" She was out of the car and moving towards the entrance. I had to hurry to keep up.

"You noticed his hands?" She pointed at a cart and walked through the automatic door.

"Of course, most women do. And it's not for the same reason you do. I associate large, strong hands with strength of character. Both of my husbands were quite deficient in that arena."

"Hands or character?"

"Both."

"Then why did you marry them?"

"I'll answer that question the day you tell me what happened with your one and only boyfriend and not a minute before." She squeezed a few baguettes before putting one in the cart. Several minutes later we were standing in line while I leafed through the current issue of *Star*. Benjamin was on the cover along with Jacqueline Anderson. Apparently she was pregnant by him for about the tenth time.

"You really are a trash monger, aren't you?" I quickly put the magazine back. I looked up to see John Cahill at the cash register. A high school classmate, he had worked at this same grocery store for sixteen years. He had courted us in high school, anxious to be our friend. Earnestness oozed from his pores.

"Hey Liam, I saw you on TV." His eyes were bright, his smile was genuine. "I sure wish I had been there."

"Why?" I asked.

"I could have told that guy a few things about Benjamin Graves."

"You?"

"Sure, he used to come in here all the time with that friend of his, the football player."

"They did?" I tried to picture Benjamin and Scott Jensen buying groceries together.

"Yeah, in the summer they would stop by almost every day to buy Gatorade and sandwiches. They were always goofing around, pretend boxing, faking they were on the football field and getting ready to make a tackle." He finished scanning our food. "They were so cool, way cooler than anybody at our school."

"I suppose they were," Sue said as she tried to get the credit card reader to move faster, pushing buttons before they were ready.

"So what are you guys up to today?"

"Not much, just picking up a few things for my mom," Sue said.

"I get off in thirty minutes, you wanna have lunch?"

"Thanks John, but I have a million things to do today, maybe some other time?" Sue said with her most winning smile. I saw John take a quick look at her breasts.

"Sure, anytime, just give me a call, I'm in the phone book."

"You're a pretty good liar, aren't you?" I asked.

"What are you talking about?" She opened her trunk and pushed aside bags of old clothing to find room for the food.

"What you just told John."

"I wouldn't call it that. I think of it as charity work. He wants me, he cannot have me and so I am sparing him hours of frustration."

"One step closer to sainthood."

173

"Enough about him, when are we going to see your hot friend again?"

"Not sure, he had to leave town for a few days."

"Why?"

"He had some business in LA." *So far, so good.*

"He's from LA?" She came to a sudden stop as I put my hand on the dashboard again.

"No, he's from Texas, someplace called Katy."

"You've never heard of Katy, Texas?" The light turned and with a squeal of wheels, she raced through the intersection. "Jesus, Liam, you lived in Boston for ten years, haven't you heard of Roger Clemens?'

"Of course I have. He was that chubby pitcher who made too much money and who wouldn't carry his own luggage."

"That's what you remember about him? Not the fact that he is one of the greatest pitchers to have ever played baseball? You're hopeless. Anyway, Roger Clemens is from Katy. It's near Houston."

"Next time I see Clay, I'll ask him if he knows Roger."

"Who's Clay?"

"The guy with the beard."

"By the way, did you know that all of the Clemens kids names start with a K, in honor of strike outs."

"How clever," I said. "I'll make sure to tell Jenna Bush to name her kids Frank, Faye and Ferdinand in honor of the number of fuck ups her dad's achieved in the last six years."

"Political humor?"

"What? I can't jab our president?"

"Of course you can. It's just that I have this vague memory that you voted for him."

"I did not vote for that asshole. I did vote for another asshole that I'm not proud of but it wasn't that asshole."

"Right, I keep getting Mitt Romney mixed up with W."

"You know, when I voted for Mitt I thought he was a friend of the gay community. And they wonder why we're all so cynical about politicians."

"I'm not cynical about politicians," she said as she rummaged through her purse. I reached over to hold the steering wheel, which she seemed to forget needed human guidance. She slapped my hand away. "If you accept that everything that comes out of their mouth is dishonest, what's there to be cynical about?"

"Didn't you just define cynicism?"

"Perhaps. Unfortunately, I don't have a dictionary in my purse, at least today, but it seems to me that cynicism arises from having your hopes dashed. I have never allowed myself even one moment of hope when it comes to politics." She applied fresh lipstick while steering with her knees. She came to a screeching halt as the left turn signal changed to red. A semi truck barreled past us in the opposite direction.

She found a parking space one block from the beach. She backed into the space with one turn of the wheel and without looking in her rearview mirror. The wind was fresh off the lake, and to my surprise, it didn't smell.

Sue spread a blanket on the narrow beach that lined the shore. There were a few motorboats zipping past with water skiers in tow. We had the beach to ourselves.

"O.K., enough chitchat. Who is this guy?"

I ripped off the end of a loaf of French bread, split it open, put a hunk of cheddar cheese in between and stuffed a few green grapes in my mouth. "His name is Clay Davis. He's my age and he's a friend of the Graves family."

"What? You didn't tell me that."

"I haven't really told you anything about him, have I?"

"What do you mean, a friend of the Graves family?"

The lies were flowing through my mind. I felt a vein throb in my left temple. "I told you I met him at the restaurant last week, right?

175

He came in for a drink and we started talking. He's really friendly in that way that Southerners are."

"How the hell do you know anything about Southerners?"

"Are you going to let me tell this story or keep interrupting me?"

"I could really use a beer."

"Mississippi was part of my territory when I worked for that insurance company. That was in the dark ages when you and I stopped talking."

"Why did that happen?"

"Which conversation do you want to have today?"

"Shit, I could use a beer."

"Anyway, we started talking and turns out he likes to run. I asked him if he wanted to go for a run with me over the weekend and he said yes. He's taking care of the Graves home for the summer. That's about all there is."

"Bull," Sue scooped a pile of Brie onto the other heel of the bread. "You're just getting started. How did he meet the Graves family? And if he such a good friend of the family, why didn't I see him at the funeral reception?"

Crap, I thought. I hadn't thought this through enough. "Maybe friend of the family is too strong a word, he is more of a caretaker, chauffeur, bodyguard, that sort of thing. Of course he wouldn't have been inside the house with the family."

"Of course? You're an expert on their relationship all of a sudden?"

"Of course not. He met Benjamin in LA, he was doing stunt work then he started working for Benjamin exclusively. The next thing he knew he's spending the summer in Iowa watching over their house."

"Why didn't they just close the place up for the summer?"

"How the hell would I know that?"

"Is it really this simple?"

"Sue, I hardly know him."

"If I hadn't seen you two huddled at the end of the bar last night, I might believe you." She took off her sunglasses and lifted her face to the sun. "This is what I think. He's married but bisexual and you two have slept together and he's sworn you to secrecy. Am I warm?"

"Not even tepid."

"Then he let you suck his dick and he's full of remorse and terrified you're going to tell someone." I glared at her, annoyed that she would think I would do that and even more annoyed that in some ways she had summed up my relationship with Justin. "I think I hit a nerve, didn't I?"

"No." I stood up and walked to the water's edge. I picked up a few flat stones and began skipping them across the surface of the gray water.

"Would you tell me if I guessed the truth?"

"I've told you the truth already."

"No you haven't, Liam." She walked over and stood next to me. She turned my shoulders so we were facing each other. "I've had my own share of screwed up relationships so I'm no one to judge, but you are not telling me the truth. I knew it last night and I know it now."

I looked away.

"I'm sure you have your reasons for not telling me the truth. I'm sure they are very good reasons and I'm just as sure someday you'll tell me what the hell is going on."

I took off my sneakers and waded into the lake. Could I tell her the truth? I walked further into the lake. The cool murky water brought back a memory of my dad holding me up by the waist and teasing me he was going to throw me in. I had been five or six and had cried uncontrollably until he relented. My sister Deirdre had been clamoring for Dad to do the same thing except she allowed him to toss her in. I remembered being surprised that she popped out of the water, on her feet, laughing and splashing. I had thought he was throwing me into water that was over my head.

A stream of scenes of my life with Dad unfolded in front of me: Little League, football, girls, church, all with the same theme: pushing me into something he wanted me to do and not what I wanted. Each time the scene ended the same way.

Trust. The word echoed through my brain.

I turned and looked at Sue. "You know I was in a very fucked up relationship in Boston. I didn't think it was at the time but it was. I'm still struggling with the after effect."

"What does that have to do with Clay?"

"Nothing, Clay doesn't mean anything to me, I barely know him."

"Then what's the connection?"

"I need to tell you what happened with Justin."

"Justin. God I love that name, or is it that I love Justin Timberlake?"

"Can you stop being glib for one second?" She looked at me with wide eyes.

"Yeah...sure, didn't know we were getting all heavy here."

"Sue, if I don't tell you about this now, I may never."

She looked at me warily, almost as if worried that anything she said would be the wrong thing.

"Let's get a beer," I said.

We walked two blocks to a restaurant that had an outdoor cafe overlooking a small park that formed the center of downtown Clear Lake. There were four or five tables with red and white checked plastic tablecloths, a bored looking waitress and no customers. Two Coronas arrived within seconds of sitting down. The waitress hovered; seemingly pleased to have something to do until Sue told her we had already eaten. I squeezed a lime into my beer and took a long swallow.

"I met Justin Thornton in December of 2000 at an open house for a building I was trying to sell. I ended up selling it to him," I said slowly. I took another sip, trying to remember and not remember at the same time. "He was a few years older than me, came from an old Waspy family with lots of discreet money."

"What does that mean?"

"It's a Yankee thing, these old families are richer than either you or I could imagine but you would never know it in a million years. They drive Volvos or Land Rovers that are at least fifteen years old, dress in LL Bean clothing they have owned their entire adult lives because their weight never fluctuates more than three pounds in either direction and wear one piece of jewelry other than their wedding rings, a watch for the man and a strand of pearls for the woman."

"Glad you don't stereotype. What did he look like?"

"He was really good looking."

"So descriptive," Sue said.

"We became good friends over the next year, exercised a lot together, skiing, running, canoeing, rollerblading, you name it. At a certain point Gregg told me I was falling in love with Justin but I denied it. As usual, Gregg was right."

"So far this doesn't sound particularly twisted to me." Sue finished her beer and ordered two more. The tension around her eyes had disappeared.

"Falling in love with a straight man doesn't seem screwed up to you?"

"Guess I'm jumping ahead in this story and assuming he's not straight."

I said nothing as I began drowning in a flood of memories. Was Justin gay? I had been convinced he was but I never knew for sure and it drove me crazy. "He told me he was straight. I believed him." I remembered waking up to find his hand on my cock. " One night we had sex at his initiation."

"So he was at least bisexual."

"He said he was straight."

"Straight men do not make passes at gay men."

"I know that and he knew that which was proof to me he was gay but closeted. But you know what? In the end nothing mattered because he insisted he was straight. And I was convinced he was gay and just needed help coming out. It was almost like marrying an alcoholic assuming you are going to help them stop drinking."

"You know better than that," Sue said and then frowned. "Sorry, don't mean to lecture."

"I know, trust me, I know." I ran my fingers through my hair. "Here's the worst part for me." I drank deeply. "I'm really attracted to men like him. Gregg calls them SOB stories." Sue raised an eyebrow. "Sort of Bi." I answered her unasked question.

"I have no idea what that means and I don't really care. So far all I've learned is that you get a woodie for flirtatious pseudo-straight men. There are worse things."

"It's more than that, Sue. I fell in love with him. I was crazy about him. And you know what? It was never reciprocated. I was not part of his life. I never met his parents, his friends, his coworkers. The few times we ran into people he knew, he would introduce me as his real estate broker. He put me back in the closet, the closet he would not walk out of and I let him do it." I felt a stab of shame.

"Why?"

"I…I thought I was helping him. I thought eventually he would realize how much he loved me and he would finally come out to his family."

"Did he tell you that he loved you?"

"Once."

"Once is enough."

"I thought so but towards the end when we were fighting all the time, he denied that he ever said it."

Sue rotated her Corona in her right hand, swirling the beer, not looking at me, with her forehead scrunched which I knew meant she was holding back a judgment.

"See, I told you that you were going to think less of me." I drained my beer. She pulled her chair closer to me and put her hand on my arm. "Liam, you may be completely fucked up when it comes to men but get in line." She leaned in towards me. "There is absolutely nothing in what you told me that causes me to think less of you."

"Thanks, I think." She put her arm around my shoulder.

"Come on Liam, lighten up. I'm not criticizing you."

"How is being told I am completely fucked about men not a criticism?"

"Maybe I could have rephrased that." She looked away. "What I am really feeling is sad. I know that word is the most overused word in the English language but in this context, it's the right one. I'm sad for whatever caused you to be drawn to men like Justin and I'm sad that it seems to keep you from being in another relationship. You are one of the finest men I have ever known and you deserve better."

My eyes were full as I leaned against her arm. We sat for several minutes in silence. I fought the tears that wanted to fall. I had not cried about Justin and I was not going to start now.

"What is it about this kind of man that attracts you?" She played with the hair that curled around my ear.

"I can tell you what Gregg thinks."

"I want to know what you think."

I remembered the night Gregg told me after a few Manhattans that he believed I despised myself.

"One theory is that I don't like being gay so I'm drawn to men who are in the same boat. Men like Justin who are so afraid of being known as gay they will marry a woman to keep people off the scent." I pushed the salt and peppershakers across the table.

"I don't buy that at all. I have never gotten the sense you have a problem being gay. Plus you've got the love and support of your family. Hell, your mom tells everyone she meets that her son is gay. I think she likes seeing the reaction she gets. Maybe you went through a phase. It must have been exciting trying to figure out what made this guy tick, right?"

I managed a half smile.

"What underlies attraction? The physical attraction wears off after about five minutes. Why are some women drawn to abusers? Why are some men enraptured with bitchy, controlling women? Look at me! I married two losers, in many ways completely opposite from each other but in the most important way, absolutely alike: when things got tough, they disappeared."

"But...but this is much more profound that that."

"Who's being critical now?"

"Sorry, not what I meant." I looked across the park at two teenage boys attempting to skateboard across a park bench. "Do you ever get that feeling when you are analyzing your life that your issues are more complicated than most people?"

"No."

"Well, I do." I was annoyed that she didn't feel the same way and annoyed with myself for saying it out loud. I backed off. "What I said earlier was right, you know...the marrying the alcoholic thing." She looked at me quizzically. I crossed my arms in front of my chest.

"Liam, don't you disappear on me. You are finally talking and I refuse to let you burrow under again." I sat in silence while she tapped her fingers on the table. Several minutes went by.

"I don't have anything else to say," I said.

"Bullshit."

"I'm serious. I am talked out." It seemed to me that the more I said the more defensive I was going to feel. My experience with Justin had felt unique and I didn't want someone telling me it was just a phase, even Sue. Going through a phase was something a fifteen-year-old did and it was quick and transitory.

"You told me you wanted to talk about this. It was your idea, not mine."

"I know, Sue, but it just sounds so…so ridiculous when I say it out loud. How did this relationship happen? Why did he come on to me?"

I looked around at the still empty restaurant., "I am sitting here imagining if there were actual other human beings in this town and a stranger had just listened to what I said, they would think I am… hell, I don't know what they would think but it wouldn't be good."

"Do you really care what a stranger thinks of your relationship with Justin?"

I thought for a moment. "Yes, I do."

"Why?"

"Because I have gone through so much angst about it that it has to be about something important, something even a stranger would identify with. Don't you see? My relationship with Justin says more about me than it does about him. And if it was just a phase, then what it says about me is not good."

"What should it have meant?"

I closed my eyes.

"I think there's a part of me that believes if I keep reminding myself how fucked up it was, then I won't repeat it."

"Jesus, Liam…." she stopped herself. "It's never that simple and you didn't answer my question."

I thought for several minutes. "The foundation of the relationship was screwed up from day one. It's not like it ended because we didn't have enough common interests or were too much alike or fought all the time. We ended because he claimed the entire relationship had been a lie, that he didn't want to be in a sexual or emotional relationship with a man, that he wasn't really attracted to men at all. It was as if he was trying to erase the two years we had spent together. This is what haunts me; I wasted two years of my life with a man who wanted to pretend I never existed and I was in love with him."

Sue looked startled. She turned away.

"Anyway, this has been interesting but you still haven't told me anything about Clay Davis."

"Anyway? That's how you're going to change the subject?"

Her mouth was a thin line inching its way downward. "What do you want me to say to all of this?"

"That you understand? Empathize? Feel sorry for me? Something?"

"You know the Flanagan clan is about as judging as any group gets so of course I felt like wagging my finger at you. But just don't hold up any mirrors, okay? I don't want to think about all the things I've done in relationships. And one other thing, I knew you well in high school and that was fourteen years ago. So I know you and yet I don't know you. It still feels to me as if we are on our first date. Does that make sense?"

"Yeah, it does." Did it?

CHAPTER EIGHTEEN

———∞———

Before heading to Aunt Marie's for dinner, I drove to the one liquor store in town that sold interesting beer. I bought myself two bottles of Chimay and a couple of bottles of white zinfandel for Mom, vodka for Aunt Margaret and a few packs of cigarettes for Aunt Marie. As I parked my car in front of her house, I could see the three of them sitting on her front porch. Stepping up the three worn wooden steps, I walked in giving each of them a quick kiss on their cheeks.

"Hells bells, Liam," Aunt Marie said. "You've turned into a complete Iowan. You drove two blocks?"

"I went to the liquor store." I handed her the cigarettes, which she accepted silently. I walked into the kitchen and put the beer and wine in the refrigerator and poured myself a beer. My mom was handing Marie a photograph when I rejoined them. I looked over her shoulder and recognized one of Margaret's grandsons with a blonde woman sitting next to him.

"It's their engagement announcement." Margaret was beaming. Marie took one look and threw it on the coffee table.

"I don't like her," Marie said. I started laughing but stopped when I saw the look on Margaret's face.

"What do you mean *you don't like her?* You've never met Erica so how could you possibly say you don't like her?"

"She looks just like the woman **my** grandson was engaged to before she broke his heart. I didn't like her and I don't like this one."

"Why that is the...."

"We've already decided what we're having for dinner." Mom handed me a menu. "I'm having chicken, Marie's having beef and Margaret's having seafood, of course."

"How's the food at this place, Aunt Margaret?" I asked wondering what it would be like to go through life as Marie did.

"Considering where we are Liam Conor, it is not that bad," she said.

"Not that bad?" my mom asked. "This restaurant was reviewed in the *Mason City Globe Gazette* and they said it was the best Chinese restaurant in all of North Iowa!"

"That's like saying George Bush is the best president to have ever come out of Crawford, Texas," Aunt Marie said as she lit a cigarette.

"What the hell is that supposed to mean?"

"You know exactly what I'm saying Colleen. Don't pretend to be stupid."

"Okay, okay, time out!" I said. "What's the phone number? I'll call in the order." I pulled my cell phone out of my back pocket and punched in the numbers watching the three M's as they glared at each other. I ordered their food and an order of Kung Pao chicken for myself.

"What is it with the three of you and food?" I asked. "There is so much hostility around this issue that doesn't exist with anyone else I know."

My mom and Aunt Margaret looked away from each other. Mom asked, "Can you believe how hot and humid it's gotten?"

Marie turned toward her. "Colleen, don't start you B.S. Your son asked a specific question and I would like to give him a specific answer." She turned and looked at me. "The war was going on, there were rations, and we had no money and no food. We ate potatoes every night for months, just potatoes. Do you know what a potato

186

tastes like in April that was dug up in September? Of course you don't. You're spoiled rotten just like all of our children."

I saw Margaret shoot Marie a look.

"There's no shortage of food now so why can't you all let it go? Seems to me you're reliving your childhood over and over. Don't you get tired of it?"

There was silence as the three of them looked away from each other. I drank my beer, Margaret sucked on an ice cube, Mom polished off her wine and Marie smoked.

"Mom, have you talked to Leah lately? Isn't it great that she's pregnant?" I asked.

Marie looked at me and said, "If you think that question is going to prompt a conversation without acrimony you are sorely mistaken, young man." She looked at me with animosity. "What is your problem today? Why do you feel compelled to wade into subjects that are pimples just waiting to burst?"

"How the hell was I supposed to know that? Seems to me you all would be happy that my sister is pregnant."

"Sometimes, Colleen, it seems that your son is as thick as you are. Have you told him how you feel about Leah having a baby?" Marie asked.

"No, I haven't, Marie, and I would appreciate if you could keep your mouth shut about this. Can you do that for me, just once?"

"No, I can't. This is too important."

"Marie, for the love of God, don't go down that road!"

"Why the hell not? He's her brother, he deserves to know how you feel about his sister becoming a mom, doesn't he?"

I jumped in. "You're right, Aunt Marie. I would like to know but not now. I want to have this conversation with my mom in private."

Marie looked away. "Seems to me we're all family here, not sure why this has to be a secret." She stood up. "And more to the point, I can tell you how I feel, and nobody can stop me from doing that." She went into her kitchen with her empty coffee cup.

Mom whispered to me, "Please do not bring this up again. We have already had several arguments and I am sick to death about it. It's none of her business, for God's sake. She doesn't allow anyone to say anything critical about her children and she is not going to say anything bad about mine."

"What is wrong with Leah having a baby?" I asked. I looked over at Aunt Margaret who was uncharacteristically quiet. "What's up with you?"

"Nothing Liam, other than I refuse to get in the middle of those two." She pointed a finger at my mom.

"That would be a first," Mom said.

"So where was I?" Marie sat down and lit another cigarette. "Oh yes, I was just going to tell you how I feel about your younger sister having a baby."

I waved the smoke out of my face.

Margaret stood up, her entire body vibrating with anger. "Marie Therese, shut up! Just shut up!"

There was a long silence. I looked at their faces. Marie's face was blank as she lit another cigarette from the end of the one she had just lit. Margaret was bright red; her eyes filmy with emotion. My mom looked shocked.

"Okay Margaret, I'll drop this but I want you to know that I don't forget moments like this. Oh boy do I not forget things like this."

As if the cavalry arrived, the car delivering our dinner pulled up to the curb.

"I'll get it," I said loudly as I walked out to the sidewalk to retrieve the food. My hand shook slightly as I handed the money to the driver. I over tipped.

We ate dinner in silence. Marie finished hers before everyone else, picked up her empty boxes, said she was tired and called it a night. She disappeared into the house. Margaret looked abashed; my mom looked irritated.

"See what you've done, Margaret! It's going to take months for her to get over this."

"I know, I know, I screwed up. I'll call her in the morning and grovel."

"Why do you have to apologize?" I asked. "She was the one out of line."

"Liam, be quiet," Mom said. "This is between the three of us."

I felt about ten years old and disciplined for something I hadn't done.

"It's going to take more than groveling, Margaret," Mom continued. "I figure several pounds of good coffee and at least a month's supply of cigarettes, that ought to be a start." Margaret looked chagrined. She had little money and I knew this would set her back for weeks.

"I think I'm going to call it a night as well." I pulled a hangnail. "We're back at your house next week, right Mom?"

"Yes we are thank God. We're having roast beef, mashed potatoes, green been casserole and salad." She hugged me goodbye and headed through the house to the garage in back. I peered into the house; there was no sign of Marie. I brought the bottle of vodka to Aunt Margaret, which she accepted with a grateful smile. I sat down next to her and put a hand on her arm.

"Shoot, did I screw up," she said, her voice etched in sadness. "What was I thinking? I know better than to speak to her that way."

"Don't be so hard on yourself." I put my arm around her shoulder. "Somebody needs to tell her on occasion when she is going too far."

"But not me, Liam Conor! Not me. She will take that kind of talk from your mom but not from me. I know her as well as I know myself. She must feel like I stabbed her in the back." She struggled to her feet as I put an arm out for support. "I have always been her protector. Did you know that? She and our mom never got along. I kept the peace between them." Her eyes were glistening. "I am the only person she has ever confided in." She picked up her purse and headed down the front steps to her car. I followed in her trail. "I am so annoyed at myself I'd like to slap myself upside the head. I just might do it." She raised her hand. I reached over and brought it back to her side. "I am such an idiot."

"No you're not, Aunt Margaret. It's not that bad. You'll see, she'll be fine tomorrow."

"I wish I could believe you." We hugged for several minutes, her head against my heart. "See you on Thursday for lunch." She squeezed my arm and got into her car.

CHAPTER NINETEEN

———∞———

I drove my car the two blocks home feeling the discomfort with what had happened settle deep in my gut. What was Mom's problem with Leah's pregnancy? I toyed with calling her but she wouldn't talk about it, at least right now.

Back downstairs in the safety net of my home, I settled in front of my computer. I scrolled through the usual websites seeing photo after photo of Benjamin. The one that caught my eye was of Benjamin dismounting a motorcycle. He had on blue jeans, boots, a worn leather jacket and a T-shirt that showed off his pecs. He wasn't smiling; in fact, he looked annoyed that he was being photographed.

I looked for several minutes. There was no way I was ever going to see him again. It made no sense to me that I had even met him. My cell phone rang.

"Why haven't you called me?" Leah asked. There was an edge to her voice that caused me to sit up in my chair. "Nobody is calling me. The one time in my life when you would think I might get a little attention and the opposite happens!"

I was looking at a photograph of Ricky Martin in a Speedo doing yoga on a beach.

"Liam, are you on your computer? Is it asking too much to have a few minutes of your attention?"

I felt embarrassed and tongue-tied. I was also annoyed. I was the only person Leah allowed herself to become angry with. I shut down my computer.

"I'm sorry I haven't called. I have no excuses and it has nothing to do with you being pregnant. I am thrilled for you. I hope you know that."

"Is your computer off?"

"Yes, Leah it is." I was unable to hide my anger. There was a long pause.

"I'm sorry Liam, I am not upset with you."

"Really?"

"Really." Her voice was back to normal. "I'm upset with Mom and Deirdre, especially Deirdre. No one is calling me."

"I'm sorry I haven't called, been a little self absorbed lately. I have no idea why mom hasn't called though. I guess you'll have to ask her."

"I can't do that."

"Why not, you just asked me?"

"You're different. You don't hold grudges. Plus I'm not sure I want to know why Mom hasn't called." I could hear her voice shifting; she was beginning to sound like an adolescent.

"So, how are you feeling?" I asked.

She sighed into the phone. "Physically I feel good."

"You know you're going to be a terrific mom."

"No, I don't know that. All I can say right now is, I hope so."

"How about I come up and spend a couple of days with you later this month?"

"Um…sure."

"Not exactly encouraging."

"I'm sorry." I always thought she apologized too often. "June is really busy at the shop, you know June brides and all that crap. Towards the end of June should be fine. July would be better."

"I'll call soon."

"Thanks." Leah's voice was shifting again backward in time. I hung up before the conversation circled around into one that could last an hour. I stared at the phone and then went into my living room and found a favorite photo of my dad. He was sitting on the patio, beer in one hand, a cigarette in the other, laughing at something, his head thrown back looking handsome, young and vital. I wondered what he would think about his youngest child's pregnancy; I wondered what he would think about many things.

I awoke on Thursday to a driving rainstorm. A puddle had formed on the bedroom floor. I threw a couple of towels on the water, closed the window and climbed back in bed. I loved sleeping when it was raining. I fell back asleep until my alarm went off. I forced myself out of bed even though it was still raining. I wanted to do a quick five-mile run before Aunt Margaret arrived for lunch. I didn't mind running in the rain as long as it was warm. I had too many memories of cold winter runs around the Charles River, the wind swept rain pounding and stinging my face.

I was soaking wet within two blocks of my house. I ran to the high school outdoor running track to do speed intervals. By the time I got there, the rain had stopped and the sun had reappeared and with it the humidity. It almost felt like walking into a steam room left on high. I walked once around the track to get accustomed to the heavy air. I set my stopwatch and ran a half-mile at a seven minute pace, took a break and then ran three quarters of a mile at a 6:30 pace. When I was done, I walked another lap to try to cool off, which was impossible. I thought how great it would be to have someone to share this with, someone to run with me, someone to encourage me. I shook it off. I was not going to be one of those people who spent their lives bemoaning the fact that they were single.

I walked the last few blocks to my house. I was sore, dehydrated and hungry. I stretched for a long time, my body continuing to sweat even though I was lying in front of my fan. Preparing lunch,

I wondered how much I could tell Aunt Margaret about the funeral reception. I decided I could tell her just about anything. This was old news by now. The media was onto the next big Benjamin Graves story and it had nothing to do with anything that may have happened in Mason City, Iowa.

CHAPTER TWENTY

———∞———

Aunt Margaret showed up exactly on time wearing a loose Muumuu type dress, clunky white jewelry and smelling of Chanel #5. She was carrying a large wooden salad bowl.

"You're certainly summery." I gave her a hug

"Considering summer doesn't officially begin until next week, I'm not sure that's the right word. Boy is it hot! I didn't want to turn off the air conditioning in my car."

"You know I hate air conditioning," I said. "But I may need to rethink this position if the summer continues like this."

Margaret walked over to the window fan in the dining room, the blowing air sending the fabric of her dress billowing out around her. I stood next to her and leaned down to put my face directly in front of the fan.

"It's going to be sunny and 75 tomorrow." She always knew the weather forecast. "Don't give in, Liam Conor. There aren't many of us left who have avoided the evils of air conditioning." She moved next to me and put her head on my shoulder. I pulled her in for a hug. I was able to be physical with her in a way I couldn't or wouldn't with Mom.

"I'm starved, let's eat. I've got chicken for sandwiches, we have your famous spinach salad, and I have a loaf of French bread. Sound good to you?"

"As soon as you pour me a vodka tonic, it will be perfection."

I made her a light drink and poured myself a glass of seltzer water. I brought the food out on a teak tray she had given me for my birthday. I also brought out a fan to keep the air moving around our feet. She smiled when she saw that I was using the tray. She ran her hand over my metal patio table to clear away the leaves and twigs.

I drained my glass in one long swallow. "How are things with Aunt Marie?"

"I was afraid you'd ask that." She took a sip of her drink. "Did you put any vodka in this?" I went back into the house, poured myself more seltzer and brought the vodka bottle outside to the patio. I topped off her drink; she took a sip and grinned with pleasure. "Things with Marie are quite awful, to be honest. She won't return my phone calls and she doesn't answer her door. Your mom hasn't had any luck either. I have no idea what to do."

"Mom said that Marie is the most stubborn 68 year old woman in all of North Iowa."

"How about the entire country?"

"She will get over it, won't she?"

"I hope so. I so wish I could go back in time. Wouldn't that be marvelous?"

I nodded. I would have gone back to the date of the open house, that frozen Sunday morning in December when I had first met Justin, and never gotten out of bed. "Are you ever going to tell me the whole story with Aunt Marie?"

"What do you mean?"

"Why she is the way she is. She is so different from mom and you it's almost as if she was raised by different parents."

She sipped on her cocktail and looked away. When she returned her gaze, her eyes were full. "In some ways, in many ways, she was." She paused. "Oh Liam, this is not a good story." She drained her drink and handed it to me. I went inside, filled it with ice and tonic water and brought it back to her. She took a big gulp and topped it off with vodka again. She was shaking her head.

"You don't have to do this," I said.

"I know, I know, but I think I really need to say this out loud. Maybe then you will understand why I am so upset about what I said to Marie the other night." She put her hands on the table as if to reach for something to eat. "Do you have any pretzels or chips?"

"Sure, hang on." I ran inside and poured a small bowl of pretzels. Margaret selected five pretzels that were similar in size, which she lined up in a row. She began eating them from smallest to largest. When she finished she pushed the bowl towards me.

"Obviously you know that your mom, Marie and I are close in age. But I'm not sure you've ever thought about the fact that we are exactly ten months apart." She pushed the hair off her forehead, which was damp with perspiration.

"You're right, I never have."

"Because there was no reason for you to think about it. Our mom tried for years to become pregnant and then when she turned thirty she had Marie, ten months later me and then ten months later your mom. My God, can you imagine? Three pregnancies in two and a half years. Three deliveries so close together! Our dad worked 60-70- hours a week at the railroad and was rarely home." She stood up and began walking in circles around the table. "When Colleen was born, I guess Mom sort of fell apart. She just couldn't take it. She disappeared into her bedroom for weeks. Aunt Cecelia drove up from Waterloo and became our temporary Mom." She looked up at the hazy mid day sky. "And when she left three months later, she took Marie with her."

"What?"

"You heard me, she took Marie with her." Margaret sat back down. "Marie didn't come home until she was six. When she finally did move back home, it was as if a distant cousin had moved in. We had no memory of her. I think mom thought of her that way as well, more like a niece but never a daughter. Their relationship never recovered."

"You didn't even see her at Christmas…Thanksgiving?"

"I guess the first couple she did come home but she was so upset and disruptive they decided it was easier if she stayed with Cecelia year round."

I tried to imagine what that would be like, tried to understand how you would feel if you were given away to a relative for several years, the years you needed to be with your parents the most.

"I've been trying ever since to make her feel part of our family and now look what I have done!" A tear trickled down her cheek. "Oh Liam, I am so mad at myself, I just don't know what I am going to do."

I stood behind her, my hands kneading her shoulders. She put her small hand on mine while she fought to regain her composure.

"Marie claims she remembers things those few months before she was taken away by Cecelia. I'm not sure I believe her, she was only two and a half, after all." Margaret finished her drink. "She claims she remembers that she and mom were as close as a mother and daughter can be. You need to know Liam, that none of my children know this, and neither do your sisters. Please don't repeat it."

"I won't, I promise."

"Marie told me something once, only once." Margaret paused as her voice was breaking. "She ended up hating our mother. My God, can you imagine such a thing?"

I said nothing. We sat side by side. I listened to the wind rustle the leaves of the oak tree that covered my patio and heard the shouts of children riding their bicycles up and down the alley. I thought about the childhood Marie never had. I tried to imagine the uproar today if a mom gave away one of her children to a relative because she couldn't handle the pressure of raising three babies. Would I have ended up hating my own Mom?

Margaret looked at me, "There's one more thing. Marie was in love with your dad."

"Oh come on," I said, "now we're entering Jerry Springer territory." I went inside and refilled her glass without her asking. As I sat back down Margaret said, "I probably shouldn't tell you this but I guess it's a bit late for second guessing, isn't it?"

"That would be a yes."

"As you know, your dad was three years older than your mom, which put him in Marie's class. Did you know they dated in high school?"

"No, Aunt Margaret, I have never heard any of this."

"Marie was mad about him. It was one of the few times I saw her let her guard down with a boy." Margaret sat up in her chair. "And then something happened the year your mom turned sixteen. She was always pretty but when she turned sixteen she blossomed into something quite exotic. I would go as far as to say she was beautiful"

She took a swallow of her drink and put a drop of vodka in.

"I will never forget the day your dad noticed your mom for the first time. We were all sitting on our parents' front porch. Your dad was next to Marie and they were holding hands. Marie looked as pretty as she knew how to be; she had on her favorite plaid skirt and white blouse. It was a beautiful Sunday afternoon in mid September. I think it was the 14th, no the 15th, oh shoot, I actually think it was the 16th. It was one of those late summer days that felt like an attempt to confuse you into thinking summer would last forever. It was seventy-five degrees and a bit humid if I recall." I heard Aunt Marie's voice in my head, *here we go* she would say as Margaret dredged up memories that no one else could dispute because no one else remembered this level of detail.

"So here comes your mom bouncing onto the front porch, lipstick on, a little blush, her hair parted down the middle with a lilac headband. Her figure had come in and I don't have to tell you Liam, she has always had large breasts. She was stunning, like a young Elizabeth Taylor."

I had seen many photos of Mom from her high school years and she certainly had been pretty, but Elizabeth Taylor pretty? I began to wonder if Margaret was mixing this story up with a movie she had seen as a teenager.

"I looked over at your dad and his eyes were glued on your mom. I kept looking back and forth between your dad and Marie. I think Marie and I realized it at the same time. She looked at me; her eyes full and she left the porch. Two years later she was married to her first husband and they moved to Los Angeles."

"Has anything good happened to her?" I asked, suspending my doubts about this entire story for a moment.

"Actually, no it has not. She's just one of those people that bad luck seems to follow and now look what I've done!" I was afraid she was going to start crying again.

"Maybe it's time we ate something?"

She took in a long breath and let it out slowly. "On a much lighter note, I want to hear all about the Graves funeral reception. I need something to distract me."

"Absolutely, but I don't think you need to worry about Marie, she will come around. She will remember everything you've done for her."

"Thank you Liam, that is the best thing you've ever said to me." Her eyes were full again. "Okay, enough of this sentimental claptrap, I want you to spill the beans." She smiled as she wiped away a tear.

"I do have to ask a favor and that is that you don't tell anyone, especially anyone whose last name is Flanagan. Sue hasn't told her family anything and she will kill me if her mom or aunts find anything out before she tells them."

"You know you can trust me. I must say I'm more than a little peeved I had to ask you to tell me what happened, but I'm not going down that road today. One family conflict per month is plenty for me. So Liam, tell me, what was it like?"

I smiled. "It was amazing, truly amazing. I was a nervous wreck of course, as was Sue. When the door opened and Benjamin Graves was standing there with a tear leaking down his face, I almost had to remind myself this was real and not a movie. And when the celebrities started walking by, well it was just bizarre." Margaret's eyes were dazzled. "I didn't get the sense the actors knew Benjamin that well. Isn't that a bit screwed up?"

"Of course it is, but you're not surprised are you?"

"Not now, but I guess I was that day."

"What was the highlight?" She was looking at me as if I was going to share the secret of life.

"You're not going to believe this but Benjamin Graves knew me. He recognized my name from reading the *Globe Gazette* in high school. He ran track as well and he followed my track season our senior year. I was blown away when he started talking to me."

"Oh Liam, that is wonderful. The biggest movie star in the world remembered you from fourteen years ago!" She started to say something more but she looked behind me, surprised. I turned around. Benjamin as Clay Davis was strutting down the sidewalk that ran the length of my house. He had on tight jeans, scuffed cowboy boots, a denim shirt open a few buttons with the sleeves rolled up. I felt a thump of pleasure. I smiled broadly as I stood up to shake his hand.

"Hey, y'all, what's going on? And who might this purty lady be?"

"Margaret Ashby, meet Clay Davis." He walked over to where Margaret was sitting waving at her to stay seated. "No need for y'all to stand up." He looked over. "Is this the aunt you're always talking bout?"

"Yes, this is Aunt Margaret."

"And who are you, young man?" Aunt Margaret asked.

"I…I was going to tell you about him the other night at Marie's before the shit hit the fan." Aunt Margaret grimaced. I stood next to Benjamin. "We met at the restaurant last week. He's spending the summer here caretaking the Graves home. He met Benji in Hollywood, works as his stunt double," I said in a rush of adrenaline.

"Let me tell you something, pardner," Clay said. He put a hand on the back of my neck causing a shiver of pleasure to zip down my spine. "If you ever get the chance to meet Benjamin again, I reckon ya shouldn't use that nickname. Trust me, he kinda hates it."

My laugh sounded so phony I blushed. "Thanks, not that I need to worry about meeting him again but thanks anyway."

"What are y'all up to? I hope lunch. I'm so hungry I could eat the ass end out of a cow. Pardon my French ma'am."

Aunt Margaret laughed. "Don't worry about that, I've heard worse, much, much worse." She looked at me and I knew she was talking about the loud, ugly fights she had with her husband as they began their divorce.

"We're just about to have lunch," I said, "do you mind if he joins us?"

"Of course not, you don't even have to ask, any friend of Liam Conor's is a friend of mine."

"Liam Conor?" Clay asked.

"She's the only person in the world who uses my middle name," I replied, "can I get you a drink?"

"Sure shooting you can, I would love a Shiner Bock and a whisky chaser. Can ya handle that?"

"I don't have Shiner Bock but I do have Belgian ale. Will you drink that or is that too un-American for a big old cowboy like you?"

"Guess I can choke it down as long as you bring me that whisky chaser." His gaze lingered on mine a few seconds.

I brought out their drinks but as I descended the steps, I stopped and stared at the two of them, their heads close together, smiling and laughing. While they chattered on about the weather, Texas, the Lakers, the weather, politics, I prepared sandwiches.

I caught Benjamin's eye and smiled. He'd come back, just as he said. He ran his hand across his chest. I stared where his hand had just been.

"Clay is telling me he plans to spend most of the summer here. Isn't that great? Liam could certainly use a friend, couldn't you?" Margaret said, "Liam Conor, hello? I'm talking to you."

"Sorry, what was the question?"

"I was just saying that I think you could use a friend. Liam, you need to snap to, you know I hate repeating myself."

"Actually, you're right Aunt Margaret, I was just thinking the same thing this morning when I was doing my run."

"So that was you, wasn't it?" Clay asked. "I thought it was you that I saw at the traffic light by the high school. My God fearing Mama would have said that you were indecent, strutting around in just those shorts that you can see right through." I blushed bright red.

"What is he talking about?" Aunt Margaret asked.

"Nothing, nothing important. I was running outside in the rain and got soaked. Guess I shouldn't have worn white shorts."

"I hope Father Schmidt didn't see you."

"Don't get me started on that one," I said.

"Father Schmidt is not gay, Liam Conor Ashby." She sat up straight in her chair and with a quick swallow finished what was left in her glass. "And here you are spreading that rumor again in front of a complete stranger."

"Whoa, you two. What's going on here?"

"Father Schmidt taught religion when I was in grade school," I said, "Also he's the priest at the church the three M's attend. I always thought he had a thing for altar boys and Cub Scouts but the three M's say it's not true. And I never said I thought he was gay, a pedophile maybe, but not gay."

"Liam, you know I absolutely loath it when you say this," she struggled to her feet. "Father Schmidt is a fine, decent man. Anyway,

I need to use the girl's room. I'll be right back." I watched as she methodically made her way up the stairs. Once the door slammed shut, I said, "Hey, you came back!"

"I said I would, didn't I?" Benjamin said in his normal voice. "Did you doubt me?"

"Kind of. I saw you on television and on Pablo and I figured you wouldn't want to come back to Iowa after being in LA again."

"Why?"

"Because your life is there, not here."

"Don't be so sure about that," Benjamin said, "I like it here. In case you've forgotten I'm a native Iowan."

"Sometimes I do forget that." I fought the urge to reach over and hold his hand.

"What are your plans with your aunt?"

"Just catching up over lunch, plus I have to work tonight."

Benjamin looked at his watch as Aunt Margaret made her way down the steps to the patio. "I'm not sure I've seen better looking boys than the two of you." She sat back down with a hand on Clay's shoulder. "Of course I'm biased about Liam but you certainly are one handsome young man Clay."

"Thank you Ma'am, and you're one pretty lady as well." Clay looked at me for a while and then threw his shot of whiskey back. "Do ya really think this scrawny thing is good looking? I'd like to take him to my mama's ranch and fatten him up. A few weeks of BBQ and pork rinds would do the trick."

"Your mother lives on a ranch?" Aunt Margaret speared a few leafs of spinach on her fork.

"Why yes she does." Clay took a big bite out of his sandwich. He continued talking with his mouth full. "My daddy left her a few hundred acres just west of Houston. Hell, I miss that place. Have ya ever eaten rattlesnake?" The look in his eyes was pure delight. I wondered if he realized Aunt Margaret believed everything he said.

204

"I can't say that I have but I would love to try it someday. What's it like?"

"It's a bit like of a combination of veal and fish. Have you ever had gator?"

"Yes I have, years and years ago in Florida. It was divine."

"Then you're gonna love rattlesnake."

"Can we change the subject?" I pushed my food around on my plate.

"Why?" Margaret asked.

"Because I hate snakes."

"Sorry Liam Conor, I forgot you're one of them delicate Midwestern types." Clay punched me on the shoulder.

"Liam, do you have any iced tea?" Margaret asked.

"Of course."

When I returned to the patio, I heard, "Just three times, that's all."

"What happened three times?" I asked.

"Your aunt was asking how many times I've been bitten by a rattler."

"Oh my goodness, three times? What did you do?"

"Every Texan country boy knows what to do. It's part of Boy Scout training. I think there's even a merit badge for it."

"They should have one for storytelling as well," I said under my breath.

Aunt Margaret swallowed half her glass of ice tea. "Boys, this has been absolutely delightful. One of the best times I've had in weeks. Nevertheless, it is time for me to go. I sense a lovely nap in my immediate future." She stood up, walked over to me and gave me a hug.

"I love you Liam," she whispered in my ear. She turned to Clay. "It was a pleasure meeting you Clay Davis, I hope to see more of you this summer. I'll have you over for dinner some night. Do you like pheasant?"

"Of course I do. I go pheasant huntin' every chance I can. You got yourself a date, Ma'am. Here, let me give you a hug as well. I like you already and I barely know ya."

I watched Margaret walk a bit unsteadily down the sidewalk to her car. I turned back to see Benjamin staring at me.

"Those Texas stories sure do pour out of you, don't they? Any of it true?"

"I thought you knew my entire film career?" Benjamin scratched his beard. "God this thing itches in this weather. I've made three films in Texas. All told I've probably spent two years in Texas over the last twelve."

"I kind of wonder how you're going to keep all of this straight."

"What do you mean?"

"When you meet my mom. Didn't you say you want to meet her?"

"Yes, of course."

"What happens if you tell her something that doesn't jive with what you just told Margaret?"

"I have an excellent memory."

"I hope so."

"Can we go inside?" Benjamin asked.

"Sure. Help me bring the food in."

I was setting things down on the counter when I felt Benjamin's hand on my shoulder.

"Hey Liam, come here. I've had a tough week." He turned me around and hugged me tightly. I held on, his body smelling of faded cologne and bath soap, my hands feeling the muscles of his lower back.

Benjamin asked if he could use the bathroom. Enough time went by that I began to wonder if he was sick. I was putting things in the dishwasher when I heard Benjamin clear his throat. I turned around to see him in the doorway. His wig was gone, the beard removed, the contacts out and his shirt off.

Benjamin said, "I can't stop thinking about you."

I turned away and poured myself a glass of water.

"I thought about you the entire time I was away. No matter what I was doing, I couldn't get you out of my mind." He looked worried and tense as he shoved his hands in his pockets. "I thought about being back in Mason City with you, about running with you, about swimming with you, massaging you, about holding your head while you vomited your guts out." He took a step toward me. "I thought about bathing you in the shower. I thought about holding your cock and balls in my hands." My breathing became shallow as he took another step toward me. "I thought about feeling your lips pressed against mine when I was trying to make sure you didn't die. God that scared the crap out of me." He looked around the room a few times before meeting my eyes again. "I'm a different person when I'm around you, in fact, I'm a better person when I'm around you." He turned away and walked back towards the bedrooms.

I stood for a moment. My hands were shaking as I put the glass of water on the counter. I followed him on autopilot. When I entered my bedroom, Benjamin was closing the blinds. He turned around and stepped out of his jeans.

"What the fuck is going on?" I asked.

He took a few steps toward me, put his arm around my waist and drew me close. Our faces were inches apart as he held my gaze. He yanked my T-shirt over my head and threw it on the bed.

"This is what is going on." He wrapped his arm around my waist as he pulled me against his body. I felt his cock pressing against my own. I lifted my head and this time Benjamin kissed me on the lips. We kissed softly at first, with some hesitancy. I could taste the beer and whisky on his breath. But then the kissing became more insistent and I felt Benjamin's tongue push my lips apart. I also felt my shorts being unzipped, felt the tip of my cock brush against Benjamin's. We stood in place, kissing, rubbing our hands up and down each other's backs. My hands slid down and cupped his ass.

The kissing became rougher; he was holding me against his body with urgency as our hips moved together. I felt a jolt of pleasure slide up my legs. I pushed myself back and with my hand rubbed the head of my cock against Benjamin's. Instantly we began cumming.

"Oh my God," I said. We stayed in place, hugging each other tightly, my head against his chest. Benjamin pulled away first and headed towards the bathroom. He held out his hand to me. He turned on the shower, turned back and began kissing me again. Jumbled thoughts raced through my mind: questions raised, challenged and then rejected. Benjamin stepped into the stall and pulled me in as our bodies pressed against each other. I felt his tongue inside my mouth as I brushed my fingertips across his nipples. He began washing my body just as he had done before. Every now and then he would pause to kiss me. He kissed me on my lips, my eyes, on the tip of my nose, my ear lobe. He pulled on my lower lip as his tongue darted in and out of my mouth.

I rinsed off and pushed Benjamin against the wall and began washing his body. I knelt down and washed his ass, massaging the hard muscles, pushing them together and slightly apart. He was moaning, his hips moving back and forth. I turned him around. His erection was long, thick and curved upward at the head. I took hold of his balls and washed them, holding each in my palm. I rinsed them off and then took one in my mouth. Benjamin's legs were twitching as his body continued to buck back and forth. I put my hands around his cock and put my lips around the tip. There was a loud gasp as Benjamin began pushing his cock into my mouth. I tried to take it all but it was too big and I was too rusty. Benjamin shuddered as he pushed my face away and came on my chest.

"Unbelievable," I whispered as Benjamin pulled me to my feet. He hugged me tightly against my body and kissed me. I kept my eyes open. We stepped out of the shower together and stood in front of the mirror, our hips touching. I saw that he was erect again. He knelt down and took me deep in his throat. Afterwards I sank to the floor as my legs were shaking so much. I leaned away from him. *What the fuck had just happened?*

"Do you wanna do it again?" Benjamin asked as he pulled me to my feet.

"No. Not until you answer a few questions."

"Oh come on, can't they wait?"

"No."

"Why not?" Benjamin reached down and began stroking my cock. I pushed his hand away as his dick bobbed up and down tapping the edge of the sink.

"It's too fricking hot in here, let's go sit by the fan. I can't stop sweating." I walked to the living room to give myself time to think. I pulled the shades and turned the window fan on high. I sat down on the floor, the movement of the air cooling my skin and calming me down. The word "liar" kept repeating in the back of my mind.

Benjamin sat across from me, his legs crossed, his cock erect, his balls heavy on the floor.

"I need you to tell me the truth about a few things," I said.

"Is this always how you end sex?" Benjamin smiled. I could feel the charm quotient ratcheting up.

"I asked you a question this past Sunday and it seems to me it must have been a lie. Considering you have a hair across your ass about other people lying, I'm curious, do you have a double standard?"

"What the hell are you talking about?" He leaned back on his elbows. I kept my eyes on his face.

"I asked you that night if you ever had sex with a man and you replied no. And based on what just happened it seems to me that was a lie."

Benjamin looked sheepish as he self-consciously played with his balls. "I guess it was a bit of a white lie."

"A white lie? I was putting it all out there, everything on the line and you were lying to me?"

"Okay Liam, here's the truth." His mouth began to do the movie star smile but he cancelled it. "I have never had sex with another man until a few minutes ago, however I did have sex with a boy. So it really wasn't a lie, was it?"

"A boy!" I yelled. "What the hell are you telling me?"

"Calm down, calm down. I am not a pedophile like your priest friend. I was a boy as well, in fact we were the same age, fifteen. Do you remember Scott Jensen? We were boyfriends our sophomore year in high school." He paused. "God he would kill me right now. We took a blood vow that we would never tell another living soul what happened and until right now I have honored that vow."

"What does a boyfriend mean in this context? You certainly weren't out to anyone, were you?"

"Absolutely not. No one had any idea. In fact we were so goddamn discreet sometimes even I wonder if it really happened." He stood up and walked to the kitchen. "I need another shot of whiskey, do you want anything?"

"Just water."

He walked back into the living room, a drink in each hand, his dick swaying back and forth. He collapsed onto the floor and threw his shot back in one quick gulp.

"What happened with Scott?" I asked as I fought the feeling that I had been tricked.

"Initially it wasn't particularly romantic, sort of a cliché, too many beers, two horny guys in the back of his pickup on a country road in the middle of nowhere. Started jerking off together and then we would steer clear of each other for a few days, then more jerking off, less time apart until we progressed to kissing. Once we started kissing, the whole thing became different." He closed his eyes and rubbed his hand across his chest. "I was nuts about him, really crazy. I couldn't stop thinking about him. It killed me when it ended. He said it was just a teenage boy thing that he had finally outgrown. He was going off to college blah blah blah and weren't we

210

going to remain great friends anyway?" He looked at me, his eyes ringed with sadness. "Some friend, I haven't spoken to him or seen him in fourteen years. He was one of the reasons I left Iowa right after high school. Everything in this town reminded me of him. I suppose I should thank him. If he hadn't broken my heart, I might be working the family farm with him, although come to think of it, that doesn't sound too bad."

"So you had sex with Scott Jensen in high school but never again with another man?" I knew I sounded like a prosecutor but I couldn't shake the feeling that he was reading from a script.

He shook his head. "No, not until right now."

I stared at him, several questions bouncing around in my head.

"What's wrong?" Benjamin started moving toward me. I inched away.

"I just don't understand how you can turn your sexuality on and off."

"You are over thinking."

"And you are confusing. I just don't get it, what's your trick?"

He looked at me blankly.

"How did you avoid getting an erection?" I asked. "When you hugged me at the quarry, when you bathed me."

"Oh that. Hell if I know. Guess I just hadn't gotten my head around the idea yet. Now I have. And being away from you the past few days helped me realize what I've been suppressing."

"I will never understand this."

"Now who's lying?" Benjamin asked as he began moving towards me. "Didn't you tell me you had sex with women in college? You gotta stop seeing this as black and white, it just isn't."

He opened his legs as he pulled me in. He wrapped his legs around my body and kissed me. We kissed until our lips were sore. Benjamin pushed me away until I was flat on my back. He knelt between my legs and began playing with my balls. Then he clasped his hand around my cock and in one quick thrust put the entire shaft down his throat. I squirmed with pleasure as I pushed myself in and out of his mouth. I came quickly, much faster than I thought possible. Benjamin laughed as he leaned back and said; "Now it's your turn!"

CHAPTER TWENTY-ONE

———∞———

Two orgasms later, I looked at a clock to see that I needed to get ready for work, which was the last thing I wanted. I was drunk with sex: my lips chapped, my jaw sore, my depleted balls aching. Benjamin was asleep on the bed, splayed in a spread eagle, perspiration pooling on his chest. I took a cold shower, the water stinging my skin but rejuvenating me. Not bothering to towel off, I stood in front of the window fan.

I wondered if I should wake him but at that moment I felt breath on my neck as Benjamin said, "Come back to bed." I felt his cock sliding up and down the crack of my ass.

"No, I can't. I have to work, but you can stay here. I should be home by midnight."

"Shit, I forgot you have to work. Then come to my house when you're done. We can go for a swim and I have this modern contraption, perhaps you've heard of it? It's called air conditioning?"

I laughed as I went back to my bedroom, stepping into my briefs, black socks and pants, leaving my shirt on a hanger. If I put it on now it would be soaked by the time I got to work.

"Just close the door behind you when you leave." I gave him a long kiss. Benjamin reached down to rub my crotch, which was coming to life although moaning with the effort. I walked to the back door with a look over my shoulders to see him in the doorway of the kitchen, his semi hard on hanging down his leg.

Driving to work with the top down on my convertible, the wind created waves of pleasure across my chest. When I approached the Country Kitchen restaurant, I stopped suddenly and pulled into the parking lot, hearing the car behind me slam on its brakes. In that ever-polite way of the Midwest, they didn't honk. I pulled under an oak tree and parked my car. What had just happened?

I pulled the skin on the back of my hand and squeezed hard enough to make it sting. Clearly I was not dead or dreaming or hallucinating. Had I really just kissed Benjamin Graves with a tenderness I had never experienced with anyone? Had we really just had multiple orgasms, something I didn't even know my body could produce?

There was nothing normal about this. Even if we continued to have sex, even if we saw each other all summer, then what? I knew I would never be a public part of his life. Part of me didn't even believe Benjamin would still be around tomorrow.

The worrier part of my brain began shifting into overdrive until I heard Gregg's voice in my head: *hold on Missy, he hasn't proposed yet!* I turned the radio on to a rock station, jacked up the volume and continued on to work. As I stepped out of my car, Sue was getting out of hers. She looked at my bare chest and whistled her approval.

"Why the hell didn't I fuck you when I had the chance in high school?" Stepping closer to me she took a long look from head to toe. She leaned in and smelled me around my mouth and neck. "He's gay, isn't he? You reek of sex. Fuck."

"I have had more sex in the last few hours than I have had my entire life although I suppose that's not saying much. Figured I should throw that in before you did."

"I am so jealous of you I could scream. Is he at least bisexual?"

"Hell if I know, he claims he rejects all sexual identity labels. He's into whomever he's into at the moment." I finessed with an alacrity that surprised me.

"When he's bored with you, give him my number. By the way, how is he in bed?"

"My lips feel like they're on fire, do they look swollen?"

"Don't worry, you have a ways to go before being confused with Angelina Jolie."

"I feel squeeze-dried and drained but all I want to do is go back and jump into bed with him." I opened the car and retrieved my shirt. "You know, I had given up the fantasy of ever having this kind of sexual experience with someone."

As we walked toward the restaurant, Sue stopped me. "How big is his dick?"

"I thought women didn't care about that kind of stuff."

"Usually I don't but I think he's gorgeous and since I have every intention of sleeping with him once he realizes your many limitations, I want to know."

"Do you remember your wish list from the other night?" She nodded. "I believe you requested eight inches. Well, add several."

"You bastard," she yelled as one of the cooks standing outside the backdoor of the restaurant smoking a cigarette looked in our direction. "You're lying. They don't make them that big."

"Oh all right, you only need to add two."

The evening was as busy as I hoped. Before I knew it I was walking out the back door of the restaurant. I ripped off my shirt as I walked to my car. I rubbed my hand across my chest. I was hard as a rock before I got out of the parking lot.

When I pulled into the driveway of his house, I was startled to see that none of the lights were on. I drove slowly to the back of the house, the headlights cutting angles through the darkness. Next to the pool I could see a faint light. Benjamin was nowhere to be seen. On the metal table on the patio was one large candle flickering in the faint breeze. A bucket of ice with several beers was on the ground. A bag of potato chips sat on a chair. I popped a beer and ate a handful of chips. It felt odd sitting there by myself. I took a drink of my beer as I felt two hands rest on my shoulder that then made their way slowly down my chest. I felt my nipples being tickled as I turned in the chair to find Benjamin's erect cock inches from my lips.

"I didn't think you would ever get here." He pulled me to my feet and kissed me. His mouth tasted like toothpaste. "I thought about coming to the restaurant to watch you work but I was afraid you would think I was some kind of mad stalker. Hell, I'm glad you're here." He kissed me while his hands undid my belt. He pulled my pants down and I stepped out of them. My cock was straining against the fabric of my underwear.

"I need to take a shower."

"Let's go for a swim instead."

We dove into the pool emerging side by side. We kissed, our lips pressed together as I felt a hand wrap around my cock. Two hands fondled my balls and then I was pulled forward into a long kiss. Afterwards we sat on the side of the pool, our feet dangling in the water as we drank our beer. I felt an unexpected moment of awkwardness. I looked at him; he was staring at the star filled sky.

"What are you thinking?" I asked.

"Not much of anything." He turned towards me and put his hand under my chin. "Actually, that's not true. This is what I am thinking: I have a crush on you." He pushed the hair off my forehead. "Can a thirty two year old man use that word?"

I felt my heart race. "Works for me." I tried to sound calm. I leaned over and kissed him softly, my hand on his thigh. Within seconds Benjamin's cock was hard. He looked down and said, "Not you again?"

I laughed as I playfully slapped his erection. "You're worse than I am. All that shit you gave me about being Boner Boy. I think it was just projection."

"Jesus Liam, I haven't been like this since I was a kid. I feel like one giant hard on. And you know what, I'm done, at least for today.

I don't care what he thinks." Benjamin pushed his cock down and crossed his legs. "Maybe if he disappears for a while, he'll go to sleep."

"Sleep sounds good."

Benjamin stood up, his cock springing forward and slapping up against his belly. He groaned as he took me by the hand and led me toward the house. As we climbed into bed, I was unsure which side to sleep on. Benjamin made the decision for me as he went to the left side of the bed, pulled the crisp white sheets and duvet back and sat down on the bed. He opened his arms as I slid in next to him. I put my head on his chest and within minutes was asleep.

I awoke the next morning with one leg entwined with Benjamin's. We were on our backs; his hand was on his stomach. His mouth was open and he made a slight humming noise as he exhaled. My right arm had gone numb behind his head. I carefully extricated myself. Morning sunlight filled the room.

I pulled a chair over and sat down next to him. His upper torso was rising and falling with his breath. His skin glowed in the morning light, the sunshine burnishing out the sharp edges of his muscles. A smattering of freckles were scattered across his chest. I looked at his right arm. Thick veins traversed his inner arm; light blonde hair covered his forearms and the back of his hands. His fingernails were perfectly cut, his fingers thick and long.

My eyes moved down his body. His pubic hair was light brown and not clipped in the way that was the fashion. His balls were covered in a soft down so faint they appeared hairless. His cock was slightly engorged. Long and thick, it was the same light brown color from base to tip. I raised my hand and held it as close to Benjamin's right leg as I could without touching it. I slowly moved my hand up and down the length of his leg imagining that I was touching him but also keenly aware that I wasn't. There was energy flowing back and forth that to my surprise felt better than actual touch. I looked up to see Benjamin's legs were slightly spread, his balls hanging down, his erect cock flat on his belly. His eyes were half open and he was smiling.

"I would love to kiss you good morning, but I'm afraid my breath would singe your nostril hair." Benjamin's morning voice was deep and gravely.

"It's okay, I'm having a good time. If you would just turn over for me, then I can memorize the back of your body."

Benjamin chuckled and turned over onto his stomach with his left leg raised at the knee and his ass pushed to the side. A slight ridge ran across the top of his perineum. It was covered in soft blonde hair, which I brushed with my fingertips. Benjamin moaned softly and spread his legs even further. Abruptly he sat up, rubbed his eyes and stood up. He took a step towards me and nudged my forehead with the end of his erection.

"We'll be right back."

"We?"

"Big Ben and me," he said as he closed the bathroom door.

When he returned to the room, he had combed his hair and washed his face. Water was dripping from his ears.

"Now I can talk to you without wilting the plants."

"Hang on, I'll be right back," I said. I went into the bathroom and closed the door as well. The wall in front of me was one large mirror. I looked at myself from head to toe. My skin was brown except for the white outline left by my running shorts. Looking closely at my face I realized that I looked happy, rested and sexy? I laughed a little. I had never thought of myself as sexy before. I washed my face and brushed my teeth. When I opened the door, Benjamin was sitting up in bed with an expectant puppy dog look on this face. He patted the side of the bed next to him and motioned at me. "Get that sweet ass of yours over here."

By the time we made it to the kitchen, it was mid morning. We gobbled down cereal, toast, juice and coffee.

"I don't think food has ever tasted better," Benjamin said, "I think I could just keep eating if I let myself go."

"Me too." I sat next to him stretched out on a chaise lounge, my hands behind my head. I closed my eyes and sighed.

"That is the most satisfied sigh I have ever heard," Benjamin said.

"It's how I'm feeling. I'm not sure I've ever felt this way before."

"How?"

I sat up, opened my eyes and hesitated. Benjamin was looking at me quizzically.

"I'm not sure I can tell you," I said.

"Why?"

"I'm afraid you'll think I'm some crazy lesbian who wants to move in with her girlfriend for the rest of her life after one night together."

"Crazy lesbian?"

"It's a bit of a stereotype, but they do have a reputation for moving in together after a very short dating period."

"You want to move in with me?"

I laughed. "No, no it's nothing like that. When I sighed I was thinking that I didn't want this moment to end. I wanted to stay right there, feeling exactly as I do for the rest of my life. Guess it sounds a bit nuts, doesn't it?"

"No, it doesn't. I understand exactly what you mean. I was feeling that way a bit myself earlier."

"You were? When?"

"Right before you came the first time." He stood behind me and massaged my shoulders. "Your eyes were closed and the look of pleasure on your face was so intense it was a little overwhelming. I thought how great it is that I can make you feel that way. But since we can't live our lives on the threshold of an orgasm, let's go work out. What do you say, dude?"

"Have I told you how much I hate that word?"

"You don't have to, you wince every time I say it."

219

CHAPTER TWENTY-TWO

———∞———

"Will steaks, a baked potato, and salad be enough?" Benjamin handed me a beer. It was early evening and we were sitting by the pool. "Can you handle the grill?"

"Of course. Since my dad died, I've become the de facto outdoor cook." I regretted the words the moment I said them. "Sorry, that was dumb."

"It's okay." Benjamin took a deep breath. "I was thinking that tomorrow I might go into his room. My mom asked me the other day if I would start organizing his things."

"How does she feel about you not being in Montana with her?"

"I'm pretty sure she's fine but she wouldn't tell me if she wasn't. We've never been that close."

"Really? How come?"

"Nah, I don't want to talk about that, not now."

A dozen questions raced through my mind. "I'll help you tomorrow—if you want help, that is."

"Thanks." He turned away. "Come on, let's change the subject. Ask me something, anything other than this."

I thought for a while. "What's it like to be you?" I finally asked.

"Huh?"

I looked up at the sky just as the first stars began to appear. "What's it like to have people watching you all the time?" When I looked at him, his eyes were closed. He turned away, failing to hide his annoyance.

"You did say, *ask me anything.*"

"I didn't say anything, I said, ask me something."

I started to contradict him but let it go. "I know you don't want to talk about this kind of shit with me but can you humor me just this once?"

He took a deep breath. "What do you want to know?"

"What's it like to have people watching you all the time?"

"Didn't you just ask me that?"

"Yes and you ignored me, so I'm asking again."

He let out a sigh with a turned down mouth. "God I hate talking about this with you. It makes me sound so goddamn important. And I'm not. I'm just an actor who got a few breaks. I'm no different than you or anybody else." I tried to remember if I had heard him say something like this to David Letterman. "Sometimes when people are hounding me for an autograph or when I'm photographed by twenty different people just because I walk into a restaurant, I'm embarrassed." He disappeared into the guesthouse and returned carrying two beers. "Don't you think our priorities are screwed up?"

"Of course they are but that's not what we're talking about. Obviously Americans are obsessed with celebrity but so are the British, the Chinese…most people are. Maybe we've gone too far in one direction but I certainly understand the obsession." I took a sip of my icy beer. "You must have been star struck when you were a kid, weren't you?"

"Of course I was. I wanted to be the next Harrison Ford. I thought he was cool."

"So you understand."

"To a degree, but it seems to me that people are taking it much further than just admiring an actor, now it seems like they want to be their best friend or brother."

"What's wrong with that?" I wondered if I sounded as defensive as I felt. "Hasn't it occurred to you how most people live in this country? Do you know what the average income is for a family of four?" He shook his head. "It's around $50,000. I've heard some celebrities spend more than that on flowers every year." Benjamin's face reddened slightly. "If they believe it makes their lives a little more interesting if they know as much about you as they can, what's the big deal?"

"When you put it that way, it almost sounds like something religious."

"I think to some people it is." I paused. "Do you realize how many people would like to know what it's like to be you, to be as famous as you are, even just for a day? I know I do."

"I thought you said you didn't like being followed by H Television?"

"I didn't, but then again, that day was hardly your typical day. I kept imagining burying my dad and then having some asshole with a TV camera at my front door hoping for a quote. " I took a swallow of my beer. "Maybe under different circumstances, I would like it, I have no idea, which is exactly what I'm talking about. You know, don't you, that most of the time we're jealous of you."

"What do you mean, we?"

"I'm speaking on behalf of humankind, you know, the unwashed masses."

"You can't do that."

"Why not?"

"Because I don't want to think that people are jealous of me."

"Well, what do you think they think of you?"

"That I'm a good actor, that's about it."

"Come on Benjamin, you know it's far more than this. It's unadulterated hero worship."

"I am not a hero."

"Of course not, I never said any of this was logical or true."

He closed his eyes again, his forehead furrowed. "To answer your question—most of the time I try to block it out."

"Would you miss the attention if it disappeared tomorrow?"

Benjamin thought for a moment, took a swallow of beer. "Yeah, I would. I would miss it a lot."

"I would love to swap lives with you," I blurted.

"Come on Liam, really?"

"Maybe swap is too strong a word. I just wanna see what your life is really like, not the *People Magazine* version."

"You want to see what my life is really like? Do you?" Benjamin's aggressive tone surprised me. "I'll show you, how about that? I have to go back to LA next week. Why don't you come with me? We'll fly commercial out of Minneapolis, you might as well see that part too. You can stay at my house and we'll go out. I'll get Alyssa to find a friend for you."

"You mean go on a double date?"

"You don't think the two of us could go out to dinner, do you?"

"Why not?"

He thought for a few minutes. "Nah, way too complicated, it'll be a lot easier if we find a woman for you."

"Actors aren't allowed to go out to dinner with another guy?" Warning bells began to faintly ring.

"Of course we are, but...."

"But what?"

"Too many questions, way too many questions." He put a hand on my mouth. "Stop frowning, this will be fun."

"Let's just forget I brought this up, okay?"

"No, no, I want to do this, it'll be great."

"There has to be some other way to do this."

He walked away from me and began pacing. "Of course, this time, you will have to wear the disguise, not me. If Sydney or Theresa see you, they'll wonder why the waiter from Iowa is out to dinner with me."

"I've changed my mind," I said.

Benjamin kept pacing. "Let's see…who will you be? Cousin? Friend from high school? Do you speak a foreign language?" I shook my head. "Okay, then you can't be a distant relative from Europe. Cousin will work…definitely has possibilities. How about a second cousin from Iowa? I think I have a second cousin from Davenport or Des Moines or Decorah, some D town in Iowa, named Pete Turner. This is perfect, an easy name to remember. We reconnected at my dad's funeral and you flew out to spend a couple of days with me."

"Have you been giving this some thought?" I asked.

"Why?"

"Seems scripted already."

Benjamin sat quietly for a few minutes. "You know, maybe I have. Hadn't realized it until this moment."

"Did you hear me when I said I changed my mind?"

"What?"

"I don't want to do this."

"Come on Liam, you'll never get your question answered unless you come with me."

I drank some beer, anxiety swirling in my head. "What about your family? What if they see something about this, won't they wonder?"

"They won't see a thing. The ranch is completely cut off from the outside world. No TV, no radio, no Internet, nothing."

I saw an image of Justin walking down the street with a blond woman. "Does Alyssa live with you?" I asked.

"Yes, why?"

"I was just wondering how much I have to pretend."

"Pretend what?"

"Not to be having sex with you."

He looked distracted. "I'll figure something out. Anyway, we're leaving Tuesday and we'll be back on Friday…that's plenty of time."

"I don't know if I can rearrange my schedule like this on such short notice."

"Oh…the job."

"Yes, my job, the one that pays my bills."

"Sorry, didn't mean anything."

He came behind me and put his hands on my shoulder.

"I'll show you around the studio where we filmed my last movie, go to Hyde, Koi, the Ivy, Fred Segal, Chateau Marmont. Sound like a plan?"

I started to say no and then wondered if I was being stubborn. My shoulders relaxed and he pulled me to my feet. His eyes were glistening with excitement. "This is gonna be great. You just have to dress well, smile for the camera and absorb it. We'll go to your house tomorrow and you can show me what clothes you have." He kissed me on my furrowed forehead. "Trust me, there's nothing to worry about. I will make sure you're safe."

While I was cooking the steaks, I was having a war inside my head. Wasn't I walking into the same situation again? Pretending to be Benjamin's friend and not his lover. Lover? God I hated that word. I stood staring at the starlit sky and felt a shudder of worry wiggle down my spine. I felt Benjamin's presence before he said anything.

"What's wrong?" he asked. "You look positively unhappy."

"Not sure," I flipped the steaks. "How do you like yours cooked?"

"Medium rare." He started to adjust the temperature of the grill but I pushed his hand away.

"Tell me what's going on for you…right now," Benjamin said.

"You know I only had one relationship, right?" Benjamin nodded. "And you also know that it fucked me up badly." I turned the grill down to low. "My ex-boyfriend was so deeply closeted that he never had the balls to introduce me to his family or friends as anyone other than his real estate broker. And now, here I am going off to LA with you and you're going to introduce me as your second cousin. Sound familiar?"

"This is completely different. I'm not closeted. I don't have a problem admitting that I'm having sex with a man."

"Then why do I have to be your cousin and not your boyfriend."

"First of all, Alyssa and I haven't officially told people our relationship has ended. It was pretty much over and then my dad died and it just didn't seem the right time to announce we were breaking up. "If we went out as a couple, it would appear that I'm cheating on her."

I looked at him wondering if he could possibly be telling the truth. "So if you were single, you would come out to the world as a bi-sexual man. Is that what you are saying?"

"We're not going to have that labels conversation again, are we?"

"Benjamin, it doesn't matter that you're *trying* to reject labels." He started to say something but I cut him off. "Yes, you are right now you are *trying* to do this. You must realize that almost everyone else embraces them, more than embraces them, they are definitive. You would be labeled a homo. Period."

"A homo?"

"Queer, pansy, faggot, cocksucker, fruit, whatever they want to call us."

"Okay, okay, I get it. Some people might not like it if I show up with you on my arm."

"Not like it is putting it mildly."

"Do you think it would be that bad?"

I looked at him. Could he really be this naive?

"It would be the biggest bombshell in the last century of American cultural history. That's all."

"Oh come on, I'm not that important."

"It's not you — really —in the long run, it's what you represent, surely you know that."

He continued to stare as if he wasn't understanding or didn't want to understand.

"It's one thing for a character actor to come out or a minor TV star but for America's leading man to be having sex with another man? And publicly acknowledge it? This has never happened before."

"Lots of actors have come out."

"Sure, Richard Chamberlain when he was an old man."

Benjamin walked a few feet away from me toward the driveway. He looked down for a moment as if the ground held the answer to something. "I guess the answer is no. If I were single, I wouldn't show up with you on my arm. Isn't that pathetic?" He sat down with a sigh. "Let's change the topic, okay? We're just getting to know each other; we're having a great time. Let's leave it at that."

"Does that mean the L.A. trip is off."

"No, I'd like you to come. I still think it would be fun for you to see what my life is like. And if you don't mind being someone other than yourself for a couple of days, it would be much simpler. I know that's fucked up but…."

"Tell me again why I can't go as myself?" I asked but as soon as the words were out of my mouth I knew the reasons. I had an image of a news van parked in front of my house. "Dumb question." Benjamin looked relieved.

I knew I didn't have to do this trip, I knew I could say no right now but I also knew that a big part of me wanted to go. Benjamin was going to leave in the fall or sooner and if I went with him I would see his world in a way that few people had.

"Okay," I said, "let's do this." I wondered if I sounded as nervous as I felt.

CHAPTER TWENTY-THREE

———∞———

Over coffee the next morning Benjamin was subdued. We sat near the pool, the sky cloudy, rumbles of thunder breaking the silence. Warm, damp air swirled around us with an occasional gust that created ripples across the water. I remembered when I helped my mom sort through dad's clothing two days after the funeral. She had tried to give me various things, most of which I had refused as I had little desire to have his stuff. Most had gone to Goodwill less than a week after he died. I reached across the table to hold Benjamin's hand, but it was pulled back abruptly. He looked towards the house, stood up and without a word walked inside. I remained in place wondering what I should do. The back door opened and Benjamin said, "You're coming with me, aren't you?"

"Sure," I said.

I followed Benjamin upstairs and down the hall. We stood outside the door to his father's bedroom. He had his hands in his pockets and was looking at his feet. His shoulders were trembling.

"You don't have to do this today, maybe it's too soon." I put my hand on his arm.

"No, I want to do this, I need to do this." He put one shaking hand on the doorknob and walked in. The drapes were pulled and it was almost pitch black. Benjamin snapped on the lights and walked across the room to open the curtains. He stared out the window with his back to me. It felt incredibly intrusive to go into this man's room, someone I had never met.

There was an old-fashioned four-poster bed covered by a chenille bedspread. Hanging on one of the posts was a white polyester robe with corduroy slippers on the floor. On a small table were several books with a pair of reading glasses perched on top, three of them by Tom Clancy. Several bottles of prescription drugs sat in a row next to the books. On the far wall was a large dresser that matched the bed, the top covered with framed photographs. Across the room was an old television set on a metal stand with wheels. The room was cool from the air conditioning, everything covered in a fine dust. Slowly Benjamin turned around and began looking at the photos on top of the dresser. He motioned me over.

There were pictures of Benjamin and his sisters at various ages, almost in chronological order from baby pictures to high school graduation. Benjamin was instantly recognizable in every photo. I saw that he had never gone through an ugly phase like the rest of us, even as an adolescent. I remembered a photo of myself when I was thirteen that my sisters still teased me about: my face greasy, my forehead covered in pimples, my curly hair too large for my narrow face.

"You're one of those, aren't you?" I asked.

"What do you mean?"

"One of the lucky ones, no ugly years." Benjamin let a small smile escape from his otherwise tense face.

He went back to looking at the photographs. There was a picture of him with his sisters standing huddled together. Hooded sweatshirts almost covered their faces. The Golden Gate Bridge was barely visible in the background. Next to that was a photo of them running into the ocean, Benjamin looking back over his shoulder, beckoning to the photographer to come with them, a huge smile on his face, his body tan and trim. And then a photo of Benjamin in his track outfit from high school, his body slight compared to the current version.

There were awkwardly staged holiday photos, an artificial Christmas tree looming behind them. A lovely picture of Benjamin and his dad at his high school graduation, their arms around each other's waists, the same grin etched on their faces. I continued looking at the pictures until I caught sight of a photo tucked in the back, the taller ones mostly obscuring it. I moved to the side of the dresser so I could get a better look and to my surprise saw a photograph of Benjamin with his arm around the shoulders of a good-looking kid in a football uniform. I looked closer wondering why the football player looked so familiar.

"That's Scott at a football game our sophomore year," Benjamin said. "We were twenty one points behind and he single handedly won that game for us in the fourth quarter. I was so proud of him it was all I could do not to run on the field and kiss him."

"Why is this picture in your dad's room?" I asked. "I thought nobody knew about your relationship."

"They knew we were best friends, that's all that mattered. He hung out at my house all the time. I think Dad was as upset as I was when Scott disappeared from my life. Dad never understood what happened and obviously I couldn't tell him the truth."

"He's better looking that I remember."

"Yeah, he was a knock out. You should have seen him naked. He was almost as beautiful as you." I reddened and turned away.

Benjamin opened the bottom drawer of the dresser. He started pulling out socks, boxer shorts (a few with holes in them), T- shirts yellow with age, a brown belt, a cigar box full of old coins: Kennedy half dollars, wheat pennies, an occasional two-dollar bill scattered among the coins. He tossed everything on the bed in a haphazard pile. I stared at it for a while before I started organizing it, the coins swept back into the box.

Out came pajamas, shorts, and an old bathing suit I recognized from a photo on the dresser. There were packages of underwear and T-shirts in their original wrapping.

"He didn't like to wear new stuff," Benjamin said as he handed them to me. "He wore underwear until it just about was in shreds. My mom gave him endless grief about this—among other things."

The bed was covered in clothing when Benjamin opened the top dresser drawer. He reached inside and pulled out a wallet.

"I gave this to him last Christmas," he whispered, "I didn't know he used it. He never used any of the things I gave him." Benjamin's eyes were full. We both sat down on the bed. He began pulling out credit cards, a driver's license and a few photos. With shaking hands Benjamin counted out a hundred dollars in cash, which he placed in a neat pile next to a mound of socks. As he opened the wallet to make sure he hadn't missed anything, a folded piece of paper fell to the floor. I reached down and picked it up. I handed it to Benjamin, who, when he started reading it, began to cry. He handed it back to me. "Please read this," he said.

"Are you sure?"

"Yes."

I unfolded the note and read, "Dad, I know I don't see you enough or call you enough but I need you to know that I think of you every day. I don't have the guts to say this to you in person but you were the best dad anybody could have asked for. I love you more than I can ever tell you. Ben."

"I sent this to him last year. I was really missing him." Benjamin paused as he struggled to get his emotions under control. "He never told me he got it. I thought maybe I had embarrassed him with too much sentiment. I guess not." The note fell out of his hand as he lay back on the bed and started crying. I placed a hand on his shoulder as his sobs grew louder and louder. His entire body was shaking almost as if he were having a seizure.

I was crying as well as I lay down next to him and put my hand on his heart, which was beating furiously. Benjamin was pounding his fists on the bed, snot running from his nose, his eyes bloodshot from tears. I wiped away as much as I could with the back of my hand.

We lay there for a long time. His fits of crying came in waves, almost as if he was throwing up. I held his hand and waited for it to run its course.

I became lost in memories of my own dad. I was fourteen years old and he was pressuring me to try out for the football team. I had hated football. We argued to a stalemate but not before it was very clear to me how much of a disappointment I was to him…again.

And yet I realized now that I missed him so much it hurt.

Benjamin stood up, found a box of Kleenex and blew his nose. "Can I tell you something about him?" He blew his nose again. "He was the rare person who knew who he was, and what was important in life. It didn't matter if I introduced him to the janitor at the studio or Julia Roberts, he treated everyone with the same respect and interest. And in return he expected to be treated the same way and with a few notable exceptions he was. You know what else I miss? I liked him. It was that simple."

"Whenever I could feel my ego threatening to bust threw my skull, I would call him and within thirty seconds I would feel like my old self again. Like the person I was back in high school. Sort of how I feel around you." He sat up and put his hand on my leg. "Thanks."

I felt a rush of warmth in my chest that was either an incipient heart attack or feelings I wasn't sure I wanted. "Are you up for anything today?" I asked.

"Yeah, I need to get out of this place. We're going to your house so I can see if you have any clothing that will work in LA but before we do that, I've got something I need to do. I'll meet you outside in a bit."

When I stepped outside I was surprised to see that the storm that had threatened had disappeared. It was warm, calm and sunny. I stripped off my clothes and dove into the pool. I swam so many laps I lost track. What seemed like hours later, Benjamin walked out the back door. His mouth was turned down and his eyes looked angry.

"What's wrong?" I asked.

"I just did something I should have done six months ago. I just broke up with Alyssa."

"Really?" I was startled.

"It did not go well and frankly, I'm surprised. It's not like we haven't been talking about it." He pulled off his shorts and dove into the pool. He came up beside me and sat on the edge, his feet making small nervous circles on the surface of the water. "I asked her to move out of my house—by Tuesday. I think she is more upset by that than anything."

"Wouldn't you be upset as well?" I asked. "It's kinda sudden."

"I'm blaming you," he replied, "you asked me how you were supposed to pretend we weren't fucking, and now you don't have to worry about it."

"Thanks, I think."

"You're welcome."

"You seem pretty cavalier about this."

"Do I? I don't mean to." He stood up and began to towel off. "Our relationship was nothing like you what you read about." I started to tell him that I generally avoided articles about their relationship but he kept on talking. "We were more friends than anything. If we didn't have the kinds of jobs we do, I don't think we would have lasted six months and we certainly wouldn't have moved in together."

"So what's she upset about?"

"You know, I'm not sure. She never really liked the house I live in, thought it was too big and pretentious. She makes a ton of money and she's beautiful. Plus once the news gets out, odds are the press will blame me. Don't they usually blame the men?"

"I would be upset if my boyfriend only gave me three days to move out of the house I had lived in for two years."

Benjamin looked at me with a raised eyebrow. "Are you criticizing me?"

"No, of course not." He continued looking at me. "Okay, yes I am."

There was a long silence.

Finally Benjamin said, "I suppose I deserve it but you know something? No one has the guts to criticize me to my face anymore. I'm not used to it and to be honest, I don't like it." I started to say, *well too bad*, but instead said nothing.

"What? What were you going to say?"

I thought for a moment about what it would be like if no one ever said anything negative or critical to you about anything. What a fucked up way to live. "What I was going to say was, too bad."

"Too bad? About what?"

"That you don't like being criticized to your face. What I felt was that's too fucking bad because Benjamin, when you're around me and I think you're being an asshole, I'm going to call you on it. And I expect the same in return."

"An asshole?" I saw a look on his face that hinted of a side I had not met. He walked towards the house. He put his hand on the doorknob and started to go inside but hesitated.

"As much as it kills me to admit this, I suppose you're right. And trust me, I'll let you know when I think you're being an asshole." He walked back towards me with a determined look. "What you don't know is this: Alyssa has always kept her own place. The only things she has at my house are her clothing and toiletries so it's not like she has an entire household of furniture to move."

"I didn't know that. I guess that does make a difference."

"You guess?"

"How about I just shut up," I said.

"You don't even know her, why are you defending her?"

"Because I always defend the underdog. It's my nature."

"You perceive her as the underdog? What an interesting idea. I think I am starting to figure you out, Liam Ashby. I think you're a 1950's man trapped inside a 2006 version. That's what I think. Poor fragile Alyssa, she makes $10,000,000 a year, she is beautiful, has an incredible body and unlike most people in Hollywood, actually has talent. You gotta wonder how she's going to survive."

"That's not my point."

"Then, what is your point?"

I thought for a few minutes. "I am realizing that I perceive you as someone who always gets what he wants."

For a while he said nothing. "Yeah, I suppose I am," he finally said.

I stared at the clothing hanging in my closet, frozen with indecision. Sometimes it felt as if I had a colorblind approach to putting clothing together. Not that I put stripes with checks but that I couldn't see what worked together. I tried to remember events I had been to and what I had worn. I found a pair of tan linen pants, a white linen shirt and sandals I had worn to go out to dinner with Gregg the previous summer. When I walked into the living room, Benjamin looked at me for a second and said, "You look like you're going to a fund raiser in the Hamptons. Next!"

I went back to my room and called Gregg.

"Gregg," I whispered into my phone, "do you have a minute?" Sometimes when I called him at work we would talk for thirty minutes, other times it was thirty seconds, sometimes Gregg was glad to hear from me and sometimes he was annoyed.

"Of course, Liam, what's up?" He sounded unusually good-natured.

"Don't fall out of your chair and I promise to give you all the details when we get back but…I've met someone and he's taking me to LA for a few days and I have no idea what to wear."

"Shut up!," he said." It's not that SOB story you were telling me about, is it?"

"He is not Sort of Bi-sexual. Anyway, I don't have time for that. He's in my living room right now waiting for me to show him my best clothing. He already vetoed the first outfit."

"You never cease to amaze me. You move to Iroquois nation and you find a boyfriend. Anyway, doll, I want all the details the minute you get back. Hang on while I close my door."

I turned up the window fan to high.

"Okay, since I have no idea what kind of places you're going to, let's try the Diesel jeans, that black silk T shirt I bought you at Hugo Boss and the black leather jacket I gave you for Christmas. Next try the Armani slacks I made you buy last spring for my nephew's First Communion with the Etro shirt I forced you to buy for my birthday celebration and then for the third outfit, something you bought on your own? Quelle horreur! I don't even want to imagine what that will look like."

"I already tried the linen slacks and shirt, they bombed."

"Of course they did, nobody dresses like that in Southern California."

"Thanks Gregg, you're the best. I'll call soon."

"You bet your ass you will and I expect a complete vein by vein description of his cock, got it?"

"Okay, but you'll need plenty of time for that, it's not exactly a short story."

"You bitch! I am going to kill you. First you drop a house on me that you have a boyfriend and now you tell me he is hung like Gary Cooper! I need a Cosmo, what time is it?"

"Gotta run." I threw the phone on my bed. When I walked into the living room, Benjamin was sitting on the couch with a glass of milk and a chocolate chip cooking sticking out of his mouth. "That's much better. That should work for daytime, what do you have for evening?" he asked, crumbs falling into his lap.

When I came out in the Armani slacks, I had taken off my underwear and left the shirt unbuttoned to the waist. My erection was sticking out prominently.

"Come here, let me take care of that." He put his hand on my cock and pulled me towards him. As he dropped to his knees, he said, "I can't tell you the number of women who have told me they think penises are ugly. They must all be blind."

CHAPTER TWENTY-FOUR

That night at work I was a fountain of good humor. I was rested, as fit as I had ever been and my sexual energy was on high. When I walked into the bar, Georgia Dee said, "Have you been to a spa or something? You look great."

"Actually no, Georgia Dee, he's just getting laid regularly," Sue piped in as she popped up from the behind the bar.

"Is that true?" Georgia Dee asked.

"Yes it is, but I wasn't going to advertise it. He hasn't met my mom yet and if she overhears you or anyone else talking about him before she meets Clay, I am in a pile of trouble."

"Well, hurry up and introduce us." Georgia headed towards the front of the restaurant. "Although I'm not sure anyone is good enough for you."

"What about me?" Sue asked, which Georgia Dee ignored.

"Thanks a lot," I said. "Who else have you told?"

"My mom, her eight sisters, my thirty-five first cousins, my sixty-five second cousins and Anderson Cooper. I was trying to keep it to the minimum."

"I'm serious."

"Georgia Dee."

I looked at her. She was telling the truth.

"Why do you care, anyway?" she asked.

I walked away from her not sure how to answer. Then I got it. Every once in a while the old homophobic BS I was taught as a child would roar out of the recesses of my mind and slap me across the face as if I had no control. I took a deep breath and remembered Gregg's voice. In our ten years of friendship, he always knew exactly when my mind was playing this game. *Liam,* he said almost as if he were standing next to me, *it's okay to let people know you are having sex with a man, it really is okay.*

"Sorry, I didn't mean to snap," I said as I put the bottle of cleaner under the sink.

"It's okay." She came around the bar to look at the reservation book. "Isn't everyone protective of new relationships? You have no idea if they're going to last and it feels safer to keep them a secret. At least I did."

"Yeah, you're right, among other things."

"What's that mean?"

I pulled the stainless steel dish out of the refrigerator, which held the olives, lemon and lime wedges and cherries. I threw out a fading dried out lime and then dumped the contents of the entire container in the trash.

"As much as I believe I have freed myself of all the shit I was told about gay people when I was a kid, sometimes a negative memory takes over my brain like an oil spill, coating everything with homophobic bullshit. And when it happens it feels like I still believe it. It takes a few seconds before I can recognize what it is. But it really pisses me off that it still happens." I began cutting lime wedges and handed the bottle of olives to Sue.

"I think I know what you mean but I'm not sure." She popped two olives in her mouth.

"Don't you have old prejudices that resurface now and then?"

"You mean like how I feel about red pubic hair?" She ate another olive. "God I love these things."

239

"I suppose that works, yes, how you feel about red pubic hair. You never know, maybe if you slept with a man with red pubic hair, your disdain would disappear on the spot. By the way, whoever planted that idea in your head?"

"Doesn't it disgust you to even say it out loud, red pubic hair? It's unnatural."

I began cutting the skin off a lemon into narrow twists. "We are not going down the unnatural road."

"My turn to apologize. So how did you and Clay spend the day?" She came around the bar for her purse and lipstick. "And I want details."

"I don't kiss and tell, you know better than that." I finished filling the four metal containers with fruit and then began checking the house alcohol bottles to see if I needed more. "But I will tell you one thing, I'm going to LA with him on Tuesday morning, assuming I can get Rick to work for me on Wednesday night."

"You just met and you're already traveling together." She spritzed her neck with perfume.

"Didn't seem like that big a deal to me. He has some business to attend to and I'm going along for the ride."

"It's a huge deal!" She turned and looked at me as she reached under her skirt to pull her blouse down. "Traveling together is one of the first signs that your sex odyssey might turn into a full-fledged relationship."

"You might be right."

"Might be? Of course I'm right and it makes me sick with envy. Now I'm going to have to wait even longer before I get my turn with him." She looked at herself in the mirror behind the bar, checking her profile from either angle. "How do I convince him that he chose the wrong hot thirty-two year old Mason Cityan? It should be self-explanatory and yet somehow you've bewitched him. However, I have no doubt he will come to his senses in short order. After all, the mysteries of the vagina always win, don't they?"

"He is just coming out of a relationship with a woman. Apparently it wasn't mysterious enough. I think he just missed a big hard cock."

"Please don't start bragging about your huge dick again, I believe it already."

"Clay thinks it's beautiful."

"That is not a word I would use to describe a penis. Functional maybe, serves a purpose, good in a pinch but not beautiful."

"Then I'll just have to show you mine in all its glory so you can see what he is talking about."

"Sure, why not?" I looked at her to see if she was kidding.

"You know, I have half a mind to do just that if nothing else for the shock value but since I'm afraid you might fall on your knees on the spot, you'll have to take my word for it."

She looked at me askance. "You know of course that only gay boys and hookers drop to their knees in praise of the almighty penis."

"I thought you liked them?"

"Of course I do but I don't see them as separate from the body they're attached to, like some sort of floating Macy's Thanksgiving Day parade float." She laughed. "I am getting a visual, a thirty-foot-long erect penis floating down 5th Avenue with 100 gym boys in short shorts holding the lines." She reached in her purse and pulled out a lifesaver. "Can you imagine what Katie Couric would say about that?"

"That's because you haven't seen mine." I looked around to see if someone else had said those words.

"Don't you find it rude when one makes a comment, especially a clever comment and the person one is having a conversation with completely ignores it?" she said. "But you know what? I am willing to let it go because, Billy Bragg, I want to see it. There's nobody here yet, you are going into the store room downstairs, and you are going to show it to me."

241

"Are you serious?"

"You bet your ass I'm serious. I'm sick of hearing about it already, this penis that apparently is so beautiful it should exist on its own. Now you go downstairs and work up a head of steam, I'll be down in five minutes. Will that be enough time or do you need more than that due to the extreme volume of blood needed to turn your monstrosity into an erection?"

I stood still, my heart racing a bit, feeling like I did the first time I played strip poker in college. That time I had been drunk and it wasn't so difficult. This was completely different. What the hell was she up to? "What are you up to?" I asked her. What was I up to?

"I want to see what I'm competing against. And since I am feeling expansive, I'll let you see my perfect breasts."

"Oh so now they're perfect again?"

"Yes, I decided that this morning. You'll see that I'm not wrong. Now hurry up before any customers show up." She pushed me forward, a smile on her face that I hadn't seen since grade school. I jumped forward and ran to the storeroom, which was down a flight of stairs under the kitchen. The shelves were lined with oversized cans of tomato paste, huge bottles of olive oil and enormous plastic jars filled with oregano, dill, garlic powder and basil. There was a case of Heinz dill pickles in one corner, gallon bottles of mayonnaise in another.

I felt foolish but also aroused. I lowered my pants to my knees and within seconds and to my surprise found myself hard as a rock. It stood up proud and strong, throbbing slightly as if to say, what's next? I heard Sue come down the stairs and looked over my shoulder to see her unbuttoning her blouse. She had a lacy bra on, the whiteness of it a striking contrast to her tan, lean belly. She flung her blouse onto a can of whole tomatoes and said, "Okay bud, turn around, let's see it, or hasn't Mr. Big made an appearance yet?"

I let my pants drop to the floor, my white dress shirt covering my ass.

"Before you turn around, let me see that butt of yours. Have you run it all away? I always hate a man with a flat ass." I lifted my shirt.

"Hmmm….well it's not completely gone but it's a bit small for my taste, okay, now for the show." She began making a feeble attempt at drumming noises. I hesitated, looked down to see that I had an effortless erection and turned around. I didn't look at Sue but kept my eyes on the floor.

"Oh my God," she said. "He's right, it is beautiful. Come over here, I want to get a closer look."

I shuffled over, my pants at my ankles, threatening to trip me. As I got within a foot or so I almost fell over a case of balsamic vinegar but Sue broke my fall. I swayed back and forth trying to regain my balance until she steadied me by holding onto my shoulders. My cock was bobbing up and down; I looked at it as if it belonged to another man. She bent down, inches away from it, reached over and put her hand around it, squeezing it gently. She cupped my balls and then stood back up. "Now I understand everything. No wonder he jumped your bones. God do I regret not fucking you back in high school before your declaration of homo-ness. My two ex-husbands didn't come close to that. And one more thing, why the hell have you been single most of your life?"

I pulled up my briefs and stuffed myself back inside. My heart was beating against my chest and my dick was straining against the confines of my underwear. "Okay Miss Perfection, let's see those tits you're so proud of."

With one graceful move, she reached behind to unhook her bra. She pushed her shoulders back and put both hands on her hips as she turned slowly in a circle. Her skin was brown and blemish free with a narrow white line where the top of her bikini tied around her neck. Her skin was so smooth I wanted to touch it. She had one small mole on her right shoulder. Turning to face me, I stepped closer. To me they seemed perfect but what the hell did I know? Objectively I could see that they were free of stretch marks, her nipples were pink and erect. I reached over and put my hand under her right breast.

"I am assuming most women would kill to have that set?"

"Yes, they would," she said as she put her bra back on. She turned her back to me and paused. I knew I was supposed to clasp it in back but wasn't sure how.

"Did you breast feed?" I asked, wondering why I asked.

"Of course not. Do you know what happens to breasts after being sucked on for a year and a half? Your nipples end up belly button accessories. Wasn't that an old Joan Rivers joke?" she asked. "Are you going to help me with this or just stand there?" I reached out to fasten her bra, fumbling a bit. I felt a current of energy between her body and my fingers.

"Thanks for the show," she said as she turned around to tuck her blouse back into her skirt. "Clay is one lucky man." She groaned slightly. "Gotta say, that was the flattest response I have ever gotten from a man looking at my breasts. I get it, you are 100% gay although I don't get the boner."

"We'll find someone for you, I can feel it." We walked back upstairs to the restaurant. I felt completely revved up from what we had just done.

"That was weird, wasn't it?" she asked as she headed towards the dining room.

"Really weird," I said. "What the hell is going on around here? Did somebody tamper with the water supply? The next thing you know, Father Schmidt will be having actual adults giving him blow jobs."

Sue found her purse from behind the bar and sprayed herself with another splash of perfume.

"You know Liam, I have wondered a couple of times if you and I could have a sexual relationship. Everything else about us works so well. But then I come to my senses and realize it would fuck things up for us royally. I would always wonder if you were dreaming about

244

a cock down your throat as you were kissing my lovely breasts and that is an image I really don't want to live with."

"Clay insists that we're all bisexual."

"Are you?"

"I don't think so but then again, you do have a nice rack."

"Rack?"

Georgia Dee walked towards us with the reservation book under her arm. "Where the hell have you been? Our first reservation is here." I could feel a blush spray across my face. "What the hell do you look so guilty about?" Neither of us replied as I took the reservation book from her and opened it on the bar.

"It's a party of four," Georgia Dee said. "I think the name's Johannsen or something Dutch/Swedish/Finish whatever. Do you know them?" She looked at Sue.

"Never heard of them. Maybe they're here on vacation."

"They're in the corner booth in front." She closed the book. "The dad's awfully cute and his children are even cuter. Make sure you push the lamb."

Sue checked her reflection in the mirror again and floated into the dining room with me on her heels. Cute men in Mason City were rare. I busied myself pretending to check tables for proper place settings as I made my way towards this group. From my vantage point all I could see was a broad shouldered man and three little kids. As I got closer I saw that he had bright red hair. As I walked past the table, Sue was telling them the evening's specials and to my amazement, she was sounding flirtatious.

I took a closer look at him and understood why. He was a knock out. White creamy skin, close cropped hair, big ears and nose, beautiful white teeth and shoulders that rivaled Benjamin's. He was probably pushing forty based on the number of lines around his eyes and mouth. There was a white swath of skin showing on his upper arm. He wore a wedding ring. I realized I had stopped to stare and to avoid an awkward moment, I said, "Would you like to see our wine list, sir?" Sue turned to stare at me, indignation etched around her eyes. It was if she said *what the fuck do you think you're doing* without uttering one word.

"No thanks, I'm good with a Bud." To my ear, he sounded like he was from someplace like Missouri: Midwestern accent with a hint of the South.

"Of course we do sir," I said, "Sue will have that for you in a minute. You're in good hands tonight sir, as she is one of our best." I headed back to the bar with Sue following in my wake.

"Why did you say that? Why are you even in the dining room? And why did you use the word sir? You have never used that word in all the time I've known you."

"Hell if I know, just seemed appropriate. He is older than me, isn't he?"

"Stay away from him. Clearly he plays for my team.

"How do you know that?"

"Three little children, all in a row, that's why."

"That is meaningless and you know it. And by the way, I'm sure you saw the wedding ring, so where's the wife?"

"Who knows? Who cares? Maybe she's dead." I looked at her wondering if she really did think that. "It was a joke, Liam, a joke."

"When you have to tell me it's a joke, it isn't a joke. And before you sweep in the for the kill, don't you think you better find out where the wife is?"

"She must be out of the picture otherwise why isn't she with them?"

"Big assumption. Maybe she's visiting her mother?"

"Let's hope not. With any luck, I'm right and she is dead."

"You did not just say that."

"Say what?"

"Hey, what happened to your aversion to red hair?"

"When did I tell you that? I'm not even sure what you're talking about," she said with a flick of her hair as she headed towards the kitchen.

At that moment, I looked up to see Benjamin as Clay Davis talking to Georgia Dee at the entrance to the bar. I walked over to introduce them. Georgia Dee looked at me and waved as if to say, *there's no hurry.*

"This man walks in," Georgia Dee put her hand on Benjamin's arm, "and since he is the best looking thing I've noticed in this place in about forever, I put two and two together and decided to introduce myself assuming he belonged to you. Per usual my instincts weren't wrong. Liam, you get back to the bar and go to work while I get to know your new friend, okay?" Georgia pushed me on the shoulder and turned me around.

"Look who's here." Sue stood in front of the bar waiting to place an order. "Maybe this time he won't run out the minute I start talking to him. He's not shy, is he?"

"Trust me," I said, "Shy is not a word anyone would use in a conversation about Clay Davis. I think the night you met him you were channeling either Alex Forrest or Cruella Deville. He's really a funny guy. I think you'll like him."

"I'll like him better after he dumps your sorry but cute ass and comes running to me."

"Have you given up on Eric the Red already?"

"Is his name Eric?"

"Please try to keep up."

"I am going to jump over this bar and smack you."

"Do you like it rough?" Sue grinned.

"I think you do. Here's a visual: scorching summer afternoon, Eric the Red in overalls with the bib falling down in front, shirtless and commando, the side buttons undone to show off his flawless, milky, rock hard ass, his chest a mass of muscles, a red treasure trail hinting of, dare I continue? Red pubic hair? You on the other hand

247

are prostrate over the front of a John Deere tractor combine; your Daisy Dukes hiked up so far your girl parts are screaming for relief. Your perfect breasts are shockingly white next to your tan, tight belly and adorned with nipple clamps. A horse whip appears."

"I will give you twenty minutes to stop that story." Sue put her hand on her chest and took a deep breath.

"What are y'all fussing about?" Clay said as he ambled over and sat down at the bar. "Shit, I wish you served Shiner Bock. Nothing around here comes close. Guess I'll take a PBR. Hey, purty lady, didn't we meet before?"

"Yes we did," Sue said, "We met in this very spot not that long ago. I introduced myself as a friend of Liam and you ran out of here like I had bubonic plague. To refresh your memory, I'm Sue Flanagan."

"Clay Davis." He stood up to shake her hand and remove his baseball cap. Tonight he had on heavy black glasses, which muted the blue of his eyes. "I've heard a heck of a lot about you and it's all good."

"I've heard some damn good things about you too. I'm really happy that you and Liam met—he's my best friend and he needs someone special. I hope that's you, Mr. Davis."

"Please...call me Clay. The only person who calls me Mr. Davis is our minister back in my hometown of Katy, Texas. I always feel about sixty years old when he calls me that."

"I was telling Liam that you have quite a famous family living in Katy, don't you?"

I looked at Benjamin who looked confused.

"Sue gave me endless shit that I didn't remember that Roger Clemens lives in Katy with his eight children," I jumped in, "Kyle, Kimberly, Kelly, Kunta Kinte, Knute Rockne, Miss Kitty, Hello Kitty and Katie Holmes."

"Sure shootin we do, but that wasn't the level I was aiming for when you said that Susan. May I call you Susan?"

"Sure, why not?"

"I was thinking about our Mayor John Gary Daly and his four wives. Haven't y'all read about that in the paper?"

"Can't say that I have," Sue said as she rushed away from the bar. I heard the repeated bell from the kitchen letting the wait staff know when an order was ready.

"She's a pistol, isn't she?"

"Yup, she is. By the way, is that really the name of the mayor of Katy?"

"Hell if I know."

Around 8:30, Sue sat down at the bar next to Benjamin.

"I just heard Mr. Farmer Tan 2006 tell Georgia Dee that he is coming back here next Saturday night and he wants me, little old me, to wait on him again."

"Who y'all talking about?" Clay asked.

"Oh...no one...someone...maybe my next husband...who knows?" Sue said.

"What about his wife?" I asked.

Sue blushed redder that I had ever seen before. "You are not going to believe this and you better not laugh...she really is dead!"

I stared at her for a few seconds and then did exactly what she didn't want, I let my horse laugh out of the barn.

"Oh God, not that again," Clay said. "First time I heard that noise I just about peed my pants. Figured I was going to be crushed by a stampede."

"What...what...what happened to her?" I said as I brought my laugh back inside.

"Not sure exactly. Georgia Dee asked him where his wife was and he murmured something about being a widower, and that's all I know."

"Who y'all talking about?" Clay asked.

"The hottest farmer I have ever seen in my life," I said, "that's who she's talking about."

"Really? Where is he?" Clay sat up in his chair.

"They're gone. If you want to see him, you'll have to come back next Saturday," Sue said as she applied lip gloss. "I know I'll be here. I better make it to the gym this week."

"You look great, Sue," I said. "He doesn't strike me as the kind who is looking for Demi Moore in GI Jane mode."

"I worked out with her once," Clay said and then blushed bright red.

Fuck, I thought, *he just blew it.*

"You did what?" Sue jumped off her bar stool. "How the hell do you know her?"

"Uh…. uh…." I had never seen Benjamin speechless. "I don't know her, all I meant was she was in a kick boxing class I took in LA a few years ago, that's all. I must have sounded like a typical Southern California jerk."

"You can certainly turn that accent off when you want to Clay, can't you?" Sue asked with a questioning look at me.

Benjamin stood up and moved towards Sue. "Didn't y'all tell her Liam? When I first moved to LA, I fancied myself as an actor and of course I had to lose the accent. Turns out that was the only thing I was able to learn, how to speak like a Midwesterner. My acting skills stayed at about eighth grade level. And now sometimes when I'm embarrassed, my Texas accent goes right out the window. Can y'all imagine that?"

"Sure I can imagine that. I noticed it at the Graves funeral reception," I said as I poured myself a glass of water. Benjamin looked at me with a look of where are you going with this? "Seemed to me that John Bankman's accent went from sounding like Tom Brokaw to a thug from Dorchester after his third Scotch."

"I've heard he has trouble with that sometimes," Clay said.

"Where did you hear that?" Sue asked.

"Susan Flanagan, don't you remember a word I tell you? Clay has been Benjamin's stunt double for the past several years."

"You're right, I did forget that. Anyway, I better get back to work before Georgia Dee starts breathing down my neck and you two can go back to making cow eyes at each other."

"What the hell are cow eyes?" Clay asked.

Sue stopped and walked over to Clay. She put her hands on his shoulders and pushed him back onto his bar stool. She pushed his legs apart and stood between them with her eyes opened wide. She batted her eyelids and unbuttoned her blouse one button. She licked her lips and looked askance at him. He started laughing as he took hold of her hands and held them. "You better knock that off Susan before y'all will have more than you can handle."

"Trust me, Mr. Davis, I can handle you." She put her hand on his shoulder for a moment and then walked into the dining room.

CHAPTER TWENTY-FIVE

———∞———

"Good morning Mom," I said. It was seven A.M. on Monday morning. "I was wondering if Clay and I could come over for breakfast?"

"You know you don't have to ask. Do you want omelets, waffles, pancakes or French toast? Or a combination?"

I laughed as I asked Benjamin what he wanted. We were lying in bed. Benjamin's head was on my chest. "A combo sounds good to me," he answered as he flicked a finger across my nipple.

"Before you hang up Mom, I have a question I've been meaning to ask since that night at Aunt Marie's." I hesitated. "Are you unhappy that Leah is pregnant?" I knew from experience the best time to ask her a direct question was when she was filled to the gills with caffeine. It was almost truth serum with her. With a quick kiss on my forehead, Benjamin headed into the bathroom.

"I don't think I want to get into this so early in the morning."

I stayed quiet. I had learned over the years that no response was usually the best method to get her to speak as she had a tendency to fill silence with words, sometimes words that mattered, other times words that had nothing to do with the conversation at hand.

"Oh Liam, do you really want to know?"

"Yes, I do."

"You have to promise you won't say anything to her. Will you do that for me?"

"Of course I will."

"I have two issues with this. First, I think she is just too damn young."

"Mom, she's thirty years old!"

"I don't mean age wise, I mean emotionally. I don't think she's ready to raise a child."

I started to tell her I didn't agree but knew she would clam up if I disagreed with her. "What's the second issue?"

"This is the tricky part and Liam, if you ever tell her this, I swear I will haunt you for the rest of your life."

"I didn't think a good Catholic was supposed to believe in ghosts."

"I'm Irish first, Catholic second." I could hear the emotion in her voice. "I need you to promise you won't say anything."

"I won't —I promise."

She cleared her throat, a sure sign she was anxious.

"I don't like her husband. I never have and I never will. I kept hoping they would break up and now that she is pregnant, they won't. Now they are stuck together. Having a child will keep them together for the rest of their lives."

"They might divorce?"

"Won't matter, once they have this child, he will never go away."

I was stunned. Everyone knew that my mom and Patrick didn't get along but I had no idea it went to this depth.

"Is this what Aunt Marie wanted to say the other day?"

"Yes it is and boy do I regret telling her. That woman cannot keep her mouth shut. She thinks it's her God given right to tell the world my deepest secrets. I swear if she ever tells Leah this I will never speak to her again."

"I don't blame you—this is no one's business but your own." I was worried, worried for Leah and worried for our family if she ever found out. "You're not going to tell her, are you?"

"Of course not! It's much too late for that. The baby is on the way and that's that."

"But…but I thought that Patrick moved them back here so they could settle down and raise a family."

"So he claims but you know as well as I that that man cannot stay put for more than two years. I swear to you if they move after this baby is born, I…I…oh what the hell, there is nothing I can do!" I had never heard so much despair in her voice before.

"We'll be there as soon as we can."

"Liam, please don't worry, you know I can handle this."

"But Mom, you were just…you know…sick."

"That was ages ago. Everything is fine. Please hurry, the griddle is hot." She hung up.

I jumped out of bed and rushed into the bathroom. "We need to get moving, she expects us in thirty minutes and you still need to put your stuff on."

"Why didn't you tell her we'd be there at eight?" Benjamin said a bit grumpily as he stepped out of the shower. "And what was that conversation about?"

"Oh nothing, just that she wishes my sister wasn't pregnant and that her marriage would end."

In the shower I thought about what Mom had just said and realized that I just assumed that Leah's maternal instincts would take over and she would be a fine mom. Wouldn't she?

My Mom's dog Aggie began barking and scratching at the screen door the moment we got out of the car.

"Aggie, shut up!" Mom shouted from the kitchen. She appeared at the door holding a rolled up newspaper. "This is the only way I can get that damn dog to stop making a racket. I have to threaten to beat the tar out of her about fifteen times a day. Wouldn't you think she would remember? Oh, hello, you must be Clay? I've heard a lot about you." She opened the door with her hip while wiping her hands on her apron, which was embroidered with large sunflowers.

"Pleased to meet you, Ma'am." He shook her hand. "Now I understand where Liam got his looks. You're one of the purtiest women I've ever met."

Mom blushed and tried to wave him away. "Thank you, young man. That's very kind of you." She gave me a hug as she led us into the kitchen. The island in the center was covered with an electric grill, eggs, cooked sausage, and a bowl of pancake batter. "I decided to narrow down the choices. It's just the two of you after all. Would you like an omelet or pancakes?"

"Mrs. Ashby, at the risk of being rude, I would like both," Clay said.

"Of course you would, just look at you." Mom began cracking eggs into a metal bowl. " I wish Liam ate more. He's far too thin for my taste. Look at his face, his cheek bones are popping out of his skull. He gets that from my mother, she always lost weight in her face first, never from her hips which drove her crazy. She used to claim she would look like one of those Polynesian shrunken heads before she would lose any weight below her waist!"

"I am not too thin," I said, "My weight has been the same for the last ten years. I'm just exercising more than I was when I first moved back.

"You know, you are too thin, now that I look at you," Clay said. "I didn't realize your cheek bones stuck out so much. I could skin a coon on those cheekbones. Come to think of it, you look a little bit like a greyhound."

"Are you a hunter, Mr. Davis?"

"Please call me Clay and yes I am. Where I'm from pretty much everybody is a hunter."

"Clay tells me you're from Texas, although he didn't have to tell me that, it's written all over your face...and that accent!"

"It is?"

"Yes dear, you look like a perfect Southern gentleman. You're handsome as all get out, you're charming and polite. I've never understood why Southerners have such a bad reputation. I've always found them delightful."

"Thank you Ma'am, that's mighty kind of you."

"Okay, okay," I said, "enough with the mutual admiration society."

"Liam, don't be rude. We were just exchanging pleasantries, something you could be much better at. Now, where were we?"

"Y'all were telling me how much you like Southerners."

"Of course." She poured us both more coffee. "The last few years of his life, my husband and I spent a couple of weeks every winter in either Texas or Arizona. We met people from all over the country but I have to say that Southerners were always the most polite and gracious. Although I never, ever discussed politics with them. The one time I did, oh my, the things I heard!"

"Liam told me you lost your husband. I was sorry to hear that. I lost my own daddy a year or so ago and I still haven't gotten over it."

"You poor dear, I'm so sorry for you. We're all in the same boat. Both you and Liam lost your fathers, I lost my husband and that poor Benjamin Graves lost his father as well. Arthur Graves always struck me as such a good person." I looked at Benjamin, whose eyes started to fill up and just as quickly went back to normal. "I was appalled at all the attention that generated."

Mom poured pancake batter on one end of the grill and beaten eggs on the other end. "Clay, where does your mother live?" She filled the eggs with shredded cheddar cheese and mushrooms and folded them in half.

I looked at Benjamin, whose eyes shifted nervously. I wondered if he had thought about this question. "My mama still lives in Katy. I have a couple of sisters there who keep an eye on her. She has a heart condition, too many years of smoking cigarettes and drinking. But she's doing well right now, praise Jesus." I almost groaned out loud. Mom looked uncomfortable. She was an unapologetic Catholic but she never understood the whole Jesus movement. She once said after a few glasses of wine that she didn't consider evangelical Christians to be Christians. I looked at Benjamin, who looked flustered.

"Sorry about that, Ma'am, I always forget that Northerners don't like Jesus thrown into the middle of a conversation."

"Don't you worry about that. I'm so sorry to hear about your mother." She put two pancakes and the omelet on Clay's plate. She slid two sausage patties on top of the omelet. "A strapping young man like you must eat a lot. I'll be back in a second. Aggie needs to be let out before she jumps through the door."

As soon as I heard the screen door slam shut I said, "Praise Jesus?"

"Fuck, that was stupid. I started reciting a scene from the movie I made five years ago with Reese, sort of a modern retelling of *Elmer Gantry*."

I put my hand on his leg. "It's fine, although maybe we need to write down your entire made up family history so you're better prepared for questions, although you certainly have a good imagination."

"Improvisation. I've taken a lot of classes." He leaned over and kissed me on the lips. He tasted of butter and maple syrup. I held the kiss while massaging the back of his neck.

"Liam, I thought you told me your friend wasn't gay?" Mom said as she walked back into the kitchen. She stood and stared at us with her hands on her hips. "I don't believe I have ever seen two men kiss like that before. Isn't that odd?"

"That wasn't much of a walk," I said, "and what's odd?"

"Didn't you tell me you thought Clay was straight? I swore that you did." She put an English muffin in the toaster. "It's odd that I had never seen it before, that's all."

"I didn't know at the time," I said.

"Well, now I have to worry."

"About what?"

"What are you going to do when he leaves in September?"

"Mom, come on, we just met. Don't embarrass me."

"Oh, all right, but I know what happened to you the last time."

"Please don't, Mom."

"Okay, okay, I won't go there. No one is going to accuse me of being like Marie," she said with a pointed look at me. She poured batter for three pancakes on the grill. "What are you boys up to today?"

"I'm working tonight and then I need to get ready for tomorrow."

"What's tomorrow?"

"Clay and I are going to LA for a few days. He has some business and I'm going to do a little sightseeing. I haven't been there since my senior year in high school."

"That was a lovely trip, wasn't it? We stayed with Margaret and John." She flipped the pancakes, poured two glasses of orange juice, filled our coffee cups, refilled the pitcher with maple syrup and started doing the dishes in one smooth blur of movement. "I never liked that man."

"Who?" Clay asked.

"Margaret's ex-husband."

"Why, what happened, Mrs. Ashby?"

"Please call me Colleen," she answered as she swept away Benjamin's plate. He looked at me and mouthed, *can't I have more?* I shook my head and tried not to laugh. My mom had an unusual contradiction when it came to entertaining. While she loved cooking, when she decided the meal was over, it was over. The food would be put away sometimes while people were still eating. She slid the pancakes onto my plate and looked at the clock over the stove. I knew I needed to eat fast.

"John is my husband's brother. He and Margaret were married two years before Conor and I were married. He dumped my poor sister right before their thirtieth wedding anniversary. God, I never liked that man. Anyway, why am I talking about this for God's sake?"

"I mentioned our family vacation to Southern California."

"Of course. Anyway, that was a fun trip. Your dad was in such high spirits. Liam, do you want more pancakes?" she asked me as she turned off the grill and put the bowl of batter in the sink. "We had never gone away before in the spring. It was such a relief to get away from Iowa in March. Do you have any idea what the weather is like around here in March?"

I looked at Clay, who didn't bite.

"No, Mrs. — Colleen, I don't. But March in Texas is just about perfect. Sixty to seventy degrees every day, no humidity and no bugs. It's my favorite month, well maybe my second favorite, April is my favorite month."

"You're right about that. Conor and I spent one of our best vacations in the hill country around Austin the last March before he died. It was gorgeous, all the flowers blooming, quiet, peaceful. I never wanted that trip to end. Oh, I'm sorry." I looked at her. Her eyes were full and she swiped away her tears, tears that did not come easily to her.

"Don't you worry about that Colleen. I understand totally. Why it was just the other day I was thinking about my daddy and I started blubbering like a newborn. Surprised the piss out of me."

"How did he die, Clay?" Mom asked as she wiped at her nose.

"He was killed by a drunk driver. Hit and run. They never found the guy. I swear if I ever find the person who did it, I might just tear them apart with my bare hands." My mouth dropped open slightly. Hit and run? I had a sudden urge to ask him several pointed questions to see how quickly he could make things up.

"You poor, poor boy," Mom said as she walked over and put a hand on his arm. Benjamin stood up and they hugged. To my surprise, a shudder of grief passed through Benjamin's body. When they separated, Benjamin wiped his eyes.

"We need to change the subject, Ma'am, or I just might start blubbering again."

259

"Maybe you need to cry. Personally I'm not one to do that often but I know some people can find it helpful. Like Margaret for example. She cries at the drop of a hat, especially after her third vodka."

I stood up. "Thanks Mom, we should probably get out of your hair. Do you need anything done while I'm here?"

"No, no, you boys run along. I'm sure you have other things to do than keep an old lady company." She followed us to the front door. "You have a good time in LA." She hugged me tightly and whispered in my ear, "He's wonderful." To Clay she said, "When Liam lived in Boston, it just about killed me to say good bye to him. And now I don't have to anymore! I sure wish his father was alive to appreciate this with me." She looked at her left hand. "Why don't the two of you come over for dinner next weekend? I'll ask Margaret and Marie to join us."

"Marie?"

"I am going to get her out of that house if I have to have her arrested."

"I have Sunday night off, Clay, are you free?"

"Sure shootin' I am. Looking forward to it already. Thanks again for breakfast, Colleen." They hugged again almost as if they were related.

"She's terrific, Liam." We were sitting by the pool drinking coffee. "Although I could have eaten more—the pancakes were great."

"She's really weird about food, drives Aunt Margaret crazy. Margaret always claimed that my mom withheld food the same way she withheld affection although I always thought that was a low blow, but then again…."

"I feel like I've known her a long time. I wish my mom was more like her."

"You never talk about her. How come?"

"It's complicated, really complicated. Some other time." He stood up and stripped off his clothes. "Let's go for a swim."

Later as we lay side by side on a large beach towel, Benjamin said, "We need to talk about tomorrow."

"I almost forgot we were going." I felt my heart race.

"Yes, we're going. This is what I'm thinking." He leaned against me. "Our flight is at 11:20 and we arrive around 1:30."

"Crap," I said, "I never even thought about buying a plane ticket. What do I owe you?"

"I got this one." He stuck his pinkie into my belly button.

"Benjamin, I want to pay. I'm not exactly poor. I did really well selling real estate in Boston."

"I didn't mean to insult your manly pride."

"It's not that."

"Then, what is it?"

"Guess I'm proud I did well in Boston. I paid my own way through school, I got myself to Boston. I have never asked for a penny from anybody, not even my parents."

"You don't want to be a kept boy?"

"I don't think that's funny."

"All right, next time you can pay." Benjamin sat up. "I only fly first class and I only stay at five star hotels with butlers." I looked at him with surprise. "Kidding, Liam, just kidding, at least about the butler part." I took a breath and realized my back was up about money — again. It had always been a sore subject for me. I had a contradiction about money: I didn't want people to help me financially but would be upset with them when they didn't offer.

"Let's change the subject." Benjamin said. "We should leave here around eight. And at the risk of insulting you again, I'm going to drive." I attempted a smile. "After we park the car, I'm going to have to leave you. Obviously you have to travel as yourself. Lots and lots of pictures will be taken and we can't afford to be seen in the same photo. Right?"

"Of course," I said remembering the time Justin and I had crossed the street so he didn't have to introduce me to an old fraternity brother of his.

"You should wait a few minutes but not too long. You said you wanted to know what it's like to be famous. Nothing like what you will see at the airport tomorrow or in LA will give you a better example. I know, don't say it. I sound like a vain idiot but you'll see I'm not exaggerating."

"I know you're telling the truth—it's on TV all the time."

"Yeah, I guess it is but trust me, it doesn't begin to show you what it's really like. The last time I flew commercial from San Francisco to New York, it was insane." He grimaced.

"Hell, if I'd seen you at the airport before I met you, I would've flipped out. Probably wet myself. But now that I know you for the average schmo that you are, I wouldn't even turn my head." He cuffed me on the side of my head and sat down next to me again.

"We're sitting together in first class but we have to pretend not to know each other. We can introduce ourselves, but that's it." His hand moved down and began rubbing my dick. "When we get to LA, I'll have a driver waiting for me and a separate one for you. Just look for a sign with your name on it, actually not your name, your temporary fake name, Pete Turner."

"Do you have to worry about the driver?"

"How?"

"If I get in the car looking like myself, won't he wonder why I don't come out of the house looking the same?"

"Because he signed a confidentiality statement, because I pay him extremely well and because he knows he will never work in this town again if he says anything. Plus, I have several drivers, and I'll make sure not to use the same one twice."

"Is there anyone in your life you don't control?"

Benjamin frowned. "It's not control, it's just common sense. You would do the same thing in my shoes." He took hold of my dick with both hands. "The driver will drop you off at the rear of my house. There's a small caretaker's cottage there. Just wait inside for me." He leaned forward and began sucking on my right nipple while slowly moving his hand up and down my erection. "What a nice cock you have, Pete Turner." His hand began moving faster and faster. My breath became shallow as I felt his tongue caressing my nipple, the warm sun on my face, the finger that was working its way down below my balls. I arched my back and raised my pelvis. Benjamin squeezed my balls.

"Wow," he said.

CHAPTER TWENTY-SIX

———∞———

The next morning was cloudy and cool. I was as nervous as I had been when Sue and I had driven to the Graves house on a similar cloudy day a few weeks earlier. I had spent the night in my own home, something Benjamin had not understood. However, I needed to be alone. I couldn't explain why but it felt right.

I was standing on my front steps watching the empty street. I heard a dog barking a few houses over and the rumble of a freight train passing through town. Benjamin drove around the corner in a large, black BMW with darkened windows. I walked down the sidewalk, my left side pulling me back into the house, my right side moving forward. Benjamin smiled as I opened the car door and pulled me close for a brief kiss. His hair was slicked back; he had on blue jeans, a tight white T-shirt and cowboy boots. There was a black leather jacket in the back seat. I realized looking down at my own simple outfit of chinos and a golf shirt that I was already in role: I looked exactly like some dorky cousin from Iowa.

I was quiet on the ride to Minneapolis, turning inward as I always did when I was anxious. Benjamin was quiet as well. I turned on the radio and found a classical music station. When we got to the airport, we drove into the parking garage, found a dark corner, and sat without speaking for several minutes.

"Are you ready for this?" Benjamin asked.

"Yes, but I'm worried…worried that I'm losing something."

"What could you possibly be losing?" He rubbed my thigh.

"I'm not sure, but I can't shake this feeling."

"Everything will be fine, all we're doing is going to LA for a couple of days."

"Is that all?" He gave me a funny look and got out of the car.

"In case our flight gets cancelled or anything, why don't you just go on home and we'll do this some other time." Benjamin said.

"Sure, that makes sense. I'm sure I can get a flight back to Iowa."

"Of course not," Benjamin handed me the car keys, "just drive this back home."

"How will...."

"I'll fly into Mason City when my business is over."

"Is there any need for me to say words out loud?"

Benjamin laughed, "What do you mean?"

"You've thought of everything and you seem to know what I'm going to ask before I open my mouth."

"Thanks, I pride myself on that. I've always been this way." He kissed me on the forehead. He stepped out of the car and popped the trunk. I waited a few minutes by the side of the car until I saw him head down an escalator and then moved to follow him. *Don't get too close,* I said to myself while walking faster and faster. At the top of the escalator, I looked down to see him stepping off and striding forward. I looked at the people going up. They were all snapping their heads around to stare. Some looked like they wanted to turn around and head back down the up escalator. I heard his name being repeated over and over. A heavyset, bald man pushed brusquely by me saying, "I have got to get his autograph, my daughter will kill me if I don't. What the hell is he doing here?"

A tall redhead ran down behind him, struggling to remove her phone from her purse. "You know, his dad just died, maybe he was visiting his mom in Iowa." An elderly woman with brilliant white hair in front of me said, "His mom is in Montana which is where **he** is supposed to be, but you just can't believe anything anymore."

At the bottom of the escalator, I found myself in the middle of a crowd moving quickly to follow Benjamin. When I arrived at the Northwest check in, I could see two security guards talking to him. A large group had gathered, people were shouting his name; disembodied hands thrust their cell phones into the air hoping for a picture. People were pushing forward. I moved out of the crowd to follow Benjamin to the first class check in line but was stopped by a security guard.

"But…but I'm on a flight today," I said.

"Hang on bud," a thickly set man said, continuing to block my way, "you'll get on your flight, don't worry."

I stood my ground as I felt myself being shoved from behind.

"Come on people, you need to back up," the guard said.

"But I have to get his autograph," the man who had bumped me on the escalator said.

"Sir, if you don't back up, I am going to escort you from the premises."

I looked behind me to see that the crowd had doubled in size. People were shouting Benjamin's name, begging, demanding and pleading for his autograph. Three cops surrounded him as he was led to the front of the security line. Benjamin looked over his shoulder, his eyes scanning the crowd. I wanted to wave and call his name but stopped myself. Benjamin pulled off his cowboy boots, emptied his pockets and removed his belt.

A woman next to me said, "Oh my God, he is better looking than I ever imagined." The man behind me said into his phone, "You won't believe who is ten feet away from me. Benjamin Fucking Graves! I shit you not. How the hell do I know what he's doing here? Yes, he's gorgeous, he's beyond gorgeous. No, I cannot get his autograph, he's being taken away from here like a hostage."

I looked back at Benjamin who was now surrounded by five cops. He walked through the metal detector, put his boots and belt back on and was whisked away on a golf cart.

"Okay, okay," the heavy security guard said, "show's over, let's get on with our lives."

The crowd broke up as quickly as it formed but there was still a buzz in the air as I made my way through security. People around me were still talking about Benjamin. I wanted to tell them that I knew him; that in fact he was my boyfriend, but figured I would be as credible as the nut cases declaring the end of the world while begging for money.

I stopped at a newsstand to buy some gum and saw the latest issue of *People*. Alyssa Wheelock was on the cover, looking distraught. Angled across her breasts in big black letters, it read: DUMPED!!! I bought a copy and headed towards the gate. When I arrived there Benjamin was nowhere to be found. No one in the waiting area was talking about him so clearly he had not walked by. They must have been keeping him locked up somewhere until everyone else was on the plane. I picked up the magazine and per usual it was all unnamed sources, but to my surprise they got the story correct, even down to the day Benjamin ended the relationship and the fact he told her to move out on short notice. Clearly she was the unnamed source.

As I settled into my seat, enjoying the extra legroom and a glass of orange juice, I leafed through the magazine. The usual crew: Jackie, Angelina, Helen, Rose—shopping, eating, running, walking through airports—doing all the things everyone else did and yet we decided collectively that when **they** did these things, it warranted photographic evidence. I felt the old envy pulling at me, demanding attention, demanding that someone, anyone would say that I am important, that my presence on this earth mattered.

I looked at the empty seat next to me and just as it seemed that the plane was going to leave without him, I became aware of an energy shift near the cockpit. I could hear men's voices, the laughter of the flight attendants and suddenly there he was. He stood in the aisle for a second, found my eyes but gave nothing away. There was a collective gasp from the other passengers around me. He sat down next to me but said nothing. Everyone was staring at him. The people in front of us were craning their necks trying to turn around without turning around. An attractive middle-aged woman across the aisle was rummaging through her purse a bit frantically until she found a pen and paper. She handed it across to him but before she could say anything, a flight attendant arrived, whispered something into her ear and the paper and pen disappeared back into her purse. A man two rows up stood up but with a push on his shoulders from the other flight attendant sat back down abruptly.

"What can I get for you, Mr. Graves?" a flight attendant asked him, her smile stretching from ear to ear.

"Juice will be fine. Thanks." Benjamin pulled a stack of papers from his travel bag. Silence engulfed us. Benjamin began reading. I looked over and saw that it was the script for *Alexander*. It had three holes punched along the side, the top one held by a brass tack. Benjamin looked out the window without a glance at me. He began flipping pages until he was about midway through the script.

I sank back into my seat and looked out the window at a young, good-looking man, built like a wrestler throwing luggage onto the belt. Sweat was staining the side of his shirt, headphones blocking the cacophony of the runway. He looked up at me but his face did not change—almost as if I didn't exist.

I thought about this man sitting next to me. Was Benjamin any different from this guy sweating his balls off loading and unloading luggage from countless planes filled with people he would never meet? And of course the answer was no. I had this sudden urge to stand up and tell everyone. I wanted to say yes, I am a celebrity junkie just like you and yes I understand it but it's just a waste of time. Benjamin's notoriety is unwarranted. He's just a nice guy from Iowa. He's an actor, an actor that got a few lucky breaks.

Hadn't Benjamin said the same thing to me not that long ago? Now I understood that he was telling the truth. I hadn't believed it at the time because I didn't want to believe it. All the celebrity bullshit was just that. But then I looked at the faces around me, faces etched with anticipation of something — of anything — and I knew that no one would believe a word I might say because they wouldn't want to believe he was no different from them. I instinctively knew that what they wanted was for Benjamin to say or do something proving he was worthy of our reverence. I would have wanted the same thing. I would have wanted him to tell a wildly funny story or talk to us about his next film or be an asshole: anything to add a little color to the experience. An experience all of them would be able to retell at cocktail parties for years to come.

We were in this together, we were all playing roles and so I decided to start the scene.

Speaking in a loud voice, I turned to him and said, "You're famous, aren't you?"

He looked at me with a question in his eyes.

"I suppose you could say that." I heard a snicker from the seats in front of us.

"I know I should know you but I just can't place you. Are you on television?"

"I used to be, years ago."

"Do you do infomercials?"

"No, never," Benjamin replied.

"How about *The Biggest Loser*? I'm sure I saw you on that show, didn't you lose like 150 pounds?"

"No, that wasn't me."

"Shit, how stupid can I be?" I said with a laugh. "I know who you are! You're Brad Pitt, aren't you?"

"No, I am not Brad Pitt."

"Of course you are. That's exactly who you are. You sure look older in the movies." Benjamin put a hand over his mouth to hide his grin. A young man in front of me stood up and turned around. "You are sitting next to Benjamin Graves! The biggest movie star in the world! How can you not know who he is?" He sat back down as he said to the person next to him. "Benjamin Graves is right behind me and he has an idiot next to him."

"Benjamin Graves?" I asked. "Sorry, can't say that I've heard of you." I pulled my book out of my backpack and pretended to start reading. I could feel my heart thumping against my shirt. A cell phone rang just as the announcement came on to turn off all electronic devices. Benjamin answered his phone. No one stopped him.

"Hi Sydney…no…I haven't seen it…shit," he said quietly, his head turned towards me. "Okay, thanks for the heads up." He turned off his phone, shoved it in his bag, leaned back in his seat, spread his legs and sighed.

The flight attendant appeared, "Is everything okay, Mr. Graves? More juice?" Benjamin smiled and said no. "You know, if you need to use your phone we still have a few minutes before take off. It's not a problem."

"No, I'm fine but thanks for the offer. I appreciate it." He put his hand on her arm. "I appreciate your thoughtfulness, thanks again." I thought she looked like she was going to cry. I picked up my book and pretended to read again until we were airborne. Benjamin had closed his eyes but I could see the muscles around his mouth tightening almost into a rictus.

Within minutes of taking off, the flight attendant was back. "Mr. Graves, can I get you something to drink? Bloody Mary? Best one you'll ever have on an airplane — guaranteed."

"Sure, that sounds great."

I started to say, *I'll have one as well* but she had turned her back and walked away. When the drink was served, Benjamin tapped me on the arm. "Hey dude, do you want something?"

I involuntarily winced. "Yes, a Bloody Mary would be perfect." I wondered if I sounded gay the minute I said the word perfect, then felt a burst of annoyance that I was worrying about sounding gay. As the plane continued its ascent, I felt I was descending backward, back to my time with Justin. I took a gulp of my drink, the horseradish burning my tongue, the vodka going right to my brain. Our drinks were side by side on the small partition that divided our seats. Benjamin had crossed his leg so his foot was sticking into my space. I hadn't realized before how big his feet were. I wore size 10; Benjamin must be at least a 12. His black cowboy boots were scuffed and worn.

I reached for my drink just as Benjamin did the same. The back of our hands touched, the contact held for a few seconds. I shifted in my seat as I felt my dick stir. I looked over at the woman across the aisle. Her eyes were fixated on Benjamin's face. I took another swallow of my drink just as Benjamin drained his glass. The tension around his mouth had disappeared. He had barely set his glass down when another one appeared. "Thanks, but that will have to be my last."

"Surely you'll have wine with lunch?" she asked. "We have a lovely Cabernet."

"You may have to twist my arm." Benjamin placed his hand on hers. Flirting came as naturally to him as breathing. "I bet my traveling buddy here would like another drink, wouldn't you? What's your name, dude?"

"It's Liam and sure, I'll have another one." I was high as a kite on the one drink. I felt great. Maybe I would have fun on this trip after all.

Our hands brushed again when we reached for our drinks. I felt my erection straining against my underwear. I adjusted myself, sat up slightly and pulled my pants at the knees to give myself more room. I noticed Benjamin trying to look at me out of the corner of his eye. I looked at his crotch. I could see a bulge growing on the right side. He crossed his legs. The flight attendant reappeared shooting a glance at me as if to say, *you better not be bothering him.* I turned and looked out the window feeling embarrassed and unsure why. I could hear her asking Benjamin what he wanted for lunch, if he had any particular dietary restrictions, did he want white wine with his salad or red wine for the entire meal? I looked at her but she did not look back. I continued looking at her until she relented.

"And what would you like for lunch?" she asked, barely waiting for my reply.

While the flight attendants were in the galley, I could sense a shift in the people around us. It felt like when I was a kid and the teacher would leave the classroom for a minute. Everyone would look around to see who would be the first to do something unruly.

"Excuse me Mr. Graves, sorry to bother you but I really need your autograph. My daughter is your biggest fan and she will murder me if I don't get this." I was surprised to see it was the same guy who had bumped into me on the escalator. He was finally getting his prize. I wondered if he was in first class or had come forward from coach. I saw a flicker of annoyance on Benjamin's face as he signed the piece of paper thrust in front of him. "Thanks, maybe she'll talk to me again," he muttered as he walked away.

While this was going on, the woman across the aisle had retrieved her purse but before she could find the paper and pen, a woman with a shaved head appeared, looking agitated. An earring pierced her lower lip with a cat tattoo scampering around her neck. She placed a hand on Benjamin's shoulder. He tried to pull away but she wouldn't let go.

"I can't believe you dumped Alyssa," she said. "What the hell is wrong with you? Maybe it's true what they say about you."

"What do they say about me?" Benjamin took the woman's hand off his shoulder and pushed it away. The tight muscles around his mouth had reappeared. He started to stand up, anger etched on his face. A male flight attendant appeared, took hold of the woman's arms and moved her back to coach. A voice came over the loudspeaker, "The first class cabin is reserved for first class passengers only." There was a smattering of applause from the rows behind us. The tension flowing from Benjamin was palpable.

Lunch was served. Benjamin picked at his food and sipped his wine. Several times he turned to me as if to say something but stopped himself. For the last hour of the flight he appeared to be asleep but to my eye there was nothing restful about his expression. As we began our descent into Los Angeles, Benjamin went to the bathroom. He reappeared a few minutes later looking relaxed, in control and confident. A couple of people in the front row started applauding. The applause worked its way through the plane. I heard someone shout, "We love you Benji!" People started laughing as the applause reached a crescendo. Benjamin smiled and waved towards the back of the plane as he sank into his seat.

The flight attendant knelt down next to him, "We will have security waiting for you Mr. Graves. Would you like a cart?"

"I would prefer to walk, need to stretch my legs."

"As soon as we stop taxiing, I will ask you to come to the front of the plane. You will be the first off, okay?"

"Thanks again for all your help today." He reached into his travel bag, pulled out a slip of paper and signed it, "Thanks for the best Bloody Mary I've ever had on or off a plane. Benjamin Graves." She looked at what he had written and her eyes filled up.

The second we came to a stop, Benjamin was escorted off the plane. In the terminal, I could see Benjamin in the distance surrounded by several cops. As in Minneapolis, I tried to keep my distance but found that I couldn't. Just as I almost caught up to him, I gathered my wits and slowed down to remain about thirty feet behind. I could see people noticing him but there was coolness to their reaction completely different from Minnesota. The second we emerged from the secure area, I saw a dozen or so photographers as well as several video cameras. The cameras started flashing as they jostled to get as close as they could.

Benjamin's name was being shouted over and over. "Why did you dump her Benji?" someone yelled. Another voice called, "Three days notice? Dude that's cruel." An older voice asked, "Did this have anything to do with your dad's death?" Benjamin stopped in his tracks, looked around and said, "Who asked me that?" Several people pointed at an older, bald man. The cameras were flashing over and over. The photographers looked delighted. "Why did you ask me that?" he asked again.

The photographer looked Benjamin in the eye and said, "Hell if I know, just seems to me people can get kind of weird after one of their parents die."

"The death of my dad had nothing to do with the end of my relationship," Benjamin said looking only at the bald man. "But thank you for asking me a real question." With that he broke through the crowd, walked out the front door and into a waiting SUV. The photographers were snapping away at the departing limo when someone called out, "Madonna just arrived!" With that they disappeared like a swarm of bees in search of their queen.

CHAPTER TWENTY-SEVEN

———∞———

I walked outside and saw a man dressed in a black suit holding a sign with the name Turner written in magic marker. I followed him to the first limousine in a row of at least five. I slid into the back seat and relaxed into the soft grey leather. I remembered the last time I was in Southern California when I was a senior in high school. I had been completely confused about my sexuality and about what I wanted to do with my life. We stayed with Aunt Margaret and Uncle John in their home in Newport Beach. Their marriage was unraveling and the dislike between the two of them was so intense it was like having another person in the room, a person everyone hated. Uncle John invited friends over one night and when they walked in the house, the man had made sure his Rolls Royce key chain was hanging out of his front pocket. To my dad this couple represented everything he hated about Southern California. I remembered how glad I was when we went home to Iowa.

I closed my eyes and nodded off.

I heard the driver clearing his throat and sat up with a start. I got out of the limo and saw that I was in an alley lined on both sides by tall wooden fences. There were no spaces between the slats so it felt like I was in a long bright tunnel. A flowering shrub I didn't recognize spilled over the top of the fence. There was a small wooden door bordered in ivy that was unlocked. On the other side was a narrow brick path that led directly to a small cottage. The front door was open. I walked inside and set my bag down. There was a pitcher of ice water with several lemon wedges floating on top. I poured a glass and sat down. The room was sparsely decorated with a love seat and a side chair. A vase of roses was illuminated by the strong June sunshine that poured through the leaded glass windows. I opened them and felt the warm air on my face. I breathed deeply, sat down and nodded off again.

I dreamt I was in a limousine. I looked down and with a shudder realized I was naked. The limousine stopped and the driver ordered me out. I was standing on a sidewalk and as far as I could see in either direction were tables of young people eating and drinking. They looked at me and started laughing. Benjamin and Alyssa were at the table closest to me, laughing so hard they were both crying. I felt a hand on my shoulder and woke up to see Benjamin standing in front of me. He had a backpack slung over his shoulder. He pulled me to my feet, took hold of my hand and led me into the windowless bathroom. When he closed the door, he put his arm around my waist and began kissing me with a passion that surprised me, as if it was never going to happen again. His breath was sour as if infused with anxiety. I wanted him to stop.

He pulled back and said, "What a stupid idea it was to fly commercial. It drove me crazy to be sitting next to you and not be able to talk to you or hold your hand or put my arm around your shoulder. I'm sorry I ever suggested it."

"It's okay, it was certainly interesting."

He began kissing me again. "How about a shower?" I nodded. As Benjamin turned on the water, he looked at me. "The biggest loser? Brad Pitt?"

I grinned. "I wanted to give the people around us something to remember other than breathing the same air you did."

"Guess the glamour is wearing off?"

"Okay Pete, it's time for your transformation," Benjamin said as he towel dried my hair. "Since you're supposed to be my cousin, I thought you should have green eyes. Certainly not the same gorgeous color as my own, but green enough." He laughed. "God, I'm so obnoxious. Here, pop these in."

I put the contacts in and was surprised at how much my face changed by altering one simple trait.

"I have a few wigs in the backpack, why don't you try them all on?" There was a short spiky one that made me look about ten years younger; a long haired one that made me look like a drug dealer; and a conservative one that made me look preppy, which was the one I wanted.

"I like this one," I said looking at the back of my head in a small hand held mirror.

"Figured you would," Benjamin said. "Wouldn't you like to try something a bit more daring? I really liked the spiky one."

I put it on again and before I could take it off, Benjamin was applying glue to my face and pressing on a beard dyed a blonder version of the wig. He stepped back and admired his work.

"This is perfect. A pair of sunglasses and I bet even Mama Ashby wouldn't recognize you."

I turned a few times, looking at myself in the mirror and agreed. I didn't look anything like my normal self. I felt a bit dangerous, like I could do or say anything. I stood in front of Benjamin; my legs further apart than normal, pulled off my shirt and lowered my pants to my ankles. My erection was sticking out prominently in my briefs. I put both hands on Benjamin's shoulders and said, "Hey dude, I need my cock sucked." I pushed him down to his knees. Benjamin reached forward and began sliding my underwear down. "Yes sir, whatever you want," he said. I started laughing as I tried to pull my underwear back up.

"I was just kidding, Benjamin."

"I'm not, sir," he said as he pulled my underwear down again.

As we rinsed off in the shower, Benjamin stood behind me, his arms around my waist, his still hard dick pressed up against my ass.

"We're going to run over to Fred Segal so we can buy a couple of things for tonight and tomorrow. Then a late lunch at Chateau Marmont. Back here to change for the evening. We're picking Jacqueline up around 9 and then Edwina around 9:30." He stopped and stared at me. "What's wrong? You're white as a ghost."

"Jacqueline who? Edwina who?"

"Anderson, Sharp."

"You've got to be shitting me."

"I told you this already, didn't I?"

"I don't remember."

"Not sure how you could forget that. Plus I told you it wouldn't look right if just the two of us were in a restaurant."

"I know, I know." Had he told me this? Most likely he had; anxiety always caused amnesia for me.

"Jackie is great. She's like a sister to me. We met when she was on *Best Friends* and I was on *Buddies*."

"Just friends?"

"Yes, not that that is any of your business. Here in LA, we don't kiss and tell, at least not until we're broke or dying. You can pretend to be Edwina's date."

He pulled out hair gel, deodorant, face cream and cologne. He began working on his face and hair with determination. His hands were flying around his head almost as if they belonged to someone else.

"Stop looking so nervous. All you have to remember is to hold on to Edwina's hand and keep your hands away from your nose. All right, let's go. I'm going to drive."

"Of course you are," I said wondering why he always had to announce this. "I have no idea where I am." He looked at me with surprise, almost as if he had forgotten I didn't live in Southern California.

"I need to get a few things up at the house." He picked up the handheld mirror and did a slow turn checking his profile, the top and back of his head.

"You're perfect," I said.

"I know." I looked at him to make sure he was kidding. He unzipped and peed into the toilet.

"You are kidding, aren't you?"

"About what?" He flashed an enigmatic smile at me. "By the way, Sydney's here so remember, your name is Pete Turner, third cousin from Decorah, Iowa. Can you remember that?" I had stopped listening, wondering if he really did think he was perfect.

We walked out of the cottage, the sunshine feeling extra hot on my wig covered head. Benjamin pushed me on the shoulder. "Are you listening to me?"

"Sort of."

"I need you to focus, can you do that?" I nodded.

"You're a bartender at a supper club. We became reacquainted at the funeral. We spent a few summer vacations together when we were ten or so. Got it? From now until you leave on Friday, I am only going to call you Pete."

"Got it."

Benjamin headed up the path, stopped and called, "Pete, did I leave my wallet on the table?" I kept walking until the name Pete registered. I turned around, went inside but saw no wallet. "No wallet here," I called out.

"That was a test and you failed. You only get one screw up, okay?"

"Jesus, Benjamin, give me a break," I said. "Pretending to be someone else doesn't exactly come naturally to me."

A narrow brick walkway wound through the heavily manicured garden that lined one side of the property rising gradually to a level area announced by a wooden arch covered with blooming roses. When we stepped through the arch, I saw an enormous infinity pool with a view of downtown Los Angeles that caused me to stumble over a brick. Sydney Ross was sitting at a round glass table under a green umbrella. She waved Benjamin over.

"Sydney, I'd like you to meet my cousin, Pete Turner. Pete, this is Sydney Ross."

She shook my hand with a quizzical look. "We've met, haven't we?" I shook my head.

"He was at my dad's funeral," Benjamin said, "but he didn't come to the house. You may have seen him in the church."

"I don't think so," she said. "I wasn't there long enough. I had to get to the house to make sure Theresa wasn't completely screwing things up. Good thing that I did or she would have." She looked at Benjamin. "You have reservations for four at 10 P. M. at Koi and then drinks at Hyde after that. There are going to be gobs of photographers, you know that. The *People* article has whipped up quite a frenzy. Do you want to know what everyone is saying?"

"Actually, Sydney, I don't," Benjamin said. She looked surprised. "We'll be fine, nothing I haven't gone through before. HBO must be thrilled—Alyssa hasn't gotten this much publicity since we went on our first date." He started moving towards the house. "We have a few things to do. Pete needs some LA clothing; I keep telling him he looks like he should be going to a country club to play eighteen. Will I see you again today?" he asked her as he put an arm around her shoulder. "Not sure what I would have done without you the past few weeks."

"Thanks Benjamin, I appreciate that. And no, I won't be back until tomorrow, not unless something unforeseen comes up." She stood up. She was Benjamin's height and probably outweighed him by fifty pounds. "Have you spoken to your family? They need to make sure Ted lays low while you're here."

"Shit, I forgot all about him." Benjamin began cracking his knuckles.

"No worries, I'll call your sister right now." She gave Benjamin a kiss on the cheek, stared at me long enough to make me squirm and then went inside the house.

"Who's Ted?" I asked.

"The guy I mentioned to you."

"What guy?"

He looked exasperated. "The one that looks like me who works for me who pretends to be me."

"How the hell was I supposed to know that? You've never called him by name before."

"I'm sure I have."

"And I'm sure you haven't."

"Jacqueline and Edwina." He looked so smug I wanted to slug him.

We followed Sydney up a curved stone staircase that led to a second patio. There were three sets of wicker furniture all covered in stark white pillows. Benjamin went to a side door leading to an arcade that ran the length of the house. Through various arches I could see a Spanish influenced dining room, a living room with an elaborate terra cotta fireplace and a glimpse of a gleaming steel kitchen.

"I'll give you a tour later," Benjamin said as he continued walking. He hadn't touched me once since we left the cottage.

CHAPTER TWENTY-EIGHT

———∞———

We drove a short distance in a vintage Mustang convertible but with the top up. Benjamin was on the phone the minute we left the garage. A couple of photographers began running towards us as we sped away from the house.

"They are going to be everywhere this week. I'm afraid you might see LA at its worst." He gunned the car down a hill and came to a screeching halt at a light. "We'll be there in a second. They've closed the top floor for the next hour so we can shop in peace."

"They closed down the store?"

"Not the whole store, just the men's department. They do this all the time. It's no big deal."

"Doesn't that seem weird to you?"

"No, why should it?"

"Didn't you tell me once that you're no different from anyone else?"

"What's your point?"

"I think I just made it." We pulled into a parking lot behind the store. Before getting out of the car, Benjamin made sure my beard was firmly in place. His face, normally so animated, was expressionless. He stepped out of the car just as three teenage girls were leaving the store. They began screaming his name and rushed towards him.

"Like, oh my God!" a tall thin blonde screamed. "Like its Benjamin Graves! Like, no one is ever going to believe me. Can I like take your picture, please?"

Benjamin smiled and said, "Yes you can but only if you can say one complete sentence and not use the word like. Can you do that for me?"

"Like, huh?" she said.

"Sorry, maybe next time," he said as he pointed to a back staircase that led us up to the men's department. "What would happen to teenage girls if the word "like" didn't exist?"

"Sign language?" I asked.

At the top of the stairs, two men blocked the door. They were backlit, their faces in shadow.

"Benjamin, great to see you again. You've been away too long. May I add my condolences at the passing of your father."

"Thank you Frederick, that's very kind. Let me introduce you to my cousin, Pete Turner. He's visiting from Iowa for a couple of days and we need to buy him a few things." The two men moved to the side. I shook Frederick's hand. He was in his mid-forties, jet-black hair, grey goatee and rail thin. Benjamin put a hand on his shoulder. "Frederick has the best fashion sense of anyone in Southern California."

Frederick was grinning so widely it looked like it would hurt.

"Mr. Turner," Frederick said. I hesitated for a few seconds before realizing he was addressing me. "This is my assistant, Skip. He'll take you in back and measure you while I discuss your schedule with Benjamin." He pronounced schedule the British way though he didn't speak with a British accent.

I followed Skip, who was looking over his shoulder at Benjamin. He would have walked into the wall if I hadn't tapped him on the shoulder. He had a buzz cut and tattoos that trailed down his neck then reemerged on his bare arms. He was a solid mass of muscle and without the tattoos would have been quite good looking. "I would give my right nut to jump that man," he said softly. He looked at me. "Sorry, didn't mean to say that out loud."

"No problem," I said.

We were in a room the size of a small bedroom, mirrors lining every wall. I could see my body from every angle without turning. Skip pulled a tape measure from his back pocket and looked me up and down.

"Pete, this would be a lot easier if you didn't have those baggy pants on, do you mind stripping down to your underwear?" I hesitated. "Hey, it's no big deal, if you don't want to, I can try and make this work over your Banana Republic chinos." I started to feel embarrassed and then looked at my reflection in the mirror and remembered that I wasn't Liam Ashby today. I stepped out of my pants and removed my shirt. I turned and faced Skip, puffing out my chest a bit. He stepped behind me and measured my chest and waist. He was so close I could smell what he had had for lunch— something involving hummus. I wanted to move away from the garlic smell but Skip had moved to my front, knelt down and put the tape measure behind my hips. When he brought the tape measure to the front, his hand grazed across my crotch. I jumped a little.

"Sorry about that, dude," Skip said as he marked down my measurements on a pad of paper.

"Do you mind spreading your legs a bit? I need to measure your inseam." I moved my feet wider and looked up at the ceiling. It felt like I was getting a physical and was going to be asked to turn my head and cough. Skip's hand moved up inside my leg until he pushed the end of the tape inside my underwear. I felt the back of his hand push my balls to the side.

"Do you really need to do that?" I asked.

"Hey man, do you want a thorough measurement or not?" He stood up, wrote down some numbers and walked out. I stood in the middle of the room wondering if I had overreacted. I hadn't been measured for clothing since I was sixteen and buying my first suit for Grandpa's funeral. Maybe this was the way they did things in LA?

A few moments later Frederick walked in, his arms laden with shirts, jackets, blue jeans, leather vests and coats. Skip followed with shoes and cowboy boots. I tried on what seemed like forty different outfits. My head was spinning and at a certain point it all began to blend together. Frederick and Benjamin studied each outfit as carefully as if they were picking out a new car. When we left the store two hours later, I had no idea what clothing had been purchased.

The three teenagers must have called their friends as there were now about fifty teenagers circling Benjamin's car as we walked out. They started screaming his name as he pushed his way through, trying to be forceful without appearing rude. They were demanding his autograph, which he politely declined.

"Sorry ladies, but I'm running late. Next time, I promise, I will sign everything."

As we pulled out of the parking lot I said, "That guy Skip, do you know him?"

"No I don't, he must be new. Why?"

"When your inseam is measured, are they supposed to push your balls out of the way?"

"What the fuck are you talking about?"

I looked at him, surprised by his tone. "Forget I brought it up, it's no big deal."

"Liam, tell me what happened." His face had hardened.

"I don't know, just seemed to me that his hands strayed a bit."

"Did he come on to you?"

"Fuck, I shouldn't have said anything."

"Liam, I need to know exactly what happened." He pulled over and stopped the car.

I relayed the events as I remembered them, making sure I didn't exaggerate any aspect. When I was done, Benjamin picked up his phone.

"Frederick, it's Benjamin. No, no, the clothes are fine. Hey listen, Skip was completely inappropriate with my cousin. I can give you the details if you want them, but trust me, he was way over the line. Okay, thanks." He threw his phone onto the back seat.

"What just happened?" I asked.

"By the time we get to the next corner, Skip will have been shown the door."

I sat up and unbuckled my seat belt. I turned in my seat and put a hand on his shoulder. "Come on Benjamin, it wasn't that bad. He didn't deserve to be fired."

"You have no idea what you're talking about. Let's just say I did nothing and let's just say Skip goes out on the town tonight and tells someone he fondled the balls of my cousin. Do you know what would happen?"

I felt my own anger rising with his. "No, I don't, but I think this whole thing is getting blown way out of proportion. And to be honest, I don't care." A voice whispered in my head, *why did you bring it up, Liam?*"

"I do and that's all that matters."

"Glad you're so concerned about how I feel."

"What are you talking about?"

"All you care about is how this affects you."

"That's not true!"

"Then ask me how I felt."

He glared at me and then looked out the window. We sat in silence, neither looking at each other. A couple of people on the sidewalk noticed Benjamin and a crowd began to form. He pulled away just as someone knocked on his window. At the next light, he said, "Something similar to this happened a year or so ago to a good friend of Tom Cruise. What started as a small story blossomed until it turned into a three way in a dressing room and of course involving Tom. On more rumor adding to the belief that he's gay."

"Since when are you a Tom Cruise fan?"

286

"That's not the point and you know it. The point is how the story spiraled out of control."

"Let me see if I can figure this out," I said. "Some guy, some guy I will never see again in my life, possibly makes a pass at me. And a couple of hours later, he's fired. So which story is worse, Skip telling people he fondled my balls or that Benjamin Graves cost him his job?"

"I had to react."

"Why?" I asked, my voice shaking, something I could not control when I was angry. "Don't you think having him fired makes you seem more culpable?"

"About what?"

"It seems to me that this is such an overreaction on your part that there has to be something else going on."

"You have no idea what my world is like." Benjamin's face was flushed, his skin glistening from emotion. "You have to stop these things right when they happen. If you don't, people would wonder about me, they would wonder if I had gotten soft."

"So what?" I shouted, "Who cares?"

"I do, I have to." He pulled over and parked the car. "Liam, you really don't know what you are talking about. Trust me, I did the right thing."

"I don't believe that."

"I need you to." He put his hand on my leg. "You have to. Please."

"You know what I really think is going on?" I pushed his hand off my leg. "I think the bigger point is that you are terrified of being considered gay." I felt my temper threatening to overwhelm me, my stockpile of grievances congealing into one angry lump. "Your whole rejecting labels diatribe is a smokescreen to avoid being called a fag." I hated that word but I felt like I had no control over what was coming out of my mouth.

Benjamin's forehead was covered in sweat. He inhaled and exhaled several times.

"You know what Liam? You're right, at least about one thing. I hate how they use people's sexuality against them in this town."

"And once again you ignore the real question."

"I'm not ignoring anything."

"Go ahead Benjamin, create your own reality." My anger was volcanic. "I need you to call Frederick and tell him to give Skip his job back."

He looked at me, started to say something, and picked up his phone. "Frederick, it's Benjamin again. I think I may have overreacted to the situation with Skip, is he still around?" He looked at his reflection in the rear-view mirror. "Okay, I see...well thanks." He ended the call.

"What did he say?"

"Apparently this is not the first time Skip has done this." I could see his struggle to keep his face neutral. "Frederick was looking for the right moment to fire him and I guess we provided him with the perfect excuse."

"Then it all worked out for the best." I did not try to disguise my disdain.

"Yes, it did." Benjamin fought his smile. I looked away. Was he always right about everything?

We drove in silence for a few blocks until he suddenly pulled into a parking lot and found an empty spot.

"Liam, what the fuck just happened? What are you so pissed off about? You don't know this guy from Adam and even if he didn't deserve to be fired, which he did, I don't get why you are so angry."

I thought about Justin and how readily I went along with the subterfuge with his family, all the secrets, the lies, the hiding.

"Not now Benjamin, some other time, okay?" The anger was gone. I looked at his eyes, which were shot through with worry. "There's a lot to talk about but not now."

"Okay Liam," he said just as a group of Japanese tourists started to point their cameras at him. He whipped the car into reverse and we fled.

After a quick lunch at Chateau Marmont, we drove to his house. In the privacy of his garage, he leaned over and kissed me.

"I think I could use a nap. How about you?" he asked.

"Yes, I could use a nap." What I really wanted was to be alone.

We got out of the car and walked into the house. We went up a flight of stairs that split in the middle dividing the house into two distinct wings.

"My room is down there," he pointed to the right. "You are down this hall, last door on the left. I think you'll like the room, great view and it has it own pool." Benjamin leaned forward and whispered into my ear, "This is only for the next few hours, you won't actually be sleeping there." He cuffed me on the ear and headed to his room. I looked around. Why was he whispering in his own home?

I walked down the hall, the hardwood floor glossy and slick. On the walls were paintings, some of which I recognized from an art history class I took in college. I saw a Picasso, a Hockney, a Warhol and a Rembrandt that looked like something I had seen at the Rijks Museum in Amsterdam. Could that be possible?

I wondered how large the house was but couldn't get a sense of the scale since it seemed to be on so many different levels. I could see one open door at the end of the hall, the setting sun pouring light into the hallway. As I entered the room I saw my luggage in a corner. The room had a Western theme: a large four-poster bed quite high off the floor covered in an elaborate Indian blanket with muted greens and browns in a zigzag pattern. The skulls of several animals were on the walls. In a corner was a small oval fireplace. I stepped out a sliding glass door onto a patio with the same view of Los Angeles as the main patio. Several steps down was a lap pool and a few more steps down was a hot tub. In the immediate distance

I could see a palm tree lined golf course and far beyond the Los Angeles skyline, the lights becoming more obvious in the twilight. There were morning glories, sunflowers, poppies; flowering plants everywhere I looked, with hummingbirds darting in and out of the opened blossoms.

I sat down and took off my shoes and shirt. It was warm but not hot, and a strong breeze cooled my skin. I wondered what Benjamin was doing. I tried to imagine what it would be like if we lived in this house. What would we be doing? Working out? Cooking dinner? Did Benjamin ever cook for himself or did he have chefs who did all the cooking? If he wanted to, could he ask his staff: gardeners, cooks, maids, and personal assistants to leave him alone for an evening? Could he run through the house naked without worrying that someone might be taking a photograph or a video of him?

Could we sleep in the same bedroom without it being in the newspaper the next day?

I went back in the house and lay down on the bed and fell asleep. I woke to find Benjamin sitting next to me on the bed. The door was closed and the curtains drawn. There was one light on in the far corner casting deep shadows across the room.

CHAPTER TWENTY-NINE

"What time is it?" I asked as I rubbed my eyes and tried to sit up.

"Around eight." Benjamin slid his body down so he was lying next to me. He was freshly shaved, his hair looking tousled but studied. He smelled of cologne that reminded me of lemons and soap. I put my hand over my mouth.

"My mouth tastes like a landfill."

He leaned over and said, "Okay, let me have it, full force."

"You've got to be kidding, right?"

"Yes." He sat up. "We don't have much time. They expect us in the dining room for drinks shortly."

"They?"

"Amanda and Lily. The women who run the kitchen." I sat up as well. "It's going to be cool tonight, so I was thinking you could wear the brown leather jacket, the McQueen jeans and the Gucci shirt. Oh, and the black boots of course. What do you think?"

"Benjamin, I couldn't care less. I like good clothes but this is way out of my league; just tell me what to wear and I'll put it on."

"It's all in the closet. I think they put it in order, just start right to left. Why don't you take a shower and I'll help you with the beard and wig?"

I wondered briefly if I was going to be handed a script.

"Sure, no problem," I said.

The bathroom had a shower stall big enough for six people, the outside wall fitted with translucent glass blocks. I turned on the bank of showerheads full force and became aware that I wasn't alone. Benjamin had opened the glass door to the shower but remained outside, his T-shirt pulled up over his chest and his sweatpants around his ankles. He was erect, his hands by his side, smiling at me as I held out my hand to bring him in.

"Sorry dude, we don't have time for this. I just wanted to give you a preview of how the evening's going to end." He reached down and moved his hand slowly up and down his cock a few times. He laughed aloud, pulled up his pants and left the bathroom. I washed quickly. My mind went to Benjamin's back yard in Mason City: steaks cooking on the grill, an ice-cold beer in my hand, the sky filled with stars—and silence, silence everywhere.

I looked in the mirror and realized how tired I looked. I didn't need to shave so I brushed my teeth, put in the green contact lenses and a few minutes later was back in the bedroom where Benjamin was sitting on the bed waiting for me.

"You do get ready fast, don't you?" He knelt, put the head of my dick in his mouth and let his tongue swirl around a few times. I moaned as I put my hands on his shoulders.

"Stop teasing me," he said as he stood up and started applying spirit gum to my face.

"Excuse me?" I said as I fondled his cock through the thin cotton of his pants.

"You heard me," Benjamin pulled his sweatpants down to his knees. He took my hand and wrapped it around his cock, moving it up and down several times, by now slick with pre cum.

"I said, stop teasing me." He knelt and swallowed me whole. Suddenly he stopped. "You know what, let's wait. I think this whole evening will be a lot more fun if I'm a walking hard on." He pulled up his pants, finished applying my beard and wig and left the room, quietly closing the door.

I stood in the middle of the room staring with disappointment at my unfulfilled erection. I shoved myself into Hugo Boss briefs, pulled on black socks, and Alexander McQueen blue jeans. They rode lower on my hips than I was used to but I thought they looked okay. I put on the white cotton Gucci shirt which I left unbuttoned one too many just like I had seen Tom Ford do in magazine ads. The cotton was as soft as cashmere. I finished it off with the leather blazer cut Western style. I went into the bathroom so I could see myself from all sides. I couldn't stop grinning. I thought I looked great and more importantly, doubted that even my mom would recognize me. Preening in front of the mirror, I smiled at my reflection, imagining being photographed emerging from a limousine. A wave of panic washed over me as I realized what was in store over the next few hours. For the first time in my life, I wanted a strong drink.

Before the panic built to something out of control, I picked up my wallet and put it in the inside pocket of my jacket but it felt and looked bulky. I shoved it into the back pocket of my blue jeans but wondered if I looked like a hick. I could not remember where Benjamin carried his wallet. I stood immobile with indecision. Holding my wallet in my hand, I put it in my front pocket, back pocket, coat pocket. I felt like a magician who had forgotten how to finish off his magic trick. Disgusted with my inability to decide, I pulled out cash and threw my wallet on the bed. I shoved the cash in my pocket wondering why I hadn't done that in the first place? I left the room, strode down the staircase and walked into the living room. Would I even need cash tonight?

Benjamin had his back to me as I saw him pour something clear over ice. He turned around and stared at me with his mouth agape. He had on a chocolate brown suit with a shirt that was a shade lighter. The shirt was open three buttons, the muscles of his chest prominent through the fabric. He grinned at me.

"Pete, you look great." He put a hand on my shoulder and whispered in my ear, "Fuck do I wish I had finished you off."

I leaned forward to kiss him and at the last second saw an older woman walk in through the far door carrying a plate of hors d'oeuvres. I pulled away. She offered them to me, but I declined. I wasn't the slightest bit hungry. Benjamin took several, popping them into his mouth as if they were candy.

"So dude, how about a martini?"

I thought for a second. "Yeah, a vodka martini would be great."

Benjamin did a double take and turned to the bar but another woman was already mixing the drink. She handed the martini to me in an up glass. I hadn't had a martini in about ten years. I took a sip. There was virtually no taste other than a hint of vermouth and an icy sensation. I took another drink, this time taking a big swallow. I felt a head rush but also felt my nerves calm down. Benjamin was looking at me oddly. He polished off his own drink and then filled it again with vodka. He looked at his watch, which was big, black, and clunky.

"Hey, we better get going. I told Jackie we'd pick her up at 9 and I hate being late. Bottoms up, Pete," Benjamin said as he raised his glass towards me. I took a long swallow and then another. Benjamin took the glass out of my hand. He had a worried look on his face. We walked out the front door and into a black limousine.

"Since when do you drink martinis up?" Benjamin sat down facing me.

"Since you offered."

"Yeah, but I never thought you would say yes. You always drink beer."

"I'm a little nervous, so sue me."

"Pete," Benjamin said with a look over his shoulder at the driver. "We've got a long night ahead of us. We need to keep our wits about us."

"That didn't seem to stop you from throwing back two quick vodkas."

"I can handle it, you can't." Benjamin lowered the window and gave the driver an address. He looked back at me. "Are you all right?"

I thought for a second. "I'm fine."

"Your eyes are glassy." He reached over and put his hand on my knee in a fraternal way. "We'll be at Jackie's house in about five minutes. There is nothing to be nervous about, at least with Jackie and Edwina. They're gonna seem like your sisters."

My brain could not form a response. What seemed like seconds later we came to a stop. Benjamin lowered the window and spoke into the intercom. "Hey Jackie, it's Benjamin, we're out front." A gate swung open and we drove up a circular driveway lined with spot lit cedars. When we stopped again, Benjamin jumped out of the car. I heard her voice, that voice I had heard hundreds of times over the years while watching *Best Friends*.

"Pete, get your ass out of that car, you need to be introduced properly to my friend Jackie." I got out of the car and there she was. Her dark brown hair was parted in the middle and shoulder length. She had on a black blouse that was unbuttoned enough to suggest at her breasts, tight fitting blue jeans, no jewelry and from what I could tell virtually no make up. I stuck out my hand and said, "Hi Ms. Anderson, I'm Pete Turner." I wondered if I sounded like I had just guzzled a martini. I looked at her from head to toe. She and Sue were almost identical in body type except now that I was seeing the real thing, Sue's breasts were bigger. Would I ever be able to tell her this?

"Oh so formal," she shook my hand, "please call me Jackie."

"Pete is my cousin from Iowa. We reconnected at my dad's funeral. I thought I'd show him around LA a bit. He's never been here." I wondered if we should have discussed my fake history more, since I didn't know I had never been to LA before.

"Oh Benjamin, I was so sorry to hear about your dad. He was such a sweetheart." She moved towards him and put her arm around his waist. "I really wanted to be at the funeral. I heard it was a lovely ceremony."

"Thanks, Jackie"

"We're too young to be losing parents, aren't we?"

"I used to think so but not anymore. In fact, Pete here lost his dad a couple of years ago and we're the same age."

'You poor guy." She walked towards me and held my hand. She smelled faintly of lilacs.

"Before I start crying, let's get the hell out of here," Benjamin said.

Jacqueline stepped inside the car and Benjamin followed. When I joined them, they were sitting side by side on the back seat. I sat across from them and openly stared at two of the most famous people in the country. The vodka had settled in now. I was feeling spacey and tongue-tied. However, I suspected it wouldn't have mattered that I couldn't put together a coherent sentence since I wasn't sure they even knew I was in the same vehicle. I sat back and watched. It began to feel like I was in a movie theater. The light was dim on my side while the headlights of passing cars intermittently illuminated their faces. Heads close together, Benjamin had his arm around her shoulder and he was speaking quietly in her ear. It seemed like that moment in a movie when the two stars were supposed to kiss.

"Have you two ever thought of making a movie together?" I blurted out. They looked at me with surprise. "Although I think you'd have to play siblings."

They smiled at me and continued their conversation. They had unlined, blemish free faces, perfect hair, perfect clothing, and teeth beyond perfect. No wonder they all fought aging so much. When you were this beautiful in your thirties there was no place to go but down.

The limousine slowed as we paused at another gate, then drove up a steep driveway and under a portico. Benjamin opened the door and motioned at me. I stumbled out and saw Edwina standing by the front door, her hair pulled back off her face. Benjamin pushed me forward lightly. Her face was long and angular. She smiled at us and gave Benjamin a quick hug.

"Edwina, meet my cousin, Pete Turner."

She turned to me and put out her hand.

"Nice to meet you, Ms. Sharp," I said.

"Have we met before?" she asked.

"No, that would be a definite no," I said.

"You don't look familiar but your voice sure does. I never forget a voice. Were you at the funeral?"

"Yes he was Eddy, but he didn't come to the house afterwards. Maybe you met him at the church?"

"I don't think so. Anyway Benjamin, where are we going tonight? I'm starving."

"Koi."

"Oh God I love that place."

"Let's get this party rolling." Benjamin held out his arm and escorted Edwina to the limo. Benjamin walked over to me. "You okay Pete? You're awfully quiet."

"Just a bit star struck."

He leaned forward and whispered in my ear. "In a few hours, we'll be all alone, just you and me."

Back in the limo, I sat next to Edwina as Benjamin opened a bottle of Champagne. He poured two glasses for the women but hesitated before pouring some for me.

"You want some Pete?" he asked.

"Of course he does, Benjamin." Jacqueline said.

"He had a little too much to drink at my house."

"I love your paternal instincts Benjamin, but he's clearly a grown man and he doesn't seem drunk to me. We're out to have fun tonight, aren't we?" she asked as she held her glass up for a toast. Benjamin poured me half a glass.

"To Benjamin Graves, the biggest, best, boldest, bravest actor in the world!" she said. We clinked our glasses.

"Thanks," Benjamin said," although I'm not sure I would use those words, especially the last one, but thanks."

The three of them started talking and since I had no idea who or what they were talking about I stopped listening. I took a sip of my Champagne and looked out the window. It was a while before I realized it was blackened and opaque. I drifted away for a bit and then realized I was staring at the three of them. They didn't notice. A few minutes later we came to a stop. Something was going on outside the car.

Benjamin said, "Okay, Jackie and Edwina will get out first. Eddy, can you do me a favor and grab hold of Pete's hand?"

"Of course."

Just as the door opened, I guzzled what was left of my Champagne. My heart was in my throat as I saw Edwina reach back for my hand. There was a blinding flash of cameras as people began shouting their names. When Benjamin emerged, the energy level skyrocketed. There were so many pictures being taken, I was momentarily blinded. I was pulled forward trying to smile and walk naturally but feeling like I was walking underwater. Seconds later we were inside the restaurant, the frenzy behind us. A beautiful young Japanese woman at the hostess stand welcomed us and spoke to Benjamin. I heard him say, "I think the Granite Room would be good tonight, Mitzuki. Is that okay with you two?"

"Not the private dining area?" Jacqueline said softly.

"If it's okay with you, I'm trying to show Pete as much of the LA scene as we can jam in in a couple of nights."

"It's fine with me." Edwina squeezed my hand as if to reassure me. We walked through the dining room where every head turned to look. The three actors smiled and nodded at a few people, Benjamin stopped and exchanged a few words with a man that I vaguely recognized from the last Oscars. I looked at the faces of the diners. They all looked immensely pleased with themselves as if somehow they were responsible for Benjamin eating at the same restaurant.

We were shown a corner booth with the two women in the center, Benjamin facing the room. He ordered wine for the table. I was staring at these three famous faces trying to reconnect the disconnect I felt, especially with Benjamin. I realized that when we were in Iowa, he looked like a completely different person. In Iowa he was simply Benjamin, in LA he was a movie star. There didn't seem to be any overlap, at least so far.

The three of them were discussing scripts, producers, the fact that the new Jack Black movie had bombed and Benjamin's next movie. Finally, Edwina said, "Pete, tell us something about yourself."

"Yes, Pete," Jacqueline said, "Here we are rattling on about ourselves, not that that is anything new! Tell us something, how about a tidbit about Benjamin that we don't know?"

I laughed. They looked at me wondering what was so funny. "I thought you wanted to know something about me? Wasn't that the original question?"

"You know, I suppose you're right," Jacqueline said with a flick of her perfect hair. "Sorry about that."

"It's okay. My life is not that interesting, at least not compared to yours. I bartend at a small supper club, exercise a lot, I'm single and I watch after my mom and two aunts. That's about it."

"How come a good-looking guy like you is single?" Edwina put her hand on top of mine. "Haven't met the right girl?"

"Actually, I'm gay," I said, "and no, I haven't met the right guy." I looked at Benjamin whose eyes were registering surprise. I was surprised as well. I hadn't given this part of my made-up character any thought. But as I continued to look at Benjamin, I realized there was only so much I was willing to pretend. Without missing a beat, Jacqueline said, "Well doll, stick around. You won't be single for more than a day. I've got at least five friends who would jump your bones."

"You would be perfect for Roberto," Edwina said. "He loves quiet Midwestern types. How long are you in town?"

"Just a couple of days," Benjamin said, "and we've got a full schedule. Maybe next time."

"Thanks for speaking for me Benjamin," I said. "Who's Roberto?"

"He's my stylist, a Brazilian dreamboat. You two would be stunning together."

"How about we order dinner?" Benjamin picked up his menu.

"Benjamin, what is your problem?" Jacqueline asked. "You're acting like an overprotective dad. Why can't your cute cousin have a little fun while he's here?"

"Because I know what people are like."

"We're not talking about just anybody, we're talking about Roberto. I've known him for years," Edwina said.

"Can we change the subject?" Benjamin began reading the menu. There was a long awkward silence. I decided I had had enough of Benjamin making decisions for me.

"Edwina, I would like to meet Roberto. Is he free for lunch tomorrow?"

Benjamin closed his menu with a snap, glared at me and said, "We're having lunch at the studio tomorrow, did you forget that?"

"Well then, how about Thursday?"

"We're driving to Malibu that day. Like I said, maybe the next time we're in town." He picked up his menu again.

I looked at the two women. Jackie looked puzzled, and Edwina looked annoyed. She excused herself, picked up her purse and headed to the restroom. There was silence at the table. Benjamin looked up from his menu again.

"What? What did I miss?"

"Oh, just someone acting like a jackass," Jackie said with a smile although her face was serious.

"What are you talking about? All I'm trying to do is protect my cousin from Southern California professional homosexuals."

"What's a professional homosexual?" I asked. "I wasn't aware you had that kind of expert experience with the gay community."

Benjamin burst into a loud laugh that was hollow at its core.

"Well shit, you know that I don't but I've certainly met plenty of gay men over the years, and it seems to me that the Southern California types are all the same, out for any easy lay and hopefully with someone with an industry connection. And if Roberto finds out that Pete is my cousin, well watch out—you know what will happen."

"Jesus, Benjamin, what's gotten into you?" Jackie said. "You know very well that Roberto is nothing like that whatsoever. He's got a great job; he doesn't need a thing from you."

"I've met him," Benjamin said.

"Please don't bring this up again, here she comes," Jackie whispered as I stood up to let Edwina slide back into the booth. She had her purse in one hand and her cell phone in the other. With a look of determination she turned to me and said, "Roberto is meeting us at Hyde later. Since Benjamin has you booked solid for the next two days, this seemed like the only opportunity for you two to meet. I just know you'll like him."

Benjamin started to say something but Jacqueline moved towards him and put her hand on his shoulder. She whispered something in his ear and he resumed reading his menu. I sat back and watched his face. He looked tense, tired and ticked off. I wondered if he realized he was coming across as a jealous control freak.

I was beginning to think that it was very simple: in this world Benjamin was in total control of everything. It was something I couldn't fathom. Most of the decisions I made were balanced by factoring in other people's feelings, schedules, likes and dislikes. Benjamin, however, could decide what he wanted and it happened, usually when he wanted it to happen. The waitress came by and Benjamin started ordering everyone's dinners. The two women didn't seem surprised. I was.

"I'll have the lamb chops," I said.

"I ordered the tiger prawns for you," Benjamin said, "You'll love them."

I ignored him and looked at the waitress, "I'll have the lamp chops medium rare." I gave her my biggest smile and said thanks to make sure she understood this transaction was over. Jacqueline giggled. Benjamin looked at the waitress and shrugged his shoulders. "He's my cousin— you know what they say about family, don't you?" She nodded in agreement, seemingly unfazed by who she was waiting on or what had just transpired. I tried the wine, which of course was delicious.

"What do they say about family?" Edwina asked.

"You know that old chestnut, you can choose your friends but you can't choose your family."

"In your case it should be, you can control your friends but you can't control your family," I said.

Jacqueline gasped; Edwina put her hand on top of mine and squeezed hard. Benjamin laughed his Hollywood laugh again. "You're right dude, I'm learning a lot about you I didn't know." He finished his wine. "And I'm not sure I like what I'm learning."

"Ditto," I said utterly convinced by now that this trip had been a mistake.

"Boys, boys, relax," Jacqueline said. "Is there some history here we need to know about? Do you two even like each other?"

"Of course we do. I think we're both a little tired," he said.

Benjamin poured himself another glass of wine, not waiting for the waitress. His face was expressionless. My mind drifted. Benjamin had begun to seem like a different person the minute we decided to make this trip together. I decided on the spot I was going to go home tomorrow. I didn't like this version of Benjamin.

I wanted the Iowa version. If I couldn't have that, then I didn't want anything from him.

The conversation began between the three of them again, leaving me on the outside looking in. I tried to pay attention but as before they were talking about people I didn't know. I wondered if they ever talked about anything other than their work. Our dinner arrived, which I inhaled. I could have eaten twice as many chops as they served. Benjamin ordered cognac for all of us. I didn't drink mine. I was tired and had a headache.

Constance Cabot walked by and let out a little scream when she saw Jacqueline. Benjamin made room for her and I found myself scrunched up next to Edwina. She was staring at me intently. "Pete, if I were a betting woman, I would say that underneath that beard, you look remarkably like that waiter I met at the Graves funeral reception. Do you have a cousin in that town your age, what was the name of it again?"

"Mason City, and no I don't have any relatives there other than Benjamin and his family."

"There's something fishy going on here, isn't there?" She looked directly into my eyes. "You have colored contact lenses on, don't you?"

"No, no...I don't," I stammered. She reached over to pull on my beard. Just as she was about to grab some hair, Benjamin jumped up. "Come on, everyone, let's get the hell out of here."

The three women slid out of the booth and walked away. Benjamin leaned over and whispered into my ear, "What was going on with you two?"

"I think she has figured me out, she was just about ready to yank off my beard."

"Fuck," Benjamin said, "she's too damn smart for her own good. Why didn't I invite Britney?"

"Let's go home. I don't really care if we go to Hyde or not."

"No, we can't cancel. Too many people are expecting us." He put a hand on my shoulder as we walked to the entrance. Benjamin was speaking quietly in my ear but I wasn't listening. I was watching everyone watching us. I was almost disabled from self-consciousness. Benjamin didn't notice.

CHAPTER THIRTY

———∞———

Back in our limousine, Benjamin made sure that I was not sitting next to Edwina. Champagne was opened again, glasses filled, everyone throwing it back in gulps instead of sips. I was tight next to Benjamin. I could smell his cologne mingling with the odor his body gave off when he was hot and full of alcohol: sharp and sweet. His hip and thigh pressed against my leg.

"Jackie, do you have that mirror that I love?" Constance asked.

"Of course." She handed a small rectangular gold mirror to her friend. Constance checked her reflection, smiled widely to check her teeth and then reapplied lipstick. Edwina and Jacqueline followed suit. Benjamin looked as well. He handed it to me and I aped his moves making sure there was nothing hanging out of my nose or stuck between my teeth. The car stopped, and the three women stepped out to shouts from the crowd and an endless stream of photographs. Benjamin stepped out and the roar tripled in volume. I followed him, blinded by the lights. I stopped but there was no hand there to bring me forward. I tried to follow but was blocked. I called out Benjamin's name but since everyone else was doing the same thing, my voice simply joined the chorus. I pushed forward again but got nowhere. I pushed again and this time was pushed back. I stood frozen in place. Several minutes went by; I had no idea what to do. I thought about working my way up to the bouncer and telling him that I was Benjamin's cousin but then thought they certainly had heard that line at least a thousand times. My other alternative was to get in line and hope that eventually I made it inside. Suddenly the door to the club flew open and a huge roar went up from the crowd again. There was Benjamin, scanning the crowd. He was saying something but I couldn't hear him. I stood on my toes and began waving my arms and shouting. Over the din, I began hearing people say that Benjamin was looking for someone named Pete. I began shouting again that I was Pete! I stepped forward and raised my hand but was blocked by the outstretched arms of the photographers in front of me who were furiously snapping picture after picture of Benjamin.

I felt a surge of energy and began pushing my way through the throng. The crowd began to part and suddenly I was by his side. "Jesus, Pete," he said into my ear, "I was really worried about you. What the hell happened?"

"Not sure, you four moved forward and I got blocked. Boy am I glad to see you—I just realized I don't even know your address."

"All that matters is that you're here—come on—let's go inside." He leaned over and kissed me on the temple. He held the kiss for a few seconds. The cameras went crazy. I wasn't even sure Benjamin knew what he had done. I was swept inside, Benjamin's arm around my shoulders. I could see people smiling at Benjamin, calling out his name, reaching forward as if to touch him but knowing they couldn't.

The three women were in a round booth in a roped off corner. "What happened?" Edwina asked as I sat down next to her. "We thought you had decided to call it a night. Roberto would have been disappointed. And speak of the devil, here he is!" She moved back towards Jacqueline and Constance to make room. Roberto sat down next to me and kissed me on the cheek. He had short black hair, honey colored skin and hazel eyes. He moved towards me with feline grace as his small, tight T-shirt rode up high enough for me to see his flat, muscled stomach.

I shook his hand.

"What are you drinking?" Roberto asked me as he moved closer and put his arm around my shoulder. "What was your name again?"

"Pete, it's Pete Turner and I'll have a beer."

"I'll have one too." He waved at a waiter and ordered our beer. Looking back at me he said, " Edwina told me you were cute but I had no idea you would be a knockout!" He leaned over as if to kiss me again. "I've been waiting to meet someone like you for a long time."

"What do you mean someone like me?"

"I think Midwestern gay men are the hottest this country has to offer. They aren't all jaded or opportunistic like you meet here or in New York. Plus I can tell you have an amazing body, don't you? What the hell are you doing languishing in the middle of the country?"

"I used to live in Boston but got tired of those jaded and opportunistic men you just described." Sensing that someone was watching us, I looked over to see Benjamin drilling holes into my head with his eyes. I moved away slightly. The beer arrived and I grabbed it, anything to distract me from the sexual energy radiating up and down my body.

Roberto filled the few inches I had tried to put between us. His arm was around my shoulder again and his hand on my thigh. "How do you know Benjamin?"

"He's my cousin, second, third, I can never remember which." Roberto looked at me expectantly. "I really don't know him that well, we spent a bit of time together when we were kids. We just reconnected again a few weeks ago at his dad's funeral."

"Do you know what people think of him out here?" He looked across the table at Benjamin. "Most people say he is a major league prick and a complete control freak." He began massaging the back of my neck. "I mean for God' sake, look what he did to Alyssa, kicking her out in three days? Nobody does that, not even in this town."

I drank my beer. "I have to say it's hard to believe Benjamin is that big an asshole. He seems pretty easy going to me."

"Then you've seen a side to him I never have. Didn't you find his reaction to you and I having lunch kind of weird?"

"You heard."

"Edwina tells me everything. Why would he give a shit if you and I have lunch tomorrow other than its proof that he is a control freak? And oh my God, what he did to that salesclerk... brutal dude, just brutal!"

I looked again at Benjamin who was talking to Jacqueline. Suddenly from across the room, I saw Alyssa Wheelock marching toward our table, holding a cocktail. She stopped next to Benjamin and put her hand on the table as if to steady herself. Benjamin was smiling and indicating that she should join us. Instead she lifted her glass and threw it in his face. There was a loud gasp from the surrounding tables. Benjamin stood up, wiping the liquid off his face, rubbing his eyes and pushing his hair off his forehead.

"What the fuck was that for?" His voice was soft and angry.

"I don't have time to list all the reasons...but three days to move out? Three fucking days? I knew you were a cold bastard but really Benjamin...talk about pushing the boundaries of, of, of...fuck, of everything!"

"You're drunk Alyssa," Benjamin said. "I'll have my driver take you home." He moved towards her.

"Stay the fuck away from me. I don't need anything from you. I never needed anything from you which considering how little sex we had was the only smart decision I made in our relationship!"

Benjamin's face was bright red. He moved towards Alyssa. She stood her ground as he put his arm around her shoulder. "Come on Ally, not here, please not here, not now," he said. "We can talk about this anytime you want but just not here, okay?"

He kissed her on top of her head and I could see her features soften, her shoulders slump and her eyes fill with tears.

"Okay Ben, please call me tomorrow." She looked at us, mumbled an apology and disappeared into the crowd.

"Gonna go to the bathroom." Benjamin walked away.

"Can you believe that?" I asked Roberto whose hand was still on my thigh.

"Can't blame her," he said as he moved even closer to me. He raised his hand and rubbed it across my chest.

"I knew you had a great body under that jacket. What I wouldn't do to make love to you right now." His hand slid down my torso until he placed it on top of my crotch. "Just as I thought, you're hung like a horse, aren't you? You must have Brazilian blood in you. We're going to have such a good time tonight."

He brought his hand up to my face and turned it towards him. He planted a kiss on me that sent shivers down my legs. I felt the tension of the evening begin to melt away as my body responded to the desire I was feeling for this man. I placed a hand on his stomach.

"Let's get the hell out of here." Roberto jumped out of the booth and bumped into Benjamin who took one look at me and said, "Come on Pete, let's go home. I'm tired. I've had enough." He asked the three women, "Do you want us to drop you off?"

"No, we're fine, you go home and go to bed, you look exhausted." Jackie stood up and hugged him. Roberto took hold of my hand and said, "Benjamin, Pete and I were just leaving, maybe you could drop us off at my house?"

"No, he is not going home with you," Benjamin said.

"I'm pretty sure he is." Roberto moved a step closer to Benjamin. They were about the same size but at this moment, Benjamin seemed huge.

"Pete, we're going." He elbowed his way past Roberto who looked like he was going to punch him. Benjamin put his hand on my shoulder and I pushed it away.

"Neither one of you is going to tell me what to do." I stood my ground and glared at them. They looked at me with surprise, almost as if they had forgotten what had started this argument. I put my hand on Roberto's arm. "Next time, okay?"

He frowned at me. "You sure?" I nodded.

"Don't be surprised if I don't show up in Iowa someday," Roberto said as he kissed me on the mouth and then shoved something into my pocket. Benjamin put a hand on my back and maneuvered me toward the front door. We went out together, pushed our way through the phalanx of photographers and found our limousine. Benjamin said something to the driver and we sped away.

He sat down across from me and sighed. He reached over, poured a glass of vodka on ice and handed it to me.

"I've had enough, I want water," I said.

"No, you're having one more drink, you're gonna need it."

"What the fuck does that mean?" I was furious. "I'm sick of you making all the decisions for me. If I had known it was going to be like this, I never would have come on this trip."

"You'll thank me later for saving you from Roberto." Benjamin drained his glass. "He's slept with just about everybody in this town." He poured himself another drink.

"It's not your decision to make. I don't even know what the fuck is going on between us."

"We're in a relationship, don't you know that?"

"When did you decide that?"

"About an hour ago."

"You don't get to decide things like that by yourself."

"Liam, I like you, I like you a lot. I want us to be in a relationship, a monogamous relationship. Are you okay with that?"

I sat back in my seat and closed my eyes. I wanted to laugh at the irony: here was Benjamin declaring us in the only kind of relationship I could possibly be in. Whatever annoyance I had felt with him since arriving in LA began to wane.

"Yeah, I'm okay with this." I moved forward and kissed him. He kicked off his shoes and began unbuttoning his shirt. He pulled off his pants and boxers. Sitting naked on the leather seat, his legs were spread wide, his erection standing straight up from his body. I stripped off my clothes in seconds and moved next to him. Our legs were pressed together and our hands were on each other's cocks. Benjamin put his hands on my shoulders and turned me around. He pushed me forward until my forehead was resting on the seat. He began massaging my ass, slowly at first and then faster, a finger sliding inside me.

He leaned back from my body and I heard a crinkling noise and then he spit into his hands several times. I felt the warm saliva.

"Hey, what do you think you're doing?" He didn't reply.

I felt his fingers playing with my anus, prodding, stretching it open. This went on long enough that for a second I thought this was as far as he would go. Suddenly I felt something too large trying to push its way into my body. I tried to raise up and away but Benjamin pushed me back down. It hurt like hell. I tried to squirm away from him but couldn't. Benjamin's breath was labored as he pushed and pushed to get inside me. My insides were pressed together resisting this intrusion. My own erection had disappeared as my body responded to the pain. Benjamin kept pressing against my sphincter, massaging my stomach until…until I relaxed and he pushed through. Sweat was dripping from my forehead. Suddenly the pain was gone. I felt whole, complete; felt my body united with his in a way I had thought impossible. There was a glowing sensation deep inside my body that kept growing as our bodies moved together. My erection returned. I pushed my butt back against him to receive him more fully. Benjamin's breath became shorter as his hand wrapped around my cock.

We stayed together for a long time afterwards. I didn't want the feeling of Benjamin inside me to end. He sat down and brought me up with him. He was kissing my back and shoulders, his hand rubbing across my chest.

"Can we do it again?"

"I was hoping you would say that but first, a new condom is needed." I pulled off Benjamin and realized with a stab of pain that I was sore, really sore.

Benjamin was putting on a new condom and swallowing what was left of his cocktail. I did the same to my drink. He motioned for me to come towards him. I stood over his body, my shoulders bent forward so as not to hit my head on the roof. Benjamin grabbed me by my hips and began to lower my body down. Suddenly he stopped what he was doing and said, "You know what? I think it's my turn."

He pushed me aside, pulled off his condom, found another and edged it down over my cock. I sat down on the seat, Benjamin straddled me and in a matter of seconds had my cock deep inside him. He was moaning with pleasure, the sweat pouring down his face and chest. He was bucking up and down, his cock and balls slapping up against his stomach. My eyes feasted on this beautiful man lost in pleasure.

We continued for a long time, changing positions: Benjamin on his knees, on his back, on his side but ultimately the way we started. I was playing with his nipples as he rode faster and faster on my cock. With a thrust of his hips he came. The muscles of his ass clamping down on my cock during his orgasm was thrilling. I pushed my hips up and buried myself as deeply inside Benjamin as I could.

He leaned forward and kissed me first on the forehead, then my nose and finally my lips. He pulled off of me and handed me a cocktail napkin. We wiped ourselves up as best we could. I was sore, spent and tired. I pulled on my clothing and sprawled on the back seat. I was dying for a drink of water. Benjamin tapped the window separating us from the driver and in a few minutes we were pulling into his driveway.

I heard the driver get out of the car and walk away.

Benjamin leaned forward and rubbed the top of my head. "God what a night!"

We walked into the house but this time he held my hand. There were only a few lights on in the kitchen. We each found bottles of cold water and trudged upstairs. At the top of the stairs, I headed towards my own room. Benjamin followed. Inside my room, we stripped off our clothes, threw them into a corner, took a quick shower and fell into bed.

CHAPTER THIRTY-ONE

It was late morning when I awoke with the second worst hangover of my life. I turned over on my side and tried to fall asleep again but couldn't. My heart was racing and my stomach was roiling. When I sat up in bed, my head throbbed. I sat that way for a while, my head in my hands, recreating each part of the evening until I remembered what happened in the limousine.

Benjamin's side of the bed was cold. I stumbled to the bathroom and peed noisily. Once I emptied my bladder, I realized how much my ass hurt. It felt like someone was sticking flaming skewers inside me. I could think of nothing else to do except take a hot shower, hoping it would begin the process of curing me. I turned on all the various showerheads and let the steam build. I took a quick look at my reflection. I had bags under my eyes, and streaks of blood shot veins circled my pupils. I looked jowly and puffy. I stepped into the shower and let the pounding hot water seep into my muscles. I didn't move for a long time, letting the water hit the top of my head, pour down my face and onto my chest and back. I almost nodded off. I found a bar of soap that smelled of oranges and began soaping my body. When I reached behind, I gingerly washed my butt. I winced from the discomfort.

In the cold light of a hungover day, I knew that I was going home. I wanted out of here. I wanted to be in Iowa more than anything else in the world.

Benjamin stepped into the shower. He circled me in a bear hug and began kissing me on the neck. He knelt down in front of me and took my cock into his mouth. He brought me to life while his other hand began working its way around to my ass.

"That's not gonna happen." I pushed his hand away. "It's closed for repairs."

"You liked it, didn't you?"

"Sure I liked it but—"

Later, standing in front of the mirror, I shaved while Benjamin watched.

"I don't want to hurt your feelings but I was thinking…."

"You want to go home," he interrupted.

"Yes, that is it exactly."

"I'm relieved."

"Really?"

"Yes, really. Come out to the bedroom, I have something to show you."

A laptop was set up on the desk in the corner and from across the room I could see the distinctive graphics of Pabloposada.com.

"I didn't realize you were a fan."

"I'm not but you need to see this." I stepped closer. Filling the screen was a picture of Benjamin kissing me on the temple as we stood outside the entrance to Hyde. Pablo had written over the photo in huge white letters, *Kissing Cousins!!* I read the paragraph underneath.

"Benji claimed last night that the bearded hunk whose head is stuck to his lips is his first cousin, Pete Turner. How does one become a relative of Benji is what I want to know? We've been scouring anything Mormon trying to trace the Turner wing of the Graves family and so far, guess what? The only Pete Turner we've found is a dead Pete Turner. So who is this mystery man and why are they

thicker than thieves?" I sat down on the bed. "Dinner at Koi, where we heard they walked out of the restaurant almost holding hands, drinks at Hyde and there they leave Jacqueline, Edwina and Constance behind. Who leaves that trio? We heard there was quite a fracas at Hyde, drinks flying, two beautiful boys (and neither named Benjamin) making out, and then poor or should I say poofter, Benjamin and Mystery Man depart, heads together, the bearded boy looking distraught at leaving the beautiful boy from Ipanema behind."

Benjamin was pacing back and forth across the room.

"I'm glad you want to go home, Liam, because this way I don't have to ask you to." He stopped and stared at his reflection in the mirror but his eyes were glazed over. He ran his hand through his hair. "You do not want to be around for this circus. You sure you're okay with going home?"

I nodded.

"Good. The car will be in back in a couple of hours. There's a flight that leaves around 4 back to Minneapolis. Will you drive my Dad's car home?" He slipped the keys into my pocket. "It was really stupid to bring you out here with the disguises and all this BS. I am really sorry."

"It's okay, it was fun for a while."

"Was it?"

"Sure it was, but I've seen enough." I leaned over and tied my shoes. "Are you coming back to Iowa?" I asked quietly. There was a pause as if he hadn't heard me. I asked him again.

"I hope so," Benjamin replied.

"Hope?"

"I've got some things to do. Sydney says I need to stick around to do a little damage control."

"I understand." *Did I?*

"I know you do and it's one of the things I love about you."

Love?

"Actually, I don't understand but—"

"But what?"

"Let's talk this weekend."

"Then why did you say you understand if you didn't?"

"Will you be back in Iowa by Friday night?"

"Like I said, I hope so."

"You know where I'll be. Call me if ….and when you get home."

"Don't be like that."

"Like what?"

"I think it's called passive aggressive."

"Don't start that bullshit with me. I want you to come back to Iowa. If you can't, I would rather you tell me now. I don't think that's asking too much."

"It's not that simple."

"It should be."

"I'll do my best." Benjamin sat down on the edge of the bed, his hands under his chin. "If I can get out of here on Friday, let's have dinner at my house."

"It'll have to be midnight," I said, "I'm working Friday night."

Benjamin looked disappointed and started to say something but stopped himself.

"What?"

"I was going to tell you not to work on Friday. Shit, I need to get out of here. Not sure I like who I am anymore in this place."

"I don't like who you are here either," I said, which to my surprise elicited no response. I put my own clothes in my luggage and began zipping it up.

"But what about all the stuff from Fred Segal?" Benjamin looked surprised.

"It's all in the closet." I walked to the bathroom to get my shaving kit. "I didn't wear most of it and have no place to wear it anyway. Can't you return it?"

"No, I can't." I looked at him with a why not expression.

"The only people who do that are unemployed actors. I'll bring it with me this weekend."

"Did I miss something?"

"What do you mean?"

"You just went from tentative to certain in about fifteen seconds."

"You're right, it just hit me, I need to get out of here." He stood up and walked to the door. "If I could, I would leave with you right now."

"What's stopping you?"

"Everything and nothing."

I sank into my seat on the airplane, my head and body aching. I took a deep breath and realized through my hangover that I couldn't remember a time when I had been happier to be going home. Before the plane reached its cruising altitude, I was sound asleep. I didn't wake up until it thumped onto the runway. It was a struggle to stay awake during the two-hour drive back to Mason City. There wasn't enough McDonald's coffee in the world to make me fully awake. All my energy was focused on keeping the car on the highway. Each time a semi truck thundered past me I jerked sideways. As soon as I got home, I had a bowl of soup, several glasses of water and slept for ten hours.

The next morning over coffee I realized I had thirty-six hours completely to myself. No one knew I was home and I didn't have to work. I thought about calling Mom but decided I didn't want to have to create a story about why I was home early. I leaned my head back and felt the strong June sunshine penetrate deep into my muscles. The only thing I could hear were a few birds as they swept through my backyard searching for their morning meal.

I took a stab at reading the latest Sue Grafton novel but could not stay focused and if I couldn't focus on something as simple as that, I gave in and let my mind rehash my time in Los Angeles.

I wondered how much of what I saw of Benjamin in LA was the real person, or had it been an act? Maybe a combination of both? Maybe the version of Benjamin I had met in Iowa had been the act? I felt a rush of paranoia and just as quickly pushed it aside.

Finishing my coffee, I realized my body was impatient for exercise. I left by my front door to avoid running past Aunt Marie's house and ran for two straight hours, not worrying about distances or speed, simply reveling in the exercise itself. After a simple dinner of chicken, pasta and salad, I fell asleep early, feeling my body returning to its normal state. I avoided the television and the Internet. There was no reason to see what was going on in Benjamin's world. I knew from experience that these stories played themselves out after a few days. Benjamin would survive this just as he had all the others.

I woke up Friday morning covered in a sheen of sweat. It felt as if someone had turned on the heat in my bedroom. I squinted at the outdoor thermometer outside my kitchen window to see that it was already ninety degrees and it was barely past 7 A.M.

Stuffing gym clothes into a duffel bag, I drove the few miles to the local YMCA to throw some weights around in air-conditioned comfort. After my workout, as I was undressing I looked across the locker room to see a handsome young man, with a classic swimmer's body, stepping out of his Speedo. He looked to be in his early twenties, most likely home for summer vacation. He was the best-looking man I had seen since returning home other than Benjamin. It was like seeing a tropical bird flickering around a backyard bird feeder surrounded by wrens. He held my gaze with a head-to-toe glance at my naked body. We had to be at least ten years apart in age. I wondered if I could date someone that much younger than me. Smiling, I thought to myself, *you really are a closet lesbian.*

Not for one second did I think about a one-night stand; I went right to a relationship. With a glance back at the swimmer who was still facing my direction, proudly showing off his body with his penis lengthening slightly, I felt a flush of lust.

As I walked to the shower stalls, the swimmer began to follow me but then veered off into the steam room. I continued to the shower and then went home.

When I walked out of the garage, I could hear my phone ringing. I leapt up all four of my back steps and raced into the house. "Hey there," I said with a little too much feeling.

"I doubt that was for me," Deirdre said.

Shit, I thought as I brought my voice back to normal. "What do you mean?"

"It had a tone of flirtation to it," she said. "Are you dating someone?"

"Whatever happened to hello?"

"Sorry, Liam." She cleared her throat. "Hello! What's up? Is that better?" She laughed. "Anyway, enough small talk, are you dating someone?"

"Why?"

"Because you sounded like you were expecting him just now on the phone."

I grimaced. It annoyed the hell out of me when I wasn't in control of my own information.

"Yes, I am dating someone."

"You don't have to sound so weird about it, it's not like you're having an affair or anything, right?"

I said nothing.

"Anyway, Liam, when the hell am I going to see you again?" I continued my silence. "You know, we talked more and saw each other more often when you lived halfway across the country."

"Have you and Leah been talking? The last time I spoke to her, she said the same thing." I paused. "You know Deirdre, your car does drive south. I've been home several months now and you haven't been to Iowa once."

"I've been busy. Owning your own business and raising three kids, almost single-handedly, is not easy."

There was a long silence.

"Shit, this was not the reason I called. How did we end up here?" Warmth returned to her voice. "I miss you Liam. I miss talking to you and I miss the thought of coming to see you in Boston. You know how much I loved going east. Do you realize this is the first summer in years that I haven't gotten on a plane to come see you? I miss the ocean so much, sometimes I imagine I can hear it when I'm in the backyard and then reality sets in and I realize it's just the wind in the oak trees."

"I guess I took it for granted."

"Trust me," she said, "a couple of years back in Iowa and you'll understand what I'm talking about. None of the lakes around here cut it, especially Clear Lake."

I kicked off my shoes and threw my gym bag onto the kitchen table.

"Sue and I had lunch on the beach there last week. It doesn't smell like dead fish anymore."

"When am I going to see you again?"

"Soon. Leah invited me up the first weekend in July. Are you guys around?"

"Of course we are. Are you staying with us?"

"I told Leah I'm staying with them."

"The kids will be disappointed. You know they love having you around."

"I love being around them."

"Are you coming up Friday night or Saturday morning?"

"Saturday morning."

"I'll talk to Leah. Why don't you plan to be here around 11? We'll have a BBQ. Hey, why don't we have scallops on the grill? We

321

can pretend we're in Provincetown again! Do you remember that dinner we had last summer at The Mews? God, that was a perfect evening."

"I'm staying at Leah's."

She hung up.

CHAPTER THIRTY-TWO

After taking a cold shower and still being covered in sweat, I stood in front of the window fan trying to dry off. I remembered the last time I had stood in front of the fan with Benjamin behind me. My dick called out to me but I ignored him.

It was too hot to put my work clothes on so I threw on a pair of gym shorts and sandals and headed to work.

As I walked in the back door of the restaurant, Sue walked into the kitchen.

"Jesus Liam, put some clothes on. You're indecent. Do you have any underwear on?" She pulled my shorts down slightly in back. "You don't." She moved in front of me and grabbed the waistband and yanked them forward and then snapped it back. "Just because Lindsay Lohan runs around showing off her girl parts doesn't mean you have to do the same thing. Anyway, can you believe what is going on with Benjamin Graves?"

"What are you talking about?"

"You don't know?"

I shook my head.

She looked at me askance. "That makes no sense. You are a total celebrity whore. Anyway, his photo is everywhere. Everyone is saying that he's gay."

"Gay?" I asked. "Everyone?"

"You heard me, he was seen kissing some guy on the temple, some guy named Pete Turner that Benjamin claimed was his cousin. But guess what? Poor old Pete bit the dust several years ago. Can you believe he could be so stupid? Why would you make up a story like that when it was so easy to disprove?"

"I have no idea."

"Benjamin was doing his best Sean Penn impersonation last night, pushing a few photographers around. Did you know that he's dating Jacqueline Anderson?"

"I didn't know that either."

"Have you gone on some kind of celebrity fast?"

I walked away from her and into the bathroom to change into my work clothes. The next thing I knew I was standing behind the bar and setting things up for the evening. I slid my hand down to make sure my zipper was up. I was biting my lower lip and staring off into space as Sue came up next to me. She put two fingers on my triceps and squeezed, hard.

"Hey, that hurts! What the hell are you doing?" I pulled away and began rubbing my arm.

"Just making sure you aren't dead. You had no expression on your face. What's wrong with you?"

"Nothing, guess I'm not completely awake." I rubbed my eyes for effect. "I think I'm still on West Coast time."

She turned me so we were face to face. She stared deep into my eyes and said, "You're not high or drunk are you? Because if you are I am going to send you home on the spot!"

I started laughing at her poor imitation of Sydney Ross.

"This makes no sense to me," she continued. "You were on the West Coast and you know nothing about the Benjamin Graves fiasco?" I shook my head. "Have you lost your infatuation with him since you've been riding Clay Davis?"

My head snapped around at her insinuation. "What's that supposed to mean?"

"Oh, I don't know, Texans, southern accents, cowboys, sodomy, it all sort of blends together, doesn't it?"

I glared at her. "I have never asked you what you do in bed, have I? Even once?"

Sue blushed bright red. "You're right, I crossed a line. I'm sorry."

I began counting the money in the cash register.

"You know Liam, people are saying this could jeopardize his next movie. Some investors are threatening to pull out their money." Her voice was warm.

Benjamin must be flipping out. "Just because he kissed his cousin on his forehead? That's enough to cancel a 100 million dollar movie?"

"You don't listen to me, do you? That is the whole point of this— he wasn't Benjamin's cousin."

"So maybe the press screwed that up as well. They do make things up in case you weren't aware of that."

"The press did not make that up. Apparently Benjamin told about fifty people on Tuesday night at Hyde." She said Hyde as if she had been there.

"Okay, let's assume they were friends. I still don't see what the big deal is about the kiss. You see male actors kissing each other all the time on awards shows."

"They weren't at an awards show, he wasn't his cousin, and he kissed him on the forehead. How many men do you know who do that?" She had that look on her face that said, *Don't even try to argue me out of this.* "Let me rephrase, how many straight men do you know that kiss each other on the forehead?"

"Temple."

"What?'

"The first time you told me this story you said he kissed him on the temple."

"Temple, forehead, whatever. Does it really matter what part of the head he kissed?"

"My point is that it is easy to screw up details. Maybe he didn't even kiss him."

"You are a piece of work, Liam." She moved to the end of the bar and yanked her purse up, a purse big enough to cover her for a four-day weekend in New York. She pulled out a magazine and marched towards me holding it up in front of her. There on the cover of *People* was Benjamin kissing me on the temple. It was similar to the one I had seen on the Pablo Posada website but this one was a close up of just our faces. Benjamin's eyes were closed and I was looking up at him almost with adoration. I felt the color drain from my face.

"Are you all right, Liam?'

I moved to the end of the bar and sat down. What a fucked up mess we made.

"Yeah, I'm fine, think I might have picked up a bug in LA." I stared at the photo. The only good part was that no one would be able to tell who it was. Even I barely recognized myself. Sue came up behind me and put a hand on my shoulder.

"You know, without that beard, he could be *your* cousin and not Benjamin's."

"What…what are you saying?"

"Calm down Mister Man, don't you see the resemblance?"

"No fucking way."

She pulled her hand away and looked at me quizzically. I looked again. Was my first reaction to the photo just wishful thinking? At that moment, Georgia Dee came up behind us. She glanced at the magazine and continued around the bar to put more money in the cash register.

"I'm adding another $200, we're going to be busy tonight." She slid the bills into their respective slots. "Can you believe what a mess that poor boy is in? Why would he say he is his cousin if he isn't?"

She pushed the cash register drawer shut, looked at me and said, "Everyone is saying that he could be your cousin although I don't really see the resemblance."

"Who is this everyone you are talking about?" I asked, my voice an octave too high. "Jesus, aren't there more important things to worry about?"

Our first customers began arriving. Georgia Dee headed towards the hostess stand and Sue to the dining room. I could feel the sweat dripping down my sides. If Sue and Georgia Dee saw the resemblance and Sydney Ross acted like she knew something odd was going on—and Edwina! I remembered with a thud that she tried to pull my beard off. We were so screwed. This story was going to come out. I felt my emotions splitting in half: my paranoia versus my anger at all the pretense.

"God damn it, Liam Ashby," I said, causing two men sitting at the end of the bar to laugh out loud. *No one is going to put you back in the closet, no one, not even Benjamin.*

I knew that I would never out him but I also knew that I was done pretending. If Benjamin wanted me in his world, it was only going to be as me. I felt my resolve begin to buckle the moment it expressed itself as I knew this would mean the end of our relationship, a relationship that had just begun. Benjamin would never risk everything for me. A vein in my forehead began pulsing and I began backpedaling. Maybe it wouldn't kill me to let things continue as they were. Neither of us were being harmed, were we?

I am being harmed and so is Benjamin, floated through my brain. There was no way you could lie like this and not experience the ramifications. My resolve returned and I began to hear music swelling in the background. The music became a triumphal march as I fantasized about being proclaimed the man who helped Benjamin Graves comes striding out of the closet, in one move reshaping the way the world viewed Hollywood's leading men: for better or for worse.

In a daze, I poured two draft beers and made a gin and tonic. For better or worse. I was walking down the aisle of a church, Benjamin by my side, the church overflowing with family and friends. My

327

mom, aunts and sisters were in the first two rows. Sue was the best man. Brad and Angelina, Ben and Jacqueline, Gwyneth and Chris were in the row behind them. Jennifer Hudson was singing *Ave Maria* while wiping away tears.

With a start I felt a tap on my right cheek. Sue was staring at me holding a glass of water.

"You're scaring me. You look terrible. Drink this water and sit down. I'll make the drinks for a few minutes." She pushed me onto a barstool. Moving behind the bar, she poured two draft beers for the guys who were still staring at me.

Probably wondering if I have something contagious. Can you catch anxiety?

The restaurant and bar filled to capacity within the next hour. I had no time to think about anything except my job. Around midnight the building emptied as if there had been a fire drill. We were all so tired that as soon as we had finished our closing routines, we left. Georgia Dee hadn't even asked me to stay for a stinger.

As I pulled out of the parking lot I waved goodbye to Sue. She yelled out her window that she would call me, as she wanted to hear everything about Los Angeles. I hoped she would forget. I didn't want to talk about it. It had been a mistake, a huge mistake.

I picked up my cell phone and then set it down. What was the point? He was in LA and most likely wouldn't answer. I grabbed my phone and pushed the number almost as if my hand belonged to someone else. He answered. He sounded drunk.

"Please tell me you are pulling up my driveway," Benjamin said.

"You're home?"

"Yeah, please hurry."

There were no lights on in the back of the house either inside or outside. I had barely stepped out of my car when I was swept into his arms. We kissed deeply, Benjamin tasting of Scotch and sadness.

"Let's go to bed," he whispered in my ear. "I am talked out." I realized he was not as drunk as he had sounded on the phone. He led me by the hand into his house, upstairs and into the bedroom, there was a bottle of Johnnie Walker Blue Label on the bureau with two glasses. He poured two fingers each, we clinked glasses as Benjamin held his up for a toast.

"To us, Benjamin and Liam." His eyes glittered with emotion. "To no one else, not my family, especially not my family." He swayed a little and put his hand on the wall. "Not my colleagues...not my many fake friends, in fact, not even my real friends, no one else." He threw back his drink and poured two more fingers and raised his glass again.

"Here's to you Liam, the only person I have ever been myself around." He pulled me in for another embrace.

I looked him in the eyes and said, "Let's fuck."

CHAPTER THIRTY-THREE

—————∞—————

The next morning I woke up alone in the bedroom. I glanced at the alarm clock. I think we had fallen asleep around three but I wasn't sure. Now it was eight. I sat up in bed and swung my legs over and remembered. We had been on our sides, I was deep inside Benjamin who was moaning, laughing and crying in quick succession. I had asked him—as I wiped away the tears—what was wrong and he had said, nothing, absolutely nothing was wrong. We had fallen asleep with my body firmly pressed against his back.

Walking downstairs I could smell coffee and bacon. Benjamin was on the patio reading the New York Times on his laptop. The sky was royal blue and the air was dry and warm.

"Where does all this stuff come from?" I asked.

"What stuff?"

"The food, the coffee, you know, all the supplies in this house."

"I bought it, I brewed it, and I cooked it."

"You?"

"Well who the hell do you think did this? Singing mice?"

"I thought you had lackeys."

"Maybe it's true what they say, the pretty ones are always dumb," Benjamin said as he drained his coffee cup and turned off the computer. "Who in the name of God did you think was doing all this before?"

"Guess I assumed there was stuff left over from the funeral."

"I will have you know that I have been to the Hy-Vee just down the road, three times in the last three weeks." He stood up and squeezed my right nipple. "And I have rather enjoyed it. Quite. It was lovely, brilliant actually."

I laughed. He sounded exactly like Hugh Grant.

"Since you enjoy being a servant, do you mind getting me a cup of coffee with just a dollop of half and half?"

"Of course not, Master Ashby." He bowed and began walking backwards. He returned a few minutes later with coffee, bagels and cream cheese. We ate in silence for several minutes. I looked at his eyes.

"What is going on?" I asked.

"Nothing."

"Benjamin, clearly something is going on." I finished my bagel, although back in Boston we wouldn't have described it as a bagel, perhaps round Wonder bread would have been more appropriate. "I was with you in LA, remember?"

He paused. "Do you know what happened after you left?"

"Sort of, I avoided it initially but then everyone at work was talking—" He glared at me.

"How could I be so stupid?" He stood up and began pacing back and forth across his patio. "How could I be so fucking, fucking stupid?" He yanked a metal chair towards me and straddled it with his arms folded across the top.

"We," I replied. "We were in this together."

"Thanks for throwing yourself on the pyre with me, but you had no idea what could happen." He stood up again, walked to the edge of the patio, picked up a couple of large rocks, tossed them back and forth in his hands a few times before throwing them as hard as he could towards the cottonwood trees that separated the back yard from the fields. "I did."

I didn't say anything. He was right.

331

"Do you know that even *The New York Times,* the fucking *New York Times* is running the same picture that was on that twit's blog? Can you fucking believe this? The paper of record publishing that photo? All in the name of good journalism of course. It's covered in total bullshit. They are pretending to be writing about the proliferation of blogs and how stories on blogs are moving into the greater society seamlessly and replacing old fashioned investigative reporting. Such utter fucking bullshit. What they're really doing is giving themselves permission to print that same photo and run the same story. Am I gay? As if there is nothing more important than this. How about the 2500 soldiers who have died in Iraq? Or how about the fact that our country is bankrupting itself in Iraq? Or, oh fuck, who am I kidding?"

He sat down on the chaise lounge and closed his eyes. I didn't know what to say. I knew that he was right but I also know that if I had been an outsider looking in, I would have been as interested in this story as anyone else.

"It will blow over in a week or so."

"No, no it won't. You know better than that. This is not going away." He stood up and looked at the sky, squinting in the blinding sunshine. "But you know what? No, that's wrong, do you know *who* is going away? Me, that's who."

"Where are you going?"

"I'm already there."

"What do you mean?"

"I'm taking an official break," Benjamin said. "I'm taking a break from LA, from publicity, from lying, from pretending, from all of it." He pulled me to my feet and kissed me. "I'm staying in Iowa until the last possible moment."

"The last possible moment before what?"

"Before Morocco."

"Morocco?" I felt stupidly tongue-tied.

"For my movie, you know the one I'm starring in?"

"When is that?"

He put his hand over my mouth. "I don't know, sometime late summer, early fall, stop with the questions already. I thought you would be pleased."

I stood still. My mind was racing. I had been anticipating the opposite.

"I never expected this."

"So you don't want me here?"

I looked over at him, his face a combination of melancholy and confusion. I thought for a while.

"When I was twelve years old," I said, "I wanted a Schwinn bicycle for Christmas. I wanted it so badly I didn't sleep for the two weeks leading up to Christmas. But in my heart I was absolutely convinced that I would not get one. Guess what? I got it. It was exactly what I wanted, the right model, even the right color. There it was sitting in front of the tree when I snuck out of my room at three in the morning. I stood there and stared at that damn bike wishing it would disappear. It wasn't supposed to be there. Of course the next day I fell in love with it but in those first few hours it felt to me that anticipating disappointment was more interesting than the actual bike." I looked at him. "Guess I'm feeling a bit like that now."

"So it's been more interesting for you to wonder if I'm going to stick around than the reality that I do plan on sticking around, is that what you're saying?"

"No of course not. I'm not saying this right."

"No you're not." Benjamin's lips were a straight line across his face. "In fact, I think you just insulted me."

"Shit." I tried to organize my thoughts. "Don't you see how lopsided this relationship is? We have two things in common, Mason City and we like to have sex with each other. That's it. I live here, I work here, my family is here and I'm not going anywhere. I live my life as I am, a thirty-two year old single gay man living in a small town in northern Iowa. You, on the other hand…."

"What about me?" His lips remained pressed tightly together.

"I am not going to state the obvious. I will leave it at this, you work in movies and you are flying to Morocco in a few weeks. You don't live in Iowa, never will live here and most likely cannot tell anyone that you are currently having sex with a man. The prospect that you would tell me that you are planning on staying in Iowa for the next few weeks never entered my head, especially after what happened in L.A. I guess your decision strikes me as a little odd."

"I know what's odd and it isn't my decision. And what does any of this have to do with a bicycle?"

"Maybe that wasn't the best analogy. I was just trying to point out that I was expecting the exact opposite. Think about it from my perspective, though I know that can be a stretch for you." The thin line of his mouth wavered. "I just expected that the pressure would all be so much that you would not be able to leave LA for weeks. And what about your family?"

"What about them?"

"Where do they think you are?"

"Unfortunately, they know I was in LA." Anger accented each word.

"How?"

"Somehow a copy of *People* ended up in my mom's mailbox. My sisters saw it as well."

"What did you tell them?"

"Some junk that I'm researching a role and that you're an actor."

"Didn't you just say that you were done with pretending and lying?"

"What was I supposed to tell them?"

"The truth?"

"I can't do that."

"Why not? Don't you trust your family?

"No, I don't." I looked at him with surprise. "I know that sounds harsh. I'll tell you about it later, maybe when we're running."

"How are you going to stop hiding and lying if you can't even tell your family about me?"

He stared at me for a few minutes, his face a blank. "You can be a real prick, can't you?"

"You're the one who just said he was done with lying and pretending, not me."

The mask of anger dropped. "I'm not ready yet—but—but at least I'm thinking about it."

"Do you regret having met me?" I asked.

"Why?"

"None of this would have happened if you hadn't met me."

He walked towards the pool and looked up at the sky. "That's true but then again I wouldn't know you. That would be far worse than anything that has happened to me this week."

The softness in his voice startled me. I stared at this man and wondered who he really was. My eyes became unfocused. For a moment, I was racing along the Charles River trying to leave the broken remains of my relationship with Justin behind.

"What the hell is going on with you?" Benjamin asked.

It took me a few seconds before I realized a question had been asked. "Why?"

"You're white as a ghost."

I opened my mouth but no words came out. Benjamin walked over and put both hands on my shoulders. He shook them gently. "Where are you, Liam?" He looked deeply into my eyes. "Maybe we should start over," he said. "This is not how I thought this conversation would go. To be honest, I just assumed you'd be thrilled." He cuffed me on the ear and began laughing. "Your reaction is perfect, absolutely perfect." He pulled me close. "You know what? You couldn't have reacted any better than if I had written the script."

"Why?"

"Because it's genuine, no artifice, no agenda, just you." He kissed me on the lips, pulled back and said, "I think I'm falling in love with you."

I pulled away. "No, no you're not."

"How the hell do you know that?"

"Because people do not fall in love with me."

"Maybe it hasn't happened before but it's happening now and you cannot stop it." I turned my back to him. My eyes were full. I fought my emotions but one sob worked its way through my body. Benjamin embraced me and I began to cry. I cried for everything: the loss of my dad, my mom's illness, the loss of Justin, the loss of my belief in relationships—for everything. I remembered what Aunt Marie had said to me that day I worked on her garden. She had called me abnormal for returning to Iowa. Maybe she had been right, maybe I had fled to Iowa to avoid life. I was crying so hard I had to sit down.

"I don't know what the hell is wrong with me."

Benjamin put his hand under my chin and pulled my head up. He wiped away the tears with his thumbs and pushed my damp hair off my forehead. "There is nothing wrong with you, nothing at all." He pulled me to my feet. "There is nothing wrong with either one of us. I am the luckiest man in the world."

"Me too," I said softly.

I looked up to see a jet streaking east across the sky, leaving a milky plume in its wake.

"I think I am falling in love with you as well, although I'm not sure I really know what that means."

"Of course you do." Benjamin embraced me again. We stood that way for a long time. His head was on my shoulder. I was still fighting tears as images of my dad, Justin, Gregg, my sisters, mom, aunts, Sue all flipped through my mind. Each of the people I loved had left an indelible mark on me. Yet I rarely let the tenderness I felt for them rise to the surface. I was feeling it now and it was overwhelming.

"What are you thinking?" Benjamin whispered in my ear.

I hesitated. "Can you lead the kind of life where you are not always hiding…that is, not always hiding your feelings?"

"Yeah, I think so."

"Really? Can you pick up the phone right now and call your mom and tell her that you miss her and love her?"

His lips formed that thin line again. "You were just thinking about my mom?"

"No, no I wasn't. I was thinking about mine. I was thinking about how guarded I have become. I think my mom and sisters know that I love them but then again, maybe they don't?" I pulled away from him. "I have tried over the years to resist the stereotype of the typical Irishman who only shares his feelings when he's had a few drinks. I have steadfastly avoided that but unfortunately too much in the opposite direction."

"What's prompting all of this?"

"You, of course."

"Me?"

"Yes, you." I looked him in the eyes. I felt a flush of emotion. "I, I,…I think I love you." I turned around and closed my eyes. After a few seconds, I turned back around. "Well, you're still here. That's an improvement."

Benjamin started laughing. "You're a bit odd today, aren't you?"

"Yes I am. In fact, I am so odd that the next time I see my mom and aunts, even Aunt Marie, I am going to tell them to their faces how much I love them."

"Now I'm really worried about you. I wish I could do the same thing."

"Why couldn't you?"

He sat down. "I guess I could tell that to my sisters but after what happened in LA this week they would mistrust my motives." He stood up and began walking toward the house. "And I haven't told my mom that I love her since I was twelve."

"You're shitting me."

Benjamin started to say something but stopped himself. He disappeared into the house for a few minutes. Opening the back door he called out, "Aren't you supposed to celebrate a declaration of love with something more tangible?"

"That's an odd transition."

"I work in movies and I know how this scene is supposed to end and it doesn't involve us talking about my mom." He stepped out of his briefs and kicked them onto the patio and went back in the house.

CHAPTER THIRTY-FOUR

—∞—

As I stepped out of Benjamin's car, I looked up at a sky dotted with a handful of clouds. When I was a little boy, I believed big fluffy clouds like these could support an army of angels. I frowned as I tried to remember when I had stopped being so naive.

I looked down the narrow gravel road that undulated for miles in either direction. Underneath the electric buzz of cicadas, I could hear the faint sound of cars and trucks heading west and east across northern Iowa. I looked into the chest high cornfields that lined the road and saw a monarch butterfly flickering in and out of the cornstalks, its orange and black colors a sharp accent to the green of the corn. Its graceful pattern almost seemed choreographed. Looking up I saw a great blue heron floating across the sky. Benjamin came up to me and put his arm around my waist.

We ran the first five-mile loop in silence; the only sound our breathing and the soft thud of our sneakers on the gravel. I continued on without Benjamin and ran two more loops so quickly that when I was done, I wasn't sure if I had run both.

When I emerged on the rock platform there was a cooler with paper plates and plastic silverware stacked by its side. Benjamin was not in sight. I stood still for a moment straining to hear splashing or breathing or someone walking through the woods. Only the sound of the cicadas filled the air. I sat down on the warm stones and stretched my legs. Suddenly I heard the splashing of water.

Peering over the edge, I saw Benjamin treading water and gasping for breath.

"I heard you coming up the path and jumped in, assuming you would immediately jump in as well. I was hoping to scare the crap out of you by grabbing your leg or perhaps another appendage." He took several deep breaths. "I just about saw Jesus down there."

I stripped out of my clothes and dove in as close to Benjamin as I could.

"Shit that was close, you just about decapitated me."

I grinned at him. "I think you need to be kept on your toes a bit, Mr. Number One Box Office Star three years running." Benjamin's mouth was slightly open, his eyes mistrustful. "Should I wonder if you've lost your sense of humor now?"

"You little prick." Benjamin put both hands on my shoulders and pushed me under the water. As I came up to the surface, I choked out, "Little? It seems to me the first time you laid eyes on my lovely penis, quote, it's almost as big as mine!"

"I lied," Benjamin said, "I think it's bigger than mine."

I looked into his eyes and for a second remembered who I was with but the moment passed and I was with Benjamin again.

Later, after turkey sandwiches, dill pickles and chocolate chip cookies, we lay side by side, our feet intertwined. A large cloud covered the sun sending ripples of cool air across our damp skin. Benjamin leaned on his side, looked at me and said, "Okay, here goes nothing." He cleared his throat. "How would you have handled being told in high school that, quote, you led an artist's life without the talent."

"I would have been pissed as hell."

Benjamin looked away. "I was."

"Someone actually said that to you?" I thought for a moment. "Was it Mr. Rothman?" I asked, referencing the infamous drama coach who had terrorized decades of students at the public high

340

school as well as Catholic students at the annual state drama competition.

"Nope."

"Then it must have been Mr. Tenney." I remembered the track coach I had seen yelling at Benjamin at the state track meet.

"Wrong again."

"Then I have no idea."

Benjamin stood up and walked away from me. He shook his body as if to shed it from something. He muttered something I could not understand.

"What did you say?"

"What I said is, my mother."

"That's odd, why?"

"Because she believed it. She still believes it."

"Why would your mom say something like that to you?"

"I just said, because she believes it." He sat back down heavily. "Sorry, this is not about you. It's about my mom and me."

"Hasn't she seen your movies?"

"Of course she has. She thinks they're all crap."

"I don't believe that." I poured us water. "What about *Flag Day?* What about your Golden Globe for best actor?"

"Quote: melodramatic performance in a contrived movie with an award from a fake, fixed awards show."

"That's harsh."

"I still imagine how pleased she must have been when I wasn't even nominated for an Oscar for that movie." He sat up and crossed his legs while turning to face me. "My mother caught me smoking pot when I was fourteen."

"Shit…really?" I tried to imagine getting high when I was 14. "That's pretty young. I was in college before I tried it."

"First she caught me smoking pot, then drinking, then skipping school and a few other things." His face was as red as if sunburned. "I had a couple of rough years but as soon as I started my junior year,

341

everything changed for me. I discovered theater and running; quit pot and only drank for proms and shit like that, but she had decided I was a druggie and was unwilling to ever change her mind."

"She wasn't proud of you when you were in *The Taming of the Shrew?*"

"Hell no, she thought acting was for queers, and still does."

"She doesn't use that word, does she?"

Benjamin did not respond; his face gave his answer.

"She thinks that anything related to the arts: acting, writing, music, dance, anything at all creative is for fags. You wouldn't believe some of the things that have come out of her mouth. She would never watch any movie with Cary Grant. Anytime his name came up, she would always say he wore lace on his pants."

"That's kind of a dumb thing to say."

He shot me a look. "Are you calling my mom dumb?"

"I didn't mean to."

His face broke into a smile. "That's okay, she is…a bit." His smile faded. "It actually kind of hurts to say that out loud."

"I've seen lots of pictures of you with her at various awards shows, why was she there if she felt that way?"

"My dad made her go."

I sat for a while trying to imagine having a mother like this. While my dad and I had never really talked about homosexuality, he had also never said anything derogatory. "You seemed close to her at the funeral reception."

"It was all an act." Benjamin's eyes seemed to be battling between sadness and anger.

"You convinced me."

"Pretty sure I convinced everyone, even my sisters." He reached over and put his hand on my knee. "My worry now is whether or not she will drive a wedge between my sisters and me. I gotta tell you that what happened in LA this week didn't help." I felt a twinge of paranoia that I was the cause of all of this. Benjamin said,

"Shit Liam, I know you well enough already to know what you're thinking. You have to stop worrying that you are the cause of this."

"Kind of hard not to based on what you just said."

"I didn't mean it that way. She was more upset that Alyssa moved out on short notice than anything that had to do with Pete Turner."

"Really?"

"Of course." He stood up and walked to the edge of the rock shelf and looked down into the water. "She's always assumed that I'm gay. Alyssa moving out and then me showing up on a magazine cover kissing a guy on the forehead—"

"Temple—"

"Whatever, it didn't help. I think that's why she uses words like fag and queer, hoping to get a rise out of me. I think she believes she can out me or something by getting me totally pissed off."

"Do you think she ever suspected anything was going on between you and Scott?"

"No way." He stopped talking. The battle in his eyes had stopped, and now he was angry. "I can't lie to you anymore." He walked away taking in several deep breaths. He said something so softly that I could not hear him.

"What did you say?"

"Not sure I can say this out loud, I've never told anyone." He closed his eyes. "She, she…she caught Scott and me having sex when I was sixteen."

"Fuck."

"Actually, that's exactly what we were doing." He was silent for several minutes. "It…it…was late August, we were just getting ready to start our junior year. My dad was on a fishing trip and Mom was supposed to be visiting her sister in Omaha. My sisters were in the Twin Cities at our cousin's house. Scott and I were alone. Or so I thought." He turned away from me, his shoulders slumped. "She came home a day early. Scott and I were in my bedroom. The door was open. She walked by and saw him on top of me. She let out a scream and ran away. Scott fled out the front door. I found my mom in the kitchen sobbing. She just kept moaning, how could she have a son who was a fag?"

Benjamin turned around. There were tears on his face.

"I am so sorry, Benjamin." I moved towards him to hug him but he pushed me away.

"We never spoke about it after that day. Scott and I never saw each other again…well of course we saw each other, we went to the same high school…oh hell, you know what I mean."

"So what you told me before, that Scott ended the relationship, wasn't true."

Benjamin glared for a moment. "No, it wasn't. Although he might have anyway. He was starting to talk about how he thought we were going through a phase." He rubbed his eyes. "From that day forward, I counted the days until I could graduate and get the fuck out of her home."

"Did you ever talk about this with Scott?"

"No, never. We were toxic around each other after that."

"What did you tell your dad about why you and Scott weren't friends anymore?"

"You know, I don't remember him even asking. He was so confused by the hostility between Mom and me that he walked around as if shell shocked."

"Did your mom stop giving you shit?"

"No, not at all, in fact it got worse. The more involved I was in theater, the more she would make sure to throw around queer, fag, homo, whatever she could. She was relentless."

"Is this why you hate labels so much?" I asked.

Benjamin said nothing for a long time. Finally he spoke without moving or opening his eyes. "Maybe. But more importantly I see how people are destroyed with these labels, and innuendos. I see actors tying themselves into knots trying to hide their true selves, destroying their lives with drugs and alcohol, marrying someone of the opposite sex just to get the press off their backs for a week or so and for what? They just figure out another way to attack you."

"That's it?"

Benjamin moved away. "You don't think that's enough?"

"No...no I don't."

"Why the fuck not?"

"Because it hasn't applied to you until now." I lay down on the stone, reveling in the warmth that spread across my body. "I could maybe see you developing this attitude going forward but it's already fully developed. Why?"

He looked away from me. "Because I'm paranoid. Is that a good enough reason?" The anger and disappointment in his voice silenced me.

I walked to the edge of the quarry and peered down into the clear water. I could see the bottom broken by the jagged edges of rocks. The rocks seemed only a few feet from the surface.

We gathered our things, threw them into the cooler and headed back to the car.

CHAPTER THIRTY-FIVE

———∞———

"Oh my God." Sue rushed behind the bar to find her purse. "He's here, he is really here. Shit."

She applied lipstick, adjusted her skirt and made sure her blouse was open as much as it could be without undoing another button. I picked up two ice cubes and handed them to her.

"What are those for?"

"Do you want me to do it or are you going to?"

"Do what?" Her voice was threaded with anxiety. "Damn it Liam, I don't have time for your games."

I looked at her chest, "Doll, when your nipples are singing that loudly, you need to get laid."

"I hate your metaphors."

"Your nipples are about ready to pop off your breasts and ice is the best remedy to reduce swelling."

She looked down and sighed. "You're an asshole. If you knew anything about nipples you would know that ice will make them stand out even more." She reached in her purse and pulled out two small Band-Aids. "However, these will do the trick." She rushed to the ladies room.

I did a quick check to make sure everyone sitting at the bar had drinks. I wanted to see Sue's red headed farmer again. I made my way through the dining room looking for a table with three small children. Finally I saw him, by himself, at a corner table. He was sipping a Bud light and looking around as if expecting someone. Suddenly his face broke into a broad smile showing big white teeth with a small gap. I felt a slight push on my shoulder as Sue strode to his table.

"Get lost," she whispered. He stood up and gave her a kiss on her cheek.

When I returned to the bar, I saw Benjamin as Clay Davis sitting at the end. He signaled he wanted a drink. As I poured him a shot of whiskey, disappointment washed over me. I hadn't realized until that moment that I had hoped the disguises had disappeared forever. He thanked me quietly and looked away.

"Liam," Sue said loudly from the other end of the bar. "You have other customers." There was a chuckle from the men seated near her. I poured them two more beers. "I don't mean them, I mean me. I need a Bud light and two Cosmos." She came behind the bar and whispered in my ear, "He is going to wait for my shift to end and then wants to buy me a drink, can you believe this?"

"Not really, he is way hotter than you." I filled a shaker with vodka and a splash of cranberry juice. "Just because he is a forty-year-old with the body of a twenty-five year old, perfect teeth, huge masculine hands, and shoulders wide enough that he probably needs to walk sideways through doors, of course he's after you, a double divorcee with two children."

"You know, just because we're friends, doesn't mean that I can't kick the shit out of you. Do you really like his hands?"

"I didn't notice them. I just threw that in to see if I could get your nipples to pop off their Band-Aids." She punched me on the shoulder hard enough to hurt, yanked the shaker out of my hands, poured two Cosmos and headed back to the restaurant. The Bud light was still sitting on the bar. I picked it up and followed her. As I approached his table, Sue was taking an order at an adjacent table, fidgeting in place.

"Your waitress is a bit busy right now." I placed the beer on his table. "Hi, I'm Liam Ashby, one of the bartenders here."

He stood up and shook my hand. "Karl Johannsen, nice to meet you." His hand was enormous, the skin rough and worn.

"Sue will be right with you." He was still shaking my hand.

"No worries, I saw her." He looked in her direction. He was wearing beige cotton pants and a light blue golf shirt with the John Deere logo. "Do you know her by the way?"

"Yes, I do."

"Girlfriend?"

I laughed. "No, no, nothing like that. We're just friends."

"I'm relieved to hear that. I think she's cute as all get out."

"Me too."

"Liam," Sue said, "don't you have drinks to mix?"

"Yes I do, I just didn't want Karl's beer to get warm." I stuck my hand out again. Karl gripped it so hard it hurt. I looked him in the eye only to see him staring at Sue's breasts.

When I got behind the bar I looked over at Benjamin who looked away again. His glass was empty. I filled it and walked away.

By the end of the evening, the red headed farmer was sitting at the opposite end of the bar, his head popping up every time someone entered. I had ordered Benjamin a hamburger after his sixth beer. He was now sipping brandy and zoned out. I couldn't tell if he was relaxed or drunk, though I suspected the latter. From across the bar I saw Sue motioning to me. I followed her into the empty dining room.

"Will you please do me a huge favor?"

"Of course...anything."

"I need you to close out my book. I need some time in the bathroom and I'm afraid Karl is going to lose patience and disappear." I nodded yes as she handed me a pile of receipts. Back behind the bar, I organized her checks with a glance at Benjamin and Karl, both of whom were lost in their own worlds. I wondered what was going through Benjamin's mind. Sometimes I thought I knew him and other times he was a complete stranger. We had barely said two words to each other. He seemed embarrassed and apologetic about the disguise so why was he even here ?

I looked over at Karl. I wondered how long it had been since he had had sex: isolated on a farm with three little kids—probably a very long time. He waved at me and asked for another Bud light.

Sue walked into the bar. She had freshened her make up, brushed her hair in a way I had never seen and unbuttoned her blouse to a level that Georgia Dee didn't permit in the dining room. She sat down next to Karl, crossed her legs, smiled at him and ordered a vodka tonic, tall with a lemon. Karl had turned towards her with a look of pure lust on his face. I gave Sue her drink and left them alone.

"You about ready to hit the road?" I asked Benjamin. He sat up in his chair.

"This music is great, who the hell is that?" he asked.

"I have no idea, I don't really get jazz," I said, "Georgia Dee will know, she's in charge of the music."

"I think I will ask her." He slowly moved off the bar stool, stretched his upper body and walked to the front of the restaurant. A few minutes later he walked back to the bar while looking over at Sue and Karl. "So that's the famous farmer. I want a closer look." He picked up his brandy and walked towards them. He looked over at me and said, "Joshua Redman."

"Hey, y'all." His voice sounded large in the empty bar. "How about the four of us have a drink together? Liam, you're done for the night, right? I'm Clay Davis and of course I know this purty lady, how are ya Susan?" He leaned forward and kissed her on the lips. "Well howdy, you smell good enough to eat."

Karl stood up and thrust his hand forward. His face had hardened the moment Benjamin kissed Sue. "I'm Karl Johannsen, who are you?"

"He's Liam's boyfriend," Sue said.

"What?" Karl looked perplexed.

"Liam is gay and Clay is his boyfriend."

"You're both gay?" Karl reached for his beer.

"You seem surprised." Sue took a sip of her drink.

"Guess I am."

"Why?" I asked, wondering where this was going. Iowa was full of Evangelicals who were doctrinaire about the Bible, or at least the parts that supported their positions.

"Never mind," he said.

"No, no, tell us," Benjamin said and sat down next to Sue.

Karl was blushing bright red as we stared at him. "Well…I've never met a gay man before."

"You're shitting me," Benjamin said. I had walked around the bar and was standing facing the three of them. Benjamin reached over and held my hand. Karl glanced down at our hands then looked away.

"The ones on television don't look like you guys."

"What do they look like?" Benjamin sat up in his chair.

"Hey, hey, enough with the homo inquisition," Sue said. "Give the poor guy a break. We're in Iowa, remember? Not exactly the hot bed of the queer community."

"Sorry," Karl muttered, "I didn't mean to offend anyone."

"No offense taken," Benjamin said as he let go of my hand and spread his legs. "I could use another drink, how about you Liam?"

I poured him some more brandy and opened a Stella for myself. Sue was looking at me with confusion in her eyes.

"Where do y'all live?" Benjamin asked as he put a hand on Sue's shoulder. Karl stiffened for a second, looked at the two of us and relaxed.

"I have a few hundred acres near Marble Rock," he said.

"How long have you been farming it?" I wondered if that was the way you asked that question.

"My wife and I came back a few years ago when her dad died and we took over."

"Y'all are married?"

Sue uncrossed her legs, sat up and turned in her chair. "Yes Clay, Karl was married." She looked at me with an expression that said, how could he forget this?

Karl closed his eyes. "She died two years ago."

"Oh my God, I'm sorry." Benjamin emptied his glass. "What happened?"

"Cancer," he said. He looked at us with angry eyes. "I don't want to talk about this." He picked up his beer and finished it in one long swallow.

"Clay," I said, "How about if you and I go home?" Benjamin nodded as he stood up.

"Will you be all right?" I asked Sue. Her lips were tight as she nodded yes.

"It was a pleasure to meet you, Karl." Benjamin shook his hand again. "And I'm awful sorry about your wife." I shook his hand as well and we headed to the parking lot.

CHAPTER THIRTY-SIX

———∞———

The air was rich with humidity and a blustery, thick wind as we walked out of the restaurant. The pine trees lining the end of the parking lot were shaking as if by an invisible hand. I took off my shirt and T-shirt. Benjamin followed suit and then stepped out of his pants. He had on madras boxer shorts that he started to pull down as well.

"Shit, guess I can't do that, can I?" He pulled them back up.

"That was awkward," I said. "Guess you forgot his wife died?"

"Did I know that?" Benjamin's speech was slurred.

"Yes, obviously you forgot."

"Forgot what?"

"Are you drunk?"

"Yes."

"We'll get your car tomorrow." I turned his shoulders and pointed him towards my car. Benjamin collapsed into the passenger seat while I lowered the roof and tossed our clothes onto the back seat. I wanted to feel this air; it reminded me of the time on Cape Cod when Hurricane Bob was approaching.

"I don't want to go home yet," Benjamin said. "What the hell is there to do around here?" I looked at my watch. It was 1:30 in the morning.

"Nothing, absolutely nothing."

"Don't you feel like dancing? I sure do." He turned on the CD and pushed buttons until he landed on a Justin Timberlake album. He turned the volume up high and jumped out of the car and started dancing. I was mesmerized with this beautiful half naked man in complete synchronicity with the music.

"Come on Liam, get your ass out here and join me!"

I bounded out of the car. We began dancing, moving so well together it almost felt rehearsed. The sweat was pouring off our foreheads and down our chests. We were facing each other only inches apart, energy ricocheting off our bodies. We were both aroused, our crotches would briefly touch and then we pulled back a few feet and then move in together again. We danced for several songs until soaked with sweat.

"Boy do we need a swimming pool." I tried to mop the sweat off my forehead but it was a seemingly endless flow and I just let it run down my face.

"I've got a great idea," Benjamin said as he got back into the car. "You drive and I'll tell you where to go." We pulled out of the parking lot and drove in a direction opposite to either of our homes.

"Where the hell are we going?" I asked.

"Turn right."

A couple of miles later, we pulled into the empty parking lot of the Mason City Country Club.

"Turn your lights off and go as far as you can," he pointed to the far right corner. I turned off the car as Benjamin slithered out of his boxers, his cock slapping up against his stomach. I felt nervous as I looked around wondering if there was a security guard. How would I explain a naked priapic man sitting in my car? In the dim light I noticed a hedge that was perpendicular to the corner. I wanted it to swallow my car whole, like a python.

"You asked for a swimming pool, didn't you?" Benjamin opened the door, stepped out and disappeared through the hedge. I sat for a few seconds, picked up his underwear and tried to follow. I did not immediately see an opening until a hand materialized which I grabbed. I walked through, the branches barely touching my body. It was so dark I could barely see him on the other side.

"I used to do this all the time in high school." Benjamin began unbuttoning my pants. "Glad to know people are still doing this."

"Doing what?" My pants were pulled down to my ankles and then my underwear, my own cock bouncing out as if freed from jail. "And what others? Where are they?"

"Go skinny dipping in the pool." Benjamin knelt down in front of me and put my cock in his mouth for a few seconds. "Scott and I did this once but he was so terrified he couldn't get it up." He stood up. "Come on, let's cool off."

"What did you mean by others?" I was peering through the darkness for any kind of movement and we were out of there.

"Just that the secret entrance through the hedge is still there. Obviously it would have grown back after sixteen years unless somebody else was doing this."

I looked back at the hedge but all I could see was a solid wall of green. "Aren't you afraid of getting caught?" I asked.

"Hell no, there's nobody here. Did you see any cars?"

"No, but you never know."

Benjamin stepped around the corner of a one-story cinder block building onto the cool rough cement surface that surrounded the pool. "I worked here for a couple of summers in high school as a groundskeeper. There's no security, no caretakers, no live in help. Do you see any lights on?" I looked over at the clubhouse lined with enormous glass windows and all I saw was our reflections bouncing back at us.

"I can't take this anymore." He walked back towards the building. He ripped his wig and beard off and threw them on a table. He stretched his arms wide and spread his legs. "God, I haven't felt this good...in forever."

I had a moment of feeling star struck again. I had not seen Benjamin out of disguise in Mason City except in the privacy of our respective homes. Seeing him in public as himself made him seem naked on a completely different level. My cock throbbed as if in pain.

"That thing looks like it is going to explode." He reached over and slid his hand back and forth a few times. "My God, it's leaking." He wiped his hand on his leg. "You're a nasty little boy, aren't you?" I lunged forward to try to push him into the pool but he sidestepped me. I teetered on the edge until Benjamin touched me slightly on the shoulder and I toppled in. The water felt incredible on my feverish skin. I swam back and forth several times, the cool water rushing through my legs. Pausing near the diving board, I looked up to see Benjamin standing on the end bouncing higher and higher, his toes pointing as if he was trying to reach the sky. As he landed back down on the board, his cock slapped up and down and side to side. Finally he jumped up and out, his body arcing in a perfect semi circle, his erection flat against his belly. No matter what happened, I knew I would never forget this sight: Benjamin as if in flight, etched against the ebony sky.

He rose next to me and wrapped his legs around my waist. We kissed. I reached down and began rubbing our cocks together.

"Come on, let's go take a shower." Benjamin led me into the locker room. He walked through the blackness as if he was holding a flashlight guiding us around the many wooden benches bolted to the floor. The building was open to the sky. As we soaped each other's bodies, the warm water enveloped us in a sheen of safety. I kissed every corner of his face. It was so dark it was as if I was kissing someone blindfolded, which added a layer of thrilling anonymity. I let my hands graze over his body, feeling the muscles of his legs in a new way. I massaged the area behind his knees, surprised at how vulnerable it felt. I massaged his feet, discovering a ridge on his heel that felt like a scar. I moved my hands up his body and cupped his balls. They seemed heavier than I remembered. I pressed my thumb against his perineum eliciting a groan.

I washed under his arms, between his legs, under his feet, all the while slowly massaging his cock bringing him closer and closer to orgasm. Just as it seemed he was going over the top, I would let go and rise to kiss him. Once Benjamin was under control again, I started pulling slightly on his cock until I brought him to the brink again. I did this over and over until finally all I had to do was wrap my hand around his cock and he came. His legs almost buckled as his body convulsed in pleasure. We were laughing as I stood up to kiss him.

"I think we've pushed our luck far enough," I said, "let's get the hell out of here." As we walked out of the locker room, we heard a car door slam and we froze in place.

"Fuck," Benjamin whispered. We stood still side by side, barely breathing, waiting to see if we could hear anyone approaching. I felt my cock shrink to cold water size. After several minutes, we could see lights coming from the direction of the clubhouse.

"Where are our clothes?"

"Fuck if I know, let's get the fuck out of here."

"I can't," I said, "my keys and wallet are in my pants. You stay here and I'll go look. It doesn't matter that much if I get caught, you on the other hand—"

I began looking around the edge of the pool, under a few tables but found nothing. I looked over at the dining room, which was now backlit by lights behind the bar. Someone was heading toward the pool. I began frantically looking under every table until I remembered I had left them by the hedge.

"Come on Ben, we need to go now," I said too loudly. Benjamin came toward me and we ran around the building. I picked up my clothing and looked for the opening we had walked through. Seeing nothing but a straight wall of hedge, I shoved myself through. I pushed and struggled but made it to the other side on pure fear.

The branches scraped against my face, my chest, and my legs. I felt something warm drip down my cheek. I yanked the car keys out of my pocket and threw my clothing into the back seat. We jumped in side by side as I started the car, ripped it backwards and roared out of the parking lot, spewing rocks and dirt in our trail. I sped down the highway until I remembered we were both naked and I slowed down to the speed limit. I turned into the parking lot behind my old high school and we dressed.

"Hey, you're bleeding," Benjamin said when we got back in the car. He reached over and wiped the trail of blood from my face and smeared it on his pants. He looked intently at my face. "Do you need stitches?" I looked in my rearview mirror and felt the cut. It didn't hurt and it didn't feel that deep. My heart was still pounding and sweat was running down my sides. I wondered what would have happened if we had gotten caught?

"Hey what do you think that guy at the country club is going to think when he finds a pair of boxer shorts, a wig and a beard?"

"I can't imagine." It seemed like the beginning of a bad joke.

"I think we should go back."

"Are you nuts?"

"Yes."

"No way."

"I want that stuff back."

"Benjamin, there is no way in hell I am going back there." I turned right on the highway, heading for home. Benjamin looked at me, looked back in the direction of the country club, twitched in his seat, and said nothing.

CHAPTER THIRTY-SEVEN

I sat in my car glancing at my watch every few seconds. It was already 6:45. I knew Mom would be on her patio, wine glass in hand looking at her watch as well. I honked the horn. Mom expected me to be on time. With Aunt Margaret you could be forty-five minutes late and she didn't care, but not Mom. Cocktail hour was exactly that and then we ate. I knew she didn't like losing a portion of that hour to anything. I honked the horn again.

Benjamin emerged from the house stuffed into a pair of blue jeans. He had on a tight black T-shirt and a pair of old cowboy boots. I was dressed in plaid shorts, sandals and a golf shirt. I felt like a wilted rose next to a new blossom.

"Sydney just called me." He turned the air conditioner on high. "She wants to know when I'm coming back." He closed his eyes. "I told her not for a while."

I looked out the window at the rose bushes that lined the driveway, which were beginning to look neglected. "How'd she take it?"

"Not well...not well at all." He sighed. "She doesn't understand why I'm in Iowa and she's sick of lying for me."

"What are you going to do?"

There was a long silence. When he opened his eyes they were angry. "I'm doing it. I'm staying put." He forced a smile. "Come on, let's go eat."

Five minutes later we pulled into my mom's driveway. To my surprise, Aunt Marie's car was parked next to Mom's. I tried to clear out my anxiety over what Benjamin had just told me and focus on the moment.

"Do you have your story straight?" I asked.

He inhaled deeply and let it out in one long breath. "Sure shootin, I do." He sounded forced to me. I tried to take a deep breath as well but only got halfway down my lungs. I knew what Aunt Marie could do.

He stepped out of the car and stood up straight. "I could sure use a shot a whiskey," he said loudly as he walked into the house. "Colleen, we're here, y'all ready for us?"

I sat in my car for a moment trying to imagine feeling that comfortable with someone I hardly knew. It was almost as if it was his house and not mine.

I looked around at the things in the garage as if to reassure myself that this was my mom's home and not Benjamin's. In the corner was a small table where she sat and did crossword puzzles when it was too hot to sit on the patio. Next to it was the workbench with Dad's tools lined up exactly as he had left them. She had moved it to her townhouse almost as if it were a museum piece, everything just as it had always been. The small refrigerator in the other corner was filled with beer and pop. Everything exactly where it was supposed to be.

"Liam, what the hell y'all doing out there?" Clay called out. "Your beer is getting warm."

I walked inside glancing out at the patio where Aunt Marie was sitting, smoking a cigarette. She nodded at me without a smile. In the kitchen, Aunt Margaret was at the counter with her vodka tonic in place, Clay with a Budweiser and a shot glass full of whiskey, his hand on her shoulder. Mom was pouring herself a glass of wine. On the counter was a basket of potato chips with her homemade dip in a small metal bowl, a cutting board covered with cheddar cheese, garlic rounds, pickles and olives. A mason jar filled with beet pickles completed the offering. I poured myself a Stella Artois into a frosty glass mom had pulled from the freezer.

"I sure as hell don't know how y'all drink that sissy beer." Clay threw back his shot of whiskey. He had barely set it down when mom filled it again.

"And I don't know how you drink that crap you're drinking. It tastes like dirty water to me."

"Are you having your first argument?" Aunt Margaret drained her glass and pushed it in my direction. "That is so cute."

"How did you get Aunt Marie out of the house?" I mixed a drink for Aunt Margaret, one half vodka, the other half tonic.

"It was the damndest thing," Mom replied as she looked at the drink I was holding with a raised eyebrow. "She kept saying no but when I mentioned that Clay was coming and that he was from Katy, Texas she said yes. Just like that! Can you imagine?" I felt a flutter of worry and looked at Clay who was polishing off his beer. "Liam, you do know—" Mom started to say.

"What have you boys been up to?" Aunt Margaret interrupted as she took a sip from her drink with a nod in my direction. She gasped. "What on earth did you do to your face?"

Mom spun around and put on her glasses. She marched up to me and stared at the cut on my cheek. "Have you seen a doctor?"

"No, it's fine."

"I'm not so sure young man." She moved in for a closer look and a waft of Estee Lauder Beautiful perfume filled my nostrils. My sisters and I liked to tease that mom was a closet doctor. She always had an answer or a cure for most ailments, and usually she was right. "If you see even a hint of an infection, I want you to see Dr. Maloney immediately." He was her doctor and Mom believed he was infallible, something she used to reserve for the Pope. "Now how in the name of God did that happen?"

"It was my fault, Colleen," Clay said quickly. "We were horsing around. I had on this clunky ring I wear sometimes and it cut him on the face. I've apologized about fifteen times." I wondered when he thought that up.

"Accidents happen, Clay," Mom said as she put the back of her hand on my cheek. "I just hope it doesn't leave a scar."

"Me too." Clay said. "We wouldn't want a pretty little thing like him flawed." Mom and Aunt Margaret laughed a bit uneasily.

"What's so damn funny?" Aunt Marie asked as she walked in and stood next to me.

"Y'all must be Marie." Clay walked around the counter and shook her hand. "I've heard a lot about you. I'm Clay Davis."

"I bet you have," she replied.

"Marie, would you like a whiskey sour?" Mom asked a bit nervously. Marie hated having alcohol pushed at her.

"Why the hell not? It's not like I have to be anywhere tomorrow." A look of gratitude washed over Mom's face. She always assumed that a cocktail took the edge off anyone. I had seen the opposite happen too many times. I suspected Mom was terrified that Marie was going to say something inappropriate to Margaret. As far as I knew, they hadn't spoken since their argument over Leah's pregnancy.

Mom put Marie's drink directly in front of her. She pushed it aside.

"So Mr. Davis," Marie said.

"Please call me Clay."

"Why? I don't know you at all."

Clay looked at me, his face a blank.

"As I was saying, Mr. Davis." She looked at her drink. "Colleen, can I get a cup of coffee?" Mom's hand shook a bit as she filled her percolator with water. "I hear you're from Katy, Texas."

"Yes Ma'am, I am." The glib tone in his voice was gone. "Born and bred."

"What do they say about women born in Texas?" Marie stared intently at Clay.

"Born, bred, bedded and wedded."

Marie let out a small honk of a laugh. "That's it, I knew it was something like that." I started to breathe. "Where did you grow up? What part of town?"

"Do you know Katy?"

"Yes, I know it well," she said with a note of challenge. "My second husband Glen was from Katy."

"Mom, did you know that?" I asked, trying to not sound nervous.

"Of course I did and if Margaret hadn't interrupted me a minute ago, like she does every ten seconds, I would have told you as well."

"Why didn't you tell me sooner?"

"I don't know, guess it didn't seem that important." I picked up my beer and looked at Aunt Marie, who was glaring at Aunt Margaret.

"So Mr. Davis, what part of town did you say you lived in again?"

"Actually Ma'am, I didn't say. My daddy had a ranch just west of town."

"Had?"

"He's no longer with us." His eyes watered.

"I'm sorry to hear that. What about your mother?"

"Mama still lives on the ranch with my kid sisters. They take awful good care of her."

Marie sat up in her chair. "What church did you go to?"

"We weren't church going people." Mom filled his shot glass again.

"That's odd, most southerners are."

"Well, it was a long drive to the Methodist church, and we made it most holidays."

"Did you know Glen Rogers?"

"Can't say that I do."

"That's odd as well." She poured cream and sugar in her coffee and took several sips. "My second husband was Methodist and Glen was the pastor at First United Methodist when you were a little boy."

"You don't know how old I am." Clay said.

"You know, you're right," Marie said. "You got me on that."

"Is this a contest?" I asked, which Marie ignored.

"Guess I assumed you're the same age as Liam."

"I am."

"Then he was the pastor there when you were a boy."

"Like I said, we didn't go that often."

"She looked at the shot glass full of whiskey and the beer in Clay's hand. "You're an odd Methodist, Mr. Davis."

"How's that?"

"Surely you must have heard that expression about Methodists?"

"Which one?"

"They don't drink, swear, smoke or spit," she said without a trace of humor.

"Clearly **you** didn't convert." Clay said, his eyes glowing with energy. Marie said nothing as she took a sip of her coffee. She opened her purse, found her cigarettes and lighter. Without a word she walked out to the patio, coffee cup in hand. Clay threw back his whiskey and asked for the bathroom.

"What the hell is this all about?" I asked. "Why is she grilling him? Mom?" She handed me another beer. "She's not going to start again, is she?"

"Liam, what are you talking about?" Mom started putting away the snacks. "She's just trying to get to know your friend."

"Then why is she calling him Mr. Davis? Since when is she so formal?"

She walked over and put an arm around my shoulder. "Liam, calm down. She's still annoyed with all of us, just be thankful she's here at all. This has nothing to do with either of you."

"Why didn't you tell me that Aunt Marie knows Katy the first time you met Clay?"

"I forgot." I looked at her wondering if she was telling the truth or if I was becoming paranoid.

Mom began putting dinner on the table. Margaret was sipping her vodka tonic, staring into space acting as if she had stumbled into the wrong wedding reception. Clay came out of the bathroom with a smile on his face as if nothing had happened. I felt annoyed with all of them. Marie for being Marie, Mom for not telling me about the Katy connection, Margaret for being so passive and Benjamin for his ease with lying. But mostly I was annoyed with myself. *Why were we lying to my family?*

Yet, somehow when we were eating Mom's pork roast, twice-baked potatoes, salad, homemade bread and a strawberry rhubarb pie, everything seemed normal again. Clay was telling them story after story about his job as a stunt double—another lie—and dealing with the out of control egos of the actors, none of which he mentioned by name.

"One time the scene called for the actor I was working for—"

"Was it Benjamin Graves?" Aunt Margaret blurted. "I would give my right arm to meet him."

"No, no it wasn't him and trust me purty lady, he would love to meet y'all as well. As you would expect, he just loves older women from Iowa. I think y'all would remind him of his own mama." Aunt Margaret beamed as she put her empty wine glass to her mouth. She seemed surprised when nothing came out. I filled it to the brim.

"You've met his mother?" Marie put her hand over her wine glass that Mom was trying to fill. "How would you know his mother?"

I felt tension strike through my alcohol haze.

"At the funeral," Clay said.

"Oh," Marie removed her hand and Mom filled it half way.

"Anyway, this actor was supposed to fall out a ten story building and land in a pool."

364

"I think I saw that movie," I said, "wasn't it—"

"No, it wasn't," Clay said definitively. "This movie was never released. Anyway, I go flying out this window and fall into this pool which had the coldest water known to mankind. I thought my privates had just about disappeared inside me, sorry for the crudeness." Mom smiled, Margaret chuckled, Marie sat stone-faced. "I jump out of the water and they tell the star he has to jump in and act like he had just fallen ten stories. You should have seen the look on his face. He knew how cold the water was, everybody was talking about it. He stood there all pissed off and demanded they heat it to 80 degrees, which they refused. We were almost done shooting and we had all figured out by then it was going to be a bomb."

I wondered what part, if any, of this was true.

"So this big movie star stood there all pouty and whiny refusing to jump in so the director walks up to him and pretends to listen like he's going to give in when suddenly he pushes this guy into the pool and they start filming." Clay let out a laugh that echoed off the walls; Marie grimaced as if it hurt her ears. "The camera's rolling, the actor screaming and thrashing and swearing, saying words I cannot repeat in polite company. The director's yelling at him to get in role so they can film, threatens him with several retakes and the actor realizes that if he does this right, he can get out of the water and go home. He goes under water again and then pops up looking all determined, but in the meantime his hair was off kilter." He let out a horse laugh to rival mine.

"You gotta understand this was one of the biggest questions in Hollywood, did this guy have fake hair? Now we all knew. The director kept filming and didn't say a word. We were all busting a gut trying not to laugh. They finish the scene and he goes flying to his trailer, shivering so violently I thought his teeth were gonna pop out. A few seconds later he comes running out of his trailer, screaming that he was going to destroy this director if anyone saw this film, blah blah blah. The director was acting all innocent as if he had no idea what had happened, which made it even funnier."

"I'll bet it was Ben Affleck," Margaret said.

"I'd love to tell y'all but we signed documents. It would have ruined this guy. His whole image was based on his authenticity."

"Tell us another story," Margaret demanded, sounding about six years old. Clay went off in a different direction while I thought about his secret and my complicity.

The stories continued until it was after ten o'clock, well past Mom's bedtime. She was yawning but I could tell she was enjoying herself, otherwise she would have kicked us all out over an hour ago. The tension between Margaret and Marie had lessened over the course of the evening to the point where they were finally looking at each other. At one point Margaret had leaned towards Marie and said, "I cannot tell you how sorry I am, it kills me to know that I hurt you." Marie had looked at her with no expression, nodded slightly and then to my surprise reached over and touched the back of Margaret's hand lightly. She kept her fingers there for a good minute and then smiled. The tears rolled down Margaret's face.

I stood up and said, "Come on Clay, let's get this kitchen cleaned up so these girls can go home to bed."

"Liam Conor Ashby, you know better than that." Mom picked up the remaining dishes including Margaret's coffee cup, which she had just topped off with a shot of Kahlua. "There's nothing left to do but these few things, you boys scurry on home. Aggie and I are ready for bed, aren't we good girl?" I looked over at her dog. She was standing dutifully in the doorway to Mom's bedroom. She looked cranky.

"Do you boys want to come by my house for a nightcap?" Aunt Margaret rummaged through her purse for her car keys.

"No thanks," I said, "but we will follow you home."

"When am I going to see you again?" Mom asked.

"Not sure, I'm going to Leah's next weekend, I think we're having dinner at Deirdre's on Saturday night. You coming up?"

"No, no, not the right time, some other weekend when it isn't so crazy."

"Colleen, are you sure you don't want to join us in Minnesota?" Clay asked.

"Us?" I replied.

"Hell yes, us. You don't remember inviting me? Are y'all having short term memory problems?"

"When did I invite you?"

"Yesterday, when we were running." He stood next to me and put his hand on my shoulder. I knew I had not invited him.

"You two have fun in Minnesota. Give your sisters a hug for me." She wiped her hands on her apron. She looked at Clay who was telling Margaret and Marie good night. "I sure like your friend, he seems like one of the nicest, no nonsense men I've ever met and my Lord is he good looking."

I hugged her. "I love you, Mom."

She pulled back quickly and looked at me almost as if she hadn't understood what I said. She nodded. She turned to Clay and hugged him, he held onto her as if it was the last hug he was ever going to get.

On the drive to Aunt Margaret's Benjamin was quiet.

"You know that I didn't invite you to Minnesota, don't you?"

"Of course I know." Benjamin looked away. "I don't have to go."

"No, no, I want you to come, just thought it was odd that you lied about the invitation."

"Lie is a pretty strong word." He continued to look away. "I guess I wanted your mom to know how much you mean to me, that's all." He turned towards me, "Do you know how lucky you are?"

"About what?"

"Your mom, Aunt Margaret, hell, even Aunt Marie."

CHAPTER THIRTY-EIGHT

———∞———

We left Mason City early Saturday morning in a driving rainstorm. There had been tornados in the area the night before, and the siren had awakened us at 3 A.M. We had heard banging noises and looked out the window to see the metal patio furniture sliding around as if on a bucking cruise ship. Bolting out of the house we dragged it inside. We were soaking wet, the rain stinging our faces, the wind howling through the cottonwoods, torn leaves on the ground as if it were late October.

Afterwards, with the wind slamming against the house, we laid in bed remembering the worst summer storms of our childhoods. Considering we had only lived a few blocks apart, it was odd that we didn't remember the same storms. We had fallen asleep again with Benjamin's back pressed firmly against my chest.

Benjamin was driving his dad's BMW. Mozart was playing on the radio. I pushed back my seat and closed my eyes. The week had zipped by: work, exercise, sex, good food and wine, movies, reading, long conversations, each day passing seamlessly into the next. I realized for the first time in my life that I had experienced an entire week of living completely in the moment. With a sigh, I realized I was in the past and worrying. I looked over at Benjamin and began to think how I was going to feel when he left. Then I remembered it was only July 1, we had several weeks, didn't we?

Crossing into Minnesota, Benjamin slowed down due to side-by-side semi trucks blocking both lanes. He started honking his horn. I turned up the music. I thought about the fact that even though I had fully expected us to stay with Leah, somehow we were staying with Deirdre.

"What are you thinking about?" Benjamin asked as he roared past the trucks that had finally gotten out of our way.

"My sisters."

"What about them?"

"Nothing you don't already know." I turned the music back down. "I wish they got along better."

"Nothing you can do about it."

"I know that, it's just that I hate seeing Leah give in all the time." The Mozart ended and a Bach cello concerto began.

"What are we going to do this afternoon?" Benjamin asked as he changed the station to country western. I tried to switch it back but he pushed my hand away.

I paused before answering; I hadn't told him that the plan was miniature golf and go-kart racing. It was such a classic Midwestern summer activity with kids that I had felt illogically embarrassed. "There's this small amusement center just on the other side of the Mississippi. We're playing miniature golf and a few other things."

"You're shitting me. Why didn't you tell me sooner?"

"You don't have to do this. I can take my nephews and niece and you can hang out at Deirdre's house."

"Are you out of your mind? I love miniature golf! I haven't played since high school. It was one of the things I did every summer with my sisters. I'm pretty good at it too."

"Who isn't? It's not exactly hard."

He looked over at me. "What's your best score?"

"How the hell am I supposed to remember that?"

"I do. In fact, I should call Lake Links in Clear Lake to see if my score is still the course record."

"Course record?"

"Yes, Liam Ashby, and don't think I haven't noticed the sarcasm in your voice." He scratched his balls. "I shot a 21. You do realize that means I had 15 holes in one."

"That's impossible."

"Just wait and see, my cynical friend, wait and see."

As we pulled into my sister's driveway, the front door burst open and Chris, Andrew and Emily rushed down the steps yelling Uncle Liam, Uncle Liam! Benjamin looked at me and squeezed the back of my neck. I stepped out of the car and bent down to hug them one at a time while they clamored for my attention.

"Hang on guys," I said standing up. "I want you to meet my friend." They stopped talking at once as if a mute button had been pushed. "Clay, meet my three favorite people of all time."

"What about me?" My sister Deirdre asked. I had not seen her come out of the house.

"Four." I said giving her a quick hug.

"Hi, I'm Deirdre."

"Clay Davis. Pleased to meet you, Ma'am. I've heard a lot about you."

"Ma'am?"

"Clay's from Texas."

"What have you heard about me?"

"That you're pretty as all get out and that you have a terrific family." He grinned at her with his perfect white teeth. "I also know that your brother loves you."

She stared at Clay, her arms folded across her chest, a look of skepticism on her face.

"Where's Derek?" I asked.

"Golfing, where else?" She sighed. "He's supposed to be home by noon." I laughed. "Okay, two at the earliest."

"How about Leah?"

"I tried to get them to join us this afternoon but they decided to just come for dinner— guess go karts and miniature golf aren't their thing." She sighed again. "You boys hungry?"

"Sure shootin I am."

"Clay's always hungry."

Deirdre looked at Clay and then at Liam. "Of course he is, just look at him. You don't look like that if you don't eat well, something you need to start doing more of, Liam. You are too thin."

"God, not you too!"

"What does that mean?"

"Mom keeps telling me the same thing."

"Then it must be true."

"I weigh the same."

"Your benchmark is too low." She said this with finality as her children ran around the house to the backyard. "You guys are staying in the boy's room. Why don't you take your stuff upstairs and I'll get lunch ready." Clay headed upstairs first as Deirdre whispered in my ear, "He's gorgeous! Where the hell did you meet him in Mason City?"

"At the restaurant."

"What's he doing in Iowa?'

"It's a long story. I'll tell you later."

Benjamin was looking at the posters taped to my nephew's bedroom walls. Andrew's side was covered with photos of Brett Favre and Chris' side with Derek Jeter. There were twin beds shoved in opposite sides of the room. The room almost looked like it had a line drawn down the middle, each side distinctive with its own toys, books, and clothes.

"They're sports nuts. They get that from their dad."

"Would they like to meet them?"

"Who?"

"Brett and Derek."

"You know them?"

"Not well but yeah, we've met a few times."

"And how would you tell them you know them?"

"Fuck, I forgot that." He reached up and turned on the ceiling fan. "This is getting kind of old, isn't it?"

"More than kind of old, it is really old. Deirdre just asked me how I met you. I want to tell her the truth."

He sat down on a bed and leaned back on his elbows. "What would happen if you did?"

"I have no idea."

"Me either."

"Hey you guys," Deirdre called upstairs. "Lunch is ready."

Benjamin stood up and kissed me lightly on the lips. "Food always wins over courage."

I sent Benjamin downstairs and I walked down the narrow hallway to the guest bathroom. The orange shag carpeting was worn and stained. I passed Emily's bedroom, which was so crammed with stuffed animals you couldn't see the bed. The bathroom had a distinct odor of urine. Deirdre claimed that her sons peed more on the floors and walls than they did in the toilet. The wallpaper was peeling around the edge of the shower. The tile floor was covered with a piece of carpeting that never seemed to dry out, giving the room a damp stale feel. The sink was covered with old toothbrushes, the bristles worn and flattened, and a mostly empty tube of Crest lying in the sink. I washed my face and hands. The only towel I could find was on the floor behind the door.

Walking into the kitchen, I saw Emily sitting on Clay's lap. My nephews were on either side of him. Deirdre looked at me and rolled her eyes. Clay was telling them a rattlesnake story that involved great daring and a minor bite thrown in for dramatic effect. Their eyes were wide and Emily was looking a little pale.

"Enough about reptiles, it's time for food." Deirdre plucked Emily from Clay's lap and set her on a stool. Her arms looked strong with small biceps popping out as she lifted her daughter. Clay stared at them and said, "Howdy, I wouldn't want to mess with you Deirdre. I think your arms are in better shape that your tiny brother here."

"My Uncle Liam is not tiny," Andrew said with determination.

"Sorry little fella, tiny is the wrong word, you're right." He thought for a moment. "How about scrawny, does that work for you?"

"I don't know what that means," Andrew said.

"It means the same thing, Andrew," I said, "Clay and your mom think I am too thin."

"Can we talk about something other than your poor diet and malnourished body?" Deirdre handed us paper plates mounded with turkey and ham sandwiches, potato chips and dill pickles.

"How about this? Why aren't we staying at Leah's?" I asked. I felt a rush of anger I didn't try to hide.

"Well, talk about jumping to a new topic," Deirdre laughed. "You'll have to ask her. When she found out you were bringing your friend, she said you should stay here." She took a bite of her sandwich. "I really don't have a clue what happened." She said this with her mouth full, a sure give away. Whenever uncomfortable topics had arisen over the years, she always started eating. Full mouth meant she didn't have to talk. She took a bite of a pickle and shoved a few potato chips in as well.

I pulled her plate of food away. She looked at me with feigned innocence. "Oh, all right. It was my idea. I'm sure you're not surprised by that. I'm being selfish."

"About what?"

She pulled her plate back and took another bite. I waited patiently while she chewed and swallowed. "I wanted to host you the first time you showed up with a boyfriend." She took a sip of water. "We've been waiting for ten years Liam, for God's sake. I was beginning to think it was never going to happen, especially after that asshole you dated in Boston. I never understood what you saw in him." I glared at her. She saw this, blushed slightly and walked to the sink to refill her glass. "Other than he was good looking. However, and it is an enormous however, compared to Mr. January sitting next to you, Justin looked like Don Knotts." Benjamin laughed and spit out a half eaten potato chip. Deirdre swept it into the trash bucket.

"Anyway, as the oldest, I think it is my responsibility, in fact, my duty to host your new boyfriend." I looked at Benjamin who had inhaled his lunch. "It's really that simple. No subterfuge—Leah completely understood." I said nothing and finished my lunch. Nothing with Deirdre was ever this simple.

She began putting silverware into the dishwasher and out of habit turned on the television that hung from underneath a cabinet. "God, he's beautiful," she said. I looked at the television and saw Benjamin's face. The camera was in tight, his green eyes jumping across the kitchen counter, his look serious and sober. Deirdre turned up the volume. I looked over at Benjamin who had turned bright red.

"I am deeply honored to welcome you to the Princess Diana Memorial Concert," Benjamin's voice said over the television as an image of Diana with her sons at an amusement park flickered across the screen.

"Liam, did you hear that Alyssa Wheelock sold the story of their breakup to *People* for over a million dollars. Can that be real? So tacky." She closed the dishwasher. "Oh, who am I kidding, I'd sell just about anything for a million dollars." Her sons looked at her. "And if you don't stop peeing on the walls, I might just sell the two of you!"

"Can y'all turn that off?" Clay asked. "He kind of bugs me."

"No, we cannot," Deirdre said. "I forgot this is on today." She turned the volume up even higher. "Why does he bug you?"

I looked at Benjamin who sat frozen in place. I jumped up from my chair and said, "Anybody ready for miniature golf?" My nephews and niece bounded to the floor and ran upstairs.

"Talk about changing the topic again. Is your A.D.D. acting up?" Deirdre asked. "Guess I'll have to tape this."

"Deirdre, did you know that Clay was a child prodigy at miniature golf?"

She laughed. "I still want to know why Benjamin Graves bugs you. Maybe you can tell me over dinner." She turned to me. "Being gifted at miniature golf is not exactly like being a young Mozart, is it?" I started to laugh, glanced at Benjamin who looked engaged and competitive and felt my own competition rise to the surface.

"God, don't you two start, okay?" Deirdre said. "It's miniature golf, not the US Open." She opened a drawer and pulled out a pad of paper. "Per usual, Derek isn't here when he is supposed to be." She left a note telling him where we would be. "You know Liam, I'm at the point where I won't wait anymore. I give him five minutes and if he isn't in the car, I leave." Clay frowned, started to say something but stopped. Deirdre looked at him, her eyes daring him to challenge her. "Do you have a problem with this, Cowboy Clay?"

"Not really, Ma'am. Guess I was just feelin' sorry for your husband, standing in the driveway while his wife has left him in the dust."

"If you call me Ma'am again, I am going to slug you. I am only one year older than Liam and in case you've forgotten my name is Deirdre." She got in the back seat with her kids. "You're not some sort of southern, right-wing homosexual are you? My God, do they even exist?"

"Deirdre, calm down, okay?" I said as I backed out of the driveway. "It's not our fault that Derek is late, again."

"Sorry," she said quietly.

We drove the few miles to the miniature golf course. It was on an old, four-lane highway with a Dairy Queen on one side and a faded sign announcing the entrance to the Twin Cities last operating drive-in on the other. It all felt a little seedy and dirty and I loved it. My nephews raced into the shack and began trying out various putters, swinging them wildly while I paid. I grabbed the clubs from their hands and reminded them they were holding putters and not baseball bats. Andrew and Chris started arguing over who was going to be on my team.

"Let's flip a coin." I pulled some change from my pocket. "Since you're the oldest, Chris, heads you play with me, tails you play with Clay, okay?"

"What about me, Uncle Liam?" Emily asked, her small hand reaching out to hold mine.

"You're gonna play with your mom, right? Remember what happened the last time?" She shook her head no. "Your brothers got all impatient with you." Both Chris and Andrew started protesting loudly. "Yes, you were kind of mean to her," I said kneeling down to look Emily in the eyes. "This way you can play behind us and your mom can give you a few lessons. You're gonna be as good as they are by next summer, I promise." I leaned in. "You're riding with me in the go-karts." She smiled broadly and threw her arms around my neck. When I looked up Deirdre mouthed thanks.

I flipped a quarter high in the air while Chris yelled tails. It was tails.

Benjamin immediately pulled him over. "Hey little dude, y'all are now on the winning team. We're gonna kick their skinny asses." Clay put his hand on Chris' shoulder and they walked several feet away. He knelt on the asphalt and began speaking quietly to Chris while sketching a few things on the dirt that lined the parking lot.

"What are they talking about, Uncle Liam?" Andrew asked.

"I have no idea. All that matters is that we need to concentrate. If we want to win, we need to stay focused. Don't let your brother or Clay trash talk you or get under your skin. I have a feeling that's what they're going to try." We walked to the first hole. My heart was thumping, which didn't surprise me. I could get worked up watching billiards.

"Since we won the toss, we get to decide who goes first," Clay said. "We want y'all to start."

"Is that in the rule book?" I asked.

"My rule book, little man, my rule book." He swung his putter back and forth with evenness I had only seen watching golf on television. Then he did a few back bends and leg stretches as he started fumbling with the club as it twisted in the air. Somehow he passed it between his legs all while he seemed to be on the verge of tipping over. He teetered and tottered, the club moving over his body as if guided by unseen hands. He bent over and touched his toes and announced, "Okay, now I'm ready."

The first hole was up a ramp, through a windmill and down to the hole. I stood over the ball remembering the many rounds I had played as a kid. It was the one summer activity I was good at, other than running faster than David Meeker, the neighborhood bully. I hit the ball firmly, watched it race up the ramp, down the other side and into the hole. Andrew let out a yell, put his ball on the small rubber mat and smacked his ball. It raced through the windmill, hopped into the hole and popped out, resting a few inches from the cup. He quickly putted out as I turned around to watch Clay and Chris. Clay hit his first and it rimmed out of the cup and careened over to a corner. I turned to high five Andrew but he wasn't next to me. Looking back, I saw Andrew emerge from behind a small evergreen. He stood behind Chris ready to shout or do something to distract him. Just as I started to tell him not to, Chris whipped his club up and back and the head of the club hit Andrew firmly in the forehead directly over his right eye. There was a loud thunk. Andrew slapped his hand to his forehead and stood there without moving. When he pulled his hand away, it was covered in blood, which started gushing down his forehead. Deirdre screamed, Chris began to cry and Benjamin yelled, "fuck!" I jumped forward and knelt next to Andrew. There was a gash in his forehead several inches long, the skin neatly split in two. Andrew looked at me, the blood pouring into his eye and said, "What happened, Uncle Liam?"

I held my hand on the cut, the blood gushing through my fingers. Someone handed me a towel, which I held firmly against the wound.

Benjamin said, "I'll call an ambulance." His voice was calm and authoritative, with no trace of a Texas accent. I looked over at my sister who was fumbling through her purse looking for her phone. Benjamin waved her off and called 911.

"Where the fuck is Derek when I need him the most?" She spoke softly.

"Deirdre, that is not the issue right now. Do you have all you need for the hospital?" I asked.

"Like what?"

"Insurance card, credit card, ID's, all that crap." I pulled Andrew into my lap and pressed him against my chest. He was limp in my arms.

"Of course I do," she snapped. At that moment, Derek pulled into the parking lot. He looked over at us and waved with a big smile. Then he saw Andrew in my lap and the color drained from his face. Deirdre walked over to him and they started arguing. Chris was standing a few feet away, repeating over and over, between sobs, how sorry he was. Clay picked him up in one arm, Emily in the other and they walked a few feet away. I looked back at my sister who was shouting at her husband. He was trying to walk towards us but she kept blocking his way.

Moments later the ambulance arrived and the paramedics took over. Andrew was moaning in pain as he was lifted into the ambulance with his mom at his side. Derek followed in the car. I put Chris and Emily in the backseat. Chris' eyes were wild. I knelt and hugged him. He cried on my shoulder.

"Andrew's gonna be fine Chris, trust me, okay?" He nodded but his eyes were doubtful.

When I closed the door to our car, Benjamin pulled me aside. "That could have been much worse, he could have lost an eye." He spit on the ground. "What a fuck up."

"What do you mean?"

"Your brother-in-law."

CHAPTER THIRTY-NINE

Two hours later we were sitting on Deirdre's back deck, cold beers in hand while Chris and Emily watched a *Harry Potter* movie in the family room. Deirdre had called to say they were on their way home. She was hovering between rage and tears.

"We certainly got a taste of suburbia today," I said as I put my beer on the deck. I was drinking too fast.

Benjamin gave a half smile, "Yeah, we did, kind of makes me sad."

"Sad? Why?"

"Didn't you want this when you were a boy?" Benjamin polished off his beer. "The house, the kids, the yard with the croquet set, back to school night, baseball games and Halloween, especially Halloween. Didn't you always want to celebrate Halloween with your own kids?"

"Suppose so." I picked up my beer again.

"That's a bit half hearted."

"I guess I sort of knew all along I wouldn't have this kind of life." I pulled two more beers out of the cooler that sat in the shade by the house.

"Oh, that's right. You've known you were a homo the second you popped out."

"We are not having that conversation. Anyway, I've gotten to spend many holidays with Deirdre's kids, especially Christmas and summer vacations. And I have been here for Halloween a couple of times as well. What about your niece and nephew? Don't you do this kind of stuff with them?"

Benjamin looked away. "No. My sisters don't believe in Halloween or the Easter Bunny or Santa Claus. They're raising their kids with no mythology, no mystery, no fun at all."

"Why?"

"I have no idea. Probably some book one of them read. They are always reading the latest crap on child rearing, no doubt trying to make sure they don't do the same shit our mom did."

"You need to spend Halloween here. It is a blast, a lot more fun than Christmas."

"I would love that but it's not exactly around the corner to fly here from Morocco."

That stopped me cold. Had I really forgotten he was leaving? I was planning our twenty-fifth wedding anniversary and meanwhile, he was leaving town in a few weeks.

"Maybe next year," I said weakly.

Several minutes of awkwardness were interrupted by the slam of the front door. Derek walked out the back door looking grim as he placed Andrew in my lap. Andrew was pale, his eyes filmy with a huge bandage covering the top right half of his forehead. His shirt was stained with dried blood that had turned a brownish color. He leaned into my chest with his head on my heart. I wrapped my arms around him.

"Thirteen stitches, thirteen damn stitches, can you believe this?" Deirdre said as she pulled a beer from the cooler. She did not offer one to her husband. "I cannot even imagine what that ambulance is going to cost or the emergency room. He could have lost an eye!" A sob ran through her body. She angrily wiped her tears away. "None of this would have happened if you had been there Derek, none of this!"

Derek looked at me and started to say something but she cut him off.

"I don't want to hear any of your excuses about your slow round of golf or about traffic, none of it! It's all bullshit, it's bullshit every, single, time. You were late for our wedding and you will be late for my funeral." She let out another sob that rattled through her chest. "What an idiot I am. What kind of man is late for his own wedding? I should have walked out of that church and never looked back."

I stood up, handed Andrew to Benjamin and walked over to her. I put my hands on her shoulders. I spoke quietly. "Deirdre, I know you're upset but you are going to upset Andrew even more. Can't you at least wait until the two of you are alone?"

The tears were sliding down her face. She looked up at me and then down at her feet. She let herself cry for a few minutes. She did not move towards me for an embrace but neither did she pull away. She brushed away her tears and went back into the house.

"I am sorry," Derek said.

I wanted to yell at him, to demand that he change his behavior, but I knew from experience that the more he was challenged about his behavior the worse it got, plus this was not my fight.

I heard the front door open and then my sisters talking in the kitchen. My sister Leah let out a gasp and then burst out the back door and without saying hello, scooped Andrew out of Benjamin's arms and walked out into the back yard. Benjamin looked at his empty lap and then at me.

"That must be Leah?" he said.

"Yes, that is my sister Leah," I said loudly. "This is Clay Davis." I pointed at Benjamin. She looked over her shoulder and gave a small wave.

"Sorry for the inside look at Ashby family drama." I put my hand on Benjamin's leg.

"Apology not needed, this is *Leave it to Beaver* compared to my family. Clearly y'all love each other which...."

Later after everyone had either left or gone to bed, Clay, Deirdre and I were having a drink on her back porch. A strong wind was keeping the mosquitoes at bay.

"What a day." Deirdre stretched her legs out in front of her and arched her back like a cat. "I am so tired I am beginning to see double."

"Why do you think the accident wouldn't have happened if Derek had been there? It's not like we weren't watching them," I asked.

"I know that, I was there after all. We were all watching them."

"Then, what was your point?"

"You know him, Liam. I'm surprised I have to explain this to you." She sat up and took a sip of her Amaretto. "You know how paranoid he is, he worries about everything and always expects the worst to happen. I think he would have seen the few times Chris was swinging the club back and forth like a wild man and made sure he stopped."

"I saw that too. I tried to stop him." Clay shook his empty beer can.

"I know, Clay, and I appreciate that. It's just that, hell, this is so hard to explain, it's just that Derek always expects another bad thing to happen. He absolutely hates surprises of any kind, everything has to be mapped out. When we go on vacation, every day is scheduled, every route memorized, when we are going to stop for lunch, oh my God, it never stops. Anyway, he would have stood next to Chris on every hole and he would have always known where Andrew was. This accident would not have happened. The one time his compulsive behavior would have served a good purpose and he was on the golf course, again."

"Do you dislike him this much?" I asked, surprised that I asked.

Deirdre yawned loudly, stood up and kissed us both on the cheek and said good night.

"That's one way to avoid answering a question," Benjamin said.

Upstairs in the kid's bathroom, I brushed my teeth and washed my face while Benjamin watched me, sitting on the edge of the toilet.

"It does smell like piss in here," he said. We exchanged spots while he brushed his teeth. His beard was still on and he studiously avoided getting toothpaste on it.

Back in our room, he asked, "Does she hate Derek?" He pulled off his beard and sighed with pleasure.

"Hate is a strong word although this was a level of dislike I have never seen before. I think she's just tired."

"Dude, that's more than just tired, I know that kind of female anger. God I'm glad I dumped Alyssa's sorry ass, should have done it a year ago." He stripped off his clothes and fell into the twin bed, his feet dangling over the end. I fell into my own bed and was asleep in seconds. I was dreaming I was trick or treating with Benjamin as himself. I was telling everyone that my boyfriend had a Benjamin Graves mask on. I awoke to a scream and a yell. The door to our bedroom burst open and a figure dove into the other bed. I could hear Emily sobbing hysterically. I pulled on my shorts and ran down the hall.

"Now what?" I yelled.

Deirdre was sitting on the floor with Emily in her lap. Derek was behind Deirdre with a hand on her shoulder.

"Emily says she saw a strange man come out of the bathroom," Deirdre said.

I knelt and put a hand on her knee. "Did you forget that Clay was staying over tonight?"

"It wasn't him Uncle Liam, it wasn't him." She started crying.

"Are you positive?"

"Why would she lie about this, Liam?" Deirdre asked.

"I'm not saying she is lying, maybe she forgot? Are you sure it wasn't Clay?"

"He didn't have a beard," my niece said empathically.

Fuck, fuck, fuck! Benjamin must have needed to use the bathroom. I looked down the hall towards our bedroom. The door was open but it was dark inside.

"Clay is certainly a sound sleeper," Deirdre said.

"Your boys are too," I said knowing I sounded ridiculously defensive. "You must have had a nightmare," I said hoping she would agree.

"No I didn't Uncle Liam, I was awake and I saw a man just as big as Clay but, but.."

"But what?"

"He didn't have a beard." She paused looking anguished. "I...I...I don't think he had a beard." She started sobbing.

"Where did he go after he left the bathroom?" Derek asked.

Shit, we're busted, I thought.

Emily looked at her dad and said, "I closed my eyes."

"Maybe he went downstairs," Derek said, "I'll check things out."

Deirdre picked up Emily and took her into their bedroom.

"Make sure Clay isn't dead," she said as she closed her door.

I went into our bedroom, closed the door, and turned on the light. From under the covers I heard, "Are you alone?"

"Of course I am," I snapped.

"That was so fucking stupid of me." He sat up, squinting in the harsh light. "I really needed to pee and just assumed everyone was asleep. When I came out of the bathroom, there she was, right across the hall with her light on. She screamed as if she had seen a ghost and I ran down the hall. Why didn't I use the bathroom downstairs? What an idiot."

"It's okay Benjamin, she'll be fine but I need to sleep. Fuck, what a day." I turned off the light but sleep was not something that happened for a long time.

Sunshine awakened me the next morning. I had been dreaming that Deirdre was on *Oprah*, talking about the record amount of money *People* had paid her for her inside story on the outing of

Benjamin Graves. I got out of bed and looked across the room at Benjamin, who was sleeping on his back, the sheets pushed to the floor. The room was stuffy and warm. I turned on the ceiling fan, shut the blinds and left Benjamin to sleep.

No one else was up. I made a pot of coffee and began washing dishes, something Mom usually did. When I finished cleaning the kitchen, I poured a cup of coffee and went out the front door, picked up the newspaper from the middle of a rose bush and sat down on the concrete front steps. I leaned back and let the warm July sun seep into my bones.

What a mess floated through my mind and yet, and yet, something else was going on, just under the surface. Was I happy? Could that be possible? An injured nephew, a traumatized niece, an angry sister and a famous boyfriend who was pretending to be someone else. What a mess. I smiled.

CHAPTER FORTY

———∞———

We were speeding along Interstate 35, the mid-afternoon sun intense on my face. Benjamin was driving. We had cut our trip short. On Sunday, Andrew and Deirdre were exhausted and in bed, Derek was withdrawn and Leah wasn't answering her phone, so we left. Chris and Emily were sad that we were leaving but I assured them we would be back soon. We? I shook my head.

"Do you know you shake your head more than any other person I've met?" Benjamin asked.

"Maybe it's because I have such an interesting internal dialogue going on."

"Or you're nuts?"

"That's always a possibility." I looked out the window. Stretching for miles in either direction were enormous wind turbines planted on the curving patchwork ground. I felt the buzz of my cell phone.

I answered without looking to see who it was. "Hello," I said impatiently.

"Don't you use that tone with me, Missy," Gregg said.

"Sorry, Gregg, odd timing, that's all."

"What does that mean?"

"Clay and I were talking."

"Talking? Why aren't you fucking like every newly formed couple does day and night."

"We're in a car, he's driving eighty miles an hour and it's daylight."

387

"That never stopped me. Why haven't you filled me in yet?" I knew what he wanted but didn't want to give it to him. "I cannot believe you haven't told me. Spill it. What does his dick look like? How long? Cut or uncut? What word comes to mind when you think of his balls. Lemons? Eggs? Softballs?"

"I can't really talk right now."

"Why not?"

"He's sitting next to me."

"So?"

"What's going on?" Benjamin asked.

"Gregg wants me to describe your cock to him."

Benjamin burst out laughing. "Y'all are shitting me."

"No, it's something he insists on with all his friends. He must know what their boyfriend's cocks look like. It's how he decides whether the relationship is going to last."

"Exactly, which is why I knew Justin was…." I pulled my phone away from my ear.

"So tell him," Benjamin said. He unzipped his shorts, raised his hips slightly and slipped them down to his ankles. His cock flopped across his thigh.

"I can't do this." I felt aroused and foolish.

"Yes you can." Benjamin and Gregg spoke at the same time. Benjamin's cock was now standing straight up against his belly.

"Put me on speaker phone," Gregg demanded. "Hi Clay, I'm Gregg. It would be polite for me to say at this point that I've heard a lot about you but that would be a lie. Liam has gone underground since he met you. You're not some sort of mass murderer, are you?"

"No sir, can't say that I am."

"You're Southern? I adore Southerners."

"I'm from Texas."

Benjamin pulled his cock down between his legs and let it slap up against his stomach.

"I'm waiting," Gregg said.

Benjamin ran his hand up and down his cock a few times.

"All right, already." I looked at Benjamin's cock. "Well, it's on the large side."

"Inches, we want inches."

"I've never measured it."

"I have." Benjamin answered. "It's eight and three quarters inches."

Gregg gasped. "No fucking way."

"Yes sir, that is the truth."

"I told you it wasn't a short story," I said.

"So y'all have told him what it looks like," Benjamin said.

"No, no, nothing like that."

"All he told me, Clay, was that it was large but since Liam has only seen three erect penises in his entire life, his own, Justin's and mine, I figure he had no idea what large meant in this context."

"You've seen Gregg's erection?"

"Of course he has. We've shared rooms many times and I always have a morning hard on, in fact I absolutely insist that my friends wake up with morning woodies."

"He's kidding," I said.

"I thought you told me that you two have never had sex," Benjamin said with a noticeable lack of accent.

"We have never had sex and I have seen his erection once when he got up in the middle of the night to pee when we were sharing a bedroom in Provincetown. I had insomnia, he turned the light on and there it was, inches from my face. I was six inches away from six inches!" I grinned at Benjamin.

"You horrible, horrible bitch, you know I am closer to eight!"

"Only if you start measuring from your asshole."

"Liam Ashby, if I were there right now...." Gregg started laughing. "God I miss you. Anyway, back to Clay's cock."

Benjamin looked at me expectantly.

"Okay Gregg, it's just shy of nine inches, stands straight out from his body but curves at the head. His balls remind me of ripe lemons. He has blonde pubic hair and doesn't manscape, doesn't need to. Did I forget anything?"

"Didn't you say it was beautiful?" Benjamin asked.

"No, I didn't. You said that about mine."

"Before you two start fucking and end up dying in a fiery combination of metal, corn and hog parts, let's change the subject," Gregg said, his voice a pitch higher than normal. "Liam, are you coming on Wednesday or Thursday?"

"Where are y'all going?" Clay asked.

"To Provincetown, in ten days—didn't I tell you that?" I said.

"No, I don't think so."

"Bring him as well," Gregg said. "You'll have your own bedroom. Steve isn't coming down that weekend after all."

"Thanks Gregg, I think I will take y'all up on that offer. That's mighty kind of you."

I looked at him, pleasure pulsating through my chest.

"So when are we going?" Benjamin asked.

"Thursday, home on Monday."

"Desperate to see you both," Gregg said. "Counting the minutes." He hung up.

"Are you serious?" I asked as he pulled his shorts up.

"Damn straight I am."

"But…."

"But what?"

I remembered there was a shared bathroom for the guest rooms. "There is absolutely no way we could stay with him."

"Why not?"

"Shared bathroom."

"Oh."

"I need to tell you about my nightmare. Do you remember when Deirdre mentioned that Alyssa sold her story to *People*?"

"Alyssa would never do that."

"Well, I dreamt that my sister did, and it wouldn't be hard to substitute Gregg in the same nightmare."

"You don't trust him?" He hit the brakes hard as we came over a hill to see both lanes blocked by enormous trucks.

Did I? I imagined if the roles were reversed and Gregg was dating Benjamin. I knew I would never betray his trust and I didn't think he would betray mine but then I thought about Deirdre. She was broke, her marriage possibly teetering, three kids, college educations looming.

"I just don't know.

"Of course if I just went public, we wouldn't have this problem any longer."

"Are you shitting me?"

"Yes." He laid on his horn. The truck in the passing lane slowed down even more. "We wouldn't' have *that* problem but we would have a million others."

"If I were a woman none of this would be happening," I said. Benjamin moved back to the right lane, slowed down to sixty and set the cruise control.

"Certain aspects wouldn't be happening like with your family and Gregg, that is true, but you do remember what happened at the airport. That is my life, at least right now. Which is why I have gone in disguise many, many times, long before I met you. Why do you think I'm so good at it? So even if you were a woman, would I want to go to Cape Cod, go out to dinner, the beach as myself? No, I wouldn't." He turned and looked at me. "I've never been to Provincetown, hell, I've never been to Cape Cod. I want to relax and take it in without all that other crap. Hey, why don't we rent a house?"

"What will I tell Gregg?"

"Tell him I'm a privacy freak."

"I've already bought my plane ticket and didn't you say you would not fly commercial again?"

"I'll arrange a jet, you can use your ticket some other time."

"I am assuming you know that Provincetown is the Mecca for gay men from all over the country. It will be crawling with homos." I turned the air conditioning down.

He looked at me with a raised eyebrow. "Liam, I haven't been living under a rock the last ten years. Didn't I tell you that I've met many gay guys and lesbians through my work? Don't you think they might have mentioned Provincetown once or twice?"

"I just didn't think that a big butch, straight-at-the-time guy like you would have registered that fact."

"That word reminds me of a conversation I had with Jimmy, my make up guy for that movie I made with Kate." I wondered which Kate: Hudson, Beckinsale, Winslet? "We were talking about the director, can't think of his name. Anyway, I asked Jimmy what the director's story was. Was he or wasn't he gay?"

"I thought you rejected labels."

"You're never gonna let that go, are you?" I shook my head no. "Jimmy replied, I'm sure he has inclinations towards being gay—he's not fully registered—but definitely has inclinations. I thought that was the funniest damn response."

I smiled.

"You're not laughing."

"It's not really a laugh out loud kind of comment, is it?"

"I did."

I thought for a minute. "It reminds me of one of those old *Laughter is the Best Medicine* stories from *Readers Digest*. I don't think I ever laughed out loud once all the years I read those things when I was a kid. I did smile quite often and once or twice I had to cover my mouth to prevent a small guffaw from coming out."

"You're giving me shit, aren't you?"

"What makes you think that, Mr. Graves?"

"Everyone laughs at my stories."

"You are kidding, aren't you?"

"Sort of." Benjamin let out a minor smile. "They do usually laugh when I tell a funny story."

"Doesn't that get annoying?"

"What's annoying about everyone thinking you're hysterical?"

"But what if you aren't?"

"I am."

"You just weren't."

"That's your opinion."

"That is exactly my point. Senses of humor vary like personality types. If everyone laughs at your stories regardless of what comes out of your mouth, then they are sycophants and you're...you're...." I stopped myself before I said, you're a fool.

"I'm a what?"

"I was going to say, then you're foolish." I decided that sounded less harsh than fool.

"Foolish, huh?" He started driving faster. "First humorless and now I'm foolish. Any other terms of endearment for me?"

"Didn't you ask me to always be honest with you?"

"I didn't mean it." He slowed the car down and his face relaxed. "I suppose you have a point but can we change the subject?"

"Okay," I said, wondering how many Aunt Marie genes were buried inside me. "I don't think you have a real sense of what P-town is like on a busy summer weekend."

"I've been to plenty of summer resorts."

"Name one that has a 75 year old transvestite in a stars and stripes bikini, pulling a red wagon holding her sound system, and standing in front of Town Hall singing Frank Sinatra songs."

"No fucking way."

"That's just the beginning. Cher on a scooter, drugged out muscle boys, dykes on bikes, lipstick lesbians, gay tourists from Des Moines, bears...."

"Bears?"

"Chubby, hairy, shirtless men in leather."

"I don't think Cher needs work so badly she is doing the summer circuit in Provincetown."

I laughed.

"That wasn't supposed to get a laugh," Benjamin said, looking confused.

"I see I have my work cut out for me." I sat up in my seat. "I have two weeks to get you in shape for Homo Disney World."

"I'm in great shape."

"You don't mind letting yourself go for the next two weeks, do you? Several gallons of ice cream would be a good start."

"Why would I do that?"

"You need a paunch or something to bring it down a notch."

"Am I detecting a jealous streak?"

"Maybe."

"Were you jealous of Justin?" he asked.

I glared at him.

"Hey, look at that. I got one of those famous Liam looks. Now *that's* funny."

"No, it isn't. Do you like being reminded of fucked up relationships? Can I tease you about Alyssa?"

He was quiet for several minutes. "No, I guess you can't. Sorry. I won't bring his name up again."

We rode in silence for several miles. As we crossed into Iowa, Benjamin asked, "Should we stay in Provincetown or some other town?"

"You know this is going to be expensive to do this at the last minute."

"You do realize that I'm loaded, don't you?"

"I realize that, but it doesn't affect me, does it?" I wondered how loaded loaded was.

"You're a piece of work. You'd be surprised at how many people are obsessed about how much money I have."

"I'll call a couple of realtors when we get home," I said, not asking the question I knew he wanted me to ask.

"You know what? I'll handle this, or at least my guy will. Just give me the names of towns where we should stay. The key things are I want to be on the water and I want privacy."

"We should stay in Truro then, it's the next town over from P-town." I felt a stab of annoyance wondering if he thought I couldn't handle this.

"Done. So, tell me, what do you like about Cape Cod the most?"

I started to answer but then I thought about the things I loved: riding my bike through the dunes, the air perfumed by fallen pine needles; swimming in the ocean at the very tip of the Cape, the setting sun a burst of orange on the horizon; visiting friends in Truro, having drinks on their deck; the only sound the waves rolling across the beach.

"I think it is better left unsaid. You'll get to discover it on your own and I will get to relive it through your eyes. It's a really special place."

"I'll arrange the jet. We'll fly out of Charles City." We pulled up in front of my house. "Do you want to go for a run and a swim?"

"That sounds great. I'll be there soon."

"How soon?"

I ran into the house without answering him.

When I drove around the back of his house, Benjamin was ready, running shorts and shoes on, his skin glistening with sunscreen.

"It's all set, we've got a house in Truro."

"It was that simple?"

"Apparently."

"Rental car?"

"Handled."

"Bikes?"

"Of course, the only thing I didn't find out is whether there is a golf course in the area."

"You play golf?"

"Yeah, I love it. John Bankman and I play at his club every chance I get."

I had a flashback to the last round of golf I played with Dad. He had shot his best round and I had played my worst. I wanted to throw my clubs in the marsh that lined the road leading from the back nine. The next time Dad asked me to play I said no.

"I haven't played in a long time."

"Did you ever play golf with Derek?" Benjamin asked.

"Never. He is too good and he is too obsessed. Do you want to know why he was late for his wedding? " Benjamin nodded. "Apparently he was playing the best golf of his life and he tried to squeeze in an extra nine."

"Hard core man, that's hard core."

"That's Derek."

CHAPTER FORTY-ONE

———∞———

When I arrived at work the next night I was exhilarated. Everything was going so well it was beginning to feel like I had stumbled into a fantasy. Never, not once in my life had I expected to feel like this. Every part of my being was hungry: for sex, exercise, food, and for the first time in my life-reciprocated love.

Seeing Sue at work, I felt a rush of emotion that was overwhelming in its intensity. Then I saw Georgia Dee and felt the same thing. I wanted to tell them how much they meant to me, how much I loved Sue, how much I admired Georgia Dee, but I didn't. It reminded me of being pleasantly buzzed on alcohol when others in the room were sober.

"You look odd," Sue said plopping down on a bar stool and rummaging through her purse. "So odd that I am not sure that I, the person who knows you better than anyone, including your Texas longhorn," she said exaggerating the word long, "really knows what is going on."

She came around the bar, put a hand under my chin and looked into my eyes. "I get it, you're besotted, aren't you?" She pushed my chin away, found a glass, filled it with ice and water. "Well, enjoy it bud, it doesn't last." She took a sip of water and walked away. When she turned back, her eyes were full. "Really, Liam, enjoy it. Do you know how rarely you get to experience this and how short it lasts?

Sometimes days, other times if you're lucky a few months or so and then it all turns to shit."

She grabbed her purse and walked to the bathroom. I wanted to tell her she was wrong, that it could last longer, it could last years and that she would find it again someday, but then a voice countered that Sue was right and I was naive at best and no doubt headed for another disappointment. I shook my head violently as if to empty it of any other voices—I wanted no other voices, just the besotted one. Besotted? Where in the hell did she come up with that word?

She came back to the bar, her face flushed. "Sorry for the melodrama. I hate it when I act like that." She shoved her purse into a corner under the bar. "I should be excited. Karl is coming tonight, with his kids." She said the last few words under her breath. "He's gotten so skittish since the homo inquisition. It takes him forever to return my calls and then we only talk for a few minutes."

"We weren't that bad, were we?"

"No, no, you were fine. I think that somehow he just doesn't believe that the two of you aren't hitting on me somehow and playing some odd game with him."

"I don't know about this one, Sue, he seems to be living in some weird parallel universe where no gay people exist. Clearly, Clay and I need to make out in front of him."

"Can we schedule that?" She groaned. "Did that sound as lame as I'm afraid it sounded?"

"Yes."

"Let's just talk to each other like normal people, okay?" she said.

"Okay, let's go back a step. He thinks Clay and I are pretending to be a gay couple while secretly hitting on you? Is that it?"

"That seems kind of dumb, doesn't it."

"Dumb is one word."

"I must be wrong."

"I hope so. Ask him out!"

"Didn't I just say that I'm going to do that?"

"Tonight," I said.

"Hell no, I am not ready to do that tonight. His kids are with him."

"I suppose that would be a bit awkward. You need to get him alone." I began emptying the dishwasher and placing wine glasses on the shelf behind me. "Let's see, why don't you tell him I want to talk to him about the other night, have him come into the bar."

"I have no idea what I would say to him."

"How about, would you like to go out to dinner with me?"

"That feels a bit retro and passive."

"How about, I want to go out to dinner with you."

"I don't think I can do this." She walked into the dining room.

The evening was quiet. It was the 4th of July and most people were at family BBQs or the fireworks at Clear Lake. When Sue placed an order for a Bud Light and two root beers, I knew that Karl et al had arrived.

"How does he look?" I placed the drinks on her tray.

"Better than ever."

"Why so morose?"

"He barely smiled at me when he sat down." She stood up straight and tucked her blouse in the back. "How can I ask a man out on a date when he won't smile at me? And what the hell did I do to him?"

"Maybe his mood has nothing to do with you."

"Perhaps but, oh hell, I am feeling so paranoid about this. You know what? I can't wait. I am sending him into the bar as soon as I deliver their drinks. I need to get this over."

She almost ran into the dining room. Moments later Karl walked in heading straight for me. He had on a white golf shirt that was too big and baggy chinos. I smiled at him but he did not smile back; some might even call it a glare. I turned away from him. He was a few steps from the bar when Sue came out of the kitchen and intercepted him. She took him by the hand to the other end of the bar. I wanted to hear what they were saying but kept my distance. Suddenly the conversation grew louder.

"Are you asking me out on a date? Well, hell…."

I looked down at them. Karl was shaking his head no. He put a hand on her shoulder and whispered something in her ear and then went back to the dining room without acknowledging me. Sue stood there for a few seconds, her body rigid, and then walked over to me.

"What happened?" She was pale and her eyes were moist but I knew she would not cry.

"He said, I don't date pushy women, especially the kind that ask men out and I don't date women whose best friends are fags."

" He did not say that!"

"Well, not exactly but you get the gist."

"What did he say—exactly?"

"Quote, 'Are you asking me out on a date? Hell, I can't do that.'"

"That's it?"

"Yes, that's all he said. The rest I read in his eyes."

"He really didn't say anything else?"

"Well, he also said that he couldn't date someone who hung out with the kind of people I hang out with."

I felt an old anger, an anger that seemed to have been with me my entire life. "Fuck him."

"That's what I thought I was going to do." She looked at me, her face covered in disappointment and walked back into the dining room.

"What a fucking asshole," I said to no one in particular. I wanted to go in and tell that prick what I thought of him but figured he probably wouldn't care. She came back to the bar and ordered two martinis up.

"I think you should ask him out again."

"Are you crazy? I'm not even sure I can ask him what he wants for dinner."

"No, I'm not, maybe you misinterpreted what he said. Tone it down, don't ask him out to dinner, try lunch or suggest you meet for a cup of coffee."

"What is your problem? He said he couldn't possibly go on a date with me, and now I know he is just another homophobic hick."

"Maybe he is and maybe he isn't. And if he is, the only way he is going to change is to meet people who will convince him of the errors of his ways."

I poured Bombay gin into a tumbler and began shaking it violently back and forth. "After you have coffee with him, the four of us will go out to dinner."

"I am not going to be used as bait for your homosexual agenda."

"I don't have an agenda." I poured out the martinis. "Well, maybe I do but so what? The only way people get over their bigotry is by getting to know the people they are afraid of."

"I thought the whole point of this was for me to find a boyfriend, not to be the queer Rosa Parks." She picked up her tray. "Did that analogy work?"

"No, it didn't"

She said softly, "Maybe I will ask him out for coffee."

CHAPTER FORTY-TWO

———∞———

"So how big is this plane again?" I asked, coffee swirling in my stomach.

"You're not afraid of flying, are you? You seemed fine on the flight to LA," Benjamin said.

"That was a real plane, not a puddle jumper." I picked a hangnail on my thumb, which started to bleed. I put it in my mouth to stop the bleeding.

"This is not a puddle jumper, it's a Gulfstream 550," Benjamin said.

"I will ask again, how big is it?"

"Hell if I know, I think it can seat fifteen or sixteen."

"Sounds tiny to me."

"Just relax Liam, it's a great way to fly, you're gonna love it."

"Do you own it?" I went to work on my other thumb.

"Hell no, do you know how expensive it is to maintain your own plane?"

"You're worried about money?"

"Of course not, but I don't need to own a plane. This is easier."

"John Travolta owns his own plane."

Benjamin laughed as he exited off the highway. "Don't get me started on that one."

He drove into the parking lot of the small Charles City airport and parked his car underneath an oak tree in a far corner. He pulled a baseball cap and large sunglasses out of his bag. "Here's the drill. The plane is over there." He pointed at a silvery jet shimmering in the harsh sunlight. "I'm going to grab my bag and high tail it over there. "

"Tell me again why you're not in disguise?"

"Because I'm tired of it." He was scanning the parking lot. I looked around as well; we were the only two people in the parking lot. We both got out of the car and went to the trunk to get our luggage, the July heat and humidity hitting me like a hot slap across the face. Benjamin pulled the cap down as low on his forehead as he could and hurried across the parking lot. I followed, walking as slowly as I could. Walking the few steps into the plane, sweat pouring down my forehead, I was greeted by a middle-aged woman who could have been Susan Sarandon's sister.

"Hi, I'm Michelle." She took my luggage from me and stowed it in a cabinet. "Can I get you something to drink?"

"A glass of water would be great. I'm Liam by the way." She smiled warmly at me. There was something so calming about her that I momentarily forgot about my small plane phobia. I looked into the cabin wondering where Benjamin was. There were four white leather seats facing each other, and behind them was a couch with two more leather chairs and then behind that a table and chairs set up for dinner. There were several vases full of roses in a variety of colors. A Beethoven piano concerto was playing softly in the background.

I sat down in one of the chairs, sinking deeply into the soft leather. Michelle handed me a crystal glass with ice, water, and a wedge of lemon. She walked to the front of the plane as Benjamin emerged from the back, eating an apple. He was bending forward slightly, the top of his head almost touching the roof.

"Does this seem like a puddle jumper to you?" He grinned and took a large bite.

"It's not exactly a 747." I drained my glass of water.

Michelle asked us to take our seats and fasten our seat belts. I tightened mine so much it hurt. Benjamin sat across from me, his legs spread wide, his right foot playing with mine. "What are you so afraid of?" His mouth was full of apple and there was juice on his chin.

"Turbulence, dying, lightning strikes, dying, violent turbulence, you know, the usual stuff." The plane accelerated and moments later we were airborne. "You know it's been a very long time since a small plane with a famous person on board crashed into an Iowa cornfield," I said between gritted teeth.

"Didn't that happen in the middle of a blizzard?"

"I'm talking about odds, not weather."

"That's an interesting thought. I wonder what the odds are of my dying today in Iowa. Where's my computer?"

"You're kidding, right?" I said as the plane bucked and swerved. I grabbed onto the arms of my seat and closed my eyes. "I think we just dropped several hundred feet."

Benjamin laughed, "We need to get this boy a cocktail."

"Yes, a cocktail would be very nice, in fact, two or three would be just about ideal."

I closed my eyes and tried to relax but found myself anticipating the next round of turbulence. I looked up at the roof of the plane; it looked too close, the walls seemed to be closing in on me and Benjamin seemed to be almost sitting in my lap. A coffin, I was sitting in the middle of a coffin.

"You're not looking well, Liam," Benjamin put a hand on my knee, which he massaged several times.

"I'm not—" I said. At that moment Michelle emerged from the front of the plane. Benjamin sat up abruptly, whipping his hand back as if my knee was on fire. He flashed her his Hollywood smile.

"My friend Liam needs a drink, one very strong drink."

I looked at my knee where his hand had been. "I would like a very spicy, very strong Bloody Mary, quickly, please."

"Make that two," Benjamin spread his legs again and winked at her. "Thanks Michelle."

"What time would you like lunch, Mr. Graves?"

"In about thirty minutes." She nodded and walked back to the front of the plane.

"Was there something wrong with my knee?" I asked as the plane rocked side to side several times. My heart was racing. I felt a complete lack of control and I wanted off this plane.

"Why?"

"You jerked your hand back as if you were about to be bitten by a snake."

"I did not."

I shot him a look. "Yes, you, did." He blushed slightly.

Michelle reappeared carrying a tray with two tall bright red drinks with leafy celery stalks and large stuffed olives. She placed them on a table alongside two bowls of pretzels and cashews and paused. I took a swallow of my drink: it was perfect, strong, rich and spicy. I took another large swallow and felt the tension begin to dissipate. The ceiling height increased by several feet and Benjamin was where he was supposed to be: across from me.

"I think I'll be fine now," I said, sinking into my seat. She nodded and disappeared into the galley. The alcohol was zipping through my brain. I took another swallow and then another. I grinned: bold Liam had arrived. "This is pretty amazing, isn't it?" I looked out the window and unbuckled my seat belt. I reached over and squeezed his leg. "I think I finally understand what you sacrificed when we flew on Northwest." *Sycophant*, a voice yelled.

"Sacrificed is too strong a word."

"Perhaps, but compared to this, flying commercial must feel like a Greyhound bus."

Michele reappeared with two more drinks. Benjamin's glass was empty, mine was right behind. She placed a fresh drink in front of me and then handed us menus. There were pages of wine choices, liqueurs, and cocktails. The food choices were salmon, filet of beef or a vegetarian casserole. I pushed the menu away. The alcohol had taken over and I was in no hurry to eat. I stretched out my legs and leaned back in my seat. Benjamin did the same.

"How did Gregg take it when you told him we aren't staying with him?" he asked.

"He was relieved. Turns out he was just about to ask us to rent a hotel room." I shoved a handful of cashews in my mouth. "All of his roommates decided to come this weekend after all so there wasn't room for us. God I miss him."

"What?"

"I really miss Gregg. I can't believe I'm going to see him soon." I sat up in my seat and reached for my drink. "Have I ever told you my idea for a movie?"

"You're not going to pitch a script at me, are you?" Benjamin groaned.

"Hey, you're the one treating me like a mogul. I might as well act like one too." I sat up and leaned forward with my forearms resting on my legs. "*Billy Elliott* meets *The Music Man*."

"You watch too much TV." Benjamin took a swallow of his drink leaving a rim of red on his upper lip. I stood up, put my hands on his knees and licked off the tomato juice. I pulled away and sat back down just as the plane seemed to shimmy sideways. I waited for my heart to race: it didn't. "Did your parents ever talk about the parade held in Mason City when *The Music Man* opened?"

"Of course they did, it was the biggest thing that ever happened here."

"I'm pretty sure it was the summer of 1962." I ate half my celery stalk. "I've got this idea. The movie will focus on a thirteen-year-old boy growing up in a gritty, ethnic, maybe Italian or Greek, blue collar family, difficult childhood. He's drawn to other boys but doesn't understand why, maybe throw in an abusive father, passive mother. He wants to play the piano but his dad won't let him—he wants him to be a football star. However, this kid is scrawny, musical and uninterested in football. He wants to be a concert pianist."

I leaned forward again. Benjamin was staring at me intently. "His mom has secretly let him study piano with a nun at his grade school. The kid's been practicing for years on a piano in the music studio in the basement of the school but only after all the other kids have gone home. His dad thinks he is being tutored for his problems with science courses." I sat back in my seat and thought for a moment. "His best friend is a tom boy named Sue who thinks he is a pansy for playing the piano. She wants him to play baseball, which is her passion."

"Pansy?"

"Hey, it's the early sixties." I popped a large stuffed olive in my mouth. "There's a competition coming up in Mason City. His teacher, Sister Thomas Aquinas entered him, assuming he had told his parents but he only told his mom. His mom doesn't want to tell his dad knowing he will go ballistic but she also knows that if her son competes, the truth will come out. The kid secretly wants his dad to be there but is afraid to ask. Eventually his mom decides it will be better to tell the dad as soon as it's over." I could see the set, a small piano in the corner, beaten down music stands shoved together, the shades drawn, and the light dim. "Don't you see? The kid wants to come out of the closet about his music." Benjamin stood up and started pacing.

"The kid gets wind of *The Music Man* premiere that's going to happen that summer. There's lots of family drama, maybe a little violence, death of a grandparent, shades of *Dandelion Wine*." I was lit, excited and flushed. "There's a stew of family issues that boil over that summer culminating in the parade. He goes to the parade by himself and when he sees the marching bands from all over the country, the movie stars, the thousands of people lining the street he learns there are other possibilities for him than staying in his small hometown. For the first time he feels hopeful."

"Why?"

"Through the parade! It's a metaphor for another world, another life for him where he is allowed to make choices about how he wants to lead his life."

"What about the piano competition?"

"The movie ends with the kid playing some challenging piece of music in the school gymnasium. When he sits down to play he sees his dad standing at the back of the room." I stood up. "The kid starts nervously, in fact stops playing, frozen with stage fright. He looks down at his mom and she has a steely look in her eyes. She nods her head mouthing, 'you can do this!'" I looked over at Benjamin whose eyes were filmy.

"And of course he does, right?" he asked.

"Yes he does, the audience goes crazy and the movie ends with he and his dad walking hand in hand back to their house."

"Why did the dad show up?"

"The mom hadn't realized how good her son had gotten until Sister Thomas Aquinas told her she should come hear a rehearsal. Once she hears him play she goes home and lays it on the line with her husband. She finally stops being a doormat. She tells him that he is going to lose his son if doesn't learn to accept him as he is. The dad realizes how much he loves his son and how wrong he had been to push him into sports."

Benjamin thought for a moment. "This might have possibilities."

"You haven't heard the clincher yet…drum roll please…it will be directed by Ron Howard." I smiled triumphantly and reached over for my now empty cocktail.

"What does that have to do with anything?"

"Are you having a fake blonde moment?"

"I am not a fake blonde." Benjamin unzipped his pants and looked at his pubic hair. "Take that back, I am a fake blonde."

"Ron Howard was Winthrop in *The Music Man*, you know, the kid brother with the weird lisp. You know that as well as you know the color of your hair." I grinned. "On second thought…."

Benjamin stood up and started pacing. "Shit Liam, that's brilliant. Built in audience, built in hook, built in publicity. The marketing will create itself. The press will eat this up. "Where's the screenplay?"

"What screenplay?"

"There's no screenplay?"

"Nope."

"Then write one!"

"When did I ever tell you I could write screenplays?"

Benjamin picked up his phone and punched in a number. "Ron, it's Benjamin, call me." He flopped down in his seat. "Of course I'll play the dad."

"How do you think you can play ethnic? You're the poster child for WASPS."

He turned his back and when he turned around he had puffed out his cheeks and stuck out his gut. "Janice, I'm gonna kill ya this time." I started laughing. He sounded exactly like Tony Soprano.

"Midwest Italian, I need Midwest Italian, not New Jersey."

"Fuck if I know how to do that."

Michelle walked down the aisle and picked up our glasses. "Have you decided on lunch, Mr. Graves?"

"I'm going to have steak. How about you, Liam?"

"Me too, meat sounds great." I grinned again at Benjamin who grinned back. When Michelle disappeared into the galley, Benjamin stood up and put his hand around my waist and pulled me into his arms. He slid his hands underneath the waistband of my underwear and began massaging my ass. He kissed me as he brought his hands around front, one hand cradling my balls as the other hand slid up my belly.

"Unfortunately this may have to wait until we land, unless we're really quiet."

"Not sure that's possible. Maybe next time you should charter a plane with a bedroom."

"Okay." He pulled himself away and sat down. I wanted to kneel in front of him and finish what he had started but at that moment Michelle appeared again with salads and wine. Benjamin attacked his food as always, polished off with a slug of red wine.

"What do you think of the wine?" His salad had disappeared in about three bites.

"You do realize that one of us has to be able to drive in a couple of hours."

"Good point." He reached over and poured my wine into his glass. "I'll play the dad, maybe Kate could play the mom. Ron is gonna love this, this movie will get made, trust me."

"It's that simple for you?"

"Right now it is, as long as my movies keep making money."

"Unbelievable."

"What is?"

"The world you live in, the power you have."

"Whatever."

"Don't dismiss me." I looked down and my glass of wine was full again.

"So you're right already." He looked peeved. "What am I supposed to do, not use it?"

"Of course not. I guess I just want to remind you—I think I would want to be reminded if I were in your shoes."

"In my shoes is not where I want you." He leaned forward and put both hands on my knees. This time I noticed Michelle as she strode forward with our lunch. Benjamin removed his hands but in a smooth manner. She placed a Wedgwood plate in front of me with at least a twelve-ounce filet surrounded by asparagus. Next to it she set a metal cylindrical tube lined with parchment paper

410

and overflowing with French fries. I popped one in my mouth. I grabbed another and ran it through the juice from my steak. It was sensational. I looked over at Benjamin who was laughing.

"I love it when I meet a fellow dipper." He plopped several French fries on his plate. "You do realize that in some circles it's frowned upon. The last time I had lunch at Buckingham Palace we were quite firmly told exactly what we could and could not do whilst dining with the Queen."

"You, you had lunch with Queen Elizabeth?"

"With about a hundred others."

He attacked his steak as if it were still alive and needed to be gutted. He took a huge bite, wiping his chin before the blood ran onto his shirt. "I got the sum total of about thirty-seconds with her when she walked through the receiving line. Not a big deal."

I started to remind him again that this was a big deal but decided not to. I took a bite of my steak and felt this odd sensation. Initially I couldn't decide what I was feeling and then realized I was jealous. Here was this guy, same age, similar background, and yet he was having lunch with Queen Elizabeth and I was having lunch with my mom and aunts. How did this happen? Was he really that talented? I looked at him, he grinned at me and I realized none of this mattered.

Michelle swept in and cleared away lunch.

"Can I get you anything else, Mr. Graves?"

"No, we're fine Michelle, everything was perfect, as always. That was one of the best steaks I've ever eaten." I could feel the charm quotient ratchet up. She didn't seem to be buying it any more than I did.

"We'll be landing in about ninety minutes or so. I will remind you when we are about fifteen minutes out." She kept her eyes on Benjamin. "If you decide you do want anything else, just buzz me."

She poured us coffee and disappeared again. Benjamin looked at his watch. "We've got about an hour to play a game."

411

"Really? A game? I hope it's called nap."

"Not even close, it's called orgasm." He pulled up his shorts so I could see the outline of his erection. My jealousy disappeared instantaneously.

"Where's the game?" I looked around for a box. "I think I've seen that in a game store in Provincetown."

"There is no actual game, it's played in our heads."

"What the hell are you talking about?"

"Patience my little man, you need to learn patience." He grinned at me. "Okay, here's how it's played. It's really quite simple, the winner is the person who has an orgasm first within the timeframe we have before landing."

"Hell, that won't be difficult, I could come right now in about thirty seconds."

"But you cannot touch yourself, did I mention that?"

"How the hell do you do that?"

"Through your mind." Benjamin was sounding far away, almost as if he had already started playing. He unzipped his jeans and pulled them down to his ankles. Then he pulled off his shirt.

"What about Michelle?"

"She will not come in here without being asked. However, you cannot scream like a howling monkey when you cum, like you usually do."

"You're the one who sounds like he's delivering triplets."

"We're losing valuable time Liam, or I should say, you are. I'm pretty good at this."

"Of course you are." I lowered my shorts to my ankles and pulled off my shirt as well. I was rock hard. It was bobbing up and down; I unselfconsciously stroked it without thinking.

"Cheating already, Liam?"

I yanked my hand away. I sat back in my chair and spread my legs. The air from the overhead vents was blowing on my crotch sending shivers of sensation across my cock and balls. I looked over

412

at Benjamin who had closed his eyes. I focused all my attention on his cock looking at each detail as if I had never seen it before. While I was finding this erotic I wasn't remotely close to coming. I had no idea how you could do this without touching yourself. I closed my eyes and tried to calm my mind. Flashcards of sexual images crossed through my mind: Benjamin asleep in bed next to me that first night, the sheet slipping off his ass; the sex we had in the limousine. I remembered him bathing me in the shower, his soapy hand between my legs, one simple movement up and down my cock.

I opened my eyes. It took all my will power not to grab hold knowing that with one pull it would be over. Benjamin's eyes were half open, his nipples were erect and his belly was moist. For a moment I thought he had won but then realized it was pre cum that had dripped onto his stomach. Closing my eyes again, I was tight inside Benjamin's body. We were on our sides and Benjamin was laughing and crying as he pushed hard against me, drawing every inch of me inside him. I felt my legs bucking almost as if I were fucking him.

I realized that my body was beginning to build towards an orgasm.

I looked again at Benjamin who was sitting up in his seat, his balls hanging off the edge. It was a jolt of sexual adrenaline. I moved off my seat and knelt on the floor so that the head of my cock was inches away from his. I moved it slowly back and forth never getting any closer but pretending we were touching; it felt like we were touching. I moaned, fighting with my hands so they stayed at my sides.

"I can't stand much more of this Benjamin, I feel like I'm going to explode but can't."

"Just relax, we're almost there."

I looked down again and imagined burying my face under his balls, taking each one in my mouth and then sticking my tongue deep inside his body. Suddenly I was there, or at least I thought I was there. I leaned back, my cock straight up over my body, my hips involuntarily pushing up and down. I felt an orgasm building and then....and then....nothing.

Benjamin was moaning softly. His arms were away from his body and his palms were facing up. His hips started moving up and down, his balls shaking back and forth, his cock flat on his stomach. Sweat was running down the side of his face. He licked his lower lip and suddenly began shooting stream after stream of cum up his chest. His body rocked up and down and then he was quiet in his chair. He had barely made a sound. I watched, open mouthed and amazed. Looking down at my own cock, I brought my hand closer again.

"Don't Liam, just try one more time, okay?"

I shook my shorts free and spread my legs wide and concentrated with all my might. I kept building and building and building but couldn't go over the top. I was wild with unreleased sexual energy. Just as I was ready to stop, I felt something near my cock. I opened my eyes and saw Benjamin's foot, the big toe hovering over the head of my cock. I wanted physical contact so badly I pushed my hips up high but Benjamin jerked his foot away at the last second. We did this several times until I was a few seconds ahead of him; the tip of my cock grazed his toe and it happened. I had to slap a hand across my mouth to not cry out. My butt continued to lift up and down off my seat, my legs were shaking uncontrollably. I felt something wet on my forehead and wiped it away.

"That was fucking unbelievable." Benjamin handed me a towel. He was wiping off his chest and crotch. He pulled up his jeans and put his shirt back on. "That was the best ever."

I sat back with my eyes closed, my breath slowly returning to normal. "Who taught you that?" I asked.

"Punch."

"What???"

"You know, Punch, the singer?"

"Of course I know him, well I don't know him, I know of him, you know what I mean. You played this game with him? Isn't he straight? What's his wife's name again?"

"It wasn't just with him, there were a few others there as well." He stood up and found a bottle of water in a cabinet. "Once again you are too hung up on this straight/gay thing especially relative to this particular event. It had nothing to do with who was sitting across from me, it was about the power of my mind over my body."

"I was thinking about you."

"Ditto."

"You were thinking about you as well?"

"No, no," he laughed. "I was thinking about fucking you that first time in the limo—man was that hot."

"I was thinking about that as well, among other things." I wiped off my chest as well as I could, feeling sticky and sweaty.

He pointed at me. "Don't forget your chin. Michelle might wonder what it is."

At that moment her voice came over the intercom advising us to take our seats as we would be landing shortly.

"Shit" Benjamin said, "I was going to have my beard and wig on before we landed.

"Why don't you stay on the plane while I deal with the rental car?" I asked shifting into role. "This airport is tiny. I think the rental cars are in a lot in front of the terminal. When you're ready, head toward the parking lot and I'll honk to let you know where I am."

"Sounds like a plan." He finished his coffee just as the plane came to a smooth landing. He leapt out of his seat, bouncing around the plane like a ten-year-old. "I cannot believe I am finally here; I have wanted to come to this part of the country my entire life." He pulled a bag out of the overhead compartment just as Michelle emerged from the galley. "Hey Michelle, can I have about fifteen minutes?"

"Of course Mr. Graves." She backed out of the room as he dumped the contents of the bag onto the chair, his wig, beard, spirit gum, dark glasses and baseball cap.

"See you in a few, dude."

"Can we have a moratorium on that word for the rest of this trip?"

"Sure dude, anything you want." He reached over and grabbed my ass as I headed to the front of the plane. I flung my bag over my shoulder and stopped for a moment at the top of the stairs.

At the bottom of the staircase, I looked up at the hazy blue sky dotted with large puffy clouds. The sun was hot on my skin and I could smell the ocean and hear the waves crashing over at Race Point Beach, a short distance away. The air carried a whiff of the scrub pines, which never failed to remind me of the incense used at Catholic funerals. I ran across the parking lot, I wanted to get started immediately. I could not believe how much I missed this.

The rental car was a dark blue Camry. I grimaced as the locked in cigarette infused air poured out of the car. The driver's seat had a burn hole and the floor was dotted with sand. I threw my bag onto the back seat, turned the air conditioning on high and waited for Benjamin. As he walked out of the terminal, he stopped for a moment and began turning slowly in a circle. I thought he was lost until I realized he was simply taking in the sights, smells and sounds. I beeped my horn to let him know where I was. He jogged over to the car, threw his bag on top of mine and jumped into the car.

"Where are we going first?" He took a deep breath and lowered his window. "This car smells like ass." He waved his hands as if to transfer the outside air into the car. He stuck his head out the window and breathed deeply. "My God, the air is so sweet."

"Let's go find our house, take a shower and then we can either go for a walk on the beach or head into Provincetown." I pulled out of the parking lot and turned left. "But first we're gonna stop for a second at Race Point." I drove the short distance pointing out the bike path that intersected the road. 'There are bike trails that go for miles all over the dunes. We'll do that tomorrow."

"Do you have this entire weekend scheduled?" Benjamin turned off the air conditioning and pulled off his shirt.

"Maybe." I smiled as I paid the entrance fee to the parking lot. The young woman in her park ranger uniform was staring at Benjamin's chest. I handed her a $20 bill. "I think it would be a refreshing change if I were in charge for a while."

"What's that supposed to mean?" He looked at me with feigned outrage.

"This is the first stop in our *If It's Tuesday, it Must Be Belgium* tour of the outer Cape." I looked over at Benjamin who was wriggling out of his jeans. He reached over the back seat and pulled a pair of shorts out of a side pocket of his luggage. He pulled on his shorts, found a pair of flip-flops and hopped out of the car. "Where to?' I pointed to our right as I pulled my shirt off and threw it on to the growing pile in the back seat. At the top of the boardwalk, we both paused as we looked down on Race Point Beach.

"It's incredible," Benjamin said taking hold of my hand.

"Wait until you see Long Nook in Truro."

"Is that scheduled yet?" He grinned at me and headed towards the water. Every color jumped out at me: the orange of the lifeguard's bathing suit, the tan, burnt bodies of the sunbathers, the blue water pounding against the shore, the snow-white gulls shrieking overhead, the brown sand, hot against my bare feet.

"When are we going swimming?" Benjamin stood at the water's edge, the waves rhythmically covering his legs.

"It's not too cold for you?"

"Hell no, the Pacific Ocean is much colder than this."

"Tomorrow."

"Is that before or after the bike ride?" He sat down next to me, turned on his side and placed a hand on my stomach. I was

417

surprised at how comfortable he was touching me in public. Even in Provincetown Justin would bristle if I touched him in public.

"During," I stood up. "I know a path through the dunes we can take to a pretty deserted beach." I brushed the sand off my butt. "Ready?"

"No, I am so relaxed I could fall asleep right here." He lay flat on the ground and closed his eyes.

"Come on, your allotted time for the first stop of our tour has expired." I yanked on his hand until he reluctantly stood up.

We drove the several miles to Truro with all the windows down, the wind whipping through the car. I turned onto Route 6A which hugged the Cape Cod Bay side. It was lined with motels, condos, single-family homes, all sitting on the beach. As we drove further into Truro, we passed a row of two room cottages, each painted white and named after a flower: Salvia, Primrose, Pansy—God I hated that word.

Our house for the weekend was on Knowles Heights Road, which cut across a tall dune that faced back towards Provincetown. I pulled into a circular driveway blocked by a gate. The road was lined on both sides by cedars as it descended towards the water. I could see the flat top of a modern structure at the end of the driveway.

"Now what?" I asked. Benjamin's eyes were closed.

"Hell if I know, you're in charge for the weekend, right?" He didn't open his eyes.

"Asshole."

"Our relationship must be deepening," he opened his left eye. "I am now officially an asshole." He sat up and blinked his eyes several times. "It's 7999."

I punched in the code and watched the gates glide open. I coasted down the driveway and stopped in front of a one-story building flanked by two identical boxy additions. To me it looked like a prefab home that had been dropped by a helicopter and then nailed together.

Benjamin was grinning madly as he jumped out of the car. He raced over to a clay pot overflowing with geraniums. He lifted it up and pulled out the key. Running into the house he threw his bag on the counter and raced upstairs.

"Liam, get your ass out here, the view is incredible!"

I followed him out onto the deck. It was about ten feet from the edge of the dune with no obstructions blocking our view. The wind was strong coming off the water, the tide was high and the waves were dotted with white caps. Across the bay was Provincetown with its familiar granite monument dominating the landscape. The shoreline of the outer cape curled in on itself as if embracing the harbor.

"This is fucking amazing!"

"Better than California?"

"Yeah, I think it might be. It's so different here, the air, the smell, the history, and the view of Provincetown. I have to go swimming now." He stripped off his clothes and began moving towards the wooden staircase that descended to the beach.

"Uh Benjamin? This isn't a nude beach. The nude beach stop is at Long Nook which is day three of our tour from 1:15-2:45."

"Huh?" He looked down at his cock, ran back in the house and emerged wearing blue and orange swimming trunks that hung below his knees.

"Coming with me?" he asked.

"No, I don't think so."

"Oh come on Liam, come to the beach with me."

"No."

"No?"

"I could try this in another language, nyet….."

"I get it, but what I don't get is why?"

"I need aspirin and a nap." I rubbed my temples.

"But we just got here."

"Benjamin, come on, we're going to be here for several days." I realized how tired and thirsty I was. "I'll be good as new in an hour."

He turned his back on me after shooting me a look of disappointment and headed down to the beach. My initial reaction was relief that I was going to have some time to myself, but then wondered if I was kicking into an old habit. Whenever I had come here with Gregg, he had insisted on a nonstop party. I had resisted in the only way I knew how, going for long runs, extended bike rides or afternoon naps. Was I simply on autopilot? I never napped at home. I looked at the staircase, took a step towards it and then found the first bedroom, stripped off my clothes, fell on the bed and was asleep instantly.

CHAPTER FORTY-THREE

—————∞—————

I awoke an hour later with Benjamin curled up next to me, his leg over mine. I slid out from underneath him and quietly left the room. We had two hours before we were due at Gregg's. I walked down a staircase surrounded by windows, some two stories high, others octagons, an eyebrow window high up on the wall. They were all closed. I shivered and began shutting off the air conditioning and opening any windows I could.

The kitchen was overrun by stainless steel appliances. The cabinets were white and the floor was sunset colored terra cotta. It faced away from the water with sliding glass doors opening onto a small garden filled with flowers and herbs. I made a pot of coffee and opened the side-by-side Sub Zero refrigerator looking for half and half. It was packed with food: soft drinks, fruit, cheese, cold cuts, a pasta salad, several different kinds of beer including Affligem Ale and Westmalle. I found the half and half on the bottom shelf lined with four different kinds of milk: whole, 2%, skim and soy. The freezer was overloaded with packages of meat, ice cream, cookies and pies. I opened a cabinet next to the stove, which was stocked with every kind of spice in alphabetical order. There were shelves of crackers, cereals, and pasta. An entire floor to ceiling cupboard was filled with alcohol. I started laughing at the excess.

"What's so funny?" Benjamin was standing in the doorway; his hair tousled, his eyes sleepy, his erection pointing straight at me.

"This kitchen has enough food to last us six months."

Benjamin walked over and hugged me, his hard on poking me in the leg.

"I'm sorry I was such a jerk about swimming. Not sure why I need to do that."

"Do what?"

"Try and run your life."

"How was your swim?" I asked trying not to smile.

"I didn't go. As soon as I got down there I realized how pooped I was. I came right back up and fell asleep." He kissed me on my temple. "Maybe we can go tonight after dinner?"

He began sniffing the air. "I would kill for a cup of coffee." I poured him a cup and we walked upstairs to the deck, the late afternoon sunshine warm on our skin. Benjamin was pacing around looking at every possible view.

"What are you doing?" The coffee was hot and strong.

"Checking to see if any of our neighbors can see us."

I looked around as well. The way the house was situated, combined with the scrub pines that blocked one side of the deck guaranteed some privacy. Benjamin looked over at the stairs coming up from the beach.

"Anyone could come up those stairs, couldn't they?" he asked. He didn't wait for an answer. "What are the odds someone would?"

"Pretty slim but I suppose it could happen."

He touched his face as if to remind himself that didn't have his beard on.

"Fuck," he said.

"There must be something we can do so you don't have to be in disguise all weekend."

"I'll just wear my beard and hat, it's no big deal, we're not going to be here that long and we're wasting time. You must have something scheduled for the next fifteen minutes?"

"We're due at Gregg's around 8 which means 8:30. He hates punctual people." I finished my coffee. "Let's get cleaned up and go into P-town. You need to see Commercial Street and you need to see Ellie."

"Ellie?"

"I told you about her. She is a 75-year-old former man, who wears a bikini and sings Frank Sinatra songs in front of the Town Hall."

"Just like back home." He grabbed our coffee cups and headed into the house.

I parked the car in the public lot in the center of town. We had spent far too long trying to figure out what to wear. Benjamin was looking to me for guidance and I had none to give. Gregg had always told me what to wear when we were going out for the night. Benjamin had first come out of the bedroom dressed like a cowboy and then a surfer and then in his straight boy bathing suit.

"I can tell by the blank look on your face that this is not working." Benjamin stepped out of his clothes and stood in front of me.

"Did you bring any shorts?" I asked.

"Of course." Seconds later he came out wearing madras cotton shorts that were a size too big.

"Where did you get those?"

"Younkers," Benjamin said referencing the department store in Mason City. "And no smart-ass comments. I can shop, cook, pay bills, wash a car and mow a lawn. So anyway, how do they look?"

I looked him up and down. "Without a shirt they look great but...hey, I know what you can wear." I rummaged through my luggage until I found a small black tank top.

"I can't fit into this." He frowned as he held it up for scrutiny.

"That's the point. Try it on."

Now I looked at Benjamin as he got out of the car. The beard and wig were on, sunglasses, the black tank top plastered to his

423

body which stopped just above his hip bone. The shorts were baggy and hung low.

"How do I look?" he asked as he jumped in the air and turned completely around.

"Great."

"What else is new?" He walked over to me and planted a kiss on my mouth. "Let's get this show on the road. I may sing a few songs with Miss Ellie. Hey, is this like New Orleans? Can we walk on the street with a drink?"

"Not allowed, although I have seen a few fierce lesbians doing it. I think the cops are afraid of them."

I took hold of his hand and we walked the short block to Commercial Street, the main street that runs the entire length of town. We turned left but not before stopping to watch an elderly policeman who directed traffic at one of the busiest intersections. He was short and pot bellied but moved with fluidity as he twirled, hopped, pointed, and blew on his whistle, all while directing cars, trucks, bicycles, skateboarders, drag queens on motorized scooters and shell-shocked families up and down the street. I never knew if he was a real cop or one of the locals. Benjamin had a huge smile on his face as he imitated a couple of the cop's moves.

We walked down the street, cut through a parking lot and then upstairs to Pepe's Wharf, a restaurant/bar that sat on the beach.

"Well howdy, this is perfect." Clay Davis had arrived. We went straight to the bar. The bartender was a forty something woman in a white tank top, tattoos up and down her arms, five earrings in each ear, a gold hoop in her eyebrow and a studded leather collar around her neck. "Y'all got Shiner Bock?" Clay asked.

"You hot mess, you know better than that." She had a southern accent to match his. "We're in Yankee country. Where y'all from?"

"Katy, Texas Ma'am."

"I'm from New Orleans myself. What'll you boys have?"

"I'll have a Cape Codder," I said.

"What the hell kind of sissy drink is that, boy?" Clay asked.

"The exact kind of sissy drink this sissy wants," I said with a smile. She grinned back at me and poured a drink that was more vodka than cranberry juice.

"And you, tough guy, what do y'all want?"

"Hell, it feels like we're in the tropics somewhere." The sun was beating down on us and the air was not moving. Benjamin had sweat running down the side of his face. I wiped it off with the back of my hand.

"I'll have a shot of tequila and a Corona, no lime."

"You're my kind of drinker. What's your name?" She placed a shot of tequila on the bar.

"Clay Davis and this here is my friend Liam." He reached across and shook her hand vigorously.

"Friend or fuck buddy?" she asked.

"He's my fuck buddy." Benjamin grabbed me around the waist and kissed me.

"You're one hot fucking couple, that's for sure."

Benjamin threw back the tequila and she poured him another which he popped back as well.

"Thanks Ma'am." He took a long swallow of his beer.

"Knock that off Clay, we're not in Texas, you can cut the Southern bullshit charm. I know all about your kind."

"What about my kind?"

"All you care about is pussy or cocks depending on which way ya travel."

"Cocks in my case, in case you hadn't noticed. By the way, what's your name?"

"Toni."

"She read your beads, didn't she muscle boy?" An older man in a kaftan and pearls, heavy makeup and a straw hat sitting next to me called out. "Hmm... that girl reads em like a book and it don't take no long book either, she reads em on the first page."

I looked at her/him wondering why she sounded like a black woman from Louisiana and yet looked like an odd Boston Brahmin.

"You got that right Lu Lu, I read this boy the minute I saw him." She started mixing a shaker of martinis. I looked at my empty glass and wondered where it went.

"Hey Toni, my fuck buddy needs another cocktail."

"What are two beautiful boys doing in a place like this?" Now Lu Lu sounded like Vivien Leigh in *Gone With The Wind*.

"We're here to paaaaaaarty!!!!" Benjamin cried out. "Where's my tequila?"

Toni reappeared and poured him another one. "You're not driving are you Mr. Hot Mess? I'd hate to see a fine piece of man flesh such as you splattered all over the highway."

"No, no need to worry, my fuck buddy Liam is in charge of everything this weekend." He leaned his head over my shoulder and began inching his hands closer and closer to my crotch. I stepped away as I had a pulsating hard on.

"We're here for hours, having dinner with a friend so we have plenty of time to sober up."

"Didn't meant to rain on your Mardi Gras, just that I've seen it too many times." I was surprised how serious she had become. Lulu leaned over and whispered in my ear, "Her younger sister was killed by a drunk driver about ten years ago." She smelled of alcohol and petunias.

"Lulu Mae, you butt your nose out of my affairs. You hear me?" Toni was radiating fury. "Damn, woman, what's private should stay private. How would you like it if I started sharing some of your secrets." At that Lulu stepped back and collapsed on the bar stool, fumbling through her bag until she found a Chinese fan decorated with a large peacock that she began waving furiously in front of her face.

"Why, I would just die if y'all did that. It....it would be unforgivable, Miss Toni."

"Then, button your lip, ya hear?" Toni turned to wait on customers on the other side of the bar. Lulu continued to fan herself. Her face was sagging as if all the energy had been sucked out from underneath her cheeks.

"This is turning into an odd sort of Tennessee Williams play, don't you think?" I whispered to Benjamin.

"This is perfect, you couldn't have managed this better for me if you'd wanted." He placed his empty beer bottle on the bar. "Barkeep, una cervesa por favor."

Toni finished what she was doing with her back to us. I could almost see the anger radiating up her spine but when turned around, her face had hardened back into irony and her shoulders were square. "You got it, dude."

I was high as a kite from the second drink. I turned away to face the water, my hand on Benjamin's shoulder. There were children playing in the shallow water; two or three golden retrievers chasing after sand covered tennis balls and an older woman trying to teach the fundamentals of wind surfing to a bunch of college kids. There were purple, black, and yellow kites in a variety of shapes and sizes hanging in the sky. The kites were so high up you couldn't tell who was anchoring them. The breeze had picked up again and it felt cool against our burned flesh. Benjamin's nose was red from the sun.

"I can't believe how much I've missed this."

"I can't believe you ever left." He massaged my lower back.

"I didn't technically live here, I only vacationed here and never for more than two weeks at a time. Plus, this place never felt like my home."

"Why didn't you move here instead of Iowa?"

I thought for a minute. "Because the problems I had in Boston would have been the same here except on a smaller scale. Most of the people I knew as friends or clients were buying homes here so I would have traveled in the same circle. Plus this place is more a theme park than it is a town, at least in the summer."

"So?"

I began to feel defensive. "Haven't I told you all this before?"

"Yes, but I want to hear it again." Benjamin threw back his tequila and pushed the glass away.

"I don't want to talk about this, at least not now."

Benjamin pulled me between his legs, both hands on my ass and kissed me for several minutes. "Deal."

"Let's go," I said as I adjusted myself. "Nice to meet you Toni, and you too, Lulu." I shook both their hands.

"You boys here all weekend?" Toni was pulling two draft beers.

"You bet we are, and trust me, we'll be back, same time tomorrow," Benjamin said with his big smile.

"I'll try and save ya a seat." Toni smiled at both of us showing two rows of perfectly symmetrical white teeth. It changed her entire look—she went from looking like a biker chick to a school librarian absent the tattoos and earrings.

"I'll be here as well, lads." Lulu now had a British accent. "It'll be brilliant I say, absolutely brilliant."

We ran into the men's room and stopped to pee: our streams arced and crossed each other, both of us grinning and aroused. Benjamin took a quick look in the mirror to make sure his wig and beard were firmly in place and then we disappeared into the parade of people on Commercial Street.

There were young, tattooed lesbians in shorts and tank tops walking hand in hand; straight families with trails of children cramming ice cream and taffy into their mouths, their Midwest accents mixing with a smattering of French-Canadian accents. Chubby hairy men in leather chaps were walking in packs down the middle of the street, their girth forcing people to get out of their way.

Before we saw Ellie we heard her. From a distance her pleasant, baritone voice singing *Fly Me to the Moon* rang out over the crowd noise. Benjamin started laughing and pulled me forward rushing through the crowd and bumping a few shoulders.

"Oh my God!" Clay exclaimed. "My momma and daddy would not believe this."

Standing in front of us was a tall, thin, homely man holding a small microphone. He had shoulder length straggly hair and a narrow face with prominent cheekbones. He was wearing a bikini top and ruffled skirt that barely covered his ass. Under his skirt were panties that matched his bikini top. Black pumps finished the outfit. From a distance his legs looked good in the heels; it was only up close that you saw the droopy skin of an old man. The sound system was in a red wagon, the kind I had pulled as a little boy. There was a sign on the sidewalk describing how Ellie was a seventy-five year old man living his dream as a showgirl. He segued into *My Way*. Benjamin sat down to listen.

Ellie had a good voice, not much range but it was pure, on pitch and delivered with style. Benjamin was staring at him so intently that he began staring back. When he finished, Benjamin jumped to his feet and let out a yell. He reached into his pocket and threw several bills into the coffee can next to his wagon. He walked over to him and they began speaking quietly. He handed Ellie more money and he beamed.

"Ladies and Gentlemen, we have a special treat tonight—a guest singer. All the way from Katy, Texas, I give you Clay Davis!" He handed the microphone to him as he began fiddling with his sound system apparently trying to find a specific song. I felt my heart race and started backing out of the crowd. But Benjamin took my hand and pulled me forward. I pulled back again until I realized this could turn into some kind of odd push pull exercise. Benjamin put his arm around my shoulder and kissed me lightly on the forehead.

The music started and from the first note I knew it was the Dolly Parton song, *I Will Always Love You*. I looked around at the mass of smiling faces staring at Benjamin. I did not see doubt in any eyes. Were they all lit or was it the expectation that Benjamin would sing well because he was so good looking?

I could feel the rigidity in my spine. I picked a hangnail, looked down and was relieved to see no blood.

Benjamin began singing softly but as the song built, he relaxed and let his own strong baritone deepen and mellow. When the song hit its peak, he fell to one knee and sang the verse in the same style as Whitney Houston, even to the point of reaching the final notes. He was terrific. When he finished the song, he stood up and kissed me on my lips. He turned and faced the crowd and bowed several times. The applause was building to a crescendo and more people were stopping to see what had happened. Others were calling out, demanding another song. Ellie was quick to grab the microphone away.

We pushed our way through the crowd. People were patting him on the back, some even tried to shove money into his pockets. He was laughing, acknowledging them, grinning but always moving forward. We walked quickly up the street, found the first bar and jumped inside. Benjamin was catching his breath, his face covered in sweat, his T-shirt an odd pattern of sweat stains.

"You are unbelievable, do you know that?" I knew I sounded irritated and pleased at the same time.

"Yes I am and yes I know." He gestured at the bartender. We were in a straight bar, people huddled over checkers, chess and backgammon at tall tables that lined the window facing the street. I knew from its reputation there wouldn't be another gay couple in the place. Benjamin ordered our drinks as we tried to find room at the bar.

"God that was fun." He threw back two quick shots of tequila and drained half his beer in a single swallow.

"You have a good voice."

"I know."

"No false modesty for you, is there?"

"Why should there be? I sing well, should I pretend that I don't?"

"I guess not, but it does sound kind of boastful."

"Something you could do a lot more of Liam Conor." He started looking for the bartender. "Were you as miserable as you looked back there?"

"Yes."

"Why?"

"I have always hated public displays. They seem artificial and phony to me."

"There was nothing phony about what I just did."

"Okay, I can accept that it was genuine but to me the more important question is, was it necessary?"

"Necessary? Of course not. I mean, come on, how much of what we do or say is really necessary?"

"Then why do it?"

"Because it was fun, and you know what?" Benjamin asked without a second to wait for an answer. "You disappear into the drapery too much."

"Isn't that a different topic?"

"No, it isn't, not at all." Benjamin gestured for another round. "You need to find your voice, not a singing voice, God knows you can't do that, but your own sense of who you are, what you have to contribute, all the unique things that make you the wonderful man you are." He drank another shot of tequila.

I groaned. "Not another psychiatrist in the family."

"I'm right about this and you know it. You're too reticent with your sisters, too deferential with Aunt Marie and too young around Aunt Margaret." He paused for a second. "Who's the psychiatrist?"

"Aunt Marie." I felt a flare go off in my drunken brain. "You have no right to evaluate the relationships I have with my family. You barely know them, for God's sake."

"Maybe I don't but you have to admit that Aunt Marie is usually right, isn't she?"

"Anything else?" I asked.

"You're too damn self conscious. I've watched you, and sometimes you act like there is a video camera trained on you all the time and you're worried how you will look when it's replayed." He pushed his shot glass away and stared at me. "I can see you are withdrawing." He shook my shoulder. "You know I am only telling you this for your own good."

"Fuck if I don't hate it when people say that to me."

"You're right, it was condescending."

I drank half my beer in one swallow. "My father watched me like a hawk from the day I entered junior high."

Benjamin looked surprised. "Why?"

"Your dad didn't?"

Benjamin shook his head no.

"I suspect he was trying to figure me out, trying to see what kind of son he had produced. His eyes were on me all the time." I had never told this to anyone. "But before we go any further, let's talk about your relationship with your mom and sisters." I shoved a couple of pretzels into my mouth. "Let's see, you barely speak to your mom." I inadvertently spit a piece of pretzel on his chest, which I flicked away. "You never talk about your sisters—I don't even know their names. All I know is that they don't let their kids celebrate Halloween or any other fun holiday. I assume they live in California?"

"Marin County." Benjamin looked at me, his eyes angry. "Let's get the hell out of here."

CHAPTER FORTY-FOUR

—∞—

We stopped at a liquor store where Benjamin bought two bottles of wine. Turning right on Conant Street, we walked halfway up the short block and I stopped in front of a narrow, two story building with a small driveway on the side. To the right of that was the parking lot for the local health club: Mussel Beach.

"Here we are," I said.

"Looks kind of small." Benjamin was looking around at the side of the building almost as if expecting another wing.

"It is small. The first floor has a kitchen, dining room and living room, and a half bath. Second floor has three tiny bedrooms and an even tinier full bath. It does have a great roof deck, however."

As I was looking at the house, I saw Gregg looking down at us, staring in disbelief at Benjamin. My eyes filled with tears as I ran around to the side door. Gregg came running down the steps, threw his arms around my waist and lifted me off the ground. He set me down and pushed away to look at me and then picked me up again. So far we hadn't said a word to each other.

"You look fabulous, you asshole. You've had work done, admit it."

I shook my head no as I returned his gaze. He had on his standard outfit: tan chinos, boat shoes with no socks and a blue pinstriped Oxford shirt, the sleeves rolled up to his elbows and the collar unbuttoned at the neck. He was tan and looked rested.

"You look pretty fucking fabulous yourself, dude." *Where the fuck did that come from?* I pulled him to me and we clung to each other for a few seconds. Did I really miss him this much or was it the booze? I never trusted tears after I had been drinking. I pulled away from Gregg and heard Benjamin clearing his throat.

"Well shit, aren't I being rude. Gregg Santelli, meet Clay Davis." I turned sideways to open up our group and gestured at Benjamin who shuffled forward. He shook Gregg's hand and started to pull back but Gregg wouldn't let go. He was looking at Benjamin from head to toe, taking in every aspect of his body and face.

"This is a joke, right Liam?" He let go of Clay's hand. "You're a professional model or actor or—" I saw Benjamin flinch slightly. "And my clever yet sleazy friend has hired you for the weekend. I'm right, aren't I?"

"Why would y'all say something like that?" Benjamin shoved his hands into his pockets causing his shorts to slide down his hips, showing a wide swath of skin.

"Because you're too perfect. People like you do not exist except in the movies or on a runway."

"Didn't we tell him that day on the phone that I do work in movies?" Clay looked at me.

"Gregg doesn't listen, never has, never will."

"Are you an actor?"

"No, no, I'm a stunt double."

"For whom?"

"Benjamin Graves."

Gregg let out a little scream and covered his mouth. "Shut up!"

"Something else I told you on the phone." I punched him lightly on the shoulder.

Gregg stepped back and began scrutinizing Benjamin again. "Perhaps you did, I am having a vague memory. Let's go inside. I want to see you in unflattering light. I know Benjamin Grave's body better than even he knows it. We'll just see if you can pass as his stunt double."

He turned away and jumped up the stairs. "Plus Daddy is dying for a cocktail, what will you boys have? Hell, why am I asking, I already know what you're having."

"He doesn't believe me," Benjamin said as we followed Gregg inside.

"He takes pride in doubting everything, says it makes him a better lawyer. He believes you- he's just doing his thing when he meets new people."

"His thing?"

"He likes to make them jump through hoops. You'll be fine, he's really a pussycat underneath."

I put my arm around his shoulder and guided him to the house. We stepped inside an overly bright kitchen renovated to appear as if we had stepped back to the nineteen fifties.

"Y'all could film a period movie here and not change a thing."

Gregg handed us margaritas. "I absolutely loathe this look but what can I do, we're just measly tenants. Hey, wait a minute, Clay Davis is not the name in the credits for Benjamin's stunt double."

"I don't use my real name Gregg, I like living under the radar," Benjamin said. Gregg blushed slightly and positioned Benjamin underneath the brightest light in the room. He moved in close and looked at his eyes and then spread his arms as if to measure his shoulders. Turned him around and put his hands on his waist.

"Gregg, for God's sake, he's not a prize steer at the Iowa State Fair."

"Calm down, Missy, I'm just checking a few things out." He looked at Benjamin's face again. "You could be his twin." His forehead scrunched. He seemed to be holding something back. He drained his margarita and said to Clay, "Mr. Davis, will you please take your clothes off?"

I was taking a swallow of my drink that I spit all over the floor. "Have you lost your fucking mind?"

"How am I going to be fully certain if this man is truly Benjamin Grave's stunt double if I don't see him naked?"

"How about you take his word for it?"

"Pish posh, won't do." He handed his empty glass to me. "I've seen every one of Benjamin's movies multiple times and I know exactly what Benji's stunt double looks like naked." He put his hands around Clay's neck as if to measure him for a shirt. "You do know, Liam, that Benjamin will not take his clothes off any longer after the uproar he caused showing his love muscle back in that horrid movie he made with Richard Gere. In every movie since, this man in front of us has done Benjamin's nude scenes." He put a hand on Clay's waist. "You must be completely comfortable naked in front of a crowd, aren't you?" Clay nodded yes a bit sheepishly.

"So drop them!"

I looked at Benjamin who was grinning drunkenly. He seemed to be enjoying himself. He pulled off his tank top and tossed it on the kitchen table where it made a slapping sound from all the sweat it contained. He was swaying back and forth. He unbuttoned his shorts.

"Clay should have a mole on his right cheek, upper quadrant and another mole near his left nipple that at first blush looks like a third nipple." Gregg was standing in front of Clay staring at both of his nipples. "That's odd, where is the mole that is supposed to be there?"

"We're stopping this right now," I said walking over to Clay and handed him his wet tank top.

"It's okay Liam, I don't mind. Your friend is right, I have been naked in front of lots of people. It's not a big deal."

"So where are the moles?"

Benjamin hesitated for a second. "I finally had them removed. Too many people just like you have been complaining on the internet that I shouldn't have obvious markings on my skin different from Ben, so off they went." He stepped out of his shorts and turned his back so Gregg could see there was no mole on his butt cheek.

"See! All gone."

Gregg's mouth had dropped open as he stared at the physical perfection of Benjamin's back and butt. Benjamin turned around and Gregg got a good look at his cock and balls.

I glanced at Benjamin over Gregg's head and mouthed, "Put your shorts back on."

Benjamin stepped into his shorts and pulled the tank top back on. "God damn I'm famished, what y'all cooking tonight?"

"Dinner is swordfish on the grill with a pineapple salsa, corn on the cob, which of course Liam will not eat since it wasn't picked five minutes ago, salad, bread, and pomegranate sorbet for dessert."

"How can we help?" Clay asked.

"Gregg has everything under control as always. Let's go up on the roof while we finish our drinks and I can get the grill started." He put a hand on Clay's shoulder and pointed him towards the back door. When Clay left the room, Gregg whispered to me, "I'm sorry, not sure what came over me, guess I am just overwhelmed by how beautiful he is."

I was surprised. Gregg did not apologize often.

"Other than being drop dead gorgeous, what's he like? Maybe I should rephrase that: what's wrong with him?"

I thought for a minute. "He can be controlling, not unlike you, and he likes having things done his own way and on his own schedule, also not unlike you—hell, I think I'm dating you!"

"Well, he could pass for my twin." Gregg made sure our drinks were full as we headed to the stairs. He stopped at the first step and blocked the way.

"Obviously I'm a little drunk….." He looked up the stairs. "Liam, I really miss you. When are you coming home?"

"I miss you too." I put my arm around his shoulder.

437

"So answer my question."

"This isn't home."

"It's more home than Iraq or wherever you disappeared to."

"I live in Iowa, I…O…W…A."

"I was a few letters off, it's still a four letter word that starts with I."

"There's no q in it, no stan at the end, not Idaho, Indiana or Illinois."

He picked up his drink waving his hand in front of my face. "Whatever. Anyway, I have one thing to say to you Liam Conor and one thing only: your gorgeous friend is a stunt double for Benjamin Graves, right?" I nodded.

"This means he will be leaving soon unless somehow every movie that Benji makes for the next two decades are filmed in Iowa. Then what? Will you follow him around the world or come to Boston, your real home."

"I'm not thinking that far ahead."

"Bullshit, that is utter bullshit. You wouldn't know how to live in the moment if your life depended on it, which in this case it may. You are Irish, you worry too much and you are always anticipating the next problem and expecting the worst."

"You know what?"

"Oh God, here it comes, the long Liam lecture."

"What y'all doing down there, my drink is empty," Benjamin called down to us.

"I've changed, Gregg."

"Fiddlesticks." He climbed up the stairs to the roof deck.

The sky was hazy with humidity, which blocked the stars. The sun had set and a full moon was rising in the direction of Truro, difficult to see through the haze. The granite monument that dominated the center of town was ablaze, spotlights illuminating it as if it was full daylight. I was drunk enough that I had no idea what the conversation had just been about.

I walked to the edge of the deck and thought about what was going on in town. I imagined some groups going out to dinner; newly met couples going home for quick sex; others napping, others strategizing the right moment to take whatever their drug of choice was for the evening; older couples in for the night waiting for friends to come over for a BBQ and then an after dinner walk using their dog as an excuse to look at the parade of handsome young men; their faces a combination of sadness and envy as they remembered their own time some thirty or forty years earlier, different costumes yes, different body types of course, different drugs (maybe) but the same ultimate hope: finding someone for a few hours or maybe with luck a little longer.

Gregg and Benjamin were standing in the corner looking out at the bay, the wind strong from the southwest. The wind was whipping various rainbow flags, cocktail hour flags, American flags and Canadian flags. They made a snapping sound as the wind raced over the buildings. Benjamin had set his drink on a table and had his arms wrapped tightly against his chest. I put my arms around him. He was covered with goose bumps.

"You're freezing. Gregg, do you have something he can borrow while we have dinner?"

"Of course. I'll throw that in the wash—are your shorts wet as well?"

"No, they're not," I said.

"Kidding Liam, I am just kidding, sometimes I think your sense of humor has been surgically removed."

Clay let out a loud guffaw. "Well, shit man, I've told him the exact thing many times. Sometimes he just needs to lighten up, don't y'all think?"

"We need to get you out of those clothes, again." Gregg put a hand on Clay's arm.

"Is it asking too much for you to cut the sexual innuendo?" I whispered to Gregg.

"Yes, of course it is. It will probably be months before I see you again and odds are I will never see this chiseled hunk of manhood again."

"Thanks for the vote of confidence."

"Anytime doll, you know me, always there to throw a wet blanket on anyone's hopes or aspirations."

The kitchen seemed balmy after the cool wind on the roof. Gregg threw Benjamin's T-shirt in the dryer and gave him a large purple sweatshirt with "provincetown" across the middle. I began setting the table as I aways did whenever I had stayed with Gregg over the years. We had a routine almost as if we were an old couple. I looked over at Benjamin who was sitting in a corner staring at us. Gregg pulled a bag of corn on the cob from the pantry and handed it to Clay.

"Decorative will only get you so far in this house, mister, make yourself useful."

Clay grinned at him, dumped the corn on the floor and began shucking it with gusto.

"The water will be ready in a moment, the salad is made. I'm going to scoot upstairs and cook this lovely fish." He held the platter in one hand, did a few twirls and ran upstairs.

"How long did you cook corn in your house when you were a kid?" Benjamin asked.

"Your accent just disappeared, are you aware of that?"

"Of course I am, I'm just testing myself to see how easily I can move back and forth." He pulled the leaves off an ear of corn. "Y'all should just stop fussing." He smiled at me. "That's one of your favorite words, isn't it?"

"What are you talking about?"

"Your famous interview with Jesse Clinton."

"Shit, I forgot all about that."

"I haven't." He dumped the corn on the counter. "That's when I fell for you. I thought you moved with such animal magnetism when you jogged away from him, the camera outlining your firm buttocks that I just knew I would plunder one day. You were so graceful and sexy. Oh, oh those blue eyes, they just jumped out at me…amazing!" He put the back of his hand on his forehead.

"You are an asshole, aren't you?" I was laughing as I put an arm around his waist and pulled him in for a kiss.

"Yes I am but I am your asshole. You're stuck with me now."

"How did you remember that interview?"

"Because I—"

"Dinner is served," Gregg called out as he came down the stairs. "Drop that corn in the water, two minutes only, if it is a second longer I will know and I will not be happy."

"But, that's not how my mama cooked it," Clay protested.

"We are not having this conversation again Clay, trust me on that." I picked up the corn, threw it in the water and set a timer for two minutes.

"Places everyone, this one act is about to begin." Gregg placed the fish on the table, steam rising and the distinctive smell of grilled swordfish filling the room. He dressed the salad, delivered the corn, doled out the salsa and poured wine while pointing us to our designated chairs. He of course was at the head, and Benjamin and I sat across from one another.

"One quick toast before my gorgeous dinner is ruined." He raised his glass. "To Liam Ashby, my best friend, the person who taught me what friendship is all about. And to Clay, a friend more gorgeous than my dinner, something I didn't think possible. Cheers to both of you!"

Gregg's face was free of irony. He was smiling at me but his eyes were sad. I picked up an ear of corn, slathered it in butter and pepper and took a bite. It was mediocre at best, probably picked days earlier.

"I know what you're thinking Liam, don't say a word, we've all heard your tired diatribe about corn, it's as tedious as your lectures on the evils of pornography. Has he shared that with you, Clay?"

"No, no he hasn't." Clay said with his mouth full of corn. He had kernels stuck to his cheeks. I made a gesture that he should wipe his face, which Clay ignored. Gregg started laughing.

"There is nothing sexier than a gay man who eats like a straight man. Clay Davis, you are a keeper!"

"What? What are y'all talking about?" Clay had swallowed half his glass of wine and taken a huge bite of his fish.

"I guess pornography wouldn't come up, would it?" Gregg sipped his wine. "That usually doesn't come up as a topic until the sex gets stale." He picked up his knife to start buttering his corn but his hand froze in mid gesture. "You two together, oh my God, if that were filmed I bet even Rush Limbaugh would watch. Oh, why did I say that? Quelle horreur!!"

I took a bite of my fish. It was delicious: fresh, moist, just the slightest hint of an herb I couldn't place. I stopped talking, stopped thinking, I was so hungry all I could do was shove food in my mouth. I cleaned my plate, ate three ears of corn, polished off my salad and sat back in my chair completely sated.

"How did y'all meet?" Clay asked as he pushed back from the table and poured us all more wine.

"You haven't told him?" Gregg asked. "How you followed me home one afternoon, forced yourself into my apartment and had your way with me?" His voice was rising in pitch, his tone quavering, his eyes darting from side to side.

Benjamin laughed. "You're a pretty good actor, y'all know that?"

"Why I am not on stage, I will never understand."

"We met at the public library," I said. "I know that sounds boring and mundane but that is how it happened."

"In a stall!"

"In the reading room."

"He followed me into the men's room, forced me into the last stall and took my youth in one quick thrust. It was over in seconds, he left me on the floor covered in his bodily fluids, my pants around my ankles."

"We were both looking for the latest John Updike novel." I got up to put a pot of coffee on.

"I was, but not you, not you Liam Conor Ashby, you were looking for another conquest, another young man to have your way with."

"He's older than me." I picked up the plates and loaded the dishwasher.

"That's a bold-faced lie. Just look at us, who has retained his youthful pallor while the other one has turned brittle and jaded?"

"We met at the library, went and had coffee, then lunch the following week, then dinner and the next thing we knew we were friends. It was that simple."

"I find it hard to believe that y'all haven't had sex." Clay spread his legs wide and scratched his balls.

"I just told you young man, are you listening to me?" Gregg sat up in his chair. "He is a beast, he wouldn't leave me alone for years. I had to change the locks, change my phone number, why I even thought of changing my identity!"

Clay laughed and burped at the same time. Gregg's head snapped around as if the belch had punctured his routine. His face relaxed.

"Well it hasn't been for lack of trying. I think Liam is adorable and he knows it but alas, he doesn't find me attractive. Nevertheless, after years of Jungian and Freudian analysis, I recovered. I finally realized he has no taste in men." Clay laughed again. "Of course, present company excluded."

CHAPTER FORTY-FIVE

We were walking down Commercial Street, Gregg in the middle, Benjamin and I on either side. The street was even more crowded than before. Benjamin had a grin from ear to ear.

"I need a drink and then I am going to dance all night long. I have energy to burn!"

Gregg linked his arm in mine and we surged forward. "Come on boys, get the lead out, we only have two hours until the music stops." We turned left on a narrow side street, the A House ahead of us with a line of thirty or so men snaking down the street.

"Shit, we are never gonna dance." Benjamin complained.

"Follow me, I have friends in influential places," Gregg said as he marched to the front of the line. The bouncer smiled at Gregg, they kissed and we walked inside. I could hear various people grumbling about who did *she* think *she* was. Benjamin whispered in my ear, "Just like being in LA."

"How did you pull that off?" I asked Gregg who was paying our cover charges.

"Bribes and a blow job or two, works every time."

We walked into a wall of people. The music was thumping and the small dance floor was jammed with men dancing, most shirtless and soaked in sweat.

"What can I get you to drink?" Gregg shouted at us.

"Water for me," I replied.

"Oh come on Liam, we're here to party."

"One of us has to be able to drive home."

"You're staying with me and I won't hear of anything else. How about three shots of tequila?"

"Hell yes, I'll take two and a cold beer as well." Clay reached in his pocket and pulled out a $100 bill which he shoved in Gregg's hand. Gregg pushed his way to the bar, leaned across and kissed the bartender on the forehead.

"More bribes?" I asked as Gregg handed me a shot of tequila and a wedge of lemon. Three bottles of Corona, their sides glistening with moisture, stood side by side.

"Yes of course."

I threw back my tequila and sucked on the lemon. I hadn't done a shot in years, and now I remembered why. I chased it with several swallows of beer while Benjamin drank both his shots and sucked down his beer.

When the music changed, Benjamin took hold of our hands and pulled us forward into the heart of the mass of sweating, dancing men. He ripped his shirt off over his head and shoved it into the back of his shorts.

"I love this song!" he shouted over the music as he began dancing.

"Are you gonna dance or just stand there like an idiot?" Gregg asked, pulling off his shirt. I took my own off and Gregg pulled me in for a hug. We danced close together, moving in synchronicity that came with years of practice. I looked at Benjamin. His head was thrown back, eyes closed. I pulled him in. We had our hands around each other's waists. Benjamin kissed Gregg on the cheek and then me on the lips.

"This is perfect, just perfect. I never want it to end."

What seemed like only minutes later, the lights came up and the music stopped. We had not left the dance floor once. Our clothing was as wet as if we had jumped into a pool.

"Fuck," Benjamin said, "I was just getting started. Isn't there someplace else we can go?"

"Only if you have a helicopter to take us to Manhattan. We could probably be there in an hour," Gregg said. Benjamin looked at me as I started to put my shirt back on.

"Why are you covering up? Don't be a prude." Gregg stopped me. "Let's go stroll Commercial Street."

We walked outside and when I felt the warm air I realized I felt dehydrated, tired and sober. I yawned.

"I would kill for a slice of pizza," Gregg said.

Gregg propelled us back to Commercial Street. With the bars closing so early, everyone gathered in front of Spiritus Pizza, the local pizza shop, another chance to find someone for the evening.

"Anybody else want one?"

Benjamin had his arm around my shoulder. I put mine around his waist. I saw my reflection in a window and realized I had never done this before: walked down Commercial Street without a shirt. It was like having a dream where you are the only naked person in a room. However as I looked around I realized that people were staring at Benjamin.

Gregg jumped up the two steps and disappeared into the restaurant. Seconds later he was back with three slices of cheese pizza.

"Wow, that was fast." Benjamin grabbed the first one and began devouring it.

"None of these boys actually eat this stuff, they just like gathering here," Gregg said.

"That was the best pizza I have ever eaten," Benjamin said. He had sauce on his chin, which I wiped away with the back of my hand. "I could eat about eight more."

"Now now, Mr Davis." Gregg put his hand on Benjamin's muscled stomach. "We wouldn't want this lovely tummy of yours to look like mine."

I looked at my watch; it was 1:30. I yawned again.

"Let's go home."

"I told you Liam, you are staying with me tonight."

"I am completely sober and I want to take a shower and sleep for at least ten hours." Gregg started to argue with me until he saw the look on my face.

"Never mind. When your jaw starts clinching like that I know arguing with you is a waste of breath. Plus I really don't want to listen to your orgasmic moans all night. Clay, does he still sound like someone has just shot him when he comes?"

"How the hell do y'all know that?"

"One time when he stayed with me, I heard him having an orgy with himself in the shower, I thought a cat had been run over on the street. Anyway boys, thanks for a great evening. See you tomorrow, or I guess I should say later today at Tea Dance?"

"What's Tea Dance?" Benjamin asked.

Gregg gasped. "You really are too good to be true, gorgeous, hung and innocent, all in one delectable package." He kissed us both on the cheek. "Run along boys, I need to say good night to my many many friends before calling it a night. Rumors abound that Paul—the erstwhile geneticist—may be looking for me."

CHAPTER FORTY-SIX

———∞———

I woke to the sound of the wind rattling the blinds. Benjamin was sleeping on his side, the sheets around his feet. I looked at the clock and jumped out of bed; it was already past ten. I put the coffee on and drank several glasses of water. I was as thirsty as if I had just run ten miles in ninety-degree heat. I poured two cups of coffee but before I could leave the kitchen, Benjamin walked in, his face puffy, hair tousled.

"I will kill you if you don't hand me that cup of coffee this second." His voice was gravelly from too much alcohol. I handed it to him and we walked upstairs to the deck.

Benjamin lay down on a chaise lounge and closed his eyes. "I am never going to drink again."

"Yes you will, in fact probably in a few hours." I sat down next to him and tried to pull him up. "Come on, we've lost almost half the day. We have a lot to do."

"I'd be happiest if you let me go back to bed." He sat up and put his feet on the deck, shaking his head side to side.

"We're going for a bike ride. You'll feel much better when this is over, trust me."

"I trust you…but this is one time I think you're wrong." He closed his eyes but I pulled him to his feet.

Twenty minutes later we were rummaging through a box of bike shorts. "I can never wear these when I go riding in Los Angeles," he said.

"Why?"

"Too faggy, or at least that is what everyone would say."

I found a dark purple pair with yellow stripes on the side. Benjamin settled on a white pair and when he pulled them on, you could see the outline of his cock draped across his thigh.

"There is something obscenely sexual about these shorts," he said.

"How far do you want to ride?" I asked, feeling unfocused annoyance.

"Around the block." He slumped his shoulders and his knees buckled.

"I'm going to ignore you."

We went into the kitchen and grabbed two bottles of water and a few energy bars. When I got on my bike I said, "We're going to the dunes first, do a complete loop, maybe two and then we'll head back here. If we're up for more, we can zip down to Wellfleet. Ready?"

Benjamin looked like he was about to fall asleep standing up. I felt surprisingly strong and raced down the hill and out to Route 6. I looked back to see Benjamin far away, struggling with his bicycle as he slowly made his way to me.

"It will get better." I took a long swallow of water.

"I'm ready for a Cuban."

"What?"

"A pork sandwich with cheese, pickles and mustard. A big bag of potato chips, a chocolate brownie and the biggest fucking Coca Cola you can buy."

I handed him a Cliff bar, which he inhaled. We headed towards Provincetown on Route 6. I looked back to see Benjamin far behind again but as the miles disappeared, the gap began closing until he was inches away from my back tire.

It was a perfect beach day, mid eighties with a slight breeze coming in from the ocean. We slowed down as we rode through the parking lot at Herring Cove Beach. I looked at a crowd of guys my age walking toward the beach and remembered the many times I had come here with Gregg. My unfocused annoyance grew.

"This is where all the homos come." I said over my shoulder. "You go down that path a bit and you enter a strange enclave of topless lesbians fortified by walls of plastic coolers, Tupperware, salad spinners, pasta makers, radios and nude infants. They usually have enough food and beer to last for a week but like clockwork everyday at three, it disappears in a caravan of wagons."

"Food? Beer?" Benjamin was panting with hunger.

"They won't serve you, they won't even see you." I felt anger building that didn't feel like it should be mine. "The men gingerly make their way through this miasma of dyke-ness and head to our own section or I should say sections. Section one is for the gym bodied Speedo boys so that all the older homos passing through to their own ghetto get a good look at what they cannot have. The Speedo boys throw Frisbees, jump in and out of the water maniacally, play paddle ball, all while slathered in sunscreen with a number so high, it would take a nuclear explosion to turn their skin the slightest shade of pink. Every fifteen minutes, a duo is sent out to wander down the beach to remind the other sections what they are missing."

"Is it really this rigid?"

"Would I lie about something like this?"

"Yes, I think you would."

"Section two is for the lower class of gym boys, the ones who go faithfully but you can't tell by looking at them as their diets don't match the exercise effort. They have their coolers and beer, just like the lesbians but on a much smaller scale. They stay close to section one hoping that one of the gym boys might still be high from the drugs they took the night before and might deliberately get lost in the dunes hoping for a quick blow job."

"You're making this up."

"Do you want to see?"

"No, not today." He guzzled the rest of his water.

"Section three is for the more free spirited, somewhat older crowd, maybe pushing forty, still wishing they could hang with the twenty-four year olds but knowing how foolish they would look if they did. They keep to themselves, smoke a little pot, sleep, read, maybe slip off into the dunes for a hand job or two."

"And once you get past this section?"

"Section four is the wrinkle room. And it is not pretty. Much older, deeply tanned men in groups of two or three trolling the tops of the dunes like characters from *The Lord of the Rings*. Their goal is to find someone at least ten years younger and suck the lifeblood out of them. But if they can't find a victim, they usually turn on each other. You'll see them in groups sitting behind scraggly reeds, playing with themselves, their blood infused cocks propped up by too small cock rings and too much Viagra."

"You sound like you hate all of this."

I thought for a minute. "Yeah, I guess I do." I got off my bike and stretched my legs. The anger was diffuse, brittle, yet ready to emerge with the slightest provocation. I turned and pointed off far in the distance. "See that light house way down the beach? There is a breakwater that you can walk across that begins at the end of Commercial Street and deposits you toward the end of the Cape. We'll go there tomorrow. That's my idea of going to the beach."

"Do I smell onion rings?"

"There's a fast food stand over there." I pointed across the parking lot.

"All I see are cars." Benjamin was licking his lips.

"It's about a half mile from here—" but before I could finish, Benjamin was racing away from me.

I stayed where I was, my emotions pivoting through my chest, a quartet of voices arguing in my head. I had been here many times with Gregg and had never liked it, not once. A voice emerged from the chorus and began telling me why I hated this scene but I turned it off.

When I arrived at the fast-food stand Benjamin was happily inhaling a bacon cheeseburger, onion rings and a milk shake.

"Now I'll be good for another fifty miles." The milk shake was on his upper lip and on his beard. I stopped myself from wiping it off with my finger when I saw a family of four at the next picnic table staring at us. I handed Benjamin a napkin.

"Come on, let's go," I said. He gave me a puzzled look.

As we slowly rode through the parking lot Benjamin asked, "What happened back there?"

I ignored him. He asked again.

"I don't know," I snapped.

"Jesus Liam, no need to bite my head off."

I took in several deep breaths, looked into his eyes, saw his worry and relaxed.

"Just old paranoia," I said, knowing I was dodging.

"About what?"

"Well, I wanted to lick the milk shake off your lips but stopped myself when I saw that family staring at us."

"What family?"

I looked at him: was he really that oblivious?

"Why didn't you?" he asked. "What the hell do you care what they think? This is what I've been talking about, that video camera was on again. You know Liam, your life is not going to be replayed on the nightly news."

"Would you have?"

"Absolutely."

"As Benjamin Graves and with another man?'

Benjamin shook his head. "It's not that simple."

"Yes it is," I said and rode away struggling with the urge to speed up and not look back.

At the end of the parking lot the bike trail began. It was narrow and bumpy as it snaked through the dunes and then up a steep hill where we paused at the top. We could see the ocean on one side, and in the other direction, undulating dunes stretched out for miles. My mind kept replaying our conversation while my eyes pretended to be taking in the beauty of our surroundings. I went first as I let my bike fly down the steep hill, the warm wind whipping over my face. The path turned sharply at the bottom. I braked to make the turn and waited for Benjamin.

I could hear him whooping before I saw him. He hit the turn without any attempt to slow down, his bike threatening to skip out from under him, his right knee scraping the ground as he righted himself and came to a sliding stop in front of me.

"That was fantastic. Wow!"

I looked down. "Your knee is bleeding."

"So what? It was worth it." He wiped away the blood that trickled down the front of his leg. He brushed off his knee and then washed it off with the water remaining in his bottle. "Where next?"

I looked at him. His eyes were clear, sweat was pouring down his face and chest. I got off my bike, walked over to him and kissed him.

I felt like I wanted to cry.

He looked at me with a confused expression. I pulled away and said, "We could go towards that light house," I pointed to our left, "but the path isn't in great condition so you end up walking at the end."

"I'm too revved up to walk. I need to bike, hard aggressive biking." He moved towards me. "Are you going to tell me what is going on?"

I shook my head no.

453

We rode our bikes up and down the dunes, racing, challenging each other up the hills and then flying down the other side. Benjamin took every curve at full speed, seemingly unaware he could end up speared on a scrub pine. After a couple of hours, we found a private, shady spot several feet from the path. We stripped off our clothes and let them hang on a low branch to dry.

"This is the best, Liam. Hell, I'm glad you made me do this. I feel like a new man." Benjamin was sitting on the sand. I straddled him, put my arms around his neck and kissed him again.

"Come on Liam, tell me, what the fuck is wrong?" he asked.

I thought for a few minutes. "I think this is possibly the happiest and unhappiest I have ever been in my life." I looked up at the sky. Was that the truth? Not seeking answers from anything or anyone in that direction, I looked back at Benjamin. "Do you understand what I'm saying?"

"No, not really. What are you unhappy about?"

"I think…I think…hell, I know that I have never been happier and yet there seems to be so many obstacles, so much shit." I rolled off of him and lay down on the warm sand. He moved over next to me. I felt like I had so much I wanted to say out loud, all the things I saw him doing that to me were contradictory, all the things inside me that drove me crazy but just when I thought I was going to say something, I worried about telling him too much and I shut down.

"Is this where you expected to be in your life?" Benjamin asked after a while. He put his head on my chest.

I felt instant relief at the change in the conversation. "You mean, lying nude in the sun with a movie star?"

"No, no, that's not what I meant. When you were a little boy, what did you think you would be doing when you were an adult?"

"Lying nude in the sun with a movie star."

"I'm serious, Liam." He sat up and brushed sand off his chest.

"Hell if I know, I didn't think that far down the road."

"You had no ambitions?"

"Of course I did but everything was colored by the fact that I was confused by my sexuality and had no idea how any of that was going to play out." I sat up next to him. "Just think if being gay had been a normal part of our society when we were kids, no odder than being left-handed. You're ten years old and fantasizing about your life. It could have changed everything for me."

"I suspect you're right."

"It hasn't exactly held you back," I said.

"It never entered my head when I was a kid that I was any different from anyone else."

"But you were, you slept with your best friend."

"I know that, it's just that there wasn't much of a struggle for me. I was attracted to girls, then I had my time with Scott and then I was in LA and dating women."

"What about your mom?"

"I didn't mean that I had no problems—not at all—as you obviously know firsthand. I just meant that I always felt normal, one of the guys, that sort of thing."

"You really do have it all, don't you?" I felt envy coursing through my body.

Benjamin's face went slack as he turned away from me. He stood up, brushed off the sand on his ass and pulled on his biking shorts.

"I don't have it all, not at all. I can't live my life the way I want to."

"How would that be?" I wanted him to say it out loud.

He knocked me lightly on the forehead. "Anybody in there?"

"Fuck you."

He smiled gently. "With you by my side, of course."

"What?" *He said it.*

"You heard me and please don't remind me of the stupid things I said to you when we first met. I am well aware how most people are and know for certain how the press would react if I introduced you to the world as my boyfriend."

I pulled on my shorts and then sat down to put on my shoes and socks. Boyfriend?

"What's wrong?" he asked.

I didn't know how to answer.

CHAPTER FORTY-SEVEN

———∞———

Benjamin decided on tan cargo shorts and a lemon yellow tank top. The wig and beard were firmly in place and he had on a pair of wrap around sunglasses I had not seen before. Steaks were thawing in the refrigerator. I was fighting the urge to call Gregg and tell him we weren't going to tea dance but I knew he would be annoyed with me plus I thought Benjamin should see it—once.

We stopped at Pepe's for drinks with Lulu and the bartender. A couple of drinks later we were making our way down Commercial Street again, the crowds noticeably larger with the weekend approaching. It was one of the hottest afternoons I had ever experienced in Provincetown. Usually there was a breeze of some kind but today it was dead calm. The men were as undressed as they could get away with, sweat glistening on their naked torsos. Benjamin had grabbed my hand as we left the bar and now had his arm around my shoulder.

We stood in line at the Boatslip waiting to pay the cover charge, Benjamin fidgeting at my side. Gregg had left a voice mail saying he was going to nap and would meet us around 6. I recognized a few people I had met over the years, people I didn't know well, people I had danced with, maybe flirted with.

Benjamin turned to me and told me how much he hated waiting, waiting for anything. Finally we were inside and we went immediately to the dance floor. We danced to several songs, shirts off, sweat soaking our shorts. I nodded toward the bar and left him on the dance floor. When I returned I stood on the side watching Benjamin dance. He was in the middle of a loosely formed circle, not dancing with anyone in particular but I could see that some of the guys were trying to act as if they were dancing with him.

"I swear to God that hunk in the cargo shorts has the exact same build as Benjamin Graves," a man standing next to me said to a friend. "I know that body better than I know my own." My head snapped around to see if it was Gregg. "He is the same height, his pectoral muscles are identical, his calve muscles are a perfect match. Oh my God, wouldn't you die if Benjamin Graves was here in disguise?"

"Are you high?" his friend asked. They slid onto the dance floor and got as close to Benjamin as they could. I drank my water and rejoined him. He smiled broadly at me, pulled me into his body and kissed me on the mouth.

"God I love to dance," he shouted in my ear, "and I need a drink." He wiped his forehead off with the back of his hand and then removed his sunglasses to wipe the sweat out of his eyes. I heard a gasp behind me. I looked at Benjamin's face: he had forgotten to put the blue contacts in. The two most famous green eyes in the world were staring back at anyone who was looking. I stopped dancing.

"Oh my fucking God, it is him," someone said. I pulled the sunglasses out of his hand and replaced them just as someone took a photo on their camera. I took him by the hand and guided him back onto Commercial Street.

"Do you know what is going on?" I asked. I was walking quickly, moving us down the street and back to the safety of our car. "You forgot to put the blue contacts in."

"The fuck I did."

"Turn around." Benjamin looked behind to see the group of men following us only a few feet away. They were rushing through the crowd trying to close the gap. Someone pointed a phone and took another picture. I pulled him forward as we almost broke into a run. "We need to keep moving, just keep moving." We were still a few blocks from our car. I toyed with stopping at a store or a restaurant but when I looked behind us again, the crowd seemed to have doubled in size. I heard his name shouted a few times. Startled tourists looked around trying to see Benjamin Graves. Seeing no one who resembled him they continued on their way scrounging for cheap T-shirts and bland taffy.

Suddenly two large leather clad men stood directly in front of us.

"Are you Benjamin Graves?" the larger of the two asked.

"Leave us alone." I tried to push him aside. He spun me around by the shoulder and shoved me backwards and into a wall.

"This has nothing to do with you Mary so butt out. Hey Phil, try to remove his sunglasses." I moved forward but the shorter, hairier one blocked my way. He had at least fifty pounds on me. A growing crowd had formed a half circle around us.

The taller one reached out to remove Benjamin's sunglasses but just as they were about to be removed, in one quick motion, Benjamin flicked the hand aside, grabbed hold of his arm and twisted it behind his back and pushed him down to his knees.

"It is none of your fucking business who I am, asshole. Get the fuck out of my way." He shoved him with his foot and he toppled over on his back. The shorter one moved aside and I quickly joined Benjamin. We ran to the car.

Back in the safety of our house, we nursed two Cape Codders. On the deck next to us was a bucket of ice filled with a sweating bottle of Grey Goose, a mostly empty bottle of cranberry juice on its side. The sun was beginning its slide into the ocean. Benjamin had said very little since Provincetown. My cell phone rang.

"Where the fuck are you?" Gregg barked into the phone. "I'm at tea dance nursing a too clean dirty martini and you are nowhere to be found."

"Sorry, Clay got a migraine. I should have called." I surprised myself at the quick lie.

"Yes, you should have," he said. "Am I going to see you tonight?" Just as I was going to say no, Gregg said, "You know what, this is better. I'm pooped. I'll see you tomorrow night plus I think Paul just smiled at me." He hung up.

"You just lied as well as I do," Benjamin said. He emptied his glass in three long swallows. "Do you know how sick I am of not being able to be myself with you?" He stood up to make another drink. "Alyssa and I would go out dancing or to the beach or restaurants...."

"What does she have to do with this?"

"I'm getting there." He poured himself a strong drink and topped off my glass. "My point is I've gotten used to all the attention. It can be annoying, sometimes infuriating, but I know what to expect. If I worry that a situation might spin out of control, I bring security with me." He sat down, his back up against my knees. "But when I think about us going out into the world as we are, no disguises, no fake names, it terrifies and enrages me. It terrifies me because of my worry that something could happen to you and it enrages me because I know the scene would be ten, fifty, a hundred times worse than what we just experienced." He leaned his full weight against me. "They wouldn't leave us alone, ever."

"No they wouldn't, would they?" I ran my hand through his hair. "But—we would be together."

"I want to be able to spend a weekend with you here or in Boston or wherever, like normal people do."

"But you're not normal." I felt his back stiffen. "You know what I mean, you can't lead a normal life anymore. I read an interview once with some actor who said, once you become as famous as Brad Pitt, you can't stop being Brad Pitt, and you can't stop being Benjamin Graves."

"I know that but I understand those issues if I have a woman on my arm. It is completely uncharted territory with you by my side."

"You wouldn't be the first celebrity to come out of the closet."

"God I hate that expression, such a cliché." He sat up and pulled away from me.

"They're just words Benjamin." I stood up and walked to the edge of the deck, the water turning from gray to black. "This topic keeps coming up even though we keep telling each other we're not going to talk about it."

"I know, I know, it's my fault," Benjamin said.

"I would tell my family and friends in a heartbeat," I said. "Do you think Aunt Marie would care who you are?"

He laughed. "She's probably never heard of me."

"Oh, she's heard of you. Aunt Margaret loves you. Every time one of your movies comes out, she talks about you nonstop for a week. Your name has been banned in Marie's house on a number of occasions." He walked over next to me. "So why do you keep bringing this up?" I asked. He put his arms around my waist and kissed me on the back of my neck.

"Because I've never been happier and I don't want this to end. That's pretty simple, isn't it?"

"So tell the truth."

"Right now I think I can but ask me tomorrow and you might get a different answer." He turned me around. "Why are we like this?"

"Gay?"

"No, no...why can't we just be who we are? Why is this such a huge fucking deal?" He walked away from me. He started to say something and then went silent. He sat down and put his head in his hands. "If I bring this up again this weekend, I want you to slap me, okay?"

CHAPTER FORTY-EIGHT

———∞———

We found a parking space in the small rotary outside the Provincetown Inn, the last hotel on Cape Cod. The breakwater, a long line of broken concrete, formed a path that stretched out for a mile or so in front of us. It cut across the water providing access to the outer most tip of the Cape. The tide was going out which left an enormous section of damp sand dotted with broken shells and sea grass. To our left the retreating water opened up into the bay. The tip of the Cape curled around with a lighthouse dotting the end almost as if a Christmas ornament. Benjamin was standing at the beginning of the breakwater, his face turned up to the sun. The beard, wig and blue contact lenses were in place.

"I've never seen anything like this." He turned side to side while taking off his T-shirt. I did the same, reveling in the warm wind that splashed across my chest.

"Come on." I took hold of his hand and led him forward. I had done this walk so many times I couldn't remember how I felt the first time. As we moved further from the road, the space between the rocks grew wider, the blue green water rushing through several feet below. In many places we had to jump across to the next rock. Benjamin began walking faster and faster and jumping higher while his backpack slapped against his body. He stopped to watch a few people fishing, said hello to a young couple taking photographs and watched some kids swimming in the clear water.

"If we step down to the sand and go that direction," Benjamin pointed to his right, "where will we be?"

"Herring Cove and homo heaven…or hell, depending on your perspective."

"We certainly know yours!"

"Maybe I was a little harsh."

"A little?" He punched me lightly on the shoulder.

I knew he was right, I had been too critical. However, I also believed as firmly as I believed anything that you could be a part of a community and still be yourself. Whenever I had walked through the crowds at Herring Cove over the years, I would look at the groups of lesbians with all their food and drinks, or the gym boys and their cliques and wonder if they knew they had all bought into stereotypes.

Then I would step back and realize that everyone did this. How many preppy guys had I met over the years, including Justin, who felt it necessary to dress a certain way, speak a certain way almost as if they had no choice. How many straight men had I met who within five minutes of meeting them let me know they liked women and were fanatical about sports.

"Hey Liam, where are you?"

"Missing Gregg."

"Why?"

"He always pulled me up short when I was judgmental."

"He's a good friend, isn't he?"

"Yeah, the best."

"I don't have a close male friend, well…except you."

"How come?"

"You know, I have no idea."

Toward the end of the breakwater, I jumped down onto the sand. We cut an angle towards the beach that was protected by a line of rolling dunes. When we reached the top of the dune, Benjamin dropped his backpack, kicked off his sneakers and ran down to the water. I looked in either direction: we were completely alone. Benjamin dove into the water and began swimming parallel to the shore. I found a spot and spread out our blanket. I pulled off my shorts, lay down on the blanket and let the sun seep into my body. I could hear the water pulling at the shore, the sea gulls calling, and I closed my eyes. Suddenly cold water splashed on my forehead. Benjamin was wiggling his body like a dog making sure that most of the water fell on me. I sat up.

"You didn't tell me this is a nude beach." He toweled off his back and stepped out of his shorts.

"It's not, and if we get caught they will fine us. Although I've never seen a park ranger come out this far. Some summers you never see them at all."

"Perfect." Benjamin threw himself on the ground and put my soft cock in his mouth.

"The fine for this activity is a lot more than for public nudity."

Benjamin pulled away and flipped over onto his stomach. "Does this make me one of those old trolls you were talking about?" he asked me over his shoulder as he spread his legs. "Guess we have a double standard here, don't we?"

I straddled him, my erection sliding up and down the crack of his ass. I lay down on top of him and began kissing the back of his neck. He moaned and pushed his hips up. He maneuvered his body so the tip of my cock was pressing into his body.

"Liam, I want you inside me…now." He was up on his hands and knees.

"But, but…I don't have any lube or condoms." He reached behind and grabbed my cock.

"Not necessary. I'm negative, you're negative, right?" He pushed back and drew me deep inside him. He pulled up so we were both kneeling. I was struggling not to come instantly. He put his hands on my ass and stopped my thrusting motion. "Easy, easy, we have lots of time." He took my hands and put them on his stomach. We knelt that way, not moving, my cock surrounded by his heat. Benjamin was running his hands up and down the mounds of my ass. He began to slowly and slightly move forward and backward.

I groaned, "I don't think I can hold back much longer."

Something caught my eye and I looked to my left. In the distance I could see people walking towards us.

"Fuck."

"What's the matter?"

"Look." He turned his head and pulled off my cock and in one quick motion put on his shorts. I knelt there, my hard on throbbing. I moaned in frustration and put my shorts on as well.

"You'll see, it'll be better this way." He leaned over and kissed me on the cheek. "Isn't it always better to wait for something?" He reached into his backpack and pulled out an apple. He sat facing the approaching twosome who turned out to be an elderly couple pulling a wagon filled with easels, paint and an old coffee can packed with brushes. They said hello as they walked by with a few random comments about the perfect weather. As soon as they were a distant silhouette, Benjamin pulled off my shorts as well as his own. I was still hard. He spit in his hand and covered my cock with saliva. Kneeling over me he slowly eased me deep inside him again. He kissed me on the mouth as he began moving up and down. Suddenly he stopped, stood up and pulled his shorts back on again. I turned around to see two men standing on top of the dune staring at us.

"I thought you said no one ever came out here," he said.

I slid into my shorts. "Did I say no one? I meant very few."

I walked toward the water glancing over my shoulder to see the men had pulled off their shorts, sporting two average sized erections, one pointing left, the other right. They moved down the dune and headed toward Herring Cove with a few glances back. I sat down on the edge of the water letting the waves roll across my lap. The cool water did nothing to diminish my erection. I leaned back, looked up and Benjamin began kissing me.

We heard the roar of a motorboat before we heard the catcalls. A group of college boys went zipping by. They were drinking beer, which they held up as if in a toast. Two of them were mimicking having anal sex while another pretended to give his friend a blowjob.

"Great, that's exactly what we need right now." I was disgusted. In all the years I had vacationed here, I had not seen anything like that.

"They're just jealous." He began kissing me again. "And who wouldn't be?" He pulled me to my feet and pushed down our shorts.

"I don't think I can do this again." I looked down at my partially erect cock. "Anyone could come walking over the dune again."

Benjamin ran up to the dune looking in all directions almost as if he were an Indian scout looking for soldiers. He bounded back down the dune, his cock bouncing up and down and side to side.

"There's no one coming. We have plenty of time. Now we are going to finish what we started." He was slicking my cock with saliva. Turning his back, in one quick motion I was inside him.

We stood that way, neither wanting to finish the sensations we had started and stopped and started and stopped. I slowly pulled out and then just as slowly reentered him. I repeated this several times until I felt his sphincter clamp down on my cock and I let go. I reached around to feel his cum splash across my hands. We jumped into the water just as the ferry from Boston went gliding past. We laughed as we dove into the cooling water, kissing and embracing as we washed off.

After devouring sandwiches, we both fell asleep. I woke up an hour later feeling as if I had slept all night. Benjamin was snoring lightly next to me, curled on his side, his face relaxed and happy. I looked at him and my eyes filled with tears. What was going to happen to us? I turned on my side and let my fingers strum over his shoulder. A tear dropped onto the sand. We lay that way for a long time, the rhythm of the waves lulling me in and out of sleep.

When we returned to our car, Benjamin said that he was starving—again. I suggested that we go home and cook something but he claimed he would pass out from hunger if he didn't eat within the next thirty minutes.

"Do you really want to go into Provincetown again after what happened?" I threw my bag into the back seat.

"Sure, I mean, what are the odds that the few people who might have seen something will recognize us?"

"This is a small town."

"I need a double bacon cheeseburger and onion rings pronto." The decision had been made. "Where's the nearest place?"

I took hold of his hand and we walked up Commercial Street toward the center of town. It was even hotter in the late afternoon sun, the air heavy and smelling of low tide. We sat down at the first outdoor cafe we found, our tank tops sticking to our salty, sweaty skin. Benjamin ordered the biggest and strongest margarita they knew how to make. The young, twinky waiter seemed oblivious to Benjamin's charms.

"Does it concern you that Tad, our prepubescent waiter, isn't bowled over by you?"

"He isn't?" Benjamin took a big swallow of his drink, the salt covering his top lip. "Of course he is, everyone is." He grinned at me. I took a long drink of my Corona, the taste instantly taking me back to my lunch with Sue at Clear Lake, which seemed a lifetime ago. Benjamin signaled to Tad, who sullenly walked toward our table. I listened to a few minutes of Benjamin's flirting and then tuned it out. I didn't care if he won this boy. I turned away from them and stretched my arms high. Someone caught my eye across the patio and I turned in my seat to see who it was. With a sharp intake of breath, I saw Justin staring back at me. He looked as shocked as I felt. He was sitting next to a small blonde woman, her hair pushed off her face with a white headband. She was talking on her cell phone and looking in the opposite direction. I turned away.

"Hey Liam, you all right?" Benjamin put his hand on top of mine.

I said nothing, I had no idea what to say, and I wanted to leave. "No, not really."

"Why? What happened?" Benjamin was looking from side to side.

"Please don't move and please don't turn around when I tell you this, do you promise?"

"What the fuck is going on?" Benjamin twitched in his chair.

"I need you to promise."

"Scout's honor."

"Justin Thornton is three tables behind you."

"Your Justin?"

"My ex-Justin."

"You have got to be shitting me—where the fuck is this twerp?"

"Benjamin, you promised." I finished my beer while Benjamin waved at Tad again who hurried toward their table, a big smile on his face. I saw Benjamin hand him a fifty-dollar bill. He ordered another round of drinks.

"Point him out, I want to see him."

"Okay, sit still. There's a bathroom inside the back of the restaurant. When you get up, look to your right and you'll see a guy, dark hair, nice looking, sitting next to a thin blonde. That's him and I'm assuming his wife Penny."

Benjamin had a grin on his face that I didn't trust. He stood up, looked over but walked into the restaurant. After a few minutes, he emerged from the building but walked straight back to me, looking disappointed.

"What's the matter with you?" I asked.

"Well hell, I was all set to talk to him but for the first time in my life, I couldn't think of any bullshit to say to someone. My mind went blank."

"Good." I took another slug from my beer. With a start I felt a hand on my shoulder.

"Liam, Liam Ashby, hey, it's great to see you again." Justin was standing next to me, a smile plastered on his face, his right hand raised for a handshake. His eyes seemed unfocused. I felt a spike of anger. I had had no intention of speaking to him but my Midwestern upbringing took over. I stood up, reached forward to shake his hand but instead found myself stuck in an awkward bear hug. "God, it's great to see you dude." He stepped back. His hair had fallen into his eyes and he pushed it off his forehead. I remembered how much Justin disliked his always out of place hair. My hand moved forward to help him, as I had done on many occasions but I stopped myself at the last moment. Out of the corner of my eye I saw Benjamin with a bemused look on his face. I looked again at Justin and realized he was very drunk.

"You look great man, where the hell you been keeping yourself?"

"I thought you moved to Winchester," I said.

"We did, we did but I still come to the South End every once in a while." I raised an eyebrow.

"Y'all gonna introduce me or do I have to introduce myself?" Benjamin stood up, towering over Justin.

"This is my boyfriend, Clay Davis. Clay, this is Justin Thornton." I felt like I was introducing two new clients at a business meeting.

"How do y'all know each other?" Benjamin asked without a trace of guile.

"Liam sold me my first house." Justin tottered back and forth several times.

"Among other things," I said feeling the anger I had been holding back move up my body in a volcanic spasm.

"What did y'all say?" Clay put a hand on Justin's shoulder.

"Justin and I dated for a while," I said loudly. A moment of panic crossed Justin's face as he looked back at Penny who was staring at us with a confused expression. "In fact, we were lovers, weren't we Justin? We were lovers for a couple of years."

"Why did y'all break up?" Benjamin was massaging Justin's shoulder. I looked at him critically. While he was still trim, he had lost his musculature and he looked older.

Justin stood stock still, no words emerging.

"Cat got your tongue, Justin?" Benjamin was standing too close to him. Justin slid a few feet away. He took a deep breath and seemed to regain his composure.

"Yes, Liam and I did spend some time together a few years back."

"Is that what you call it? Spending time together?" I reached for the table to steady myself.

"Are you still living on Union Park?" Justin asked.

"I moved home to Iowa," I said with instant regret.

"You did what?"

I froze. I never expected to see Justin again and I had not prepared a story that contained enough truth without giving him anything in return.

"Liam's Daddy died a couple of years ago and he moved home to take care of his Momma." Benjamin's accent as thick as I had ever heard it.

"Conor died?" Justin moved toward me but I stepped back. "I'm really sorry to hear that." I had almost forgotten that Justin had met my parents.

"So, Justin, why did y'all break up?" Benjamin was grinning but his eyes were angry.

There was a long awkward silence that I refused to break. I wanted to hear his answer.

He cleared his throat. "No particular reason, it just ended, you know that happens, people go their separate ways."

"Didn't y'all tell me, Liam, that Justin proposed to a woman, Petunia or Priscilla? Talk about a leopard changing his spots."

"Yes Clay, that is what he told me. I believe her name was Penny, in fact, is that her?" I pointed across at Penny who jumped a little.

"It was great seeing you again Liam; give Colleen my best." He shook my hand brushing past Tad who almost dropped Benjamin's burger and onion rings. I watched him plop down in his chair and polish off whatever he had been drinking while signaling for another. Penny was talking to him but he was staring off into the sky. Something he had done to me countless times whenever he didn't want to talk about something.

"Liam, this weekend just keeps getting better and better. Hell, the only thing that could top this off is if the real Cher came flying by on a motor scooter." He covered his burger in ketchup and began devouring it. He bit an onion ring in half, the onion sliding out of the crust and slapping against his chin.

I could feel the anger in my gut, in fact I felt sick. And I was pissed at myself, pissed that Justin could still get under my skin.

"Spent time together! Can you believe what that cock sucker called our relationship?"

"I have never heard you use that word before." Benjamin's mouth was full. "It's kind of hot, will you say it again?"

"Cock sucker, cock sucker, cock sucker." I added resonance and volume each time. The young lesbian couple at the next table starting laughing.

"He has Tourette's." Benjamin finished his lunch.

"I need to pee and then I want to go."

"But you haven't eaten your lunch."

"I don't want it." Benjamin slid it over as I got up from the table. I walked to the men's room without a glance in Justin's direction. I stood in front of the urinal replaying our conversation in my head, remembering the exact words, wishing I had said so many things. I lost track of time. Someone was standing next to me. I looked over to see Justin at the next urinal, one hand on the wall, the other hand stroking his cock.

"I can't believe how hot you look, Liam. Have you always looked like this?"

"You're drunk." I peed noisily into the urinal, zipped up my pants and turned to walk out the door.

"Why in such a hurry?" He reached over and grabbed my crotch. I pushed his hand away. Justin continued stroking his own, now erect cock. I tried to hold my eyes at face level but looked down for one quick second. It was just as handsome as I remembered.

Justin moved closer to kiss me. He pushed me against the wall and pressed his body hard against mine. I put both hands on his chest and shoved him across the tiny bathroom. He hit the door of the stall with a thud.

"You're drunk and you're an asshole." My rage was at fever pitch.

Justin continued stroking his cock; he shuddered, turned his body and came into the urinal. He stood there for a moment as if in shock, zipped up his pants and stumbled out the door. I washed my hands and threw cold water on my face. The anger had left with Justin. When I returned to the patio Justin and Penny were gone.

"What just happened?"

"I don't want to talk about it."

"Yes you do and yes you will."

I looked at my empty plate. "Where's my food?"

"I ate it," Benjamin said as he looked around for the waiter "What do you want?"

"Nothing, I'll just finish my beer and we can go." I took two long swallows. "I cannot fucking believe this, after all this time to have this happen is such bullshit!"

"Have what happen? Did he do something to you?"

I sat down and closed my eyes. "Guess you could say that."

"Tell me what happened."

I paused as I realized that underneath my numbed state was a layer of sexual excitement. I wondered if things could get more fucked up. "He made a pass at me."

"He did what? I will kill that mother fucker." Benjamin stood up from the table looking in several directions. The lesbians at the next table were watching and waiting. "Where the fuck did he go?"

I looked at the two women. "Clay, please sit down. He's long gone, trust me, nothing happened."

"I want to know everything. Start from the beginning." His face was red, sweat pouring down his temples. He waved at Tad who scurried over with another margarita and a Corona.

I lowered my voice. "I was standing next to the urinal rehashing what I had said to him, kicking myself for not saying more. After a few minutes I realized he was standing at the next urinal…he had his cock out…he was beating off."

"I am going to kill that fucker if I ever see him again. What a sleaze bag."

"He tried to grab my crotch, I pushed him across the room but meanwhile he never let go of his cock. He hit the side of the stall and then turned and unloaded into the urinal. It was over in seconds."

Benjamin was looking intently at me. Softly he said, "Was he that kind of person when you dated?"

"What do you mean?"

"Someone who hung out in public bathrooms or locker rooms hitting on anything with a cock."

"Hell no, my God, we only had sex that one time in the middle of the night."

"Are you sure?"

"Absolutely."

"You might want to think some more about this Liam. You don't become that kind of person overnight."

"What possible difference does it make now?" I asked. Benjamin scowled. "I believed him, he just wasn't a very sexual person." Benjamin let out a long breath and his shoulders relaxed.

"Tell me again what you saw in him?" he asked.

"Oh God, you sound like Gregg."

"Really, I want to know, tell me."

I could feel the burn on my forehead and shoulders and pushed my chair into the little shade there was.

"I thought he was everything I wasn't. He was Protestant, straight or so I thought, Ivy League, worked at a bank that his family had owned for generations. He was handsome, funny in a way I had never experienced before." I remembered sailing with him off Cape Ann while he did a spot on imitation of George Bush. "He came on so strong. He would call me all the time to go biking, skiing, rollerblading, hiking, sailing, running. We were always doing something—plays, symphony, dinners, rock concerts, folk singers in Harvard Square, the Celtics, even the Bruins. I saw and did things I never would have done on my own. He was always challenging me, challenging me to try harder, run faster, climb higher, listen more carefully to music, to think about the world in a way I had never done before. We never talked about the same thing twice. I thought I had met my best friend."

Benjamin said nothing, a frown etched in his forehead.

"It never occurred to me that we would…have sex. It did to Gregg of course; he thought Justin was a closeted liar from the get go."

"If Gregg did, why didn't you?"

I took a sip of his margarita. "Because I didn't want to believe it."

"Did you meet his parents? Siblings?"

"No, no I never did."

"Why?"

"There was always an excuse."

"Didn't you find that odd? He met your parents obviously."

I squeezed the lime into my beer. I remembered my dad's reaction to Justin. Dad had always been demonstrative with other men, a hand on the shoulder, a touch on the arm. He never touched Justin once.

"How did you know for sure his life story was true?"

"That was easy to research on the internet and at the New England Genealogical Society."

"You spied on him?"

I reddened. "I did a little research on him. It was no big deal. I just started to have a few doubts. But there was no reason to doubt him, it was all true."

"How many times did Gregg meet him?"

"I tried a few times to have them over for dinner, meet for coffee or a beer but it was awful. They hated each other immediately, it was almost feral. Gregg cannot tolerate closet cases and instantly decided Justin was a classic one. As was his fashion whenever Gregg was around a closet case, he turned into the biggest queen this side of the Mississippi. Every time Gregg camped it up, Justin disappeared into himself. "I gave up. The last time we were all together was here in Provincetown. What a major fuck up that was!"

"Did you think Gregg was wrong?"

"Yes...no...sort of." I blushed. "I don't know what to believe. Gregg told me he thought I was in love with Justin. I denied it of course, at least early on. I told him I loved him but as you would love a brother." Benjamin started to say something but stopped himself. "You don't have to say anything Benjamin, I've said it all to myself before."

"Did you ever try to initiate sex with him?"

"No, never, absolutely never."

"Nothing even vaguely sexual?"

I thought of the many times we were naked around each other. In various locker rooms, Justin standing naked in the sauna doing a variety of yoga poses while I watched and admired his perfectly proportioned body. We had gone skinny-dipping in the rivers of the White Mountains and had even gone on a nude hike one muggy late July day on a path deep in the woods of northern Maine.

But there was no arousal, it was innocent, wasn't it?

"We were naked a lot around each other but I always thought it was just something good friends did." My face was bright red. "We even went on a nude hike once."

"What does your Aunt Margaret say—'I'm gonna slap you upside the head.' Jesus, Liam, what were you thinking? Did you seriously think this was normal behavior? A straight guy befriends an openly gay man and yet never introduces him to his friends, family, siblings, work associates. Your best friend hated him and you just admitted you had moments where you thought he was lying."

"I am done talking about this." I stood up.

"Oh no you're not. Sit down." I stood where I was and glared at him.

"All right. I'll pay the bill. At least sit down until I do that."

I sat back down on the edge of the chair looking in every direction except at him.

"Let's get this out in the open once and for all, okay Liam?"

I did not reply.

"You sit there and act like you have this all figured out inside your head but you don't, do you? And I suspect what just happened with Justin will fuck you up even more and you'll carry around that piece of shit in your heart for the rest of your life." He reached over and grabbed my hand. "He is not worth it, not in the slightest."

"How can you say that? You didn't know him."

"I just met him."

"No, you did not." I remembered the first time I met Justin. The man Benjamin had just seen was a pathetic imitation.

"Who did you fall in love with? Which Justin Thornton?"

I sat in silence for several minutes until Benjamin cleared his throat.

"The Justin that no one else met," I said.

"I suspect that version wasn't real either."

I stood up, anger coursing through my chest. "Why the fuck do you think you're an expert on this guy after meeting him once?"

"LA is full of his type. Most of the actors I've met are just like him. They want you to think they are these big macho types with a trail of girlfriends but meanwhile they're getting their cocks sucked in a cheap hotel or picking up tranny hookers or marrying a lesbian. He is cookie cutter."

"Justin was not like that."

"At least not with you," Benjamin said. "But it sure sounds to me when two guys go hiking in the nude there must have been a slight sexual edge? Was he hoping to run into a few strippers along the way?" He smiled. I didn't.

I looked him in the eyes. "I want to talk about you. I recall a few times when we first met where you took your clothes off at the drop of a hat. Just another closet case?"

"It was different." He pushed his empty glass away.

"How?"

"Give me a few minutes and I will give you a few perfect answers." It was another of his glib responses but this time he wasn't smiling.

"You know it wasn't any different, you just won't admit it."

"First, I never said to you I was 100% straight. What I told you—at the time—is that I reject all labels."

"But you also told me about a hundred times that you weren't gay." I slid my beer towards him but then took it back. "Then in a complete about face you announced you were a proud homosexual."

"I was acting with a capital A. Isn't that what you told me at the time?"

"Admit it, the story is the same, just the main character changed." I looked down. Had Gregg been right all along? Was Benjamin just another SOB story?"

"It's not the same. Not at all." I looked into his eyes again, but he looked away. "Oh all right, there were some similarities, at least when I first met you but not any longer. I love you. I've told you that many times. Did the cock sucker ever say it to you?"

"Once." It was the one time Justin had gotten painfully drunk.

"There you have it, there's the difference."

I lowered my voice. "Then when are the disguises going to stop? Aren't the two of us now in a different closet of our own making?"

"No...not at all...it is not the same thing at all," he said quietly. "The disguises have nothing to do with how I feel about you. They're all about keeping the world at bay."

"Really? That's what they're all about?"

Benjamin thought for a moment. Tad dropped off the nachos, a mound of food that neither of us reached for. Under the hot sun the cheddar cheese began to pool in a greasy pattern along the edge of the plate.

"Well, here we are talking about this again." Benjamin looked around to see that the lesbian couple had left. "What did I tell you this morning? Disposing of these disguises would take a level of courage that I don't think I have. You know by now what would happen if I took it off and you and I went walking hand in hand down this street, don't you?"

"Then stop being so critical of Justin."

"You're defending that asshole?"

"No, I'm not defending him, but I am struck by the similarities between the two of you and annoyed at myself for not noticing sooner." Benjamin rubbed his chin as if he had been stung. "Justin didn't have the courage to tell his parents the truth, he didn't have the balls to live his life as an openly gay man and he didn't have the guts to tell his dad that the Thornton family name might end with him. It's the same thing, Benjamin, it's all about integrity, honor and having the nerve to tell the world who you are and who you love. Clearly Justin is a coward. Are you?"

Benjamin stood up and walked into the restaurant. I waited, picked at the nachos, and waited some more. Benjamin reappeared looking dejected. He threw some money on the table.

"I am a coward," he said. He picked up his empty beer bottle and took a drink of nothing. "I was going to do it, I was really going to do it."

"Do what?"

"Take off this stupid disguise."

"And?"

"I just told you, I don't have the balls." He lowered his sunglasses for a second, his green eyes blazing across the table at me. "All I could manage was taking off the blue contacts." He had a hangdog expression. Suddenly his head snapped around as he stood up and looked at the crowd walking by on Commercial Street.

"Is that Debra? It can't be. What the hell would she be doing here?" He looked in several directions.

"Debra who?"

"There, listen, there it is again." I heard a vaguely familiar but unusual laugh that rang out over the crowd noise.

"I know that laugh anywhere. What in the name of God is Debra doing here?"

The laugh rang out again and then I knew who it was. Emerging from the crowd was Debra Merchant carrying a slice of pizza, a man by her side. Benjamin called her name. She looked at him as she would a total stranger. He called her name again. He moved around the table and walked right up to her. The man next to her put his hand up as if to stop him. I watched as he said something in her ear and then lowered his sunglasses for a second. She let out a shriek as she dropped her pizza on the ground and threw her arms around his neck. Benjamin put his arms around their shoulders and moved them toward me.

"What in the name of God are y'all doing here?" His Texas accent was back in place.

"I could ask the same of you and what's with the beard and accent?" Benjamin ignored her question. "Anyway, my husband and I are here to see Elaine Stritch, she's performing at Town Hall tonight." She was bouncing around as if on a pogo stick.

"Do you want to sit and have a drink with us?"

"I would love to but we need to get back to our hotel so I can put my face on and God knows that can take a weekend!" She let out her laugh again that I had heard countless times on *Phil and Mary*. Apparently she hadn't been acting.

Benjamin looked over at me, I looked at her and she looked back at the two of us.

"And you are?" she asked.

"I'm Liam Ashby." I shook her hand. Benjamin was tongue-tied and his face was bright red.

"Are you an actor?"

"No, I'm a bartender back in my home town in Iowa."

"How do you know Benjamin?"

"I...I worked at the funeral reception for his dad."

"I was so sorry to hear about that." She stood up on her toes to give Benjamin another hug.

Benjamin started to say something but all he produced was a croak. He cleared his throat loudly.

"Benjamin, you've met my husband before." They shook hands. She turned toward me. "And this is Liam Ashby, a...a...a friend of Benjamin's."

"Liam is my...my...my...my...b...friend." I looked at Benjamin who was in such distress he looked ill.

"What did you say?" she asked.

"I am his..." I began but Benjamin interrupted.

"Liam is my friend. We grew up in the same place." He looked relieved and guilty at the same time.

"This is so freaky." She was smiling but with a question in her eyes. "First I heard the rumors that you were in Montana, then Iowa

480

and of course the Internet is abuzz that you're in Ptown which is obviously true." She laughed again.

"Do you mind calling me Clay?"

"Okay, I guess." She looked at me with a raised eyebrow

"Walk with us to the hotel," she said. She took hold of his hand. I followed behind with her husband, neither of us saying anything. Every few feet people would try to stop her for a photograph or an autograph but she waved them off, occasionally throwing out her famous laugh. When we reached their hotel, Benjamin put his hands on her shoulders and said something under his breath.

When we got to our car I asked, "What did you just say to her?"

"That I would call her for dinner the next time I'm in LA."

"That's all?"

"What else would I say to her?"

"What did you tell her about the beard and accent?"

"I lied to her." He got into the car, took off his sunglasses and looked at me, his eyes were full. "I told her I am researching a role."

I turned away.

CHAPTER FORTY-NINE

———∞———

Benjamin's hands were gripping the steering wheel as we sped along the highway. I kept looking over at him hoping and waiting for him to say something, something that was real, something that mattered to us.

"I am the worst kind of coward," he finally said as he brought the car to a stop in front of the house. "As much as it kills me to say this, Justin at least had the legitimate right to fear losing his family. I have no relationship with my mom…or sisters for that matter. I have enough money to last several lifetimes. I have nothing to lose. Except you. I'm going to lose you, aren't I?"

I didn't reply.

We sat in the car, the engine off, the windows down. Songbirds were crowding the bird feeder near the kitchen window. A blue jay swept in scattering the smaller birds into the scrub pines that lined the driveway.

"Say something Liam, anything."

"What do you want me to say?" I looked out the window. The blue jay had flown up to the eave of the roof, looking down as if to dare the other birds to return. "Do you want me to say that you're right? That we're over?"

A tear slid down his cheek. "Of course not."

"Then what is there to say?"

"That you love me?" He put a hand on my knee.

I felt an ache in my chest. I looked at him. "Yes, I love you, but…."

"But what?"

"I can't do this anymore. I did it with Justin and I've been doing it with you. I won't hide anymore." I started to get out of the car. "What would have happened if you had told Debra that I was your boyfriend? Would she have told other people?"

"I have no idea, but most likely she wouldn't have said anything to anyone."

"Then why didn't you tell her the truth?"

His face turned into a scowl. "Do you think this is easy for me?"

"Of course not."

"Then give me a break."

"No, I won't, not anymore. You just asked me if you're going to lose me and now you're antagonistic?" I walked into the house slamming the door behind me. Benjamin followed me slamming the door even harder.

"I'm beginning to think you're all talk." I poured a glass of water.

"Who's all talk?" He popped a beer. "If I told the world we're a couple, would you move to LA with me?"

"What?"

"You heard me, would you come with me? Would you support me? Would you put up with the shit storm that would ensue? Would your family be okay with photographers stalking them? Do you think Colleen would be okay if someone followed her into church some Saturday evening? How would she feel if we were at her house for dinner and there were fifty photographers and TV crews lined up on the street waiting for us to leave?"

"That wouldn't happen," I said.

"Don't lie to me Liam, you know it would be even worse than that. She would have to move. Look at what my parents had to do, they walled themselves off in their home, in a house they hated. This would be so much worse."

"So you can't lead your life the way you want because you're protecting my family? Is that really what you are trying to convey to me?"

"It's just part of it, part of the fall out, that's all."

"So quit making movies."

He stopped dead in his tracks as he ripped the beard off his face and threw it on the counter. He now had a tan line that threatened to split his face in two.

"Why would I do that?"

"Seems to me if you stop making films and move to a small town in Iowa with your boyfriend, stay out of trouble, stay out of the New York and LA scene, this will all blow over in a few weeks."

"But I like making movies, I'm good at it, plus I have contracts. I have commitments for four films over the next five years. I just can't walk away."

"Then you're stuck. You won't give up your job even though you have enough money to last you forever. And yet you're paralyzed at the thought of 'us' being over."

"Why can't we leave things as they are? I'll come back to Iowa every chance I get. You don't have to do anything."

"Except hang out with someone in disguise who uses a fake name, continue lying to my family and friends and never be able to tell the people I love who you really are. Is that what you expect me to do?"

"It's worked so far." His face was trying to break into a boyish grin but it seemed like it hurt.

"Not anymore," I said.

He stood in place, staring at nothing. "I can't talk about this."

"Why not?"

"I'm pooped, I need a nap."

"When are we going to talk about this?" I asked.

"Back in Iowa," he said. I started to argue with him but with a jolt to my gut, I knew in that moment our relationship was going to end.

When I didn't say anything, Benjamin smiled with relief.

"We're going to make this work Liam, I just know we are."

No, we're not.

"How about we stay in tonight?" he asked.

My mind was blank. "Sure."

"Are you joining me for a nap?"

"No," I said abruptly. He frowned.

"I'm calling Gregg to have him come here," I said, walking away without waiting for a reaction.

Gregg seemed relieved at the thought of dinner in North Truro. I invited him for 7:30 knowing it would be 8:30 at the earliest. In the refrigerator I found a drawer full of various colored peppers, sweet onions and white mushrooms. There was chicken thawing on a shelf almost as if someone knew we were eating in.

I was moving slowly, feeling like I was walking underwater. Everything was different now. For the first time in my life, I knew what it was like to love someone and have it returned, and it was going to end. The thought of going back to Mason City now, without Benjamin, struck me as if I was entering a parallel world where nothing ever changed: treated like a young man forever.

I set the table, filled a plate with cheese, crackers, olives; chilled the glasses for cosmos, anything to stay busy. I felt a lump of sadness in my chest I could not shake. My eyes filled. I wondered why I had ended up in the same place. I believed I was a person of integrity and honesty and yet both of my relationships were built on a pyre of lies.

Was there something I should have done differently? If I could start over with Benjamin was there one moment I should have altered? One moment when I should have known to stop before we began?

I went upstairs to check on him. I heard the shower running and left him alone. I changed my clothes and went back to the kitchen to set the table. I poured myself a glass of wine. I looked out the window and thought about the conversation we had just had; the same conversation we had been having ever since we left Iowa.

A part of me knew that our lives were too different: clearly Benjamin was not willing to give up the life he had created. And I wasn't willing to join his, was I?

I felt a pain in my gut and pressure behind my eyes and I knew, I knew how deeply I had fallen.

My practical voice jumped in to remind me that we hadn't known each other very long. It warmed to the moment, telling me that this was going to end and I would never see Benjamin again. The pain disappeared and my eyes dried.

I heard a knock on the door and spun around in surprise. The clock above the sink showed 7:30 on the nose. To my shock, Gregg was standing at the door carrying a brown bag with several bottles of wine. I looked at my watch and pretended to faint.

"I'm on time for once, so shoot me." He barged into the kitchen as if he owned the place. He turned a few times appraising its features. "Guess it'll do, not my taste by a long shot. Anyway, where's your Texas side of beef?"

"He's still getting ready."

"Perfect, that gives us time to talk." He looked at my wine glass. "Where's my cocktail?"

"I wasn't expecting you for at least another hour." I began preparing cosmopolitans.

"That was the old Gregg, the Gregg that got to see you often. The new Gregg, who only gets to see you in drips and drabs, is punctual." He turned away from me. "It puzzles me how much I miss you."

I handed him his drink and we clinked glasses.

"You are going to crap when I tell you who I saw today," I said. I took a sip of my drink thinking it needed more vodka.

"Julia Roberts?"

"Nobody famous."

"Your sisters?"

"No."

"My future husband?"

I took another sip. It definitely had too much cranberry juice. "I saw Justin Thornton and his wife Penny." I watched him carefully. He flushed, his eyes narrowed, the muscles around his mouth twitched, dragging his lips down into a frown.

"I hope you didn't talk to them." He took a drink and scowled. "I'm making the next batch."

"I did talk to him, he came over to us. I had no choice."

"What did that cock sucker say to you?"

"He was completely shit faced but friendly, sort of like running into an old fraternity brother. Then he started hitting on me, well not exactly hitting on me while Clay was around but he did follow me into the bathroom." Gregg's eyes widened. I couldn't help but smile.

"Are you fucking kidding me? What did he want? What did he say? How does he look?"

"He wanted to give me a blow job. He kept telling me how good I looked. He on the other hand is going to seed." I smiled again at the wave of pleasure this produced.

"Wait, wait a minute there. This asshole who supposedly only jerked you off once now wanted to have public sex? Doesn't that strike you as fucked up?"

"Yes of course it was fucked up."

"So, what happened?"

"I pushed him away and he jerked off into the urinal and fled. Never saw him again."

"He jerked off? In front of you? What did Clay say?"

"Only that he wanted to kill him. Oh, and that he wouldn't be surprised if Justin had been having anonymous public sex for years."

"I couldn't agree more. My God, what a sleaze although I do find the thought of this curiously arousing."

From the top of the stairs I heard, "Where's my drink?" Gregg spun around as if disoriented.

"That just can't be," he said. He looked up at Clay who was standing on the staircase completely in shadow. "Now I get it. Of course! Of course you would know how to do a perfect Benjamin Graves imitation. Tell me again why you're not an actor?"

I followed Gregg's gaze wondering if Benjamin had forgotten his Texas accent again.

Benjamin came down the stairs, the light illuminating his feet and then slowly making its way up his body. When his face emerged, it was as Benjamin and not Clay. I set my drink down and walked a few paces back. Gregg's mouth was open and his drink slipped in his hand, splashing onto his sandals. He looked at me.

"What the fuck are you doing to me? Where's Clay?" He looked again at Benjamin and then at me. His eyes were furious. "Liam, what the fuck are you up to?" Benjamin stood next to him and poured himself a drink.

"God damn it Liam, who the fuck is this?" He looked back and forth between Benjamin and me, his eyes glazed by shock. I found my drink and threw it back. Gregg fumbled for the pitcher and filled his glass to the brim. Benjamin took a step towards Gregg, who moved across the room.

"It's me—Benjamin," he said quietly.

Gregg glared at him. "It can't be," he said.

"Let's go sit down. It's a long story." Benjamin walked across the kitchen and put his arm around my shoulder. He kissed me on the lips. "Liam is my boyfriend and I love him." I looked closely at him. He must have put bronzer on, because the tan line was gone.

"But…but…you're straight! Aren't you? What about Alyssa?"

"We broke up."

"I must be hallucinating. This cannot be happening. Things like this do not happen." The color had drained from his face. He reached for his glass and almost knocked it over. "I have been in love with you for over a decade and now here you are standing in front of me and you are fucking my best friend?" He leaned against the wall. "How the fuck have you kept the fact that you are gay out of the press?" Suddenly he yelled, "I knew it, I just knew it. Why didn't I trust my instincts?"

"What are you talking about?" I asked.

"I knew that was Benjamin's cock the second I laid eyes on it." He set his drink on the counter and grabbed for a chair. "I saw Benjamin Graves' cock in the flesh. Oh my fucking God, this is way too much. I need air." He grabbed his drink and looked at me. I pointed at the staircase and he went up to the deck.

"What is going on?" I asked, feeling pleasure and anxiety wrapping around my stomach.

"Trial run."

"Trial run for what?"

"Don't be dumb, Liam. For what's coming next."

"What's coming next?"

"Not sure yet, let's see how tonight goes."

"I thought you said you are a coward."

"I am a coward. I'm not exactly on display here, am I?"

"But why do you trust Gregg not to say anything?"

"Because he's your best friend and because you love each other."

We climbed the last few steps. The wind was whipping across the front of the house, lightning flashing on the horizon. The air was full of moisture, the bay a jigsaw puzzle of white caps. Gregg was leaning against the railing, his empty glass on the table, the pitcher of cosmos in his hand. He reached across and touched Benjamin on the face.

"You are real, aren't you? Thank God. I was afraid I had lost my mind."

Benjamin took the pitcher from Gregg and filled their glasses. We sat down across from each other. No one said a word.

"This is awkward," Benjamin said as he stood up and put his hand on my shoulder. "Somebody say something."

"How about this?" Gregg said. "My best friend moves home to some Podunk town in the middle of nowhere...."

"That Podunk town is our home town," Benjamin said.

"You know what I mean. Liam moves to a no doubt lovely small town in no doubt a lovely state in no doubt a lovely portion of the country and meets the biggest movie star in the world, who happens to be a closeted gay man who happens to fall in love with said best friend. Does this make sense to you? Would you star in this movie?"

"Please don't use that phrase, closeted gay man. I hate that," Benjamin said.

"They're just words that happen to be true, aren't they?" Gregg asked.

"We are not having this conversation," I said. "There are a million other things we can talk about."

"Like how much I love your best friend." Benjamin pulled me towards him and kissed me hard on the lips. Gregg gasped and then frowned.

"How does my best friend in the world lie to me about something this big for the last two months?" he asked. "How does that happen?"

I blushed bright red.

"Because I asked him to." Benjamin took a step towards Gregg who stepped away.

"That's not good enough." Gregg snapped. "We have no secrets between us. Or I guess I should say, had no secrets."

"I wanted to. You have no idea how badly I wanted to tell you."

"Then why didn't you? I've known you for over a decade. How long have you known him?" He pointed his finger at Benjamin.

"Since Memorial Day," I said quietly.

"So you put a two month relationship ahead of our ten year friendship." His voice was clipped. "Glad to know where I stand."

"Gregg, give him a break. It's not his fault, it's mine," Benjamin said.

"This has nothing to do with you and has everything to do with the apparent and appalling lack of trust my best friend has in me."

"I'm sorry." I walked to Gregg and put my arm around his waist.

"That's it?" Gregg tried to pull away but I didn't let go.

"What else is there to say? I can't rewrite history. I figured if the roles were reversed I wouldn't be able to keep your secret. So I told no one, not even my mom or my sisters."

"Aunt Margaret?"

"Nope, no one, not even Sue."

"God I love that little filly." I snapped my head around to see if Clay had returned.

"You don't have to do that accent tonight," I said.

"Well shit, I like Clay."

"Are you telling me that you have been pretending to be Clay Davis for the past two months?"

"Yup."

"And no one has figured you out?"

"You didn't, did you?" Benjamin grinned.

"Fuck you," Gregg said. "I knew it was you the first time we met but it didn't make sense so I wiped it away."

Benjamin walked towards him but Gregg put a hand out to block his way. He picked up his drink and went back downstairs.

"That went well," Benjamin said.

"He's in shock. Hell, I'm in shock too."

"I am **not** going to lose you." Benjamin kissed me and hugged me tightly against his body.

"Give us a minute." I pulled away from him and jumped down the stairs two at a time, nervous energy shooting sparks up my spine. When I entered the kitchen, Gregg was opening the door to leave.

"Hey, come on Gregg, where are you going?" I crossed the room and closed the door. He moved to the center of the kitchen, his arms across his chest. "Do you have any idea how hard this has been for me?"

"I can't imagine how much you're suffering. You're fucking Benjamin fucking Graves. How bad can that be?"

"It's not about that. It's about lying. I've been lying to every person in the world I love. Do you have any idea what that's like?"

"Of course I do. I lied to my parents about being gay. You know that."

He was right, this was no different.

"It's not the same," I said. "We all did that." He started to protest but I kept talking. I had to convince him this was different. Wasn't it?

"Save your breath Liam, a lie is a lie. Period." He opened the refrigerator and poured us both a glass of wine. He sat down at the kitchen table. I felt relief wash over me. "Yours are on a bigger scale but the underlying truth is the same. You are lying about whom you love, again. It doesn't matter that he is who he is, this is no different from Justin."

"Goddammit, Gregg. It *is* different. I didn't lie to my parents about Justin or to you or my sisters or anyone else."

He looked away. "Okay, I'll give you that but you are still protecting him by not telling your family the truth just as you protected Justin from his. And look at how that turned out." He paused. "Is Benjamin that ashamed of liking cock?"

"No, not at all. He loves it."

"Did you have sex the first time you met him?"

I felt my face turn bright red. "He told me he wasn't gay."

"Oh my God Liam Ashby, I am going to have you committed. How you met another Justin is beyond me."

"He is not another Justin. He is only hiding because of who he is. You know as well as anyone what would happen if this all came out."

"This- as in your love for each other? You are both cowards."

"Fuck you. It's not that simple and you know it."

"Thanks Liam, but I can handle this now." Benjamin walked into the kitchen. He opened the cabinet filled with liquor and poured himself a shot of tequila that he threw back and refilled. "Liam is simply trying to protect me. Does that make him a coward?" Before Gregg could respond, Benjamin said, "I'm the coward, plain and simple. It is driving me crazy that I don't have the balls to do anything about it other than this, this, hell I don't even know what to call what I am doing right now."

"Well if you aren't willing to do this anywhere else, then you're just being a cock tease," Gregg said with finality.

"Is life always this black and white for you, Gregg?" Benjamin asked. "It's not for me."

"You have a responsibility—a duty—to come out," Gregg said. "You have a duty to tell the world you are in love with another man."

"Let's think this out? I tell Oprah that I am in love with a man. It's all over the papers, magazines, on every talk show. Every headline will be that I was and am a closeted gay man. Then I go back on Oprah and tell her that actually I'm bisexual, which is the truth. You know where that story will end up, just another closeted actor who isn't willing to fully commit to another man. Meanwhile Liam is going to be hounded, bombarded with accusations that he is in a relationship with a man who doesn't like himself very much. Then what do I do? What would you do?"

Gregg thought for a moment. "You have no choice but to emerge from—a room that is used to store clothing—as a gay man. You have to and you have to play the game. Because if you don't people won't respect you. Most humans want black or white. They don't believe in nuance or subtlety or bisexuals." He paused. "Or keep on pretending to be Clay Davis."

"No, that is not going to happen. Liam told me so today. He told me he would leave me if Clay isn't retired." Gregg looked at me with astonishment.

"Are you fucking nuts? You would walk away from Benjamin Graves for what? Your precious integrity? A dead end job in the middle of bum-fuck Egypt living near your mom is more important than trying to stay with this man who says he loves you and all because he is pretending to be someone else on occasion?"

"It's not "on occasion," it's all the time unless we are alone in his parent's house." A thought occurred to me. "Weren't you just giving me a ration of shit about three-seconds ago because I was aiding and abetting the subterfuge?"

"That was so five minutes ago. I've come to my senses, I understand now the decision you made to support the hiding, it all makes sense now." He was looking at Benjamin differently. The anger was gone.

"What makes sense now that didn't make sense thirty minutes ago? One minute you're all high and mighty and judgmental and now you understand? I don't get it."

Gregg didn't respond. He was staring at Benjamin. The hardness had left his eyes, replaced with adoration.

CHAPTER FIFTY

———∞———

I was lying next to Benjamin who was snoring lightly. Lightning lit the sky. Rain was pounding against the windows, the wind bending the scrub pines almost to the ground. I had opened a window to hear the rain. Normally this would have put me to sleep instantly but not tonight. Tonight it was fingers drumming on my skull, reliving the events of the past few hours. Gregg had peppered Benjamin with endless questions ranging from his childhood, to sex, to his girlfriends and then back to sex. Benjamin had answered many but dodged any question having to do with his parents or Scott. He had only alluded to a boyhood fling. Toward the end of the evening Gregg had asked, what next? Benjamin's reply was I don't know.

All I knew what we were going back to Iowa on Monday which meant we had one more full day on Cape Cod.

I got up to watch the storm. I wanted to go outside and stand in the rain but the lightning seemed too close. Remembering the adoration on Gregg's face made me squirm. Would everyone react this way?

Gregg had promised us that he would never tell another living soul but I wondered for how long. He had never been good at keeping secrets, as much as he pretended otherwise. Benjamin may have started something that could take on a life of its own. When Gregg told us there were reporters in Provincetown asking people if they had seen Benjamin Graves, Benjamin had blanched. They were getting closer. Benjamin was making mistakes. I wondered sometimes if the lapses were deliberate. Did he want people to find out without having to say it himself?

I replayed our time together almost as if watching a movie. I wondered if I would jeopardize what Benjamin had created if I were in his shoes.

Benjamin turned over and reached across the bed for me. I crawled back in next to him. He wrapped his legs around me with his head on my shoulder and his hand on my stomach. I felt an upwelling of emotion. I kissed him on the lips, got as close as I could and fell asleep.

I awoke the next morning alone in bed, the smell of coffee filtering upstairs. The wind streaming through the windows slapped the blinds against each other. It was cold enough that I pulled the comforter up from the floor during the night. Shivering, I tucked it around my feet, forming a cocoon up to my chin. My mind darted in various directions; the constant theme was of worry. Each thought ended with: is our time together over?

And then I thought of what Gregg had called my precious integrity. Was he right? Was I being rigid for no reason? A voice in my head said probably but was quickly replaced by my moral voice that rushed in with banners and trumpets telling me to not give in to Gregg's squishy belief system. We knew what was right and staying with Benjamin as Clay was wrong. This voice moved into the background but I could feel its presence daring anyone else to challenge him. None did.

I turned on my phone and saw a text message from Gregg: *did I dream last night?* I responded: *no.*

I sat up abruptly, pulled on sweatpants and sweatshirt and made a decision. We had one full day left on the Cape and if I had anything to do with it we were going to spend it without talking about our future. We were going to live in the moment for the next twenty-four hours no matter how difficult.

When I walked into the kitchen, Benjamin was on his computer, his hair tousled, his eyes hidden by glasses. I kissed him on the top of his head. He had turned on the gas fireplace, which filled the kitchen with welcome warmth. I poured myself a cup of coffee and sat down in front of the fire. Benjamin sighed.

"What was that for?"

"Apparently I am being hunted." He shoved a large spoonful of Cheerios into his mouth. "And there are pictures of me walking down Commercial Street with Debra, pictures of Clay I should say. Many people are saying that Clay is me. Some photographers talked to those thugs that accosted you and a couple of the guys who apparently saw me on the dance floor without my blue contacts. Shit Liam, it's starting already. Debra sent me a text saying there are reporters lined up outside her hotel." He sighed again as he brought the bowl to his lips and drank the remaining milk.

"Okay, that's it." I stood up and put my hands on his shoulders. "Turn that damn thing off," I ordered as I turned off my own cell phone. "We are going cold turkey today, no phones, no computers, no Blackberries, no newspapers, just the two of us."

"Yes sir," Benjamin said with a salute.

"I'm serious, this is our last day here. Let's make the best of it." I felt my eyes start to fill up and I turned my back. Benjamin jumped to his feet and hugged me tightly. I pulled away. I was not going to be maudlin today.

"Since it's too cold to go to the beach, I have something else in mind which involves a bike ride, a hike, lunch and sex in that order, although the sex might be reshuffled."

"Do you ever spend a day without exercise?"

"No, at least not on vacation." The warmth of the fire radiated across my back.

We pulled on sweatshirts and packed a cotton blanket to lie on. The temperature was sixty-two degrees and the wind was off the ocean. It felt like late October. I had packed our lunch, and

Benjamin had the drinks. We had said very little to each other so far, knowing, at least for me, that if we began talking we would end up having the same conversation again.

We rode our bikes out to Route 6, the wind fresh in our faces causing my eyes to water. I felt cold and warm at the same time.

Turning left on Long Nook Road, a narrow, winding, tree covered road that led past farmhouses and wind buffeted woods, we rode side by side. We locked our bikes to a tree about three quarters of the way down the road at the head of a narrow path that quickly climbed up into the woods. We walked up a short path and then joined a fire road that rose gradually up and down, mimicking the contour of the dunes. Benjamin stopped to pee, started to say something but then stopped. He smiled at me and continued up the road.

After a few miles, we veered left down a path lined on either side by wild roses and poison ivy. It led toward the top of a dune overlooking the ocean. We stared down at the empty beach, shivering in the wind. The trail descended until we were standing in a round depression, almost as if someone had scooped out the sand. The wall of the dune slanted up and away toward the ocean, which blocked the wind. The temperature seemed to rise ten degrees.

Spreading out our blanket, we pulled off our sweatshirts and stripped down to our underwear. The roar of the ocean whipped over our heads, the wind dragging the sound screaming into the woods behind us. We lay down next to each other, our heads supported by the slope of the sandy wall. Benjamin spread out food and poured us coffee from a thermos. He pulled a small bottle of cognac out of his knapsack and offered it to me. I shook my head. He topped off his coffee. He smiled and sighed as he took a sip of the scalding drink.

He leaned back against the wall of sand and motioned to me. I lay down next to him. We kissed for several minutes. Benjamin then slid down so his head was on my chest. With a start, I realized he wasn't in disguise. I was pleased that I hadn't even noticed. I ran fingers through his thick hair, massaged his temples and then kissed him again. We lay together for a long time, occasionally sitting up to eat or drink something. I pulled out my book; Benjamin his script. The wind continued its howl over our heads. We drew closer together and Benjamin closed his eyes. The angle of light against his skin reminded me of that June morning in his parents' house. I remembered memorizing his body, wondering at the time if I would ever see him again. Now I knew it as well as my own. I hovered my hand over his chest and began running it up and down his torso just as I had done before. I could once again feel the energy snapping back and forth. I gently pulled myself out from under his body and sat up on my knees. I slowly moved my hand up and down his entire body. I felt myself becoming aroused, as was Benjamin. I moved my hand over his crotch getting as close as I could without touching him. This went on for several minutes until I could see a wet spot forming at the tip of his cock. Benjamin was moving his hips in concert with my hand.

Suddenly he whipped off his briefs, stood up and put his cock deep in my mouth. Before I knew what was happening, Benjamin came down my throat. I was so surprised I didn't resist. I looked down at my crotch and realized I had come at the same time. I sat down in the sand and pulled off my underwear that was lined with sticky semen.

He lay down next to me and within a few minutes we were both asleep. When a cloud settled in and the temperature dropped, we both woke up shivering; quickly put our clothes back on and hurried home. Benjamin lit a fire in the master bathroom while I filled the tub with steaming water. The windows were open letting the wind race through the bathroom, a hint of smoke lingering behind. Mozart was playing somewhere, half empty wine glasses on the windowsill. I had my head on his chest and his arm was around my waist. I thought about my family, Sue, Gregg and then with a clunk I was back in the future, worrying.

"Your entire body just tensed," Benjamin said. "What's wrong?"

"If I tell you, we will have that conversation again."

"What are we doing for dinner?" Benjamin asked as his hand slid between my legs.

"The Red Inn, with Gregg at nine."

"This has been the most relaxing day of my life," he said.

"Me too."

We kissed. Benjamin sat up, finished his drink and knelt before me.

I knelt behind and with a little soap and one quick thrust, I was deep inside Benjamin Graves.

CHAPTER FIFTY-ONE

———∞———

Benjamin came out of the bathroom without a wig and wearing a blonde beard instead of the usual black one. When he crossed the room, I saw that he didn't have the colored contacts in. With his natural hair, blonde beard and those green eyes, most people would know who he was. He smiled at me and tousled my hair.

"Hey, I just spent an hour perfecting this look!" I said with feigned outrage.

"It's too perfect." He messed up my hair again. "There, much better. Now you look a bit thuggish instead of that altar boy thing you've perfected."

"Since when do you know anything about altar boys?" Benjamin let out a loud laugh. "Don't answer that."

"I would have loved to have seen you in your altar boy get up." He put a hand on my crotch. "With nothing on underneath." He ran a hand around my stiffening cock.

"I was twelve!"

"I would have been twelve as well, and it would have been hot."

"We better get going, Gregg has suddenly decided to start being punctual." I pushed his hand away. We were meeting Gregg at the restaurant for a cocktail at 8:30. The wind had died down but it was still cool. We both wore cotton chinos, loafers and polo shirts.

"Have you seen my sunglasses?" Benjamin asked as he walked right past them. I grabbed them and followed him out the door.

When we arrived at The Red Inn, Benjamin kept his sunglasses on. The sun had set across the bay, the sky was pink and gray, shiny as mother of pearl. Gregg was standing at the bar impatiently tapping his fingers on the granite top.

"There you two are." He paused as he looked us up and down. "You haven't been together long enough to start dressing like the Olsen twins." He turned away with a slight frown. "A boy could die of thirst around here…barkeep," he snapped his fingers twice, "A very large, very strong, very dirty martini for moi and Clay?" He didn't hesitate for a second as he said Clay. Benjamin nodded.

"Since when do you snap your fingers at bartenders?" I ordered a Stella.

"Sorry doll for not taking your order. You are so forgettable sometimes." He grinned as he gave me a kiss on the cheek. Benjamin laughed and gave Gregg a bear hug that he returned.

"I only snap my fingers at bartenders who ignore me, ignore me on multiple levels." I looked at the bartender who was mid-thirties, bald, built, his chest muscles straining the fabric of his shirt.

"What did y'all do to Gregg?" Benjamin took a handful of cashews and stuffed them into his mouth. The bartender walked away.

"That's what he did, ignore me. Je suis decu!" He raised his glass. "Cheers boys, to a lovely, startling and most memorable weekend." We touched glasses. I felt a burst of sadness.

"Take that sour puss off, Liam. I know what is going on inside that dungeon of an Irish soul. If you're so sad about going back to Indonesia, then don't!"

I didn't bite. I turned away from them. They began talking as if they had known each other for years. I realized that Gregg had finally met someone who knew more about movies than he did. They began discussing Altman's last film, *A Prairie Home Companion,* which they both hated.

I looked out the window at the bay. The tide was out and there were several small sailboats stranded on the sand. A woman walked by on the beach bundled up in a hooded sweatshirt and jeans, her golden retriever chasing a seagull.

I thought about what it would be like in Iowa as the weather turned cold, the days got shorter, the fields covered with brown, dried cornstalks. I shivered as I wondered for the hundredth time if I had made the right decision moving to Iowa. Then I realized I would have never met Benjamin if I hadn't. I shook my body trying to let that thought in, remembering what I had actually experienced rather than what might have happened if I had stayed in Boston.

I looked at the bar. Gregg's drink was empty.

"Let's eat boys," he said, "I am withering away to nothing standing here. I don't know about you but I think an empty cocktail glass is one of the saddest sights known to mankind. Dylan, check, por favor!"

"I got this," Benjamin reached for the bill. Gregg slapped his hand away. "I make a decent living Mr. Davis. I insist. Shoo." He waved his hand in Benjamin's face who grabbed it and kissed it on the knuckles.

"I'm sure shootin' gonna miss ya Gregg. Y'all have to come to Texas sometime." Gregg raised an eyebrow. Benjamin blushed.

"Sure Clay, I would love to. Next time you're there, call me." Gregg paid the bill and went looking for the hostess.

We were seated at a table in a corner near the fireplace with windows on two sides. I stood in front of the fire for a moment to warm my hands. Benjamin still had his sunglasses on. He chose the chair facing the windows with his back to the room. Dylan brought us another round of drinks.

"What's with the shades?" Gregg pulled the olive out of his drink and bit it in half. "Did you have your eyes dilated today? Or are you so mesmerized by moi that you need sunglasses to ratchet down the dazzle?"

With that Benjamin removed his sunglasses and smiled at Gregg who dropped his half eaten olive on the floor.

"Shit!" Gregg whispered. "Your eyes."

"We're living dangerously tonight, dudes." Benjamin took a big swallow of his drink. "Danger is now my middle name." He looked from side to side pretending to wave a gun and then burst out laughing.

"But, but, but…." Gregg stuttered.

"Thank you for noticing my ass, Gregg." Benjamin reached over and held my hand. "I think it's quite a nice butt myself."

"Aren't you afraid of someone noticing?" Gregg whispered again.

"Stop whispering dude. What's up with that?" He laughed loudly and picked up the menu. "I'm so hungry I could eat a moose. Do you think y'all have that on your menu?" Benjamin asked as our waitress approached.

"Good evening. My name is Claire. I see you are all set with cocktails." She was our age, thin with mildly blue eyes but violently curly hair. "And no sir, we do not serve moose although I did see a few bears in town yesterday. Would bear work for you?"

Benjamin looked at me with a confused expression. Gregg had just taken a sip of his drink. He put a hand over his mouth to keep from spitting it all over the table.

"I'll explain later," I said.

"No, I think I got it," Benjamin said. "Bears are hairy, chubby men, right?" Benjamin looked pleased with himself. I noticed that he had not looked up from his menu.

"A gold star for Mr. Davis. He just passed Introduction to Homo, Level 3. Next topic, what is it that two girls do in bed together?"

Claire shot Gregg a look that said, *don't fuck with me.* She took a deep breath and recited the specials and left.

"So Clay Danger Davis, what's on tap for you tonight? And what's up with your boyfriend? He's awfully quiet. Did you bruise his throat?" Benjamin choked out a laugh as I reddened. "You did, didn't you? Oh my, you are a brute. Gorgeous, hung, famous and a demon in the bedroom." He fanned his face furiously. "I need a lie down. Liam, you better hire a food taster. If words gets out, my goodness, the boys will be lined up trying to knock you off."

Benjamin and I reached for our drinks.

"I said famous, didn't I? Shit. From now on my lips are absolutely stapled shut, at least on this topic. Even a Jesuit…oh who am I kidding?"

"And you wonder why I didn't tell you?" I asked.

"It's all good," Gregg said with a slurp of his martini. He looked away from me. "I ask again, what are you up to tonight Clay?"

"Not sure yet, Gregg. Just spreading my wings a bit. We'll see where this takes me. But right now, I feel a bit naked and it's feeling pretty good." He started to pull the wine list out of my hand but I wouldn't let go.

"Dinner is on me tonight and I don't want to hear any comments about whatever wine I order," I said. Benjamin looked at Gregg who shrugged his shoulders.

"I suspect by now Clay, when you hear that snippy tone out of our mutual friend's mouth, you know better than to try and change his mind. He turns into a cornered cobra."

Later, when coffee and dessert arrived, I looked across the table at Gregg who looked as sad as I had ever seen him. I reached across the table to hold his hand and he did not resist.

"When am I going to see you again?" Gregg asked.

"When are you coming to Iowa?"

"You don't really expect me to visit there, do you?"

"Yes I do expect it. You'll love it. Good food, great company, card playing, exercise, alcohol."

Gregg took a bite of his molten chocolate cake and moaned with pleasure. He grabbed at his waistline. "Exercise, huh?" He took another bite. "And you Clay, can I expect to see you when I visit sometime this fall?"

"Don't think so. I'm going to Morocco this fall. In fact, I'm leaving soon to go back to LA to start training and rehearsing."

I looked into his eyes. Was he telling the truth or playing out a story?

"Quelle domage!" Gregg said. "Then I'll just have to settle for little Liam."

"Will you excuse me?" Benjamin pushed back from the table and walked across the room with his eyes on the floor.

"Did you know he was leaving?" Gregg pushed his dessert over to me for the last bite.

"No…yes…not really."

"Thank you for being so definitive."

"So when can you come to Iowa?" I needed to pin him down so it wouldn't be so hard to say good-bye and I needed to change the subject.

"How about mid-September?"

"That's perfect. The weather is still warm. It's gonna be great!"

Gregg raised an eyebrow but said nothing. We talked about possible dates, whether we should meet in the Twin Cities first and then segued into a possible winter vacation somewhere in the Caribbean.

I looked at my watch; Benjamin had been gone for at least ten minutes. I wondered if he was ill. I was getting up to check on him when I saw him walk across the dining room without his beard. He smiled at us as he sat down again at our table. I saw all the other patrons snap around as they realized who it was. The room seemed frozen in mid motion. Claire stood at the bar, her blank face telling everything. Gregg had his hand over his mouth. I felt sweat forming at the base of my back. Suddenly two people from an adjacent table stood up and came over with their bill demanding an autograph. Benjamin said no and turned away. I saw a woman fumbling in her purse until she yanked out a camera. Benjamin turned around and looked at the rest of the room. A couple of people applauded. Several phones were pointed at his face. Just as the woman leaned over to take a photo, Benjamin stood up and strode out the building. She followed him; I could see the flash of the camera as Benjamin went out the front door.

"Gregg, go see if he needs any help. I need to settle the bill." I waved for the check.

Claire handed me the check. "Was that who I thought it was?"

I quickly added a tip and handed her a pile of cash. I told her I had no idea what she was talking about. Gregg was standing on the street looking at the lights of a retreating car.

"He took off," Gregg said. " He seemed really spooked."

I heard excited voices behind me. There were several people from the restaurant staring at us. Some were taking photos—of us. I grabbed Gregg's arm and we jogged toward the end of Commercial Street. We didn't stop until we ran out of road. Sitting down on a park bench in front of the Provincetown Inn, we caught our breath. No one had followed us.

When my cell phone finally rang, I gave Benjamin directions and waited for him to return. I was angry at what he had just done: didn't he expect people to react?

He picked us up and we drove in silence to the empty parking lot at Herring Cove.

"God, that was a rush Benjamin, I didn't see that coming." Gregg opened the door letting the fragrant air sweep through the car.

"I hadn't planned on doing that Gregg; guess I wasn't thinking." Benjamin was looking out the window.

"I agree with that statement," Gregg said, "clearly you weren't thinking but boy was it fun to see the expression on their faces." The excitement in his voice was irritating to me.

"Did you think people wouldn't react?" I asked. There was a long silence.

"Hell Liam, I don't know. I was having such a good time with you guys, pretending to be Clay and Benjamin at the same time. It seemed like I was in a movie, a movie I was really enjoying and shit, it just happened. I guess I thought maybe people wouldn't react? We're not exactly in Des Moines. I thought people would be cooler about celebrity here. And really there weren't that many people in the room." He stopped himself. "I'm not telling the truth. I didn't think this through at all."

"Did someone take a picture of you?" Gregg asked.

"I think so but if they did it was of my back."

"Why did you run away?" I asked.

"I need a drink," he replied.

We drove the short distance to Gregg's apartment. The lights were all on which meant his roommates were home.

"Shit!" Gregg exclaimed. "I would invite you up but everyone is here tonight. Plus Jeremy's new boy toy is here for a few days and I cannot stand him. He is like a little, lithe, muscled, snappy Chihuahua. He drives me mad!" He put a hand on Benjamin's shoulder.

"Well then, the only thing left to do is say good-bye." Gregg squeezed Benjamin's shoulder. I got out of the car and walked with Gregg a few feet to the front door. We hugged for a long time. Finally, I said, "It's only a few weeks, they'll fly by."

"You know it's not that Liam, it is about much more than that." He pulled away from me. "It's knowing that my best friend is halfway across the country instead of two blocks." His voice became oddly neutral. "I'm afraid we're drifting apart. Look at what happened." He pointed at Benjamin who was staring at us from the darkness of the car. "You kept from me the most important thing that ever happened to you. And I only know it because he told me—not you." Gregg hugged me again and walked into the house.

CHAPTER FIFTY-TWO

———∞———

We were halfway through our flight back to Iowa. We had said very little to each other since leaving the house. We had not turned on our phones, computers or bought a newspaper.

As the plane lurched side to side in turbulence, I pretended to read my book but kept closing my eyes, remembering every detail of the weekend. I was creating a chronology in my head, remembering the exact time we arrived, the weather, how the sun felt when we sat on the roof deck drinking cocktails, how the wind sounded as it raced through our bedroom, how his body smelled as he lay next to me in bed.

Benjamin was asleep in the seat across from me. His face was inscrutable. When the flight attendant brought our lunch and seltzer water, Benjamin sat up and looked at me, his eyes red and dejected.

"Everything is going to change tomorrow." He took a small bite from his sandwich.

"Why?"

"Because I need to get serious about my schedule. I need to start planning things. Meetings are going to start. I have to get in better shape, start cross training. Stop drinking!" He laughed awkwardly.

"I thought you said you had weeks before you had to leave." *Had he said that?*

509

"That's true but I do need to go back and forth to LA a few times. Do you want to come with me?" He seemed as surprised by his question as I was.

"No, I don't." *Was that the truth?*

He looked out the window. "There is something I'd like to do tonight. Do you think Sue might be able to come over for dinner?'

"Why?"

"She's going to meet Benjamin Graves." My eyes widened. "I figured it's the least I can do; to let your two best friends know what's been going on with you this summer."

"Jesus, Benjamin," I said. "What the fuck is going on? One minute you're hiding, the next minute you're walking through a restaurant as yourself. Tonight it's Benjamin, tomorrow back to Clay. Who is going to meet my mom the next time?" He sat back in his seat, his face reddening as if he had been slapped. "Are you done with the disguises or aren't you?"

He was quiet for several minutes. Finally, he said, "I didn't expect that reaction."

"What the fuck did you expect?"

"I'm just trying to help, that's all."

"How the fuck is this helping?"

Benjamin's eyes filled and a tear fell down his cheek that he brushed away with his fist.

"I don't want to say good-bye. I miss you already and we're still together," he said.

I felt the anger slip out of my body as if I was shedding a layer of clothing. Benjamin paused as he struggled to rein in his emotions.

"I just thought if you could talk to your best friends about what really happened this summer, you wouldn't feel so alone. Is that stupid of me?"

"No, it's not stupid at all. It's one of the nicest things anyone has ever done for me." I stood up and moved towards him.

"Why is it that our relationship is ending just as it's beginning?"

I thought for a while. "I…I think it's because neither one of us want to live a lie and yet…."

"And yet what?"

"Neither one of us wants what will happen if we live the truth." I looked out the window. "I have thought many times what it would be like if I went to LA with you either as your public boyfriend or even as your hidden boyfriend. In either scenario, I would be a prisoner in your home."

"I know." Benjamin's face sagged. "And if you stayed in Iowa, it wouldn't be much different, would it?"

"Only if we keep pretending." I frowned. "But that isn't going to work either, even if we actually wanted that. Someone is going to find out. It's close to that already, isn't it?"

"No, it isn't." Benjamin's voice lacked conviction.

"Yes it is," I said firmly. "I don't want you hurt, ridiculed, or hounded. It would kill me to see you become a scapegoat. A poster boy for all the right-wing nut cases in this country." I held my breath out of fear I was going to cry. "It will be better for you, for me, for our families, if we end this." I waited for him to disagree.

"I'm afraid you're right." Benjamin closed his eyes and let the tears stream down his face. His body shook as he cried. I reached out to touch him but he pushed my hand away. "Please, please don't touch me, it will make things even worse."

I sat back down. My tears had gone away. I was angry again. Angry at the world, angry at ourselves, angry with all the people who would have a field day if Benjamin and I lived our lives as a public couple. I thought of that crazy minister from Kansas, the Catholic Church, the Mormons. All the institutions that had figured out ways to keep us in our place.

I knew what they would do with this story. I knew what some priests would say in their sermons, I had heard it all before whenever the subject of gay marriage came up. I was radiating fury.

"Liam, what the hell is going on with you?"

"Why are we in this position? This is such bullshit!"

"You're right," he said. "It is utter bullshit and there is nothing we can do about it. Nothing."

I felt anger reverberating in my chest. "No matter what law is passed in our favor, no matter which church changes their rules to include us, there are always going to be people who hate us and I don't understand why." I sat back down. "Kind of makes you want to give up, doesn't it?" The anger was hissing out of me like a slow leak. Why couldn't he just be a normal guy I happened to meet one night in a bar? I looked at him, his eyes waiting, demanding something from me. I felt worn out. My mind went blank.

"I'm going to call Sue."

She sounded startled and wary about meeting us for dinner.

"You're not leaving Iowa?" she had asked me. I assured her that was the last thing that was going to happen. Just as I hung up, I heard her say, "Have you seen...?"

"She'll be at your house at 7," I said. I put my phone in my luggage. I didn't want to know what she had seen but I had an idea.

CHAPTER FIFTY-THREE

I was sitting by the pool, a cold Stella in my hand. Sue was running late as usual. The vodka tonic I had made her was sitting on the table, the ice quickly melting in the late afternoon sun. It was 95 degrees and humid. My T-shirt was soaked but I didn't want to be in the house with Benjamin. It seemed to me that we had both begun to live in the future and were now uncomfortable being with each other in the present.

Benjamin was preparing dinner; I was going to prepare Sue.

At that minute she drove around the back of the house. She jumped out of the car and then cringed as the heat and humidity hit her like a slap.

"What the hell are you doing outside?" she asked. She had on sandals, blue jean shorts and a coral blue tank top. "Please don't tell me that this house does not have air conditioning. I do not want to hear that!" she cried out in an almost pitch perfect imitation of Theresa Armstrong. I laughed as I rose to hug her.

"Don't take another step towards me," she said. "If you think I'm going to ruin a perfectly good shower by hugging your sweaty, muscled body, you've got another thing coming." She pretended to fan herself as she walked over to me and gave me two air kisses. She picked up the drink she knew was hers and pulled a chair into the shade. "By the way, I didn't appreciate you hanging up on me. So rude and childish." She took a sip of her drink and crossed her legs which caused her shorts to inch up even higher.

"Britney," I said, "if those shorts go any higher, I'm going to see something I'm not sure I want to see."

"Obviously you haven't seen the newspapers, Internet, magazines, blogosphere, blah blah blah or you wouldn't be focused on my girl parts." Reaching inside her bag, she pulled out a copy of a photo from Pablo Posada's website. It showed Benjamin exiting the Red Inn, his body turned, his hand in front of his face but clearly, unmistakably, undeniably, Benjamin Graves—in Provincetown.

"Can you fucking believe he was in Provincetown the same time you were? Did you see him? This is wild!"

I said nothing. My face was burning and sweat was pouring down my face. I wiped my forehead off with the back of my hand and flicked the sweat onto the grass. She was staring at me as if reading my mind.

"Okay, spill it," she said.

I took a deep breath. "Clay Davis is not who you think he is. He is really Benjamin Graves in disguise. We've been having a relationship for about two months but it's ending because neither one of us can deal...can deal with what it would be like if people found out." I blurted this so fast I wasn't sure if I had been intelligible. But when I saw the color drain from her face, I knew she had heard me. She picked up her drink and finished it. She handed me her empty glass. She looked at the photo again.

"I don't believe you," she said.

The screen door slammed shut and we both looked over at the house and there he was. Benjamin walked towards us with a half grin. He had on a white T-shirt and madras shorts. He was barefoot. His hair was tousled. I looked at him as if I had never seen him before.

"So we meet again, Sue." He motioned for her to stand up. "I'm Benjamin." He pulled her in for a hug, which she welcomed.

I went into the guesthouse to make her another drink.

I looked out the window at the two of them. They were sitting at the metal table next to the pool and he was holding her hand and talking. She was staring at him with a frozen expression on her face. I watched for a while, wondering how many times this scenario would be repeated if Benjamin and I remained a couple. It would be nothing like introducing a new boyfriend to family, friends, coworkers. Each time it would be this seismic shock of recognition, disbelief and then awe? Fawning? Envy?

Sue looked over at me and waved. She held up her empty hand and moved it to her lips as if there was a glass in it. Then she looked sad. Benjamin laughed.

"You cannot get good help in this town, can you?" she said as she snatched the drink out of my hand, "as you would well know." She nodded in Benjamin's direction.

She pretended to toast him, grimaced and set it down. "Are you trying to get me drunk?" She stuck a finger in her glass and swirled it around. "Okay, I just got the Cliff notes version of your relationship as well as a warning to not give you shit about withholding this information from me, your dearest, kindest, best looking friend. But Jesus Liam, really?" Benjamin tapped the back of her hand. "Sorry, can't help myself. Really Liam?" Benjamin stood up and went into the guesthouse after putting a finger on her lips.

"I have already had this argument with Gregg." She started to say something but then stopped. "Yes, I withheld this from my best friends and I'm sorry. What can I say beyond that?"

"There is so much to say, so many things to apologize for, so...

"Benjamin asked me to not say anything." I cut her off. "And now that we're ending...."

"You're ending already? Why?"

Benjamin returned carrying a martini, up. He was walking too fast with the drink slopping over the rim. He sat down next to Sue and put a hand on her knee.

"We both think this is the only viable option."

She sat up in her chair. "That's the dumbest thing I've ever heard. You're talking as if this is a financial transaction. What is wrong with you two? Clearly you know how hard it is to find someone you love. Snap out of it and get on with your lives. Where's Aunt Margaret when we need her? The two of you need to be slapped upside your heads, several times, hard."

"Oh come on, Sue. You know how fucked up this would be. Don't you remember what happened in LA a few weeks ago?"

"Oh my God Liam, you are so annoying. A, I wasn't in LA with you several weeks ago. B, I hate it when you assume I can read your mind and C, I knew that was you on the cover of *People* all along."

I started to say something and she cut **me** off.

"Stop assuming I've been along for the ride when I just got in the car a few minutes ago."

She stood up and moved closer to Benjamin until her face was a few inches from his. She touched his cheek, pushed the hair off his forehead, ran a finger over his lips.

"It really is you, isn't it?" She spoke so softly I almost didn't hear her.

"Yes, it's him. Can you fast forward through this part?"

"Don't be a prick Liam," she said, "you've had two months to get used to this, and I've had about ten minutes."

"What happened in LA was just a taste of what our lives would be like and I was in disguise pretending to be his cousin. Imagine for a few seconds, because that's all the time you'll need, what our lives would be like if we publicly announced we are a couple as ourselves."

"You two need to man up. What the hell is wrong with you?"

Out of her purse, she pulled several printed pages from Pablo's website.

"Cla…Benjamin, everyone is claiming that you are one of the following, in no particular order: being held captive by your family

516

in Montana, drunk and drugged and suicidal in Iowa or a gay man taking his first steps out of the closet in Provincetown. Really Benjamin, what difference would it make now?" She shoved the pages in front of Benjamin. "Since one of the rumors just happens to be true, why not tell the truth? No one is going to believe you if you return to LA and try and get back together with Alyssa. Actually if you did that, people would believe you less—it's way too obvious."

"Since when are you an expert on all of this?" I asked.

"I read more of this crap than you've ever imagined. What else do you want to know? Hey, Benjamin, how about your current Q score?"

"No, no I don't." Benjamin threw back his drink. "I'll find out all of this tomorrow. Goddamnit to hell!"

I could feel my dormant anger threatening to resurface. "Okay Sue, let's say we man up. Do you know how much I hate that phrase?" I could feel and hear the anger in my voice and tried to remember who I was really angry with. "Benjamin goes on some talk show and tells the world he's gay and living with me. Then what do you think will happen?"

"Your mom will start planning your wedding. Aunt Margaret will faint. Aunt Marie will smoke a cigarette and find something to criticize. I will be overjoyed at your happiness and the gay community will be in the stratosphere. Do you know what this would mean for gay boys all over the world? The most successful, recognizable movie star in the world coming out as a gay man? Nothing like this has ever happened, it will change the way Hollywood operates."

"You are not really that naive, are you?"

"That is not a word that is commonly associated with my name."

"Would you go see him in a romantic comedy with, hell I don't know, Cameron Diaz?"

"Of course I would, this is not the 1950's anymore. People are changing, Liam, so why aren't you?"

"You haven't had time to think of all the ramifications," Benjamin said. "I have, we have. This would kill my career."

"So what? I'm sure you're richer than Croesus, plus you only have a few years left as a leading man, then you're too old, right?" Benjamin nodded his agreement.

This was all too easy. I jumped in.

"He will be pilloried by the right wing media, he will be accused of having AIDS, they'll stir up every actress in Hollywood who ever kissed him. Then the jokes would start about what had been in his mouth or up his ass." I wanted to shock her into agreeing with me. If she didn't…then what?

"How graphic." She kicked off her sandals, sat down on the edge of the pool and let her feet dangle in the water. "I agree that it could be ugly but it will blow over. It always does."

"We won't be able to move in public without being harassed," Benjamin said. "It will be an absolute zoo. How could we possibly sustain a normal relationship?" He looked defeated.

"You can't. It won't be normal. End of discussion." She stood up and moved next to me. "If you really love each other—and based on the way you are looking at each other, you do— you'll find a way to keep the core part of your relationship, the reason you love each other, separate, protected and known only to the two of you. If you can do that, no one can touch you." She put her hands on my shoulders. I looked up at her; her eyes were full. "You know guys, you can take your home with you wherever you go."

Benjamin looked confused. He picked up the pages Sue had read from and walked into the house with a shake of his head.

"I think he just realized how much he is going to have to lie about why he was in Provincetown," I said.

"So he'll lie, celebrities and politicians lie all the time." She picked up her watered-down drink and threw the contents on the lawn. "Neither of you have any intention of coming clean about this, do you?"

"No, we don't. It seems overwhelming to me and obviously to Benjamin as well."

She rolled her eyes at me. "I've made my point. I am not going to say it again," she said. "But I will say that the two of you have been spending too much time alone. You're in some sort of bubble where you're worrying about integrity, honesty, and candor. I say it's all white noise. Nobody in Benjamin's world operates with those kind of standards, so why should he?"

"I have no idea what your point is, Sue."

"My point is that since you have no intention of telling the truth, you should figure out a way to stay together, even if it means one huge never-ending lie, that is my point." She frowned. "Okay, before the thought police come back, why didn't you tell me? To withhold this from me, of all people. I was with you the day you met him, for God's sake! I wouldn't have told a soul."

I stared at her until she shifted uncomfortably. "Okay, maybe I would have told my mom or one of my sisters but that would have been it."

"You just answered your own question." I scratched at nothing on my forehead. "Plus I had no idea where this was going. For the first couple of weeks, we were just hanging out, going for runs, swimming, working out. Just being friends. I had no idea he slept with men—I guess I should say would sleep with me. He hasn't exactly left a trail of former boyfriends."

"How many?" Sue looked at me as if she already knew the answer.

"One. One before me that is and that was a long time ago, back in high school."

"I don't believe this. No more lies, not after this."

"I swear to God this is the truth. His only other boyfriend was sixteen years ago."

"No way, who was it? Do I know him?"

"You'll have to ask him. It's not my place to tell you."

"Oh come on, spill it! Was it a teacher? The football coach? Drama coach? Did Father Schmidt kidnap him and have his way with him in a confessional?" She sat up in her chair and folded her legs close to her body. "You're killing me Liam, tell me!"

"Tell you what?" Benjamin walked out the back door carrying another martini, his face a scowl. Sue took one look at him and said, "Nothing important."

I stood up and walked towards him but he went in the opposite direction.

"What does Sue want to know?" His voice was devoid of humor.

Sue jumped in. "I just wanted to know what it's like to kiss you, that's all. Can he forget about who you are?"

"And the answer is?" Benjamin's voice softened slightly.

"The answer is yes, I don't think anymore about who you are except who you are to me." I moved towards him again and he put his arm around my shoulder. His scowl disappeared, replaced by sadness.

"What's the matter?" Sue asked.

"I just spoke to Sydney." He sat down heavily in his chair spilling his drink on his shorts. "All hell is breaking loose out there. The studio thinks I am having a nervous breakdown. The *National Inquirer* has people in Montana, Provincetown, and apparently here in Iowa as well." He jumped up. "Shit, I forgot to turn the alarm back on after Sue got here." He ran into the house and returned a few minutes later. "Everything seems fine but I think you should stay here tonight, Sue. I don't want one of those assholes following you home."

"I appreciate the offer Benjamin." Sue said his name awkwardly as if Benjamin was the made up name instead of Clay. "But I have two children and a mom who cannot handle them for more than a few hours. Plus Liam and I are old pros at being followed, right?"

"You remember that story, don't you?" I asked.

"This is completely different. They know that any new photo of me will earn them a lot more money than normal. They're going to be like pit bulls. You have no idea." Sue looked at me with a worried expression.

"I'll follow you home, Sue, and spend the night in my own bed," I said.

I waited for Benjamin to object, but he did not.

We all heard it at the same instant, our heads snapping around in unison at the sound of someone taking photos. Benjamin exploded out of his chair, yelling and racing across the yard. He ran towards a small scruffy man who had a long camera pointed in our direction. He turned to flee down the driveway but Benjamin was too fast. He took hold of the man by his neck, ripped the camera out of his hands and flung it into the pool. Then he tore the bag off the man's shoulder and threw that into the pool as well. He was shouting that he was going to have him arrested for trespassing, that he was going to ruin his career, his entire life. The man was screaming back that he was going to charge Benjamin with assault and battery. Sue and I stood frozen in place.

Benjamin let go of the photographer. He said something quietly to him, pulled out his wallet and shoved a wad of bills into the guy's open hands. He walked back down the driveway with Benjamin following. Benjamin returned a few minutes later, anger pouring off his body, and I realized I had never seen him truly angry before. He picked up the net that was used to remove leaves from the pool and scooped out the camera and canvas bag. He walked over to the fence that lined the back yard and threw them into the field as hard as he could and then disappeared into the house.

Sue whispered to me, "Another typical night in Mason City, movie star-paparazzi smack down."

The back door slammed and we both jumped. Benjamin stalked over to us, his eyes furious.

"I checked all the security monitors. No one else is on the property. Not sure how I missed that asshole." He paced back and forth without looking at either of us. "All I know is that as soon as this story gets out, this place will be swarming with his kind." He looked at me, his eyes red. "I was thinking I needed to head to LA tomorrow anyway, and this just cements it."

"Of course," I mumbled.

"And you're going with him, right?" Sue looked at me.

"No," we both said in unison. Benjamin's look silenced her.

"What should we do?" he asked.

"Here's the deal Benjamin," I said, "I'm starving. I'll start the grill and cook the steaks. The two of you can handle everything else. When dinner is over Sue and I will go to our homes. If we're harassed, we'll call the police but I don't expect that to happen. You can stay here where they can't get to you, okay?" My equanimity surprised me.

"I was hoping we would spend tonight together," Benjamin said.

"Hell yes, I was hoping and expecting that as well. But for all our sakes, I think we should each go home. Benjamin, you have a job to do in LA, right? Sue and I have our lives and jobs here. So for now it's time to get on with things."

Benjamin looked at me, his eyes dead.

"Nice, really nice," Sue said, "but I'm not buying it."

She walked over to me and grabbed my right hand. I looked down. My thumb was bleeding.

CHAPTER FIFTY-FOUR

———∞———

I lay in bed, my window fan on high. Sweat ran down my forehead, under my arms, between my legs. I was thinking about the last two hours. Dinner had been rushed. I burned the steaks. Benjamin had overcooked the corn and Sue had drowned the salad. Initially she tried to keep the conversation going but had eventually given up. We all drank water.

Afterwards Sue sat in her car while I said good-bye to Benjamin. It was brief. A quick kiss, an even quicker hug. He said he would call me in a few days when things settled down. I followed Sue down the driveway with a look back over my shoulder. Benjamin was nowhere to be seen.

No one had followed us home. I wondered where the photographer had gone. What was he telling people? Of course with no photos, there wasn't much to tell and even with photos what had the guy seen? Benjamin talking to two people that no one in LA would recognize. Had Benjamin overreacted again?

I turned on my side hoping to maximize the flow of air over my body. I felt empty, alone and adrift. I didn't want to be in Iowa anymore nor did I want to be in Boston or LA. I fitfully fell asleep wondering what Benjamin was doing at that moment.

I dreamt we were camping in northern Minnesota on a rocky beach. The sun was warm on our skin as we stood in front of each other. I walked away and lay down in the shallow water to cool off.

Benjamin straddled me, leaning forward to kiss me. I was holding onto him, pulling him closer, my hands in his hair. Then I was inside him. I pushed myself deeper and deeper wanting to be sealed to him forever. Benjamin's hands were under my hips pulling me up and in. We came together and remained together. I felt water pouring off my forehead. I wiped the back of my hand across my face to keep the water out of my eyes and woke up. Benjamin was asleep next to me. My face and chest were slippery with sweat and semen. I touched Benjamin on the shoulder and he turned towards me.

The sun woke me the next morning. I was alone.

CHAPTER FIFTY-FIVE

———∞———

I sat up and rubbed the sleep out of my eyes. Sitting on the edge of the bed, I spread my legs wide and let the fan blow against my feverish skin. I picked up the pillow next to mine and breathed deeply Benjamin's familiar scent. I looked down at my stomach and saw dried semen on my belly button. Aimlessly picking at it, I tried to figure out how I was feeling and then realized I wasn't feeling anything. I didn't know what to do with myself or how I was going to spend the day, or any day for that matter.

I rinsed off in a cold shower and sat in front of the fan again, short lived goose bumps lining my arms and legs. My stomach grumbled. Hunger pushed through to center stage. Halfway to the kitchen, I smelled coffee. My pace quickened wondering if Benjamin had changed his mind. In the kitchen, the coffee pot was almost full and there were doughnuts on the counter. I looked out the window and saw Sue sitting in the shade of the oak tree, a coffee cup in one hand, the local paper in the other. I looked at the clock, it was eight A.M., normally way too early for her. I found a pair of gym shorts, poured a cup of coffee, beginning to worry that something bad had happened. When she looked up as I walked down the few steps to my backyard, I could tell from her expression that everything was fine.

"Why aren't you eating a donut?" she asked. "Please don't tell me you don't eat them."

"What are you doing here?" I sat down on the grass, the humid, heavy air encasing me in moisture. For a few seconds, the dew covered grass felt refreshingly cool on my legs.

"Good morning to you too."

"I will rephrase: is everything and everyone okay?"

"Of course they are, why wouldn't they be?"

"So why are you here so early?"

"I am here because I knew if I were you, I would want me here."

"Huh?"

"Have some coffee." She emptied her cup at the base of the tree, went into the house and returned with the donuts and a carafe. "I figured you wouldn't want to be alone today." She sat down on the ground and handed me a chocolate frosted donut. "I wouldn't if I were you." I ate the donut in three bites and gulped the coffee.

"Thanks," I said as she handed me a glazed donut. We sat in silence for several minutes. I lay down on the ground staring up through the dense leaves and branches of the oak tree remembering the old tire swing. I could still see the look of disgust on my friend Ronnie's face when I asked him to swing with me.

A slight breeze stirred the leaves for a moment and then it was still.

She put a hand on my knee, "Are you all right?"

"I don't know."

She lay down and turned on her side to face me. "So has anything changed since last night regarding Benjamin?"

"If I answer that, are you going to lecture me?"

"No lectures today, I am just here to listen."

"My relationship is over." I looked at her intently. "It has to be."

"Does that mean you're never going to see him again?"

I felt a throb of sadness start in the middle of my chest, my throat tightened and my eyes started to fill. "I don't know." A voice inside my head said, *please, one more time, just one more time.* "He said he would be back here before he leaves for Morocco but…."

"Then I'm sure he will be."

"You know this because?"

"He just struck me as that sort of person."

"Sue, you knew Clay. Benjamin was playing a role. You don't know Benjamin at all."

"Are you telling me that Clay was a completely different person?" I nodded.

"That's bullshit," she said. "He may have had a fake name, fake accent, fake beard, fake colored eyes but you cannot fake integrity, honesty, love." She paused. "Guess you can try and fake it, god knows my second husband tried but I've learned since then to smell a phony from a mile away and Clay or Benjamin, whatever—he is not a phony."

"You're right, as usual, he's not a phony but, and I repeat, you knew Clay, not Benjamin."

At that moment Mrs. Casey drove up the alley with her dog in her lap. Seeing Sue and I on the ground, side by side, she stopped her car and waved a good morning to us. She was smiling so broadly I thought her face would crack.

"Our engagement photo will be in the *Globe Gazette* tomorrow." She poured herself more coffee. "She drives my mom bonkers. She calls once a month with some innocuous question while pumping her for information about my sisters and me. Anyway, where were we? Oh yeah, your broken heart." I winced. "Sorry, didn't mean to put you in the lonely-hearts club already."

"It's okay, it is the truth." I sat up. "God, I am so sick of talking about me. So what's going on with Karl?" Now she winced. "Did that prick dump you?"

"How can you be dumped when there was nothing to be dumped from?" There was no inflection in her voice. "We were supposed to have coffee on Friday and he didn't show up. I waited for over an hour."

"Maybe he had an emergency?"

"Don't start with the excuses, Liam. You were the reason I tried again for a so-called date, the only reason I asked him out twice in one evening. I ended up humiliating myself for nothing."

"Humiliated seems a bit dramatic."

She barked out a laugh. "You're calling me dramatic?" She squeezed her legs together. "I have to pee, don't move." She ran to the house. I lay back down on the ground. I wanted Benjamin more than anything. I closed my eyes and I was back on top of the dune in Truro, the cool wind swirling over us, my head on his stomach.

"You look miserable." She handed me my phone. "Call Northwest, buy a ticket and go to California."

"I can't do that. He doesn't want me there and I don't want to be there."

"I will only put up with your Joan of Arc for—." She looked at her watch. "Five more minutes. The only thing stopping the two of you is yourselves."

"And the lecture begins."

"This is the oddest thing, you're both single, you're clearly in love with each other." She slapped herself lightly on her cheek. "Shut up, Sue."

"Do you want to know what it was like in LA?" I asked. "Benjamin was an asshole."

"Are you rewriting history?"

"No, I am not. He was completely different, controlling, demanding, angry, shut down, all the things he isn't here. Well, except the controlling thing, he does like to be in charge."

"And you don't?" She broke a donut in half, picked up a piece and put it back in the box. "Was he like that out east?"

I thought about him dancing, singing with Ellie on Commercial Street, fucking on the beach and I smiled. "No, he wasn't, he was fantastic."

"So LA was an aberration. Why are you so hell bent on making this relationship bad? Are you deliberately trying to end this?"

"Haven't we had this conversation enough?" I asked.

"I am so frustrated with you two. I just don't get this. I can't even get a man to have coffee with me and you have this great guy who is crazy about you and you are breaking up. This is completely screwed up!" She knelt in front of me and took hold of my shoulders. "Listen to me, if you let this man go, you are going to regret this for the rest of your life."

I pulled away and went into my house.

CHAPTER FIFTY-SIX

—∞—

I was drunk with ragged energy. I woke each morning with my cell phone next to me and I would wake up several times a night to see if he had sent me a text. I called a few times but it always went to voice mail. I had to stop myself from leaving a message. Then I would be furious at myself for feeling so needy and furious with Benjamin for disappearing so completely.

I spent hours on my computer checking out celebrity websites for any information I could find. Each site offered the same story: Benjamin had been so overcome with grief that he had spent most of the summer by himself at his parent's house in Iowa.

There was no attempt to explain away any anomalies; the machine stayed on message. Benjamin was back to normal, back home in Los Angeles, ready to get back to work, and excited about his upcoming trip to Morocco. He was working out furiously with several trainers and was on a strict diet. The Internet was full of stories about how to get in the same fighting shape as Benjamin Graves. Everywhere I looked there were photos of Benjamin shirtless, his muscles so ripped they looked like tire treads.

The few times Benjamin was seen in public, Jacqueline Anderson was on his arm. Photos of them dining at Mr. Chow, walking hand in hand on the beach in Malibu, leaving a gym gripping a water bottle appeared on cue.

The only periodical that wasn't buying the story was the *Enquirer*. They were attempting to keep alive the story about the photographer who had snuck onto the Graves family's home in Iowa to find Benjamin sitting on a patio with a man and a woman deep in conversation. Benjamin had reportedly flipped out and assaulted the man and destroyed his camera and photos. However, with no evidence to support this story, it fell into the rumor mill.

Meanwhile Sue and Gregg were treating me as if I'd had a death in my family. They were being so solicitous it was beginning to unnerve me. While I missed Benjamin more than I could put into words, I did not want to be treated as if I had an incurable disease.

Gregg called me every day to let me know what was being said in Provincetown. Everyone was now claiming to have been at The Boatslip the day Benjamin was there dancing. The consensus was he wanted to get caught. Why else would he forget to cover those famous eyes? Several men were stating on their blogs they had slept with him, with grainy photos appearing of a naked, muscular blond lying on a bed, his face nowhere near the camera. The two leather bears were local heroes for having tried to unmask Benjamin. I grimaced when I saw the photo of them walking in the annual Provincetown Carnival parade, remembering their exaggerated aggressiveness.

After a week of this I put my computer away and told Gregg I didn't want to hear anymore about any of this. I alone knew what Benjamin had done all summer and it enraged me to see the massive cover up.

I realized one day while running that I had not taken one photograph of Benjamin. If we never saw each other again, the only tangible evidence I had of our relationship was his business card.

Had I been afraid he would have stopped me?

I was just beginning to believe I would never see him again until one night my phone rang, startling me out of the best sex dream I had ever experienced.

"Liam, it's me." It was Benjamin and he sounded anxious and angry.

"Hey Benjamin." I sat up to wake up. I looked at the unfamiliar number on my cell phone.

"Oh my God, I miss you so much, every part of me hurts." His voice cracked. "I cannot call you or text you. I think someone has hacked into my account or maybe my paranoia has gone over the cliff but…I'm sorry I haven't called sooner. Fuck, do I miss you."

"I miss you too." The words sounded hollow and incomplete.

"Everything out here is such bullshit, it's driving me nuts. The only positive in all of this is Jacqueline. I couldn't have done this without her." He paused. "She knows everything."

"Everything?"

"I had to tell someone what's happened to me and how I feel about you. It's eating me up. I don't know if I can go on like this." I heard noise in the background. "I'll be home soon." The phone went dead.

I was sitting in front of my television, two window fans on high trying to move the sticky air around my living room. Sue was due in a few minutes with pizzas. Benjamin was going to be interviewed on Gary Printz. It still seemed incongruous that Benjamin was doing this kind of interview, something he hadn't done in years. It seemed to me he was being moved around like a pawn on a chessboard.

Sue walked in the front door, damp hair stuck to her forehead.

"When is this summer ever going to end?" She picked up a magazine and began fanning herself. She looked at the cover, saw another photo of Benjamin and threw it on the floor.

I had a bucket of cold Stellas on the coffee table. We each opened one and began eating our pizzas as Gary Printz did his introductions. He gave a brief retrospective of Benjamin's career but mostly dealt with the photos of him taken over the past two months from his dad's funeral to Provincetown.

"I want you to know, Benjamin, how sorry we are over the loss of your dad." The camera caressed Benjamin and zoomed in on his eyes that were full of tears. For a moment it seemed he was going to lose his composure. His chin trembled softly and he took a deep breath and then another.

"Thanks Gary, it's been really hard."

"I'm sure it was a shock. He wasn't that old, was he?" Gary's sincerity seemed real and phony at the same time.

"Yes, it was a shock although he had been having health problems, but that's not what I'm talking about." He paused. His eyes filled up and overflowed. "What is surprising to me is how much I miss him." The tears were streaming down his face and Gary cut to a commercial.

I was holding a slice of pizza in front of my mouth, stunned by what I was seeing. This man who rarely did any kind of talk show or interview, who dodged every personal question he could, who had done his best to keep the world at bay from his family, was now exposing himself on television in a way that was unimaginable until that very moment.

"I can't believe what I'm seeing," Sue whispered. "Is this an act?"

"No, no it's not, he really loved his dad. But he is so private, this...this just isn't him."

The show resumed and Benjamin was back in control. The questions were softballs and Benjamin handled them deftly. He talked a great deal about his upcoming movie, about how sore he was from all the exercise, how difficult the diet was, how much he missed beer. I stopped listening to focus on how he was coming across. To me, he seemed chastened with no hint of his usual cockiness. Just a young man, clearly still in mourning, trying to get on with his life which just happened to be a life that millions of people wanted to be part of.

With just a few minutes left in the show, Gary switched gears.

"I have to ask this, please forgive me, but was that really your cousin?"

The photograph appeared on screen of Benjamin kissing me on my temple. Sue said, "That is so obviously you. I cannot believe for a second I didn't recognize you, I am such an idiot!"

Benjamin didn't hesitate. "No Gary, he's not my cousin. He's a friend of mine from back home. I was just showing him around LA."

"So why did you introduce him as your cousin?"

A look of annoyance slipped across Benjamin's face.

"I thought it would be easier. Guess I got that wrong." He laughed loudly, too loudly.

"What about Provincetown? Never having been there I can't say much about it, but I've heard stories."

Per usual, Gary missed a golden opportunity for the follow-up question that was screaming to be asked.

"Not sure what you've heard Gary, but it is a beautiful place." He shifted in his chair. "It never ceases to amaze me how something simple like going to a small town to do some research about a prospective film can cause such a reaction." He shook his head and then forced a smile.

"What's the movie?"

"I read a book recently, *Heaven's Coast* by Mark Doty. Have you heard of him?" Gary shook his head. "You should, he's a great poet and writer. He wrote about the death of his partner from AIDS. I've been thinking of optioning it for a movie."

"Would you star in this movie?"

"Possibly. Might be time for me to play a gay man, don't you think? After all, I haven't won an Oscar!" He laughed even louder this time

"With that comment, he never will," Sue said.

I wondered who came up with the Mark Doty idea and if Mark Doty knew anything about this, because his world was about to change.

"Then it must be true that you were spotted dancing in a homosexual bar a couple of weeks ago," Gary said, stumbling slightly over the word homosexual.

"Yup, that was me. I had a great time until people started recognizing me. The music was terrific. If I had just remembered the blue contact lenses!" He smiled sincerely. "God, do I love to dance."

"Not sure I knew that about you Benjamin," Gary said.

"There's a lot you don't know about me." Benjamin let loose with his false laugh one more time.

"But in a homo…gay bar?" Gary seemed incredulous.

"Why not? That's where the best music is. You should try it some time, Gary." He started to laugh again, they broke for another commercial and I turned off the television. Sue jumped up and grabbed the remote from me and turned it back on.

"What the hell are you doing? It's finally getting interesting."

The interview resumed with Gary asking Benjamin about his movie, as if the preceding conversation hadn't occurred. I groaned.

"How much longer are you in LA?" Gary leaned forward with a look on his face as if he had just asked Benjamin to explain how he had discovered the cure for cancer.

"Just a few more days. I have a few things to do, family things, then one more quick stop to do some scouting. I have an idea for a movie, actually it's not my idea, it was given to me by a great friend. It's gonna be such a terrific movie. I can't wait to get started on it. Then on to Morocco for the next few months."

"Benjamin, thank you for spending this hour with us. And once again I want you to know how sorry we all are about your dad." Benjamin's face was drawn and he nodded gravely.

"Thanks Gary, that means a great deal to me."

Sue turned off the television and opened another beer.

"How come he didn't ask him anything about who this friend is and what the movie is about?" She picked up a slice of pizza and threw it back into the box. "My God, what does it take for that guy to ask the expected follow up question?"

I smiled and then scowled. Sue looked at me with alarm.

"Sybil, what the hell is going on inside that big head of yours?"

I picked up a slice of pizza and took a large bite. I slowly chewed my food and then deliberately took another large bite.

"Come on Liam, don't be a jerk. What's going on?"

I didn't know how to answer her.

"Let's start over." Sue stood up and knocked the fan over. She cursed and set it upright. "Why did you smile?"

"I am the friend he referred to."

"How do you know that?"

"Because it's my idea for this movie."

"Bullshit. Since when have you become a screenwriter?"

"I never said I wrote a screenplay, I just have a great idea for a movie, that's all."

"So he's coming by here one more time." She opened another beer and handed it to me. "And the scowl?"

"Did you like what you just saw?"

She started to say something and I put my hand up. "I know what you're gonna say so let's pretend we already had that conversation."

"You're an asshole, Liam, you know that?" She found her purse and stood up. "You are determined to remain single and I for one am no longer willing to participate in this charade. Don't expect me to be there the next time you come crying to me about how lonely you are. You have created some impossible, idealized version of a boyfriend and you know what? If Benjamin Graves isn't it, he doesn't exist."

CHAPTER FIFTY-SEVEN

———∞———

The Gary Printz interview had the desired effect of changing the focus from Benjamin's dissolute weekend in Provincetown back to the grieving, young, newly single superstar. I read article after article describing jilted women, presumed lost pregnancies and cancelled wedding plans.

By Friday, I was beginning to think he had changed his mind about stopping in Iowa and had gone on to Morocco. I had weekend plans to have dinner with Mom and the aunts but other than that, I had nothing going on except work and exercise and no Sue.

I could feel the beginning of an old depression begin to reestablish an outpost in my brain.

I was sitting on my patio trying to read a magazine when my cell phone rang. My heart thudded a few times until I heard my younger sister's voice.

"Liam!" she cried, "I...I lost my baby!" With that she began sobbing convulsively.

"I'm so sorry Leah. When did it happen?" I wondered if that was the right question.

"This morning. I wasn't doing anything wrong, it just happened. I can't believe this, why does everything shitty always happen to me?" The sobbing returned even louder this time. I pulled the phone away from my ear.

"How's Patrick holding up?" I asked when she took a few breaths.

"Fuck him!" she screamed into the phone. "He never wanted this baby in the first place and now he's gotten his wish. Now he can divorce me and go fuck every 22 year old in the Twin Cities!"

My head was spinning. I had no idea what to say. Part of me was glad that maybe her fucked up marriage was going to end. *She's not ready to be a mom,* whipped through my brain.

"Say something Liam." She was breathing heavily. "You know how paranoid I get when people stop talking."

"I don't know what to say."

"Then I will. I'm sick of being polite, sick of worrying about everyone else's feelings. Sick of being quiet!" There was anger in her voice I had not heard before. "I need to get out of here. I'm coming to Mom's for a few days, maybe a week, maybe longer."

"How did she take the news?"

Leah laughed harshly. "She was surprisingly upset. I figured she thought I wasn't ready to have a child. Guess I figured that wrong."

No you didn't.

"I love you Leah, you're gonna be okay."

"Not so sure about that." She hung up. I instantly dialed mom. When she answered on the sixth ring she sounded like she'd been crying.

"Oh Liam, can you believe this happened to my baby?" Her voice was hoarse as if she had been coughing.

"But I thought you...I thought you said she wasn't ready to be a mom?"

"Liam, that was weeks ago, people change," she snapped. "Look at your dad, he did a complete 360 about you being gay."

"What did you say?"

There was a long uncomfortable pause.

"What did he say about it, Mom?" I asked quietly.

"Oh poop, now why did I go and open that can of worms?" She coughed a couple of times and then asked me what I wanted for dinner on Sunday.

I did not reply.

"Do you really want to know what he said, Liam?" She cleared her throat twice. "It was unkind and not very original. I think we all tend to fall back on clichés when we are uncomfortable with a new thing." She paused. "He loved you so much." She paused again. "Can't we pretend that I never said anything, just this once?"

"We pretend enough in this family. Look at Leah, she had no idea how you felt about her pregnancy but she certainly knew that things weren't right between the two of you. What did that accomplish other than make her feel paranoid that you weren't happy for her?"

"You're right. I messed up. Will you ever forgive me?"

"What did Dad say?" There was a disappointed sigh at the other end and then quiet. It was so quiet I wondered if she had set down the phone and walked away. I waited.

"Before I say this, I need you to know how much he loved you. He loved you so much he was willing to set aside his prejudices about homosexuals."

"Did he have many?"

"Yes. Many. After all, he had no exposure to homosexuals. He only knew one. You."

I knew this was impossible but kept my mouth shut to keep her on topic.

"He was no different from any other man his age that had lived their entire lives in the Midwest. They knew nothing about homosexuals other than the worst possible stories you can imagine."

"I can imagine them, Mom. I've heard them all before."

"Probably not all. There used to be many, many more stories of abducted boys being led into lives of prostitution or luring innocent men, especially soldiers, into life changing moments. Everything was linked to this. It was in the newspaper all the time. The McCarthy hearings for God's sake! Oh my, it was an awful time. Of course none of us knew any openly gay people. I had my suspicions about that woman at the library, what was her name? Oh yes, it was Betty. She ruled that library with a fist. Her arms were bigger than your fathers. I was quite shocked when she ran off with Clarence Babbitt, the wrestling coach from the public high school. She was living with a woman at the time, so we just assumed they were a couple."

"Who's we?"

"I don't know, maybe it was just me. Does it matter?"

"Yes it matters. It would be nice to know that other people in the nineteen fifties acknowledged gay people in this town."

"Maybe they did and maybe they didn't. We did not talk about this out loud." She sounded so distressed I almost stopped the conversation but realized I only had this one opportunity. She would never discuss this again.

"I am so afraid you are never going to think of your dad the same way." Her voice quavered. "Do you promise me you will still love and honor him? I need you to swear to this." Her voice rose a pitch. "Colleen Ashby, when you are going to learn to keep your big bazoo shut?"

"I promise," I said. Several seconds went by.

"At first he was shocked, just as I was and then of course just like everyone else, we assumed it was a phase you would outgrow. And, and when you didn't outgrow it, well, that was the hardest time for him."

"Was it hard for you?"

"No, no it wasn't. I saw my son. The son who was my hope, the son who brought joy into my life from the very first week when we came home from the hospital. I didn't see a label or a lifestyle, just my little boy." She stopped and let herself cry. I swiped at my tears.

"I didn't care other than worry about what kind of life you would have. Would you find someone, that sort of thing. Would you encounter prejudice or violence? I was worried sick those first few months after you moved to Boston. Then when I visited the first time and saw how lovely your neighborhood was, I calmed down instantly. Your father on the other hand—" She paused again.

"My father...what?" I failed to keep the impatience out of my voice. The longer this went on the more worried I was that she was either going to abruptly stop or tell me things I didn't want to hear.

"Once he accepted the fact that your choice to live life as a gay man was definite..."

"It is not a choice, Mom. I have known that I am gay since I was three or four."

"Sorry, I know how sensitive your group is about that word 'choice.' Anyway, he believed it was a choice and Liam, just go with me for a bit. You and your dad could have discussed the word 'choice' for hours, weeks on end and you wouldn't have changed his mind."

"He really thought I woke up one day and said, hey, I think I'm going to be a queer from now on?" I laughed, wondering what I was laughing about.

"I hate that word Liam Conor and you know it. Please do not use it again."

So, Dad thought I had chosen to be gay. I shook my head and sighed loudly.

"I know your back is up about this and I understand but I need you to see things through his eyes. He firmly believed you had chosen to be a homosexual. Of course, once that issue was off the table, he obsessed about what you did in the bedroom. You know, who did what to whom and how did you decide, that sort of thing." She said this as if she was giving the weekend weather forecast.

"He wanted to know what I did in the bedroom?" My voice was loud, too loud.

"This wasn't specific to you, he just couldn't imagine what two men did in bed together. Your father was very traditional about sex...extremely traditional."

"I could have told him."

"Yes you could have and thank God you didn't. He did a great deal of reading, even went to Minneapolis a few times and spoke to a psychologist. That seemed to help a great deal."

"He didn't speak to Father Schmidt about this?"

Mom took a long intake of breath. "I know you're upset so I am not going to say anything about that last cheap shot but boy, what a cheap shot!"

My face reddened.

"I want to finish this conversation, Liam, okay?" She didn't wait for a response. "After he saw the psychologist and after you came home a few times and you still seemed like the same lovable, caring Liam, then he finally, truly calmed down. If he was still struggling internally, he didn't tell me. Of course, when we met Justin, we did have a wee bit of a setback."

"Why?"

"Do you have to ask?"

"Yes, what was wrong with Justin?"

"Liam Conor Ashby, you are a smart man. What did you possibly see in him? I could tell he was bad news the second I met him. Your father couldn't stand him. We thought he represented the worst possible match for you. He was controlling, my God, that time he wouldn't let you order that cheeseburger and forced you to eat a salad, why I wanted to throw a hard roll at him. He was uncomfortable in his skin, shallow, evasive, acting like the two of you were roommates instead of a couple. He exuded shame like it was perspiration." Her anger rippled across the line. "Your dad's prejudices were reawakened after that first weekend. We were hoping you would meet a nice boy, just like you, but instead you found Justin. It was so clear to us that he disliked being gay we worried you felt the same way about yourself. That would have broken my heart."

Had I imagined all the good I saw in Justin?

"We were so relieved when you broke up."

No, I hadn't.

"First Dad thought I was a pedophile or a prostitute and then once he got over that gem, he decided I was filled with so much self loathing, I found another man just like me and ended up in a horrible, self hating relationship. Is that it in a nut shell?" I was seething. "Goddamnit Mom, why didn't he tell me?"

"I am never, never going to forgive myself for telling you this. Your father thought the world of you Liam. He told me that many times—especially toward the end. He told me he couldn't have asked for a better son. Okay honey?"

It was not okay but I said nothing.

"Liam, please say something…anything." She started to cry.

"I'll see you on Sunday," I said quietly.

I felt her relief through the phone. "I love you Liam."

"Love you too." I hung up.

I stood at the picture window looking out at the backyard. I saw my dad mowing the lawn, painting the garage, in control at the barbecue. I looked into the dining room and saw him carving the Thanksgiving turkey with surgical precision, a half smile on his face, a cigarette dangling from his lower lip.

I walked into the living room and fell heavily into a chair. I looked across the room. The Christmas tree was again dominating the corner, piles of presents so high they almost blocked the television. I remembered the year I bought Dad a Christmas present with my own money, the first time I had been able to do this from the money I earned as a paperboy. It was a cheap bottle of cologne from Target but I had been so excited I barely slept. Dad had seemed genuinely touched. He told me he loved me that day, probably not the first time, but the first time I remembered.

Had all that changed when I came out to him?

Throwing on running clothes, I raced out to the high school. I ran several miles on the track pushing myself lap after lap until I collapsed onto the grass under an oak tree near the empty football field. I looked up into the canopy of leaves and I was in my backyard again, Dad calling me to help him with the burgers.

I put an arm over my eyes and cried.

CHAPTER FIFTY-EIGHT

———∞———

As I pulled into the parking lot behind the restaurant, Sue was getting out of her car. I stayed in my car with the air conditioning blasting me in the face. I closed my eyes, willing my mind to think of nothing and almost fell asleep. I felt a hand on my knee and looked over at Sue.

"What the hell is wrong with you? Somebody die?"

"Leah lost her baby."

"You're kidding me."

"No I am not. She miscarried this morning."

"Oh my God, I am never going to ask that question again. How did it happen?"

"What difference does it make how it happened? Her baby is dead, that's all that matters." I stepped out of my car and slammed the door. I felt fury rising and roiling in my gut. Leaning against the car, I felt the heat from the fender stinging through my cotton pants but I didn't move. Sue stood next to me. She pulled me towards her for an embrace. I resisted but she wouldn't let go.

"I am so sorry, Liam." She put her arm around my shoulder and I stopped resisting. We stayed together. "Is there something else?" She looked me in the eyes. "Come on Liam, something else happened, didn't it? It's about Benjamin, isn't it?"

"No." I moved away from the car and walked towards the restaurant. "There's nothing else going on."

It was a typical midsummer Friday night. Sunburned golfers, a few tourists, and my regulars. The same people who came every Friday night, sat in the same chairs and ordered the same drinks and had the same conversations with their friends they had every Friday night for weeks, months, years.

Making drinks, avoiding small talk, I kept glancing at my watch wishing it was eleven instead of eight. All I wanted was to go home and sleep.

The few times I thought of my dad, a flood of sadness filled my chest so completely I thought I would choke. Sue kept a quiet distance. I knew someday I would tell her what I had learned but not now.

And really, what would I tell her? That Dad had hated learning I was gay? That he had disliked me?

When an unfamiliar face ordered a Brandy Alexander, I had a hard time hiding my irritation. I hated making ice cream drinks in the summer. The ice cream was the wrong consistency and they always came back.

I heard a commotion in the front of the restaurant as I reached up to grab the rarely used glass. The person I saw reflected in the mirror crossing the lounge didn't register. For a moment I thought I was looking at a television. Benjamin was striding towards me, Georgia Dee and the wait staff on his heels. He was smiling at me. Sue came to the bar and Benjamin waved at her.

"Hey Liam, good to see you again." He reached across the bar and pumped my hand. Sue came running across the room moving towards him as if to hug him but he stuck out his arm and shook her hand. "Sue, good to see you too."

"How, how, how do you know him?" Georgia Dee asked. She stood right next to Benjamin, her face ashen and flushed at the same time. Before anyone could answer, she said, "Well of course you know him, you worked the funeral reception."

Benjamin stood at the bar staring at me, everyone else staring at him. The cooks had come out of the kitchen, the whole scene a frozen tableaux. Sue started laughing.

"What a bunch of hicks! Come on everyone, we need to get back to work." She herded the waitresses back to the dining room and with a hand on Georgia Dee's shoulder pushed her towards the front of the restaurant.

"Liam, is there somewhere we can talk in private?" Benjamin had his hands in his pockets as he looked nervously at the people crowding around the bar.

"Sure, give me a second."

I looked at the sea of empty glasses lined up on the bar which I refilled as quickly as possible, and then led Benjamin to the store room under the kitchen. The single light bulb cast a harsh glare on the cartons of food. I made sure the door was closed tightly and then I was in his arms. We kissed urgently, tears mixing with the sweat running down our faces. Benjamin pushed me away and put his hands on my face.

"Oh fuck how I have missed you."

We kissed until I heard Sue calling down for us.

"If you don't get your asses back up here, an army of vigilantes is gonna be down there and haul you back up. They want more cocktails and they want Benjamin although not sure that is the right order. Hell with this crowd, of course it is."

We separated. I wiped the perspiration from his face and pushed his hair off his forehead.

"I'm going home," Benjamin said, "come over as soon as you can."

"You're not going back to the bar?"

"That version of Benjamin is not here tonight." He gave me another kiss and bounded up the stairs.

When I returned to the bar an array of heads turned in my direction. The look of disappointment on their faces reminded me of our high school homecoming game when we had lost in the last ten seconds.

"Anyone need a drink?"

"Where's Benji?" several people asked at once.

"He left." I went back to work.

"What do you mean he left?" Georgia Dee asked as she stepped behind the bar. "My kids are gonna kill me if I don't get his autograph."

"He had to go." I walked away.

"What was he doing here in the first place?"

"He owed me some money from the funeral reception," I lied fluidly. "Just settling his debt."

We were sitting with our feet in the pool, dirty dishes on the table, empty wine glasses on the patio. For the past twenty-four hours we had been so consumed with being with each other again we had not thought beyond our immediate needs: sex, food, sex, exercise and sleep. The few times we'd started to talk about anything, especially about anything that hinted at the future, we had fallen back into bed.

I wanted to sculpt a statue of him that incorporated the feel of his skin, the smell of his breath and his body: during sex, after exercise, first thing in the morning, his laugh, his anger, his tears. I wanted a version of him alive with me in my home even when he was halfway around the world. I wanted to never forget and I was afraid I would.

"I was thinking about tomorrow night," Benjamin said leaning back to pull the wine from the ice bucket. "We're going to your mom's for dinner, right?"

"Yup."

He took a gulp of his wine and said, "Clay is not going to your mom's. I am."

I paused with my wine glass halfway to my lips and absorbed what he said. "You're kidding me."

"No I'm not. I want your family to know the truth. And one more thing, I want ice cream and I want it now. Is Birdsall's still around?"

He jumped to his feet knocking over his wine glass, which didn't break. He picked up my glass and finished it off. I was lost in thought trying to imagine how the three M's were going to react and how I was going to react to their reaction. Benjamin snapped his fingers in front of my face.

"To answer your question, yes, it's still around," I said.

I remembered pedaling my bike across town to buy their chocolate chip ice cream. I would buy a half-gallon and it never lasted more than one evening.

"Let's go." Benjamin jumped to his feet, threw his tank top on, stepped into his sandals and got into the car. I looked at him in amazement.

"This is certainly different, you going out as you." I put on my shirt and joined him in the car.

"Get used to it." Benjamin leaned over and kissed me hard on the mouth. Ten minutes later we pulled into the small, narrow parking lot next to the ice cream store. There was a lone pickup truck parked near the entrance.

"Another frenetic night in old Mason Jar." Benjamin pulled in next to the truck. "I'm having a triple hot fudge sundae with coffee ice cream, nuts and extra whipped cream."

We walked into the shop, Benjamin leading the way. It always amazed me how this shop had not changed in all the years I had been coming. A long narrow counter stretched the entire length of the building, with metal stools covered in cracked leather. A line of small booths ran along the opposite wall. The list of items for sale was on the facing wall and as I looked at it, it seemed to me that the flavors of ice cream had never changed. The smell never changed either. It was a combination of cream, milk, chocolate, bananas and cleaning products.

549

I looked to my left, and sitting in a booth was an Amish family. The young father was in bib overalls, the mother in a long cotton dress, a bonnet holding her hair off her face, a young girl sitting next to her. They looked at us with no recognition. I laughed. Of course they wouldn't have a clue who Benjamin was. Benjamin looked in their direction, must have had the same thought as me as I saw his shoulders relax and a smile light up his face. Not his Hollywood smile, his real one.

The man behind the counter must have been in his seventies. If he recognized Benjamin, he did not let on. As he gave Benjamin his change, he looked briefly in his eyes and said, "I'm real sorry to hear about your dad, young man." Benjamin shook his hand and we went outside.

We leaned against the hood of the car and ate our ice cream. I slapped at a mosquito on my arm.

"How does it feel to be anonymous?" I asked, my mouth full of chocolate chip ice cream and hot fudge. Benjamin shoveled an overflowing spoonful of whipped cream into his mouth, leaving a smudge at the end of his nose, which I flicked off with a finger.

"I can't remember the last time this happened. It's just like the old days."

The door opened and the Amish family walked outside. I heard the little girl say she needed to use the bathroom. The mom disappeared back inside. The father stood by his truck and smiled at us.

"Think this weather's gonna break soon?" he asked.

He pulled off his cap and ran his hand through his hair. Benjamin gave a perfunctory answer. The father leaned against the hood of the truck and smiled at me. He had uneven teeth with a slight gap in the middle. His face was two toned: deeply tanned on the bottom half, white on top where his hat protected him from the sun. He had a full beard, muscular forearms and strong weathered hands. He wore a crisp white T-shirt underneath his bib overalls.

I looked away and then looked back. He was still staring at me. I looked over at Benjamin who was lost in the process of devouring his sundae. I looked again at the father. This time his stare was bolder. He looked at me from head to foot. He put his hands in his pockets. The door opened and with a jump, he walked away to help his wife and daughter into the truck. He went back around to his side, nodded at me and drove away.

Benjamin went inside to wash his hands. I looked up at the sole street lamp and it struck me that everyone I knew was trapped in their lives one way or another. This man; straight, gay or whatever he was, was trapped within the confines of his religion and family. Benjamin was trapped inside the rules of his industry and his own fears. Leah was trapped in a bad marriage. Deirdre was trapped with a man who would rather play golf than be a dad. I was trapped....

"Liam, where are you?" Benjamin put a hand on my shoulder. He reached over, took the spoon out of my hand and took a large bite of my sundae.

"I don't know," I replied.

CHAPTER FIFTY-NINE

———∞———

"So where is he?" Deirdre looked at her watch. "And why didn't he come with you?"

"He had a few errands to run." I looked at my own watch. Benjamin was thirty minutes late. Not a good sign. I had told my family that I had a bit of a surprise for them and so Deirdre had driven down with Leah. Now I wished I hadn't opened my mouth.

"There's no hurry, is there Colleen?" Aunt Margaret said. I saw her empty glass and went into the kitchen to make another one with Mom on my heels.

"I don't want you to put any vodka in that, Liam. She's had enough." She opened the refrigerator to pour herself another glass of wine and while she watched, I dumped a dollop of vodka into a glass and filled it with diet tonic water. Mom started to say something but stopped.

"Can you give me any hint of what the big news is?"

She turned the stove on under the corn. I frowned; it would be mush by the time we ate. I turned it off. Her eyes went wide but again said nothing.

"It has to do with Clay but he made me promise not to say anything. He wants to tell you himself."

"I hate surprises," Colleen said.

"Me too." Aunt Marie came into the kitchen for more coffee. "What's going on?"

At that moment I heard a car door slam. My heart jumped into my throat.

"Clay must be here." Mom smiled as she turned the water back on under the corn. I went into the bathroom and splashed water on my face. I figured there was a fifty-fifty chance Benjamin had come as himself. When I walked into the kitchen, I stopped cold. I could see Clay on the patio through the sliding glass doors. Hearing that booming Texan twang was so disappointing to me I walked to the back of the house and sat on a bed for several minutes.

"Liam, get your ass out here," Clay yelled through the house. When I joined them on the patio, Benjamin stood next to me with an arm around my shoulder. I pulled away. Leah and Deirdre looked delighted to see us together.

"Can I talk to you for a second?" I walked through the garage to the street with Benjamin trailing. When we were far enough away, I said, "What the fuck is going on? Aren't we finally past this?" I turned and began walking away, walking so fast it was almost a jog.

"Liam, come on. How many times have I told you I'm a coward." I stopped and waited for him to catch up.

"Why did you set me up?" He shrugged his shoulders. "I am done Benjamin, I am so done."

I walked back to the house, not caring whether Benjamin was behind me. On the patio, I picked up my beer and drank half while the five women stared at me.

"Did you two have a fight?" Aunt Margaret looked concerned and glassy eyed. I didn't answer. Mom started talking about the upcoming church picnic. Aunt Marie lit a cigarette, looking bemused. Deirdre moved over and put a hand on mine.

"It'll be okay Liam, everybody fights."

Somebody put a new beer in front of me, and the next thing I knew I was lighting the BBQ and cooking the pork tenderloin.

I thought about the entire summer and what had brought us to this point. Two weeks ago I thought we were over for good, then

Benjamin dropped in with virtually no warning and we resumed our lives together as if nothing had happened. Then he claimed he was moving this forward and then at the last minute backed off-again. The notion that this had been one long game was the most believable narrative-and I had lost again. I felt anger radiating across my chest and realized it was impossible to pretend anymore with my family.

'Mom, Deirdre, Leah, Aunt Margaret, Aunt Marie." They seemed surprised I was still there. "There was something that Clay was going to tell you tonight. Something kind of important."

"He's not ill, is he? Oh the poor dear." Aunt Margaret said.

"No, no he's fine."

"You boys must have broken up, is that it Liam?" Mom asked.

"Of course they did," Aunt Marie said. "He finally figured out that Liam must have a few screws loose, moving back to Iowa after all."

"It's not about that." I was impatient to finally say this out loud. "We **have** broken up but that is not what he was going to tell you. He was going to tell you that....." Suddenly I saw Benjamin walking through the garage as himself. He smiled sheepishly and stepped onto the patio.

"I was going to tell you that I have been pretending to be Clay Davis for many, many reasons, most of them pretty stupid. My real name is Benjamin, Benjamin Graves."

"I knew it all along," Marie said as she drained her coffee cup. Aunt Margaret gasped and grabbed her drink.

Colleen let out a sound somewhere between a cry and a moan, jumped to her feet and went to shake his hand. He pulled her in for a long hug. She pulled back and looked into his face.

"I had no idea you weren't who you said you were but it doesn't matter one iota. I knew you were a good kind man the minute I met you, that's all that matters. Well, on second thought, does this mean you're not a Baptist?"

He laughed. "Not a Baptist. I was raised Episcopalian."

"I knew that too," Marie said. "You were the sorriest excuse for a Baptist I've ever met." She was looking at the wall, seeming unable to look Benjamin in the eyes.

"Aunt Marie, how did you know that he wasn't Clay?" I asked.

"Have you heard of a telephone Liam?" She reached for her cigarettes. "I made a few calls to my friends in Katy. There is no Davis family living on a farm anywhere near that town."

"That doesn't mean you knew he was Benjamin Graves, only that…"

"Liam, what the hell difference does it make now?" She looked exasperated. "Your little game is over. Was it fun?"

"Episcopalian is a lot better than Baptist," Mom said.

Benjamin shot Marie a look and then turned to Colleen. "You also need to know that I love your son, brother, nephew more than anyone I have ever loved in my life. He is the only thing in my life that matters." He stepped over to me and hugged me for several minutes. We pulled away slightly and kissed.

Aunt Margaret sighed, "Oh, this is just like in the movies."

"Margaret Ashby, you dumb bunny. What movies have you seen that look like that?" Marie said as she pointed at us kissing. I pulled away and wiped away a tear. I looked at my sisters who had not moved.

"Benjamin, you remember Deirdre and Leah?"

He stepped over, pulled them to their feet and hugged them both. Their eyes were shocked. I tried to imagine the roles reversed.

"Clay….sorry…Benjamin, what can I get you to drink? A beer and a shot of tequila?" Mom asked.

"I would prefer a vodka tonic." Benjamin smiled at her. I felt myself beginning to relax in a way I hadn't for weeks.

"So, how long before the *Enquirer* gets hold of this story?" Marie said flatly.

Benjamin took a swallow of his cocktail and handed it back to Colleen. "Do you mind putting a little more vodka in this?"

"She makes a poor drink, doesn't she?" Margaret said glancing over at me.

"Let's hope they don't," I said.

"They will," Marie said.

"Why?"

"They always do."

"Who else knows?" Margaret asked.

"Sue and Gregg."

"Sue Flanagan knew this before me?" Deirdre asked.

"Does your family know…Cla… Benjamin?" Margaret handed her empty glass to Leah.

"No, Margaret, they do not."

Aunt Margaret flushed. "Can you say my name again? It has just killed me that none of your leading ladies have had my name."

"Margaret, Margaret, Margaret," he said as she squirmed in her seat. He took a drink of the refilled glass and said, "Much better. Thanks."

"Why doesn't your family know?" Marie asked. "Your mom got a problem with fairies?"

"Jesus, Aunt Marie," I said.

"Marie, if you don't stop this impolite questioning, I…I don't know what I will do!" Mom said.

"It's okay Colleen," Benjamin said. "The answer is yes, my mom has problems with fairies, and actually she has problems with any kind of sexuality. I **will** tell her someday, just not sure when."

"Not surprised." Marie spun her lighter in a circle. "She's a cold fish. I never liked her." Leah let out a small shriek.

"That's okay too." Benjamin finished his drink. "I'm not too fond of her these days either."

"What's next?" Marie pushed her empty coffee cup towards Colleen who ran to the kitchen to fill it. "Aren't you supposed to be on an airplane?"

Benjamin frowned. "Yes, I leave for Morocco tomorrow for several months of shooting. Should be done in early December if the weather cooperates."

"Liam going with you?" Marie dropped two packets of sugar into her coffee and a heavy dollop of cream. Mom set her wine glass down with a thud.

"No, I'm not," I answered.

"Why not?" Aunt Marie asked.

"I have a life here, I have a job, family, my house."

"You have no life here Liam Ashby. I have been telling you this all summer. It is simply not normal for a thirty-two year old man to move back home. You have a life with this man, so get the hell out of here. I'll keep an eye on your house and garden."

"Marie, leave him alone," Mom said. "If he wants to stay in Iowa, it's his choice."

"Stop babying him, Colleen. You baby all your children and look how they turned out."

I looked over at my sisters. Deirdre said softly, "I think we're fine."

"I'll be back for Liam. It's just that a movie set is no place for him. I work ten, twelve, fourteen-hour days, sometimes all night long. We're in the middle of a desert, there will be nothing for him to do."

"It all sounds so glamorous," Margaret said.

"Since you finally told the truth, it seems to me that this isn't the time to start lying again." Marie sat up in her chair. "Liam's not going with you because you don't want the world to know that you're a homosexual."

"It's not that simple," Benjamin said.

"If Liam were a woman, would she be going with you?"

"I don't know how to answer that, Marie." His refilled glass was placed in front of him.

"Just the truth." She exhaled a stream of smoke.

"It would depend, it would depend on lots of things. Do they have a job they can leave for several months? Are they self-sufficient enough so I don't have to worry about them? Can they handle the conditions?"

"Do they have a vagina instead of a penis?" Marie asked.

Benjamin reddened. "Okay Marie, you've made your point. The answer is probably yes, if Liam were a woman, the odds are she would be going with me. Are you happy now?"

"Yes, thanks."

"Do you think this would be easy?" Benjamin was angry. His eyes were piercing Marie's but she didn't blink.

"Nothing in life that's worth anything is ever easy."

"You would tell the truth if you were me, is that it Marie?" Benjamin spat out the words. A flicker of saliva hit the table. Margaret wiped it up with her napkin and stuck it in her purse.

"Of course I would. If I loved someone as much as you say you love Liam, it's a no brainer. The only reason not to tell is if you're a coward."

Benjamin's face was bright red and his shoulders were heaving. "It's not that simple."

"Yes, it is." Marie looked at me. "Liam, you burned the pork." I looked over and saw smoke pouring out of the grill. I yanked the charred meat off the fire and threw it on a plate. Marie stood up and disappeared into the house.

"Time for dinner!" Mom exclaimed. "Liam, please put the meat on the board in the kitchen, I'll clean it up. Girls, help me set the table."

When I returned to the patio, Benjamin was sitting close to Margaret. She was holding his hand. Her face was an expression of joy but her eyes were sad.

"Nothing is as simple as Marie makes it out. Liam knows that, we all know that. Life is full of nuance. Marie just bulldozes through, not caring how many bodies are scattered along the way," Margaret said.

"Thanks, but sometimes I wish I could do things that way. But with this, I cannot. I can't stop thinking about all the bad things that will happen."

I put my hands on his shoulder. I felt such enormous relief that the game was finally over with my family that for a second I didn't care what came next.

"I keep taking baby steps." Benjamin pulled out an ice cube and began chewing on it. "You don't think Marie will tell people, do you?"

"Of course not. She has a big mouth but when it comes to family, her lips are sealed. Plus, as you might have guessed by now, she's not exactly impressed with the trappings of fame. Me on the other hand, can we talk about your performance in *Flag Day?* That scene when you were shot? I just sobbed. I was convinced you were going to die. And when the music started, oh Sacred Heart, it was too much. I sat there crying and crying with relief that you had survived. The ushers had to ask me to leave." He put his hand on her forearm which bubbled with goose bumps.

I went looking for my sisters. They were sitting on the back porch in complete silence. I sat down on a wooden bench next to them. I noticed the silver maple tree I had given Mom for Mother's Day. It seemed to be struggling.

"Emily must have seen Benjamin that night when she started screaming in the hallway, right?" Deirdre asked.

I blushed bright red. I had completely forgotten that night. "Yes, she did. He had to pee and thought everyone was asleep."

"She still has nightmares about that at least once a week."

"Well, shit," I said.

"Yes Liam, it is shit. Why did you lie to us?"

"He doesn't trust us," Leah said.

"Apparently."

"Benjamin asked me not to say anything."

"That's the best you've got?"

"Would you have?"

"Of course I would have. This is huge!"

"That's easy for you to say now."

"We wouldn't have told a soul." Deirdre seemed disgusted with me.

"You have no idea what this has been like or how you would have reacted if you were in my shoes."

"I would have told you." Deirdre stood up.

"Me too," Leah said.

We heard Mom call us to dinner. Suddenly I felt about ten years old being called in for a weeknight dinner in the middle of an argument with my sisters. We would race through our meal so we could get back outside to continue our fight away from our parents' ears. They walked into the house.

It was so easy for them to talk about this in hindsight. I knew they would have done the same thing, didn't I?

CHAPTER SIXTY

———∞———

I was alone in my bed. Benjamin had left for the airport moments before, saying he would be back sometime before Christmas but in the meantime, I would not hear from him. No phone calls, no emails, or texts. I argued with him in the hope we could exchange at least a monthly phone call, something friends would do, no strings attached, but he said no. He terminated the conversation by saying he had a job to do and that I had no idea what pressure he was under. This entire 100-million-dollar film rested on his shoulders. He had left abruptly, almost as if annoyed with me for asking anything from him.

I lay in bed remembering the night before. After dinner we went back outside to the patio. Mom lit a few candles and turned off the outside light. Aunt Margaret tried to get Benjamin to tell Hollywood stories but he had turned her questions around and we began talking about our pasts. The smell of drying leaves, burned out lawns and gardens full of ripe fruit and vegetables worked to unlock memories.

The three M's told stories about their childhood that neither my sisters nor I had ever heard. Leah told the story of climbing up on the roof of our grade school one hot August day to find Sister Nora sunbathing in a one-piece suit. She was locked out of the school. Leah had to run down the fire escape to find the principal. Sister Nora disappeared from our lives that day.

And now Benjamin had disappeared from my life. Most likely for good.

I felt like I had experienced another death. His telling my family the truth gave me a glimpse into what my life could be like and now it was gone again. Why had he told them only to disappear? Grief gnawed at me. I didn't want to do anything. The only thing I wanted was Benjamin by my side. I lay in bed for hours that first day, dragging myself out of the house at the last minute to go to work.

After several days of this, my inherent need for movement kicked in and I started running again. I recommitted to running the Twin Cities Marathon in October. I felt like my body was moving forward but my mind was stuck in the past, not only my time with Benjamin but also remembering my childhood and my relationship with my dad. I couldn't shake the confusion I felt.

I was withdrawn around Sue and Mom and the aunts. I postponed Gregg's Iowa visit until the holidays. He had seemed as relieved as I was. I felt dried up and shut down.

I followed Benjamin's story on the Internet. There were countless pictures of him in costume for his role as Alexander. But other than photos, there was very little news. The rumors were that Benjamin was still grieving his dad and was spending every night alone in his hotel room.

As the weeks passed, I fell into a comfortable and safe routine: work, sleep, exercise, family, and Sue. The only thing out of the ordinary was running into the swimmer again at the Y. His name was Jay and he asked me out. We had dinner the night before he returned to Iowa State for his senior year. I felt like a cross between his dad and an uncle. The almost ten-year age difference seemed like a huge chasm even if I had been remotely interested in developing a relationship. Jay had tried to kiss me as we stood by our cars but I shook his hand instead.

In that moment, it struck me as odd that he would want to kiss me.

The week before the marathon was torture. I had to force myself to stop training to give my body time to rest. I was as twitchy and nudgy as I had ever been in my life. I drove up to Leah's house to spend the night before the race with her. The weather was supposed to be cloudy and fifty degrees, perfect for a marathon. I was as fit as I could be. I hadn't had a drop of alcohol since Benjamin left seven weeks earlier.

The day of the race was much colder than predicted. A wind was blowing out of the north at thirty miles an hour and there were snow flurries in the air. My goal was to break three hours but now that it was so windy and cold, I knew I needed to lower my expectations. When the race started I was in a group that for the most part was at my level so I was able to start running immediately.

From the moment the race started I knew I was in a zone. I passed runner after runner as if they were toppled bowling pins. My pace was just over seven-minute miles. I knew I could go faster but held back. My mind was blank, my body had taken over and all the weeks of training had paid off the way they were supposed to. I was completely focused on the runners in front of me, watching to see if they were struggling, resisting the urge to pass them until I was ready. The sun came out and the wind died down. Suddenly I was hot, sweat pouring down my forehead and back. I ripped off my windbreaker, hat and gloves and threw them by the side of the road.

At the twenty-mile mark I guzzled Gatorade feeling the drink nourish my depleted muscles. With a surge of energy, I zipped past the group in front of me. I was running faster and faster, my body on autopilot, endorphins pumping through my legs and chest. I could see people cheering me on but I could not hear them.

With two miles to go, my head cleared almost as if I had been in a drugged state for several months. In that moment, I knew I was moving back to Boston. Finally, I knew why I had moved home to Iowa. There was no doubt any longer that I had run away from Boston and from a one-sided relationship. Somehow I had convinced myself that I needed to live in my hometown to feel safe, or more accurately, numb.

Moving home to Iowa had been a fantasy. In Boston I couldn't admit what an enormous cluster fuck my relationship with Justin had been, but now I could. I started a list in my mind of all the screwed-up parts of our time together. Justin had hated my lists.

"Fuck him," I shouted causing several college students drinking beer to loudly echo my sentiment.

As I compiled a list, I realized that it didn't matter anymore. None of this mattered. I was no longer the man who had driven across the frozen highways last winter. During that drive I had barely reflected on why I was doing what I was doing.

Now I knew why.

I crossed the finish line in two hours and fifty-five minutes, which was twenty minutes faster than my last marathon. I was exhilarated. I scanned the crowd looking for a familiar face. A college student in a red St. John's University sweatshirt handed me a metallic blanket, which I wrapped around my shoulders. Streaks of dried sweat had crusted on my face. Someone else handed me a box full of fruit, nuts and water. An apple had never tasted better.

Working my way out of the finish area, my medal around my neck, I saw my family standing on a corner trying to stay warm in the weak sunshine. I shuffled over to them. Mom hugged me tightly, not caring I was covered in a sheen of sweat. I cried in her arms in a way I had not done since I was a little boy.

"I still can't believe you ran that far," she whispered in my ear, "Marie thinks you're nuts."

I hugged my sisters. Deirdre told me how proud she was that I finished the race and that she loved me. I wiped my eyes and nose in a Kleenex provided by my mom. As I tried to explain how well I had done, I realized they would not understand I had just run the marathon of my life.

"Honey, I am so proud of you." Mom handed me another Kleenex. She stopped herself before trying to blow my nose.

"We are too, Liam." Leah put an arm around my shoulder. Her eyes were glistening. "Aren't you freezing? I am cold to the bone." I was too busy eating a stale, hard bagel to answer. I shook my head no.

"Is there a bar around here?" Mom asked. My sisters burst out laughing. "What's so funny? It's well past lunchtime. I bet Liam would love a beer, he hasn't had a drop of alcohol since...well, since...you know what I mean."

"Since Benjamin wouldn't take him to Morocco because he isn't a woman, is that what you're trying to say, Colleen?"

Aunt Marie was fidgeting because every time she tried to light a cigarette, someone had angrily asked her to put it out. Now she was just holding one, daring someone to say something so she could wave the unlit cigarette in their face.

"I would kill for a beer," I said. "I can't imagine anything more perfect than a cold beer right now. But first I need to put on some warm clothes." Leah handed me my knapsack and Deirdre pointed me towards a McDonalds. Strangers were congratulating me as I stumbled into the restaurant. I washed my face and put on warm, clean clothing. The cotton felt like silk against my aching muscles. I stared at my reflection. I was drawn and flushed. I was exhilarated by my result, but far more importantly by the fact that I knew what I was going to do next.

CHAPTER SIXTY-ONE

It was the first time I had been back in Iowa in two months. Christmas was two days away. I rolled over, stretched my legs, and thought about my recently resumed life in Boston. Gregg welcomed me back with only ten or fifteen jibes about why it had taken me so long to finally wise up and listen to him. The spare bedroom in Gregg's condominium was now my temporary home. I had made an offer on a condo two doors down from where I had lived before and I was moving in mid-February, which was way too long. Gregg and I were lousy roommates and the bickering was beginning to take a toll on our friendship. Needing a break, I stretched my week in Iowa for the holidays into three.

I knew I needed to find a new job in Boston but wasn't sure I wanted to sell real estate again, even though my former boss wanted me back. She did not understand why I hadn't immediately accepted her offer. I couldn't explain to her that I didn't want to precisely duplicate the life I had rejected not so many months before. She would take it personally just as I would have in her shoes.

Sue was hurt when she learned I was moving back to Boston but she calmed down when I told her I would be back in Iowa over Christmas, and maybe even for a few weeks in the summer.

Mom had shed a few tears but when I told her I would be back as often as I could, she relaxed as well. Aunt Margaret was heartbroken. Aunt Marie was smug. She kept reminding anyone who would listen that she had said from day one that it was a poor fit for a thirty-two-year-old single gay man to move back to Iowa, for God's sake. She reveled in telling people that I was following her advice. I didn't try to dissuade her.

I was back in Boston. Hanging out with Gregg again, living in the South End and trying to find a new home made it seem that my eight months in Iowa had been a dream. When I added Benjamin Graves to my memories, the dream took on aspects of a movie without a happy ending.

Jay was sound asleep next to me, flat on his back, his arms across his hairless chest. His entire body was hairless as he had a swim meet the following week. I still wasn't used to the look. I worried that Jay liked me too much and I worried that most of the time I was with him, I was comparing him to Benjamin.

Over the first few weeks, I had thought about Benjamin all the time but as time moved on, I found myself going for a few hours at a time without his image in my head. Sometimes I would see a *People* cover shot of Benjamin and while I always looked, it felt like I was looking at a stranger, not someone I loved and who had loved me in return.

We had had no contact for four months. I would see an occasional article about the weather problems they were encountering in Morocco but short of that, there was no news. With no scandal, it was almost as if he didn't exist.

Jay rolled over and put a leg on top of mine. He smelled of chlorine and I was back once again sitting beside Benjamin poolside, drinking a cold Belgian beer.

When I thought about my last weekend with Benjamin what I remembered more than anything were the smells: soap washed skin, beer, grilled steaks, tonic water, limes, watermelon, freshly picked tomatoes, newly mown grass, sweat and semen.

What I couldn't remember was why we had seemingly decided at the same time that our relationship could not succeed.

I remembered that it made sense at the time but in retrospect, I wondered if we had decided or let the circumstances make it for us.

Sue had tried to bring this up the night before over dinner but I had deflected her. Grief had flooded me after Benjamin left but now it was settled deep in my gut with only an occasional sighting. But with Sue asking the same old questions again, it had resurfaced. The old hope that Benjamin was going to call, show up unannounced or even send a text telling me how much he missed me was in my consciousness again. I went to the bathroom to interrupt the conversation. Not able to look at my reflection, a voice announced in my head, with a wavering tone, that Benjamin was *not* coming back. I pushed the voice away and wiped my eyes. When I returned to the table, I immediately changed the subject, Sue protesting all the time.

When I returned to Mason City in early December, the first night at the restaurant, I found Sue and Karl kissing in a corner booth, he with a Bud and she with a Brandy Alexander. His hand was on her thigh, her face was completely alive. She had winked at me while gesturing me away.

Jay showed up the next night and four days later we were sleeping together. For the first time in my life, I was experiencing unencumbered sex and it was fun but fun was all it was.

How could I establish a relationship with someone who was still writing term papers?

Jay put a hand on my stomach. I looked again at his unlined complexion with two largish pimples on his chin, a slight hint of a mustache on his face and his tousled brown hair. I kissed him on the forehead. I looked at the clock. It was midnight. My phone buzzed as it received a text message.

"Gregg told me where you are. In Mason City tomorrow morning. Will call. FYI, Clay died in a horrible rodeo accident. B."

Then a second text. "Check out the internet."

I instantly went to people.com. His face was on the cover again. I read the headline. "Benjamin Tells All!"

I lurched out of bed, tripped over Jay's size twelve sneakers and stumbled into the living room. Disbelief, wariness, anxiety, excitement flooded my chest all at once. I sat down on the couch and tried to breathe.

Was the game starting again?

Would I play?

ABOUT THE AUTHOR

John M. Argos was raised in Mason City, Iowa. After graduating from Saint John's University in Minnesota, he moved to Boston where he began a career in the insurance industry and built a community. *Backstage* is his first novel. He and his husband continue to live in Massachusetts, splitting their time between Boston and Truro.

www.ingramcontent.com/pod-product-compliance
Lightning Source LLC
Chambersburg PA
CBHW021937110726
47901CB00003B/866